PRAISE FOR DONNA GRANT'S
BEST-SELLING ROMANCE NOVELS

· —— · ◆◆◆ · —— ·

"Grant's ability to quickly convey complicated
backstory makes this jam-packed love story accessible
even to new or periodic readers."
–Publishers' Weekly

"Donna Grant has given the paranormal genre
a burst of fresh air..."
–San Francisco Book Review

"The premise is dramatic and heartbreaking;
the characters are colorful and engaging;
the romance is spirited and seductive."
–The Reading Cafe

"The central romance, fueled by a hostage drama, plays
out in glorious detail against a backdrop of multiple ongoing
issues in the "Dark Kings" books. This seemingly penultimate
installment creates a nice segue to a climactic end."
–Library Journal

"...intense romance amid the growing war between
the Dragons and the Dark Fae is scorching hot."
–Booklist

SKYE DRUIDS SERIES

Iron Ember ~ Shoulder the Skye ~ Heart of Glass
Endless Skye ~ Still of the Night

DARK KINGS SERIES

Dark Heat ~ Darkest Flame ~ Fire Rising
Burning Desire ~ Hot Blooded ~ Night's Blaze
Soul Scorched ~ Dragon King ~ Passion Ignites
Smoldering Hunger ~ Smoke and Fire
Dragon Fever ~ Firestorm ~ Blaze ~ Dragon Burn
Constantine: A History, Parts 1-3 ~ Heat ~ Torched
Dragon Night ~ Dragonfire ~ Dragon Claimed
Ignite ~ Fever ~ Dragon Lost ~ Flame ~ Inferno
A Dragon's Tale (Whisky and Wishes: *A Holiday Novella*,
Heart of Gold: *A Valentine's Novella*, & Of Fire and Flame)
My Fiery Valentine ~ The Dragon King Coloring Book
Dragon King Special Edition Character Coloring Book: Rhi

DARK WARRIORS SERIES

Midnight's Master ~ Midnight's Lover
Midnight's Seduction ~ Midnight's Warrior
Midnight's Kiss ~ Midnight's Captive
Midnight's Temptation ~ Midnight's Promise
Midnight's Surrender ~ A Warrior for Christmas

CHIASSON SERIES

Wild Fever ~ Wild Dream ~ Wild Need
Wild Flame ~ Wild Rapture

DRAGON BORN

A DRAGON KINGS® NOVEL

NEW YORK TIMES & USA TODAY BESTSELLING AUTHOR

DONNA GRANT

This is a work of fiction. All of the characters, organizations, and events portrayed in this novel are either products of the author's imagination or are used fictitiously.

www.DonnaGrant.com

www.MotherofDragonsBooks.com

DRAGON KINGS INDEX

Alasdair (AEL-aeS-Deh-R) – King of Amethyst
- Dragon tattoo on his chest
- Power is energy absorption
- Story in DRAGON ARISEN & DRAGON KISS
- Mated to Lotti
- One of the Star People

Anson (AN – sən) – King of Browns
- Ying yang dragon tattoo on back
- Power to take possession of someone's mind for a short period
- Story in BLAZE
- Mated to Devon
- Descended from Druids
- Gift from Con is a smoky quartz bracelet, both round and princess cut stones

Arian (AR-ee-ən) – King of Turquoises
- Dragon tattoo on his left leg
- Power to control the weather
- Story in DRAGON KING
- Mated to Grace
- Gift from Con is a rose gold link ankle bracelet with a turquoise heart pendant

Asher (ASH-er) – King of Hunter Greens

- Tattoo on his left arm from wrist to shoulder
- Power to heal burns caused by dragon fire
- Story in DRAGON FEVER
- Mated to Rachel
- Journalist
- Gift from Con 4-strands of faceted chrome diopside necklace

Banan (BAN-yen) – King of Blues

- Tattoo of two intertwined dragons upon his chest
- Ability to make someone hallucinate
- Story in DAWN'S DESIRE and DARK HEAT
- Mated to Jane
- Gift from Con is a silver cuff bracelet with a dragon, wings spread, covered in sapphires

Brandr (BRAND-er) – Dragon King

- Son of Con and Rhi
- Gold and beige dragon
- Ability to dispel magic

Cain (KAYN) – King of Navy

- Tattoo on chest
- Ability to use a cone of hot sand
- Story in FLAME
- Mated to Noreen
- Dark Fae
- Gift from Con was platinum wire wrapped lapis earrings

Cináed (KIN-ay) – King of Moonstone

- Tattoo on left left from his knee up to hip
- Power that he can learn and master anything
- Story in DRAGON CLAIMED
- Mated to Gemma
- Gift from Con silver Celtic cuff bracelet with moonstones at the ends
- Druid who can sense another Druid's magic

Constantine aka Con (KAHN-stən-teen) – King of Golds, King of Dragon Kings

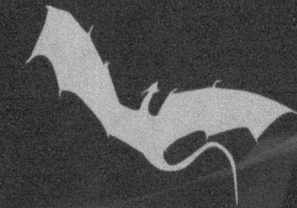

- Tattoo on his back
- Power to heal anything except death
- Best friends with Ulrik
- One of two Kings who never slept away centuries
- Puts the Dragon Kings and their future above his own happiness
- Story in INFERNO, HEART OF GOLD, OF FIRE AND FLAME, and DRAGON FROST
- Mated to Rhi
- Gift from the Dragon Kings: a crown with a jewel for every color Dragon King
- Royal Light Fae

Cullen (KUL-ən) – King of Garnets

- Tattoo on left arm
- Power to breath fog
- Story in DRAGON UNBOUND
- Mate to Tamlyn (no ceremony yet)
- Banshee from Zora

Darius (də-RIE-əs) – King of Dark Purple
- Tattoo on his back looking over his shoulder
- No discernable special ability
- Story in SMOLDERING HUNGER
- Mated to Sophie
- Doctor
- Gift from Con are cushion cut dark Siberian amethyst dangle earrings over 5 carets each

Dmitri (DMEE-tree) – King of Whites
- Tattoo draped along the back of his shoulders
- Has the ability to cancel someone's thoughts
- Story in FIRESTORM
- Mated to Faith
- Archeologist with ties to Skye Druids
- Gift from Con is a narrow bracelet made of gold interlocked with a single pearl

Dorian (DAWR-ee-ən) – King of Corals
- Tattoo down his left side from his chest to his leg
- Has the ability to turn invisible
- Story in DRAGON NIGHT
- Mated to Alexandra
- Gift from Con is a large, round sunstone gem set in a narrow rose gold beveled band

Eurwen (AYR-wen) – Dragon Queen
- Daughter of Con and Rhi
- Peach dragon with gold wings
- Tattoo along her spine
- Has the ability to shield herself
- Story in DRAGON MINE
- Mated to Vaughn
- Gift from Con Montana sapphire

Guy (gai) – King of Reds
- Tattoo on back
- Power to erase memories
- Story in NIGHT'S AWAKENING and DARK HEAT
- Mated to Elena
- Gift from Con is a teardrop ruby nestled in a platinum band

Haldor aka Hal (HAL-door) – King of Greens
- Tattoo on front and wrapping
- Ability to breath sleeping gas
- Story in DARK CRAVING and DARK HEAT
- Mated to Cassie
- Gift from Con is a large emerald pendant necklace

Kellan (KEHL-ən) – King of Bronzes
- Tattoo on chest and extending to his left arm
- Power to pull wounds into himself
- Story in DARKEST FLAME
- Mated to Denae
- MI5 agent
- Gift from Con are smoky quartz earrings

Keltan (KEHL-tən) – King of Citrines
- Tattoo on right ribcage
- Ability to cook anything
- Story in FEVER
- Mated to Bernadette
- Cryptozoologist
- Gift from Con large oval citrine pendent on gold chain necklace

Kendrick (KEHN-drik) – King of Siennas
- Dragon Tattoo on back
- Power to camouflage
- Story in DRAGON LOVER
- Mated to Esha
- Sun Elf
- Asavori Ranger

Kiril (kih-RIHL) – King of Burnt Oranges
- Tattoo on his chest
- Breath of ice
- Best friends with Rhys
- Story in BURNING DESIRE
- Mated to Shara
- Gift from Con is a Padparadscha (one of the rarest gems in the world) emerald bracelet.
- Dark Fae who turned Light Fae

Laith (LAY-th) – King of Blacks

- Tattoo on his back
- Ability to breath paralyzing gas
- Runs The Fox and The Hound pub
- Story in HOT BLOODED
- Mated to Iona
- Ancestor to Warrior, Hayden Campbell (Dark Sword series)
- Gift from Con is a large black peal and diamond pendant necklace

Melisse (MEH-LihS) – Queen of Violets

- The very first Dragon King and Dark Fae offspring
- Tattoo winding up her left leg
- Ability to breath a cone of burning venom
- Was kept prisoner by the Dragon Kings for eons
- Store in DRAGON BORN
- Mated to Henry
- JusticeBringer with his sister; part of an ancient line of Druid enforcers
- Brother to Esther (Truthseeker)

Merrill (MEHR-əl) – King of Oranges

- Power of breath a beam of searing light
- Loves to give pep talks
- Best friends with Varek

Nikolai (nyi-ku-LIE) – King of Ivories

· Tattoo on right arm and right side of his body
· Ability of projected thermography (once he sees something, he can paint or draw it)
· Story in HEAT
· Mated to Esther
· Gift from Con of mother of pearl earrings
· Sister to Henry (JusticeBringer)
· TruthSeeker with her brother; part of an ancient line of Druid enforcers

Rhys (REES) – King of Yellows

· Tattoo on his chest and shoulder
· Ability to call the night and shadows
· Constantly pushes Con, testing boundaries
· Best friends with Kiril
· Story in NIGHT'S BLAZE
· Mated to Liliana aka Lily
· Daughter of nobility
· Helicopter pilot
· Gift from Con is a 5-carat cushion cut yellow sapphire ring set in a thin band of platinum

Roman (RO-mən) – King of Pale Blues

· Tattoo on his chest
· Ability to control metals
· Story in DRAGONFIRE
· Mated to Sabina
· Gypsy
· Gift from Con are teardrop aquamarine dangle earrings

Royden (ROI-dən) – King of Beiges

- Tattoo on his back
- Power of blinding light
- Story in DRAGON LOST
- Mated to Annita
- Gift from Con raw druzy cluster ring

Ryder (RIE-dər) – King of Grays

- Tattoo wraps his entire torso
- Ability to project weakness into someone
- Has an affinity for jelly donuts
- Designs, creates, and implements all electronics
- Story in SMOKE AND FIRE
- Mated to Kinsey
- Talented hacker
- Gift from Con is a gray star sapphire ring, large oval set in a thick platinum filigree band

Shaw (SHAW) – King of Sapphires

- Tattoo on right hip, waist, and thigh
- Ability to create illusions
- Story in DRAGON ETERNAL
- Mated to Nia

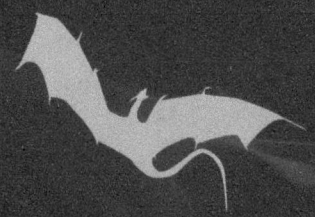

Sebastian (sə-BAS-chən) – King of Steels

· Tattoo on his right leg winding upward to his abdomen
· Can breathe lightning bolts
· Story in DRAGON BURN
· Mated to Gianna
· Gift from Con large octagonal gunmetal blue stone pendant necklace

Thorn (THAWRN) – King of Clarets

· Tattoo on his chest
· Power of sound manipulation
· Story in PASSION IGNITES
· Mated to Lexi
· Gift from Con are curving French wire 5-caret multifaceted rectangular garnet earrings that appear to float under her ears

Tristan (TRIS-tən) – King of Ambers

· Tattoo on his chest
· Power to get into someone's mind
· Reincarnated Warrior, Duncan Kerr
· First new Dragon King in eons
· Story in FIRE RISING
· Mated to Samantha aka Sammi
· Half-sister to Jane

Ulrik (OOL-rik) – King of Silvers

· Tattoo on his chest and neck
· Power to bring people back to life
· Best friends with Con
· One of only two Kings who never slept centuries away
· Banished from Dreagan for the war with humans
· Story in TORCHED
· Mated to Eilish
· Gift from Con are platinum teardrop earrings
· Powerful Druid
· Wears silver Celtic finger rings that allows her to teleport

Varek (VAHR-ihk) – King of Lichen

· Tattoo on his left arm
· Power is energy draining shadows
· Best friends with Merrill
· Kidnapped from Earth and brought to Zora
· Story in DRAGON REVEALED
· Mated to Jeyra
· Warrior
· Gift from Con are green amethyst stone armbands

Vaughn (VAWN) – King of Teals

· Tattoo on chest
· Ability of dream manipulation
· Attorney for all things Dreagan
· Story in DRAGON MINE
· Mated to Eurwen
· Gift from Con full finger ring with teal stones wound in a delicate, beautiful pattern from the base of her finger to her nail.

Vlad aka V (vuh-lad) – King of Coppers

· Tattoo on his back with wings on the back of each arm
· Ability to mask himself while in dragon form
· Story in IGNITE
· Mated to Claire
· Gift from Con is a 5-caret copper zircon set in rose gold
· First mate to become pregnant

Warrick aka War (WAWR-ik) – King of Jades

· Tattoo on the right side of his body from shoulder to hip
· Power of protection
· Story in SOUL SCORCHED
· Mated to Darcy
· Was the Druid who unbound Ulrik's magic
· Gift from Con is a gold bracelet with five jade beads.

DRAGON BORN

A DRAGON KINGS® NOVEL

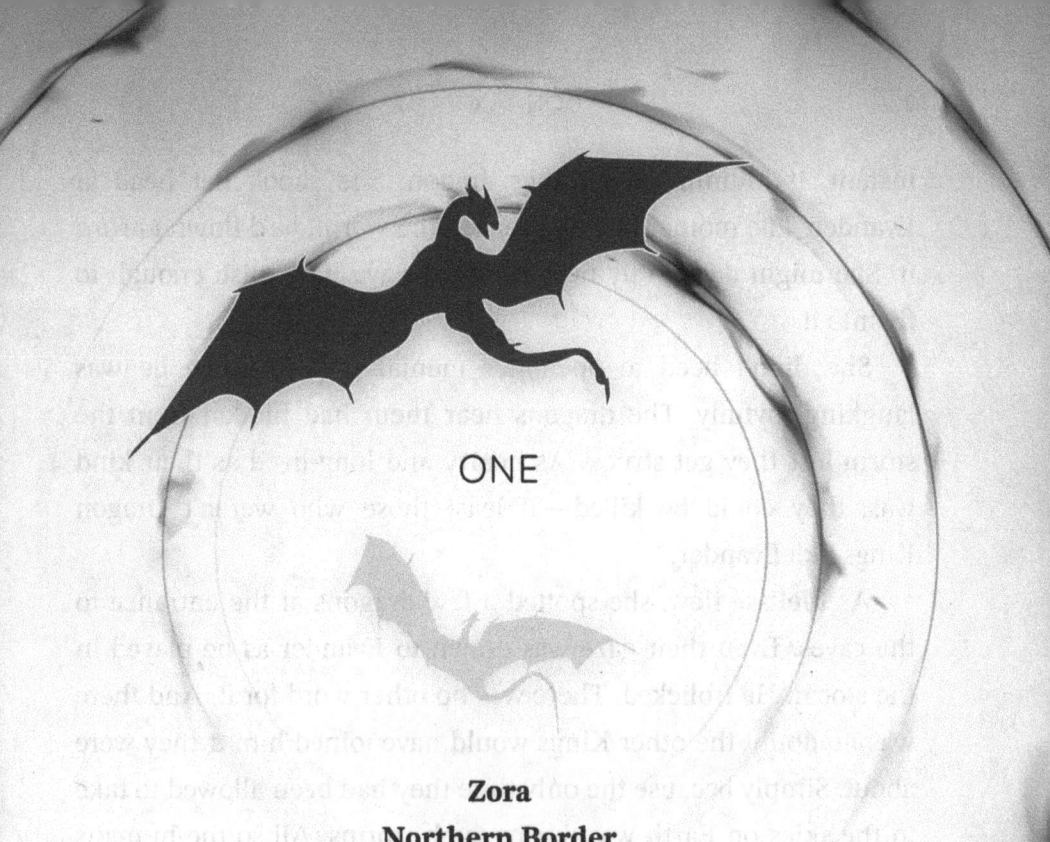

ONE

Zora
Northern Border
Autumn

Freedom had never felt so good. Melisse flapped her wings and flew toward the foreboding clouds. A flash to the left caught her attention. She looked over in time to see bolts zigzagging across the turbulent sky. Three beats later, a reverberating boom followed, rolling across the area like an aftershock. She loved the feeling of the icy rain as it pelted her scales. It was as invigorating as the frosty air of the northern climate.

Melisse tilted onto her side so her wings were perpendicular to the ground. She swung around, folded them against her, and twirled her body in the rainfall. Just as she began plummeting, she spread her wings and glided along a current.

An impressive show of lightning burst in every direction, like spidery fingers reaching for something. Or someone. For a brief instant, it illuminated another dragon. She shook her head at Evander. The moment he had sensed the storm, he'd flown *toward* it. She might dare to fly near it, but she wasn't foolish enough to fly into it.

She didn't need to open her mental link to know he was laughing joyfully. The dragons near them had hidden from the storm lest they get struck. As hearty and long-lived as their kind was, they could be killed—at least those who weren't Dragon Kings like Evander.

As Melisse flew, she spotted a few dragons at the entrance to the caves. Even their gaze was drawn to Evander as he played in the storm. He frolicked. There was no other word for it. And there was no doubt the other Kings would have joined him if they were about. Simply because the only time they had been allowed to take to the skies on Earth was during such storms. All so the humans wouldn't see them.

Melisse blinked the water from her eyes and swung back around, her thoughts turning as dark as the skies. Earth had been her home. And her prison. She had been one of the first to volunteer to come to Zora, and although she had been excited to locate the dragons that had been sent away from Earth during the war with the humans, that wasn't the reason she had joined the Kings in venturing to the new realm.

Melisse was searching for somewhere she fit. A place to call home. It certainly wasn't Earth. How could it ever be? She was the product of a Dragon King and a Dark Fae. As far as she knew, there were only two others like her: the twins, Brandr and Eurwen. They were the offspring of Constantine, King of Dragon Kings, and Rhi, a royal Light Fae.

The twins had governed Zora for centuries. They knew their

place in the universe while Melisse was still trying to figure hers out. And the more she searched for that special location, the farther away it felt. She had hoped to find answers on this realm, but so far, all she had were more questions and doubts—and far more uncertainties.

Earth had been her father's home and the place her mother had chosen to live. It was where she had been born. But if she'd stayed there, she would have had to hide both her Fae and dragon sides from the humans. And she had seen firsthand what that had done to the Dragon Kings. Why would she put herself through that?

She hadn't spent much time with any Fae outside of those mated to the Kings. Her mother had been Dark, which meant the Light didn't want any part of Melisse. And the Dark didn't trust her because she was half-dragon. So, that effectively ruled out the Fae.

Con and the rest of the Kings had opened their home to her, but she wasn't entirely comfortable at Dreagan. She still carried a lot of animosity and resentment toward all Kings. She was getting better at letting go of the past, but it would take more time.

A *lot* more time.

Which had made Zora sound so much more appealing. Imagine her surprise when she arrived to learn that the dragons detested the Kings and anyone associated with them—including Melisse. They didn't care about anyone's backstory or their reasons. They had a blanket hatred that no one—not even Brandr and Eurwen, who the dragons loved and adored—could penetrate.

Then, there were the humans on the realm. They knew about

the dragons, and their loathing for all things magical was shocking.

And terrifying.

War was brewing—a war the Kings were desperately attempting to stop. The twins helped to keep the dragons pacified, but Melisse wasn't sure how much longer Eurwen and Brandr could accomplish that. If the dragons abhorred one thing above all others, it was humans. Who could blame them when the mortals had forced their ancestors to abandon their home?

The rain faded to a drizzle before gradually stopping altogether. Melisse flew to the top of a mountain that had become a favorite and landed. She searched for Evander, finally locating him farther northeast along the border. He had been tasked with watching the northern boundary while Hector surveyed the south side near the sea. The eastern and western borders were also being guarded. That's what things had come to. Watching and waiting to see who would make the first move.

Melisse had flown over the entire swath of land claimed by the dragons. It was vast and beautiful. They had mountains and plains of flatlands, valleys and lakes, canyons and deserts—plenty of room for them to roam as they pleased. When the dragons called Earth home, they had once been in clans dictated by color. Now, they created their groupings, and the color combinations were stunning. She wished her father had been able to see such a sight. He had fought to do away with the clans, but the culture had been too ingrained even then.

She shook, sending droplets flying from her scales. Then she shifted to her other form. The dragons thought she was human. She had once attempted to tell some that she was Fae, but they didn't care to see the difference. She looked human, and that was all they cared about.

Melisse sat on the cliff's edge and let her feet dangle over the side. She drew in a deep breath and let the icy air fill her lungs. The trees were an array of yellows, oranges, and reds mixed in with the evergreens. The smell of autumn hung heavy in the air, its brisk, crisp scent a harbinger of winter soon to come.

She gazed at the thick, steely clouds hanging over her. Zora had been made in Earth's image, and it was sometimes difficult to remember that she was on another realm. Then, she would listen. She enjoyed the absence of human sound. There were no engine roars and no people noise. Utility poles weren't sticking out of the ground with lines connecting them to ruin the landscape. Nor were there any paved roads.

Zora was as wild and fierce as Earth had once been—at least within the borders of dragon land. Outside those borders, humans—and elves—had civilized their respective regions. There were cities and villages, armies, and even conflict. She couldn't put that squarely on the mortals' shoulders since her ancestors on her mother's side had raged a brutal civil war that lasted so long that it destroyed the Fae Realm. Rhi had since healed it. And from what Melisse had last heard, the Fae were slowly beginning to return to the Fae Realm.

It didn't seem to matter where Melisse went. Chaos and anarchy were everywhere. All she wanted was a place to be herself. Her mother had done the impossible long ago and moved between realms before the Fae learned how to construct those doorways and follow in her footsteps. Maybe Melisse should be like her mother and find somewhere new.

It would mean leaving everything and everyone behind,

though. She had to give it to Con and those at Dreagan. They did
their best to make her feel welcome and included, and it wasn't
their fault she couldn't shake off her past or the lingering anger
about her imprisonment. She hated to even think the word.

Once freed, she'd tried to find her footing, but nothing was the
same. Her parents were gone, and the world she'd known had
turned into a strange and hostile environment. It was noisy and
dirty, with only a few pockets where places resembled the Earth
she had once known and loved. She had even wondered if she
should've remained locked away.

Then, she saw Henry.

Thinking about the mortal made her chest ache with soul-deep
longing. She shut off those thoughts. Too often of late, she found
herself recalling his face, the curve of his lips when he smiled, and
the way his hazel eyes seemed to see straight into her. At odd
times, snippets of their conversations filled her mind, and it took
her back to that moment with him.

And always, her thoughts turned to their kiss.

It had made her knees go weak and her stomach flutter with
excitement and need. Henry had been her first kiss and left a
lasting impression that would forever be stamped in her mind so
she could pull it up day after day.

He had been kind and warm. Had opened his heart to her.
And she'd stomped all over it with harsh words. It didn't matter
why she had been in a hurry. She should've taken those few
moments and explained. If she had, maybe she wouldn't have
been haunted daily by the sight of Henry at Dreagan. He
wouldn't hear her explanations, but she hadn't tried very hard to
talk to him either. Instead, she'd left to see and experience the
world on her own. Eventually, she returned to Scotland. To

Henry. Except, he wasn't there. Then it didn't matter because she came to Zora.

Yet Henry was still everywhere for her. In every leaf that fluttered in the wind, in the very molecules that shimmered unseen around them. He was in the warmth of the sunlight and the ethereal glow of the moonbeams.

Through their mental link, Evander's voice nudged her. Melisse let him in and asked, *"Did you have fun?"*

"More than you know, lass," he replied, a smile in his voice.

His Scottish accent was as thick as her father's had been. *"Did you get struck by lightning?"*

"No' this time." Evander chuckled. *"I have in the past, though. No' a verra fun experience."*

"Yet you still race toward storms."

"Aye. It's the only way we had fun for too many years."

She leaned back on her hands. *"You can have your storms. I'll stick to the rain."*

"You doona know what you're missing," he teased, then sobered. *"I'm going to keep heading east for a wee bit. You good there?"*

"I've got you covered. You shouldn't be here by yourself any more than Hector should be on his own in the south."

"Aye, but these borders are no' as active as the eastern and western sides. I wouldna mind the company, though."

"I can leave."

"Nay. You're fine just as you are."

Melisse grinned. *"Figured you'd say that."*

"At least we have something to look at. Poor Hector has a flat coastline and water."

"Whatever," she replied with a snort. *"You think I've forgotten about the race you and Sebastian had in the North Sea?"*

Evander laughed loudly. *"Join us next time."*

"Are you sure you want me to do that? I'd best any of you." It was a boast. She was the smallest of all the Dragon Kings.

"I think you could." He paused. *"I'm glad you came to Zora."*

Melisse became uncomfortable anytime the conversation turned to such things. *"Stay out of the storms."*

"Be back in a few hours," he said and severed the link.

She blew out a breath and looked around at the mountain range. The peaks to the north were awe-inspiring. Their jagged, steep sides soared to amazing heights, their topography deeply cut by erosion. She had flown over bottomless river gorges and seen different flora and fauna with every mountain as if each peak were a world all its own.

The section she had chosen was at the base of a long, wide valley. Below her, an area of the valley looked like a bowl as the mountains rose up at its slenderest spot. A dramatic waterfall cut down the mountainside opposite her, rushing toward a river that wove a path to the south. The grass was still green, but it wouldn't hold its color for much longer. It was a beautiful location, unfortunately interrupted by giant brambles that towered over even the dragons.

A sound drew her attention to a group of pink dragons venturing out of their caves after the rain. They were the smallest of all the dragons. Perhaps that was why they were the only ones who'd kept to their clan. Though they weren't one *big* clan, as some might assume. They were divided into several nomadic groups. They continually moved, meeting at certain times of the year in larger groups. Melisse's guess was that those gatherings were to socialize, but also so the dragons could find mates—which was significant since dragons only had one mate.

Melisse watched an elder male step out of a cave across the valley and immediately fly north, straight toward the thorn forest. The vines covered the entire valley, even across the border, except for the bowl area below. She kept away from the thicket. There was an ominous air to it that unsettled her.

She sat up when she spotted a group of five Pink younglings playing close to the brambles. Melisse got to her feet, ready to jump into action, but the male got to them first. She didn't know what he said, but whatever it was, it sent them hurrying back to their families. The male paused, looked back at the thicket, then flew to the others.

Was something in there? Or was it simply parental instinct that had the male reacting so? Melisse swung her gaze back to the group of Pinks and noticed that everyone had stopped what they were doing and rushed to greet the younglings. She frowned and returned her attention to the thorns. Even from this distance, they were enormous.

The male's reaction bothered her. So, too, did the clan's reaction when the younglings returned. Perhaps she needed to shove aside that niggle of worry and take a closer look. It might all be in her head. If she could determine it was safe, it would alleviate the Pinks' fears. And perhaps even show them that she wasn't their enemy.

She shifted into dragon form and dove from the cliff, making sure not to get too close to the Pinks. They tolerated her and Evander, but they wouldn't engage in conversation. Melisse flew as low as she dared over the forest of thorns. They appeared to be huge brambles that twisted and turned around each other, creating a dense jungle with thorns protruding at every angle.

Despite her enhanced vision, she couldn't see between the

thorns to gauge if anyone or anything lay in wait. She reached the border and spun around for another pass.

She flew over again and again, constantly searching. What she couldn't locate was the *source* of the vines. They had to start somewhere, but as far as she could tell, that was well past the border, extending through the long valley. She flew higher to see into the distance, but it was too great. The only way to find the answer she sought was to cross the border, which simply couldn't happen.

Melisse returned to the mountain summit. One glance at the sky showed the sun well on its way down. She hadn't realized that she had spent so long studying the thorns. The Pinks were gathered together now, and one Pink was in obvious distress. Melisse dove toward them and landed far enough away so as not to cause alarm. Then she made her way to them. She opted to stay in dragon form in hopes it would get them to talk to her.

"*...gone! He's gone!*" a female wailed.

Melisse searched the group, but no one would look at her. Several of the small dragons were gathered around the female, and more were grouped in twos as they brought the younglings close. A set of elders spoke low, their heads together. Then she spotted the older male who had chased the younglings from the thicket earlier.

"*What happened?*" she asked, hoping someone would answer her.

The elder walked a few steps toward the forest before dropping his head. The female roared again, the pain and anguish in the sound making Melisse's throat thicken with emotion.

"*Please. I want to help,*" she begged them. "*Someone tell me what happened.*"

"*There's nothing you can do.*"

It took her a moment to realize the reply had come from the older male. *"You don't know that."*

"I didna think he'd do it," one of the youngling lads said through sobs.

"We always dare each other, but we doona go in," said another.

One of the young females shifted closer to her parents. *"He said he was going in and coming right back out."*

"But he didna, did he?" a male bellowed. Given that he held the wailing female, he was most likely the missing lad's father.

Melisse watched in horror as the families began turning to leave. One by one, the Pinks somberly made their way into the caves until she and the older male were the only ones left. She walked closer to him.

"I'm going after him," she declared.

"Then you will disappear like all the others. Any dragon who ventures into the thorns vanishes forever."

"We'll see about that." Melisse returned to her Fae form and strode to the thorn forest. At the edge, she turned and looked back at the elder. *"I'm going to find him and bring him home to his family."*

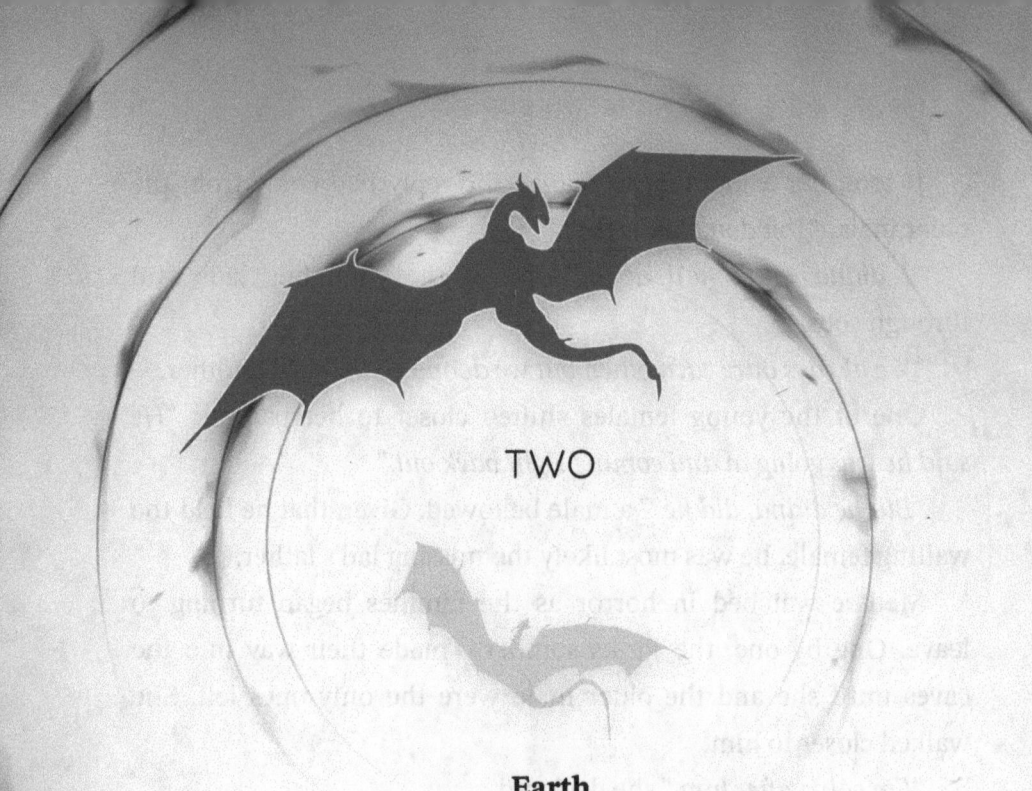

TWO

Earth
Highlands of Scotland
Spring

Time was running out. Henry felt it with every beat of his heart. His steps were long and purposeful, but his trek still took entirely too long. The moment he crossed the invisible barrier protecting the sixty-four-thousand-acre estate, the Dragon Kings had been notified. They would be coming for him.

And they would stop him.

Or they would try. He was getting through the Fae doorway no matter what he had to do. There was no time for a discussion. There wasn't time for anything.

He broke into a run. He had parked at the distillery instead of the manor, hoping to make it to the Dragonwood before one of the Kings stopped him. Which one would it be? His guess was Ulrik, the King of Silvers, since he was in charge of Dreagan while Con was on Zora.

Henry glanced to the side and spotted Dreagan Manor in the distance. His gaze went to the sky. The Kings didn't fly during the day, but that didn't mean they wouldn't if they thought the threat was significant enough. He was defying Con's explicit orders.

Which meant he was a threat.

He ran faster, pumping his legs and arms to push his body to its limit. Sweat beaded his skin, and he wished he had left his jacket in his vehicle. His lungs burned, and his legs ached, but he didn't stop. He couldn't.

He should've told his sister his plans, but he couldn't chance her passing the info on to her mate, Nikolai. They would soon learn that he was no longer on the Isle of Skye to help them with the situation the Skye Druids were dealing with.

Esther had been furious when he left to travel to Zora the first time. Unfortunately, no one on Zora had been very pleased to see him either. He understood that things were in flux there, and adding another human to the mix with the dragons didn't make things any easier for the Kings. If only Con had listened to what Henry had to say.

The instant he was within the trees, Henry let out a small sigh of relief. Even if he got to the Fae doorway on Dreagan, he would still have to get past the Kings once he reached Zora. But Henry didn't have a choice. He had to go. Something on Zora posed a threat to everyone. He had felt it through the doorway, and it was only growing darker and more powerful with each day that passed.

He wove through the trees, slowing to a jog. Daily five-mile runs kept him in shape, but he was likely to be pushed past his breaking point. He glanced behind him but saw no one following.

He looked up, but no large shadows crossed the bright sun. He looked to either side of him but saw nothing. It wasn't just the Kings Henry needed to be concerned about. Their mates were powerful in their own rights. Any of them could stop him.

His mobile vibrated in his pocket. He didn't need to look to know it was Esther. He wished he could have told her and Nikolai what he planned. He wished they could've helped him. But Nikolai wouldn't go against Con's orders, and right now, keeping the dragons on Zora calm was the Kings' main goal.

Henry ignored the call and started running again. Only the Fae could see the doorway, but he had memorized its location. He scanned the area and didn't see anyone. Maybe he could get through without interference. He picked up speed, jumping over the small stream and continuing on. He was making a lot of noise, but stealth wouldn't help him now. Only speed.

His heart thumped excitedly as he spied the area he needed through the trees. He sprinted the last bit of distance, then burst into the small glade and slid to a stop, frantically searching for the rocks he'd placed on either side of the door. But they were gone. That meant the Kings knew he might return. Henry curled his hands into fists, frustration and fear churning in his gut. He didn't have time for this.

A sound to his left drew his attention. Henry found Sebastian leaning a shoulder against a tree as he studied a wren that had landed on his finger. Years of work as a spy for MI5 kept Henry calm, even as he scanned the area for more Dragon Kings. The doorway was there, even if the markers he'd placed after returning from Zora the last time weren't. He'd just have to guess. But he would only get one chance.

"We thought you were on Skye," Sebastian said, his topaz gaze remaining on the bird. The King of Steels stood relaxed, indifferent even, in jeans and a white tee with the long sleeves shoved up to his elbows. His golden-brown hair was pulled back in a queue at the base of his neck.

Henry studied Sebastian. "I have to get to Zora."

The bird flew away, and Sebastian crossed his arms over his chest, his gaze locking on Henry. "Why?"

"I've already explained it."

"No' to me."

Henry felt the seconds ticking away, moments that could be all there was between life and death. The Dragon Kings were millions of years old and more powerful than any other being on the planet. Sebastian could take Henry's life with a snap of his fingers. He had lived with the Kings and had seen them ruthlessly cut down threats to Earth while being exceedingly generous to those they cared about. He was their friend, someone who had freely been welcomed into their world. And he would always be their friend. But right now, he stood in defiance of Con's orders, and that raised concerns.

"Henry," Sebastian pressed.

He blew out a breath. "There isn't time for this."

"Make time," the King stated flatly.

It was easy to forget how dangerous the Dragon Kings were. They never flaunted their power unless pushed, and he was pushing things. "There is something dangerous on Zora."

"Aye. There are the Star People, who apparently once enslaved my kind." Sebastian dropped his arms to his sides and pushed away from the tree as his brogue deepened. "There's the invisible foe that can kill dragons and do quite a lot of damage to a King. Then there are the elves who want to test us."

Henry shook his head and raked a hand through his hair. "I know all about that." Then the words penetrated, and he drew up. "Wait. Did you say elves?"

"A recent development," Sebastian said as he approached. "Things are no' going well on Zora. Another human walking through that doorway will only make things worse."

"I wouldn't be going if it weren't important. I've tried to explain to Con, but he won't listen."

Sebastian's eyes held his. "Then tell me."

Tick. Tock. The clock in Henry's head kept ticking away. He really didn't have time for this, but if he didn't try, he might not make it to the doorway. And he had to go through.

He drew in a breath and said, "I don't have magic. Even though I'm considered a Druid, I have no abilities. Save one. I can sense Druids."

"Aye." Sebastian's brows drew together in a frown. "Are you telling me that's what you feel? A Druid?"

"That's exactly what I'm saying."

"On Zora?"

Henry nodded and adjusted his coat as his body began cooling down. "Not just any Druid either. A very powerful, dangerous one." When Sebastian didn't reply, Henry kept talking. "I know my sister and I are a team. The TruthSeeker and the JusticeBringer. It is our job to police the Druids. Our family was nearly annihilated because of it. I know what I feel."

"And Esther?"

Henry looked away. "She can sense Druids, but she doesn't feel what I do. Not this time."

"The Kings have handled Druids before."

"Maybe. If they know where to look."

"You think you can find the Druid?"

"I know I can."

Sebastian quirked a brow. "A bold statement."

"But a true one."

The King glanced at the ground and then released a long breath. "You've been a good friend to us. I believe you."

That should've been enough. Yet, it wasn't. Not nearly. Even before Henry asked, he knew the answer. "But?"

"I have orders no' to let anyone through."

Henry nodded slowly and glanced to the right. *Tick. Tock.* Could he dive toward the area where he thought the doorway was before Sebastian reached him? Or worse, used his ability, his breath of electricity? Unlikely. But he had to take the chance. He shifted his feet, moving himself an inch or two to the right. "I have to stop this Druid."

"Is it just the Druid?"

Henry didn't play dumb. He knew Sebastian was asking about Melisse—the woman who had brought his world into vivid clarity. The woman who had him falling head over heels for her. They had a complicated relationship, made more so because of who she was.

And who he wasn't.

"I see," Sebastian said at Henry's silence.

How did he explain that the urgency propelling him to take such drastic actions was a combination of the Druid and Melisse? That it was warped in such a way that he couldn't tell which was which? He only knew one thing. He had to find them both.

"You should've told us this was about Melisse," Sebastian stated.

Tick. Tock. Henry squeezed his eyes shut for a heartbeat. "I don't know how she's involved, so don't ask. Are you going to let me through?"

"I'll pass on the information. You have my word."

"No one will see it as a threat. They'll think like you. That Druids can easily be dealt with." He moved another inch to the right. "This one is different."

Sebastian shrugged. "We face the dangers posed to us. We always have, and we always will."

Tick. Tock. "This will be a threat, but one we can stop before it becomes another enemy to fight."

"Do you plan on fighting this Druid yourself?"

Henry clenched his teeth at the reminder that he didn't have magic. Another inch. "I know the adversary is there. I *feel* it. I will find them. And if it comes down to it, and I'm the only option, then I will stop them."

His phone vibrated again.

"It's most likely Esther. Talk to your sister," Sebastian urged.

Henry pulled his mobile from his pocket and glanced at the screen to see his sister's name. He had one chance. It would likely be his last. But the catastrophe that would follow would be immense if he didn't get to Zora in time. And it would ripple across both realms in ways Henry barely understood and couldn't even begin to explain.

Without a second thought, Henry tossed his mobile at Sebastian and dove to where he hoped the doorway was. His shoulder slammed into something before he bounced off and slid from one realm into the other as the King bellowed his name. The instant Henry was through the doorway, he jumped to his feet. He didn't need to orient himself. He knew exactly where he was. So, he turned and started running to the north.

He expected Rhi to teleport in front of him or one of the Kings to swoop down and land so the ground trembled, but neither happened. He spotted dragons in the distance, but he couldn't tell if they were Kings or not. So, he kept running. He didn't slow, even when a stitch began in his side, and his legs grew wobbly.

When he reached a section of woods, he finally slowed to a jog. Seeing the lake, he made his way to it and knelt at the edge to dip his hand into the water and bring it to his mouth for a drink. He looked around before wiping his mouth and getting to his feet, ready to set off again. Only, when he moved, a woman of exceptional beauty with long, black hair and silver eyes dressed in all black stood in his way.

"Rhi." He had expected her sooner.

The Light Fae lifted one of her slim brows. Then, in her Irish accent, she said, "Henry. Care to explain what you're doing?"

"What I tried to do before."

"You can't be here."

"I have to be. There is a Druid on Zora. They're dangerous."

Rhi glanced to the left before closing the distance between them. Her jaw worked as if she were considering something. "You seem to have a destination in mind."

"North."

"How far north?"

He frowned at her question. "I'll know when I reach it."

"Hmm. This Druid, you felt them through the doorway?"

"I did."

Rhi held his gaze. "The truth, Henry, if you please. You've returned after Con told you not to. You left your sister behind. You two are a team. You're supposed to stick together."

"I'm after the Druid," he stated. *And Melisse.* He wasn't sure why he didn't tell Rhi that. Probably for the same reason he hadn't told anyone else. Because he was terrified of how interconnected Melisse was with the Druid.

"What else?"

He glanced away. Rhi was going to make him say it. "You know."

"Say it," she demanded, her silver eyes narrowing slightly. "If for no one else than yourself."

He blew out a breath and glanced north. *Tick. Tock.* "Melisse."

"What about her?"

Henry read people for a living. It was how he had gotten out of some very sticky situations working for MI5. Rhi wasn't surprised by his statement. Which meant she already knew something was going on. Was he too late? "She's in danger."

"What makes you think that?"

"I've felt it. For weeks."

Rhi hesitated as if trying to come to a decision.

"I'm too late, aren't I?" Henry asked. "Something has already happened."

The Light Fae sighed. "Melisse is missing. We can't locate her, and she's not answering any of the Kings."

"Take me to her last known location." When Rhi didn't immediately reply, he took a step toward her. "The longer we wait, the worse this will get."

Rhi's lips twisted in irritation, but she grabbed hold of him. One moment, he was standing by the lake. The next, he was in a valley surrounded by steep mountains.

"I hope you're prepared for this," Rhi whispered.

Henry swung his head to the side to find Con bearing down on him. The King of Dragon Kings usually kept his emotions carefully concealed, but the rage Henry saw in Con's black eyes would cause anyone to want to turn and run. Somehow, Henry stood his ground.

"I thought I told you no' to return," Con said in a soft voice that belied his anger.

Henry had known this wouldn't be easy. He was on Zora, which was a feat in itself. Now, he had to get past Con. "There's a Druid here."

"Then where the fuck is Melisse?" Evander demanded as he strode up.

Con held up a hand to quiet the King of Brass. Henry stared into Evander's gray eyes. Evander was angry, yes, but he was also worried. It was understandable, with Merrill still missing.

"I've felt the Druid for some time," Henry continued. "Through the doorway. Their power is...considerable. They're a threat."

Evander grunted and shoved a lock of dark brown hair from his eyes. "We'll take care of them."

"It isn't just the Druid I've felt. Melisse is tied to them somehow." Henry might as well get that out in the open now.

Con's gaze narrowed slightly. "I asked you the last time if you coming here was about her."

"It has nothing to do with my feelings." That was a bald-faced lie, and all of them knew it. Henry waited for one of them to call him on it. "The threat from the Druid has been growing. It's gotten steadily worse. And I sense Melisse in all of it. I don't know how she's connected or in what capacity, but I know that I need to find them both. And soon."

Con's gaze remained riveted on Henry. "Why?"

Henry licked his lips. "I don't know. It's a gut feeling. A certainty I haven't been able to shake for days."

"Melisse is one of us," Evander interjected. "She can hold her own against a Druid."

"Not this one," Henry stated.

Rhi put a hand on Con's arm. "There's a reason Henry was called here."

"Please. Let me help. I know I can," Henry begged.

Con swung his gaze to Rhi before saying, "Before you arrived, the Pinks told me any dragon who goes into the brambles is never seen again."

Henry looked past Con's shoulder to where he motioned with his thumb and took in the thicket of thorns. They towered above them, the dark vines twisting into unsettling forms. This was it. This was the place that had called to him.

He walked around Con and toward the brambles for a closer look. The Druid magic was strong within—stronger than anything he had felt on Earth. Powerful enough to stretch from here to the Fae doorway and across the realms.

"Melisse is in there," Henry announced. "I'm going after her."

"I'll come. You might need a way out," Rhi said.

Henry turned to tell her to stay, but Con had already taken her hand to stop her.

"Nay, my love," Con said. He whispered something, and Rhi nodded slowly.

She looked at Henry apologetically. "If you wait, I'll return with someone to go with you."

The pull of the vines was intense. He needed to get in there and quickly. "I must go now."

Con's brow knitted. "Henry."

"There's no time." He looked from Con to Rhi and then to Evander.

Rhi snorted. "Well, you won't go in unprepared."

Suddenly, there was a soft weight on his back. Henry looked over his shoulder to see a rucksack.

"Food, water, and a few other things," Rhi told him. "Find Melisse and get back to us quickly."

Henry turned back to the thorns and started walking. As he neared, he saw movement to his left and looked over to see one of the Pinks watching him. Then he entered the thorn forest. The moment he stepped inside, it was as if the very air had been snatched from him. The brambles allowed only a meager bit of light to get through, making it feel as if Henry had entered another world.

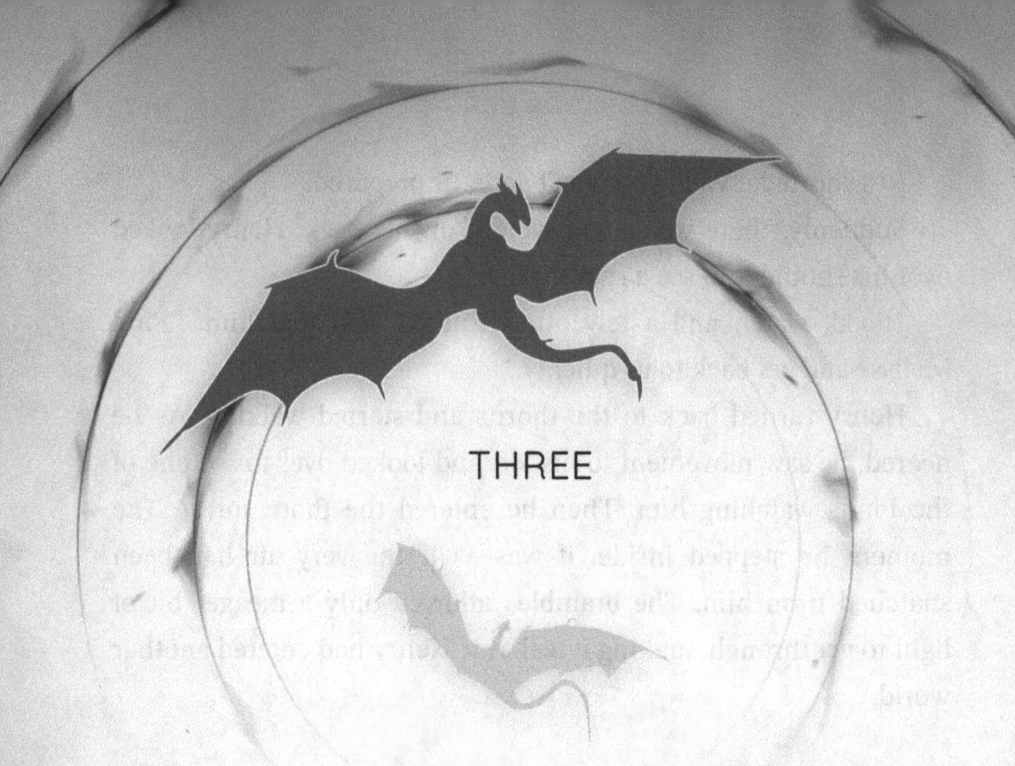

THREE

From the moment Melisse entered the thicket, she was overcome with a feeling of impending doom. Menace just out of sight, waiting for the right opportunity to strike. It settled around her like a damp cloak she couldn't shake off.

And the longer she walked among the vines, the worse it became.

Every fiber of her being urged her to turn and run back the way she had come. But she couldn't leave the youngling. The Pinks might, but she wouldn't. She carefully picked her way through the brambles. Some of them were as big around as giant oaks and wove among themselves as well as into the ground in a dizzying maze. Then there were the thorns. They came in all sizes. The largest she had seen was the length of her leg, their points as sharp as a dragon's talon. She had brushed too close to one when she first rushed into the thicket and sliced her arm all the way through her jacket and shirt.

Melisse hadn't paid much attention to the wound. She would

heal. Granted, not as instantaneously as a King, but it was still quicker than others. At least, that's what *should* happen.

She paused and looked down at her arm. The wound was only an inch and a half long, the skin only grazed. Blood welled and oozed slowly from the scratch. What concerned her was that it still bled several hours later. Melisse pressed her left palm against it, hoping the pressure would get the graze healing.

The meager light was fading quickly. Her blood might be only half-dragon, but she retained many of their abilities. Seeing in the dark was one of them. The darkness had never frightened her. She had always thought of it as a friend, a willing companion. Besides, monsters lurked everywhere. Even in the sunlight.

Melisse scanned the area. It was as if she had walked into a death zone. Everything was brown, gray, and black. There wasn't a single speck of green anywhere. No color. No life. Pockets of fog hung close to the ground, giving the space an even spookier ambiance.

The hair on the back of her neck rose. Someone watched her. Or some*thing*. She lifted her chin and let them come for her. She would show them something they hadn't seen before. Whatever hunted the Pinks had found easy prey with the small dragons. But she was something else altogether.

She couldn't wait to come face-to-face with this monster, be they human or something else. Zora was supposed to be a safe place for dragons. She imagined the joy on the parents' faces when she returned their son to them. It would go a long way in proving that she and the Kings were on Zora to help. She wouldn't stand by and allow any more dragons to go missing. This was something she could do. A way to help the dragons and prove she was one of them.

Until those thoughts went through her mind, she hadn't real-ized how much she needed those things. To be a part of some-thing. To *belong*. To be needed, loved. She could find the missing Pink, or at the very least, stop whoever or whatever was keeping them in the thicket.

Melisse lifted her hand from the wound and saw that the flesh still hadn't mended. She dropped her arm to her side and listened to see if she could hear anything. There was nothing but silence. She glanced over her shoulder, back the way she had come. There was no trail or path. No way to know where she had stepped before since the ground was hard, the earth packed.

The longer she was in the brambles, the more irritated she became. What kind of monster targeted younglings? If Con were there, he would urge her to think before acting. But he hadn't seen the grief on the mother's face. He hadn't heard her wail of sorrow. Melisse would find the youngling and any other dragons who had gotten lost in the valley. If anything else had happened to them, though...

She couldn't even finish the thought. If dragons had been slain, she would throw caution to the wind and retaliate in kind. She didn't care if it ignited the war the others were trying so desper-ately to stop. Then she would release dragon fire on the thicket and burn it until nothing remained. She wanted to do that now, but she had to make sure all the dragons found their way out first.

Melisse slowly picked her way through the vines. She could step over or go around some, but she had to climb others. It went on for hours. She began marking the ground with the toe of her boot when she thought she had gone in a circle. And her wound still slowly dripped blood.

She didn't know how long she walked before things became

blurry. Her toe caught on a vine, and she pitched forward. The spike of adrenaline jolted her awake. She saw her face headed straight for a giant thorn but was thankfully able to twist her body and land on her side away from the spike—just in time.

Her heart thudded against her ribs like a drum. She stared at the barb that would have impaled her. Dragon Kings were difficult to kill. Some called her a Queen, but she wasn't keen on testing the theory. Melisse lay on the ground for a few moments to collect herself. She hadn't realized how tired she was. The thought of getting up made her cringe.

Fae needed sleep, but dragons didn't. Unfortunately, she took after her mum in that regard. She had to sleep each night, but unlike other Fae, she only needed a couple of hours. There had been times, in extreme situations, when she had been able to go without rest and functioned well enough. There was no reason for her to feel such lethargy now.

Melisse pushed into a sitting position and slowly climbed to her feet. She blinked a few times before jumping up and down to get her blood flowing. It helped to shake her awake once more. Then, she continued walking.

It wasn't long before each step became harder and harder, and her feet felt weighed down. Like they were glued to the ground. She put her left palm on one of the enormous vines to step over it. Only she must not have placed her hand correctly because it slipped across the vine and over dozens of tiny thorns.

She hissed in pain as she jerked her hand to her chest. Already off balance, she tumbled to the ground once more. Melisse clutched the wrist of her injured hand and looked at her palm. Several small slices poured blood. She pressed her hands together tightly at her chest to stanch the flow.

Her head dropped forward as she pulled her knees to her chest. She sat huddled as frustration, then anger, then irritation welled within her. Tears pricked her eyes. She had wanted to be the one to find the youngling, but she couldn't even do that properly. It was time for her to admit defeat and let Evander know where she was. He would help her search for the Pink.

"Evander," she called through their mental link. She waited a beat for a reply before trying again. *"Evander? I went into the thicket after a youngling. The thorns cut me, and I'm not healing. It might be because of my Fae blood."*

There was still no reply. Was Evander in trouble? He should be able to hear her wherever he was, and it wasn't like him not to answer.

Melisse decided to try another King. *"Con?"*

Apprehension set in when he didn't respond either. Though there was a chance he had returned to Earth if there was an emergency. That settled her nerves. Somewhat.

"Cullen?"

Unease tightened its hold when he didn't answer either.

"Hector? Alasdair? Eurwen? Anyone?!"

Melisse hated the note of panic in her voice. When no one responded, she had to admit something was terribly wrong. She looked up at the dark vines arching and twisting around her. It was a plant. It couldn't prevent her from reaching other dragons. Unless that's exactly what was happening.

That would explain why the parents hadn't heard their son when they tried to call him back to them. She had rushed headlong into the brambles without telling anyone where she was. She should have at least informed Evander. Would the Pinks notify the

Kings? That was highly unlikely, since the dragons liked to pretend the Kings weren't around.

It wasn't as if she were completely out of options, however. She still had her magic, and she could shift. She wouldn't give up on the youngling as its clan had. She was tempted to go ahead and burn the area around her so she didn't have to look at it anymore. But she would never forgive herself if she did that, and the Pink died because of her recklessness. It was better for her to scout the area first.

Melisse struggled to her feet. Something niggled in her mind. As if there was someone else she could call for help, but she couldn't seem to connect the thoughts. Then she stopped trying. The need to lay down and close her eyes was tremendous, but she forced herself to ignore it and forge ahead. She tried to steer clear of the vines, but that proved impossible since she had to weave in and around them to get anywhere. She was careful where she placed her feet and hands so as not to slip or trip again, and anytime it became unbearable for her to keep her eyes open or stand, she took a moment to shake herself awake.

Her palm and arm throbbed mercilessly, but she refused to let the stinging consume her. She was the daughter of a Dragon King and a powerful Fae, after all. Feared by the Kings to such a degree that they had imprisoned her. She might never have known this kind of agony before, but she would endure it. Sooner or later, her body would heal the wounds. She just had to get from now until that moment.

Suddenly, her leg buckled, and she went down hard on one knee. She had to use her right hand to keep from pitching forward onto her face. Her stomach roiled at the agony running up and down her arm. It would be so easy to just sit. Just for a little while...

Melisse was about to do exactly that when she realized what was happening. Her eyes snapped open. She carefully pushed off her hand and tried to stand. She got halfway up before her leg buckled again.

"Bloody hell," she murmured.

She tried a second time with the same results. Tears of weariness and exasperation stung her eyes, but Melisse wouldn't give up. Giving up meant defeat, and that wasn't who she was.

Her eyes searched the vines near her for a plant she could grip to help her get to her feet. She didn't trust the areas of the brambles that looked smooth. Her left palm bore the wounds of such an encounter. Instead, she gripped the base of one of the giant thorns with her right hand. Her arm protested the movement, and pain shot through her muscles. She gritted her teeth and pulled herself up until she got her legs under her.

She smiled triumphantly when she was able to stand. But one step forward, and her legs refused to hold her. She landed hard on her right side. The agony left her writhing on the ground. That was when she realized that her body refused to go on. It needed rest. She closed her eyes, and the darkness engulfed her a second later.

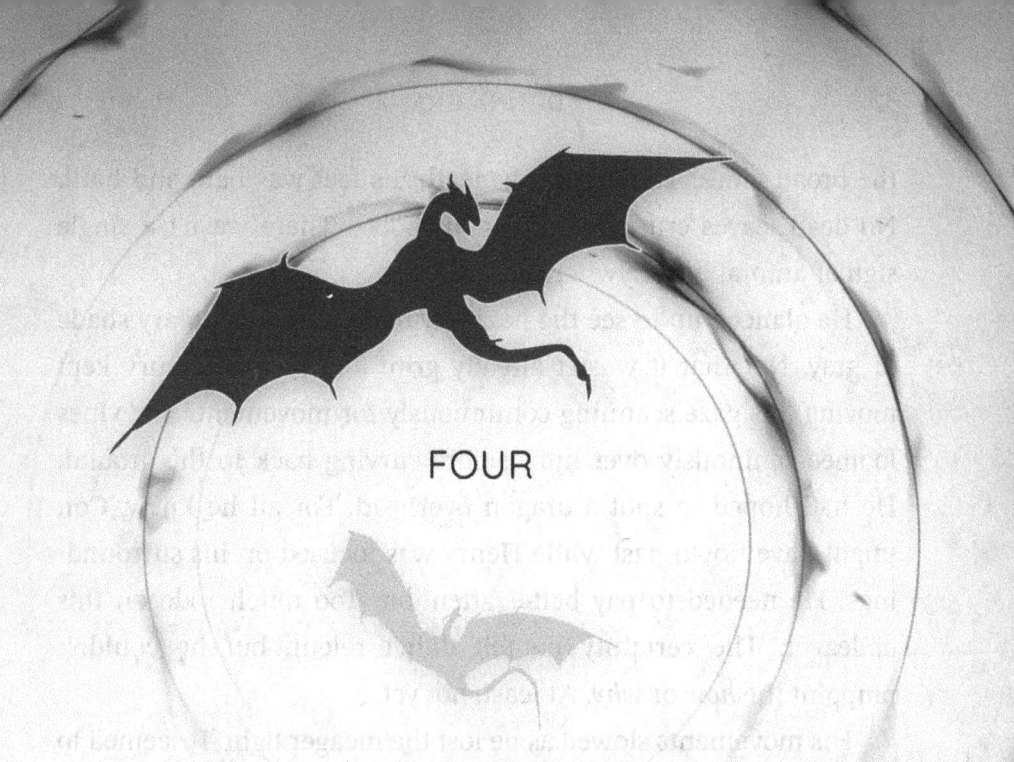

FOUR

There was no doubt in Henry's mind that the Druid was in the vine forest. He felt their presence stronger now. The Druid was there, watching. Waiting. The silence unnerved him nearly as much as the murkiness. The brambles appeared dead, but he wasn't sure they were.

The vines reminded him of snakes in how they curved and twined with one another. Seeing their hulking width disappear into the ground only to rise again gave them an ominous, menacing appearance. Which was probably exactly what the Druid wanted—assuming the Druid had created the plants. There was much Henry didn't know, and he needed to gain information as swiftly as he could. That clock in his head hadn't let up.

The air was thick, damp, and frigid. More than that, it felt angry. Outraged, even.

Wrathful.

It cleaved to everything. He gripped the base of one of the enormous thorns and used it to haul himself up and over one of the broad vines. The ground beneath his feet was bare and hard. No dead leaves crunched under his boots. There wasn't a single sign of animal life anywhere either.

He glanced up to see the hazy sky darkening to a dreary shade of gray. Not that it wasn't already grim and dismal. Henry kept moving, his gaze scanning continuously for movement. The vines loomed ominously over him, before curving back to the ground. He had hoped to spot a dragon overhead. For all he knew, Con might have flown past while Henry was focused on his surroundings. He needed to pay better attention. Too much rode on this endeavor. The certainty he felt didn't relent, but he couldn't pinpoint the *how* or *why*. At least, not yet.

His movements slowed as he lost the meager light. It seemed to go out quickly like a blanket had been yanked over the valley. It was a fanciful notion. And very unlike him. Actually, it was unlike the MI5 agent he had once been before he learned about magic, Fae doorways to other realms, Druids, and dragons.

Henry went as far as he could before his head started to hurt from squinting into the dimness. He slipped the rucksack from his back and rifled through it. He had no idea what Rhi had put inside, but knowing her, she had probably thought of everything. Sure enough, one of the first things he found was a small torch.

He clicked it on, and LEDs brightly illuminated the area. It made him wish he had done this earlier instead of straining. He shone the light into the pack to see what else was in there. He found four bottles of water, six protein bars, and a med kit. Henry drank some water, then continued on his way.

There was no indication of which way Melisse had gone. He thought about calling out to her, but something urged him not to break the unnatural silence. Was it just the Druid who lurked nearby? Or was there something else? Henry would rather wait until morning to discover the answer to that.

Unbidden thoughts of Melisse filled his mind. He had tried not to think of her, but it had been a hopeless endeavor. He'd been enamored with her from the first moment he saw her, even before he knew that she was the *weapon* imprisoned in Con's mountain. Not just caged but also hidden. Her existence had only been known to the King of Kings, passed down from one to the other before death.

Henry had known that Melisse was different, which was saying something since he spent most of his time surrounded by magical beings. Ulrik had been the one to release Melisse from her prison, but Con hadn't pursued her. Instead, he'd sent Henry after her so she might have someone to trust. Someone to befriend. And the friendship between them had developed quickly.

He still remembered the night Con had told him about Melisse and his part in keeping her prisoner. Con had warned that she could kill the Dragon Kings, something everyone in his position took seriously since only another Dragon King should be able to do that. Con had been told that if the Kings ever came under threat, it was better to kill Melisse than give her a chance at escape.

Some might envy Con his position and power, but not Henry. He carried the weight of his responsibility better than most could ever dream of doing. And one of those grave decisions had been to give Melisse her life and freedom. It had been the right call, but no one could've known that at the time. Con took the risk because he was tired of keeping Melisse a secret. There was probably much more to his judgment, but that was the reason Con had given him.

Henry turned to the side to slide his leg through a narrow

space between the brambles. Then he bent forward, pushing through to the other side, all the while avoiding the razor-sharp thorns. His rucksack got snagged, causing him to shift in several directions before he could free it and pull his other leg through.

The darkness grew with every hour, and the air became heavier. The silence was deafening. It became a tangible force that made Henry hyperaware of everything. He continued his slow, methodical process through the jungle of giant vines. There was no sign that anyone had been through the area. He didn't see any broken or bent vines indicating that Melisse had rushed through in either her dragon or human form. Nor were there any shoe impressions for him to track her. Though he noticed he wasn't leaving any himself.

He used his hand to vault over another vine, and a thorn nicked the skin at his wrist. He gritted his teeth at the instant flash of pain and brought the torch closer to view the cut. It was barely a scratch, but it warned him to be careful going forward. One wrong move, and he could end up impaled on one of the enormous spikes.

A soft laugh cut through the air. Henry stilled and covered the end of the torch to cut off the light as he swung his head toward where he thought he'd heard it. He was certain it had been a chuckle. Or perhaps a giggle. It had been faint, but there had been a noise. He was sure of it. Then again, there had been no sound except for what he caused as he made his way through the forest. He waited for the laugh to come again, but there was nothing.

Henry shook out his injured wrist and swung the torchlight to the ground before continuing on. There was no sign or sound of water, so he drank what he had sparingly to make sure he had enough for him and Melisse later. He snorted, shaking his head at himself. Melisse didn't need his help. She had magic in spades. *He* had none.

But where was she? And why wasn't she answering any of the Kings? Why hadn't she come out of the brambles? Those questions kept running through his head. Was the Druid powerful enough to hold a dragon? It wasn't as if he could fight the Druid. One that powerful would likely end his life with a look—though he honestly didn't know what he was capable of as a non-magical Druid, especially one with his title. Still, knowing that he might be walking straight to his death didn't slow him. He knew he had to find Melisse and the Druid. What he did after that was anyone's guess. He only hoped he would know when the time came.

He wasn't without skills, but they weren't the kind someone brought into a magical battle. He kept out of those since he didn't want to be a burden. It galled him to know that he came from a long line of Druids but didn't have magic, at least not in the traditional sense. He had abilities that he barely understood, but nothing that came close to being called *magic*. He'd been trying to figure out how that was possible, but he had yet to uncover any answers that he could bear. *It's just the way it is* was unacceptable.

It didn't matter what he was walking into. He had to be there. He knew it in his bones. To his very soul. It might well be his ending, but he wouldn't turn away. This was about more than just him. It was about his friends and family. It was about every occupant on Zora and Earth.

Henry blew out a breath. The malevolence within the thicket was cloying. How had Melisse not felt it? Or any dragon? Rhi? Why him? And if he had, why hadn't his sister? Everything they did as TruthSeeker and JusticeBringer was done as a team. As soon as he realized that Esther hadn't sensed the Druid, Henry knew he had to do this alone.

It wasn't that he thought he could handle things on his own. It was simply that he had been called, for whatever was about to happen. He probably should've sent Esther a text or something. What would happen if he died? As far as he had been able to tell after digging extensively into his ancestry and learning about the last TruthSeeker and JusticeBringer, he and Esther appeared to be the last of the line. If neither had any children, the TruthSeeker and JusticeBringer lines would end.

For good.

But not even that could make him turn back. He wasn't sure he could leave the vine jungle even if he tried. The Druid magic here was different, yet familiar. On Earth, the Dragon Kings were the most formidable beings, both physically and magically. If there was a Druid on Zora who was more powerful than the dragons, that was enough to make him take notice. And if that Druid also had the ability to harm Melisse? Then that being was someone everyone should be wary of.

What Henry didn't know was if it was only one Druid or many. He only sensed the magic greatest here. The inhabitants of Zora were divided between those with magic and those without. Those without had banished and condemned those with any abilities. It would seem natural for this Druid to align with the dragons.

The night dragged on endlessly. Because there were no paths, his trail wove all over the place. For all he knew, he could've been walking in circles. It was just by chance that the beam of his torch caught some color. He jerked the light back until he found the dark red drip on a thorn. He bent down for a closer look. It was unmistakably dried blood.

He began to hunt for more. It didn't take him long to find a small grouping of barbs tipped with blood. Was it Melisse's? The thorns were sharp, but could they pierce a dragon's scales? He didn't know what form Melisse was in, but he was beginning to wonder if it mattered. He studied one of the giant spikes. Dragon scales were particularly hard. They should protect a dragon from the thorns.

But that didn't make him feel any better.

Henry continued on, more determined than ever to locate Melisse. Fatigue weighed on him heavily as the hours crept by slowly. There was no more blood trail. He only had his gut telling him which way to walk, and he was beginning to doubt even that.

He rubbed his tired eyes and blinked several times. It was only then that he realized the darkness was pulling back. After another hour, Henry turned off the torch and put it into his rucksack. The enormous vines that towered overhead created a canopy that kept the valley in an almost twilight haze—light enough to see, but dark enough to make it difficult to discern objects. It was why he nearly walked past the foot. Henry jerked to a stop and stared at the booted foot to make sure he wasn't hallucinating. His gaze traveled up the leg to a body. Then, he saw long, silver hair with black ends.

"Melisse," he whispered and rushed to her, dizzy with relief.

She lay on her side, curled into a ball. Her lids opened briefly, showing him her black-ringed white eyes speckled with silver. He gently moved her hair away from her face and raked his gaze down her, noticing that her jacket had been sliced. He pulled an edge of the fabric back to get a better look and spotted the blood, both fresh and dried.

"Melisse," he said again.

She didn't stir. Henry checked her back for wounds and then gingerly rolled her over. Oval face, plump lips, stubborn chin with dark eyebrows that arched gently. He wanted to gather her against him. He wanted to kiss her and never let go. His gaze dropped to her hands, and he noticed the blood pooling in her left palm.

He had completed one of his objectives, but her condition concerned him. He shrugged out of his rucksack. First things first, he needed to tend to her wounds—ones that should've healed.

FIVE

Henry. He was there, on the fringes of her dreams, just out of reach. Like always. Melisse searched for him often when she slept. He was constantly on her mind when she was awake but disappeared in her dreams.

Except for this time.

He said her name, nothing more than a soft whisper, but it reached her all the same. The deep, silky timbre of his British accent. She loved the sound of it. She liked quite a lot about Henry. Especially the way he kissed. It made her think of their first one. Their only one. His lips had been tender and searching, needy. Desire had burned through her as hot as dragon fire. But the longing running just beneath had swept her off her feet. She sighed as she remembered the strength of his arms as he held her firmly against his hard body.

The desire in his hazel eyes.

In that moment, her very first kiss, she had comprehended soul-deep longing. And passion that not even time could diminish.

Then she had smothered the sparks of their desire with one careless comment. All she'd wanted to do was protect him, ensure that his mortal life wasn't snuffed out. Yet once those harsh words passed her lips, there was no taking them back—no matter how much she wished otherwise.

Something was near. She could sense it, even as the edges of sleep fell away. Melisse came to, feeling worse than she had before she rested. Her mind screamed at her to wake up and see who was near, but her body wouldn't respond. She cracked open her eyes to see that the night had given way to a soft gray. The longer she dallied, the harder it would be to get moving. Hadn't she been worried about something? She sighed as her lids fell closed again. She forced them open once more and caught a glimpse of jean-clad legs. She was dreaming. She had to be. It was growing more difficult to determine when she was awake and when she slept. Or maybe she had never woken.

The throbbing in her wounds yanked her from sleep's dark embrace. She wanted to roll onto her side, but she couldn't. That was when she realized that someone was there. Fear shot through her, turning her blood to ice. She blinked, and it took a moment for the face before her to come into focus. Tears burned her eyes. It wasn't Henry. Con had sent him away from Zora, and there was no way Henry would return—at least not anytime soon.

Yet those hazel eyes looked remarkably familiar. *Sunbursts.* That's what she'd thought the first time she saw him. An amber color around the pupil faded to a mix of green and blue. As if all the colors wanted to bless him.

"Melisse? Can you hear me?"

Her gazed dropped to his lips, and she noticed the dark stubble on his strong jaw and square chin. She wanted to reach out and touch him, but he was only a figment of her imagination. A dream to tease her with what could have been, what should have been. She turned her head away in hopes of making the image disappear.

Instead, a lock of her hair was somehow brushed away from her face. Her gaze jerked to the face again.

"Henry?"

His eyes softened. "It's me."

Elation shot through her, pushing away the lethargy and pain. She drank in the sight of his handsome face: short, sandy brown hair that had a hint of a wave to it, thick brows that slashed over penetrating eyes, a straight nose, and a wide, seductive mouth.

She frowned when she noticed a small, fresh scrape near his temple.

"What happened?" he asked as he slung a rucksack off his broad shoulders.

She had run her hands over their expanse. Felt the hard sinew there. How she wished she could touch him that way now. Just thinking about his arms around her made her stomach flutter. He was oblivious to her thoughts as he unzipped the bag and took out a water bottle. He offered it to her. Melisse tried to take it, but her right arm ached too much, and she couldn't move her left hand. Henry brought the bottle to her lips and tipped it for her to drink.

She sighed at the cool liquid running down her throat and pooling in her stomach. She tried to tip the bottle higher so she could drink faster, but Henry pulled it away.

"Not too fast. Tell me what happened," he urged.

"A Pink youngling came into the thicket. The parents couldn't get a response, so I went in after him."

Henry glanced around. "Dragons don't come back from this place."

"I know. I'm going to find out why and stop it."

"You're no longer on dragon land. If you're found—"

"Dragons are going missing," she said before he could finish his sentence. "I won't stand by and do nothing."

Henry's lips compressed into a line. "Con and the others will look into this. You can join them. But right now, we need to head back."

"You're lying." She knew it instinctively.

He held her gaze. "We have to get back to the others."

"I can do this. I *have* to do this."

His chin jerked to her hand. "When did that happen?" Then he looked at her arm. "And that one?"

She didn't answer because she would have to admit the truth. That she wasn't healing.

He put away the water and took out a med kit. He glanced up at her as he poured something over the cuts on her palm. She grimaced at the contact, but he didn't notice as he moved to do the same with the deeper slash on her arm. Then she saw him stiffen.

"That'll have to do for now. We need to get out of here," he said in a soft voice that didn't carry past her. "Now."

It was like being doused with water. She was instantly aware of the tension in his body. "What is it? What's going on?"

"I'll tell you as we move." He tossed everything into the bag and wound his arms through the straps. Then, he reached for her.

"Tell me now."

. . .

His nostrils flared as he stared at her. Then he whispered, "There's a Druid here."

"I can handle them."

"Melisse," he said in a clipped tone denoting his irritation.

She shifted until she got her legs under her and tried to stand. When she began tipping to the side, Henry steadied her. She didn't like how getting to her feet seemed to take all her strength *and* his help.

"You aren't healing," he stated.

He continued to keep his voice low. Was it because he thought someone was near or because the eerie silence seemed to demand it? "I will."

"We'll come back. Let's get out of here and see to your wounds."

"Why are you acting like I'm in danger?"

"Because you are!" he hissed angrily. He briefly closed his eyes and drew in a deep breath before letting it out. Only then did he look at her.

She studied his face, noting the lines of concern bracketing his mouth and forehead. "I have dragon and Fae magic. I'll be fine."

"You look far from fine. Not when I found you, and not now."

"I'm not leaving the youngling behind."

"We'll return."

She stepped back when he went to grab her arm. "The youngling might not have that kind of time. This place is..." Melisse looked around. "Wrong."

"I know."

"Then help me."

"I will."

She cut him a dark look. "Just not now."

"We need to see to those wounds."

"I'm already healing," she stated, holding up her left palm.

Henry raised a brow as blood slowly dripped to the ground. He moved closer so their bodies were nearly touching and lowered his voice to barely a whisper. "I felt this place across realms. I felt the Druid magic. The hatred here is staggering."

"I didn't feel a Druid," she replied softly.

"No one else did either. Not even my sister."

Melisse swallowed as realization hit her. Henry hadn't come for her. The pain of that was a sucker punch. "You came for the Druid."

"Yes," he said after a brief pause.

Not for her. Could she blame him after she'd made him feel inadequate because he didn't have magic? She told herself to let it go and look past the hurt. Instead, she heard herself ask, "And how do you intend to do that?"

The instant the words were out of her mouth, his expression hardened. Henry took two steps back. "I don't need you to remind me of what I lack."

Why did she feel the need to lash out? It only caused him more hurt. The chasm that had begun months ago widened. "I didn't mean that. I'm tired is all."

"We both know you meant it."

"Henry, I'm sor—" she began.

But her words were cut off by the sound of a woman's laughter. Melisse stiffened.

"Run," Henry whispered.

Melisse would do no such thing. She looked around for the woman. "Show yourself!"

"You speak as if you have the right to demand anything."

Melisse swung her head to the side where she found a woman sitting upon one of the tall, arched vines, looking down at them. Long, wavy black hair fell over each shoulder to hang to the woman's waist, but she had the top half pulled away from her face. Steely gray eyes were locked on Melisse.

The stranger wore a beige, fitted long-sleeve top with scalloped edges around the low neckline tucked into a long, dark brown split skirt with a wide leather belt at her waist and high-heeled boots.

"When we both know you don't," the woman stated.

Melisse shot her a smile that held no humor. "Do you really want to test that?"

"I already have." The stranger's stormy eyes slid to Henry.

Anger stirred within Melisse as the woman hungrily looked Henry over before giving him a sensual smile. "Who are you?" Melisse asked.

The grin vanished as the woman's attention returned to her. "My name is of no consequence."

"You're taking the dragons." Melisse had thought that perhaps the woman was from Stonemore, but she didn't have their accent. Hers was softer, crisper. Throaty.

"It is what they deserve."

Melisse took a step toward the stranger, hating how her legs trembled as her muscles fought to do as she commanded. She struggled to stay standing even as she said, "It stops. Today."

"There you go again. Assuming you have authority here. You're in my domain. You answer to me."

"Not likely," Melisse replied.

She tried to shift, only to find herself flying backward before slamming violently against a vine and then plummeting downward. Melisse saw the thorn and managed to shove herself away at the last second. She missed that spike but landed on another smaller one. It speared the back of her thigh, embedding in her flesh. Melisse bit back a scream of pain.

"Enough," Henry said as he stepped between her and the stranger.

Melisse yanked her leg from the thorn, only to fall into a heap on the ground. She gnashed her teeth together as she tried to sit, but something held her in place. Henry glanced over his shoulder at her, concern clouding his gaze. Fear slithered down Melisse's back, winding tightly around her middle. The last time she had felt anything like this was when she was a girl. And she knew she was once more in a situation she couldn't get out of.

One that would change everything.

The woman jumped to the ground, landing softly as she spoke to Henry. "You knowingly befriended a dragon, which I let slide. Now, you stand between me and my quarry. I can't allow that."

Melisse reached for her magic. She couldn't let Henry be hurt. He might not have come for her, but she wouldn't have his death on her conscience. She tried to use her magic, but it wouldn't respond. She couldn't feel it. There was nothing there. Only emptiness that made her stomach coil tightly. She tried to shift again.

Nothing. There was nothing. She had...nothing. How was she supposed to battle the stranger without the things that made her who she was? She was defenseless, exposed. Vulnerable.

Weak.

"You don't have a choice," Henry announced. "You have to go through me to get to Melisse."

The woman's nose wrinkled. "What a pity."

Then the Druid attacked.

"Nay!" Melisse screamed as the magic rushed at Henry.

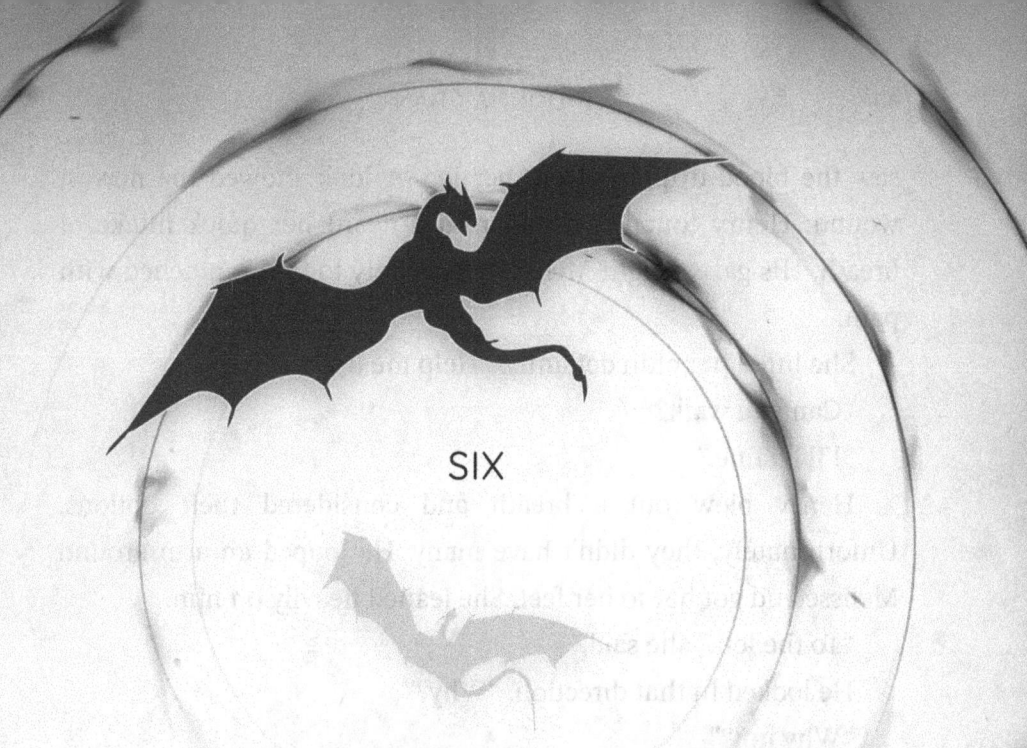

SIX

Something powerful and almost electric surged within Henry when the stranger pointed a finger at him, sparks flying. He felt rather than saw the magic shoot out. Pure instinct had him raising his hands and ducking his head as the blast came his way. Her magic was undeniably potent, unquestionably violent. It surrounded him like a vengeful beast intent on swallowing him whole.

But it never reached him.

Then, it was gone. He lifted his head to find that the woman had also vanished. Henry looked down at himself to make sure he was still in one piece, then whirled around to Melisse. Her eyes were round with shock, her lips parted in disbelief.

"You…"

He cast a quick look around. "We can talk about it later. We need to go."

"Where?"

"Anywhere but here." He dropped to one knee beside her and

saw the blood dripping from her leg. A look showed the newest wound. Henry touched her skin and heard her quick intake of breath. His gaze sought Melisse's face, only to find it pinched with pain.

She lifted her chin defiantly. "Help me up."

"Can you walk?"

"I'll be fine."

Henry blew out a breath and considered their options. Unfortunately, they didn't have many. He looped an arm around Melisse and got her to her feet. She leaned heavily on him.

"To the left," she said.

He looked in that direction. "Why?"

"Why not?"

Since he didn't have an argument, he turned them in that direction. He helped Melisse hobble around the vines. Climbing would be difficult for her, which dictated their path. They kept moving, but it was slow going. Much too slow for his liking. He pushed Melisse as hard as he dared.

Not once did she complain or ask him to stop. He knew her pain was considerable by her pinched lips and the sweat dotting her brow. When her good leg buckled, he barely held on to her and kept his footing.

"I'm sorry," she murmured.

He looked for any thorns on the vine beside Melisse before gently setting her down so she could lean against it. "We've gone far enough."

"There's no need to lie to me."

Henry removed his rucksack and pulled out the medical kit again. No doubt Rhi had included it for him, never once believing Melisse would need it. "Rest while I see to your injuries."

Melisse laughed and shut her eyes.

"Something funny?" he asked as he searched her face.

"If this is what humans feel like after they've been hurt, I wonder how any of you get up in the mornings. It's bloody awful."

Henry grinned and got to work on her leg injury. He propped her foot on the ground so he could lean down and get a better view. "We don't know any different. Have you never felt pain?"

"Not like this." She cracked open an eye to give him a brief look. "I've always healed quickly. Not as fast as a Dragon King, but quicker than a Fae."

"Lucky you."

He cleaned the puncture wound, causing her body to jerk. Henry glanced at Melisse, but she kept her eyes shut. He wished he could get a better look at the injury and make sure there were no thorn fragments left behind.

Henry worked fast. The wound bled steadily, soaking her pants. He applied a hemostatic dressing used by the military. The natural blood-stopping technology was advanced and worked as soon as it came into contact with blood. It also created a seal over the wound to create an antibacterial barrier.

Then he moved to her arm. The laceration wasn't deep. The bleeding was slow but steady. Henry cleaned it before using some clotting powder that stopped the bleeding instantly. Once that injury was bandaged, he repeated the steps with the slashes on her palm.

He rubbed his arm over his face and sat back. Melisse's eyes were still shut, but her face had relaxed. He would ask her about her pain when she woke. For now, her blood loss had at least been dealt with. Henry put away the supplies before tucking the med kit into his rucksack. He stood and turned in a slow circle.

Now that he had nothing occupying his mind or hands, his encounter with the woman began replaying in his head. He didn't understand how he was still alive. At the very least, her magic should've laid him flat. He turned his hands palms up and looked at them.

"Want to talk about it?"

His gaze jerked to Melisse to find her eyes open and on him. "I thought you were sleeping."

"Resting, as you suggested. Sit," she said, motioning to the ground with her chin.

Henry hesitated but eventually sat. He found himself staring into her white eyes, noticing the threads of silver running through them. Everything about Melisse was unusual and stunning. From her eyes to her hair to her magic. He might have befriended the Dragon Kings, but he had never fit into their world. He'd known it for a long time. Melisse had only confirmed it.

Yet he hadn't been able to walk away.

"So," Melisse began with a soft sigh, "I'll state the obvious. I'm not healing. You don't seem to have that problem."

Henry frowned. "I'm not injured."

Her gaze slid to the side. "The cut on your temple says otherwise."

The pad of his finger moved over his skin, and he felt the roughened texture of a scab. "I don't recall getting this."

"It's fresh enough that it happened after you came into the thicket." She cupped her good hand around her injured one in her lap. "There's more. I can't shift. I've tried multiple times. And...my magic is gone. I have nothing."

"There is more to you than magic."

"It's who I am. It's gone now. I don't know what I'm supposed to do."

"Fight," he replied. "You keep going like others who weren't born with such powers." He should know. It's what he always did.

She studied him for a long, quiet moment. "I thought she was going to kill you."

"I believe it was her aim to do just that."

"How are you still here?"

Henry shook his head as he leaned back on his hands. "I don't know."

"You stopped her attack. I thought you said you didn't have magic."

"I don't."

She gave him a flat look. "I know what I saw."

Henry jumped to his feet and paced a few feet away before stopping with his back to her. "I've never in my life had magic. Something about this place changed that. I don't think she expected it."

"That's for sure."

He spun to face her. "We need to get you out of here."

"I'm not sure she'll let that happen."

"We'll see about that."

Melisse looked away. "This place has halted everything magical about me. Now I know why I couldn't reach any Kings through my link." Her gaze slid to him. "It's a trap."

"Possibly."

"Her hatred for me had to begin somewhere. I've never seen her, so I couldn't have personally done anything. Add that to the fact that dragons who venture into the thicket are never seen again, and there's only one conclusion."

"A trap."

"For dragons," she added.

Henry blew out a breath. "Do you know how large the vine forest is?"

"It extends north through the valley. The mountains keep it contained, but I did see some of the vines along the mountainsides."

That's what he'd been afraid of. "Our best bet is to turn around and get back onto dragon land. We'll eventually make our way out. Con will only allow us to remain gone for so long before he sends others."

"What of the Pink I'm searching for?"

"We'll return for the youngling."

Melisse shook her head. "You can get out."

"What?"

"You aren't a dragon. If the thicket is a trap for dragons, you can get out. Plus, you'll move faster without me."

He closed the distance between them and squatted so they were at eye level. "I'm not leaving you."

"Don't be a fool."

"If this forest is one big trap, then any dragon who ventures into it will be caught."

She swallowed and looked away. "Which is why you need to tell Con and the others to burn it. And her."

"And you."

Anger flashed in Melisse's eyes when she looked at him. "Right now, she finds you interesting. How much longer do you think that will continue before she sets out to end your life?"

"I guess we're going to find out."

"Henry," she began.

But he talked over her. "How is your pain level?"

"My injuries are a little better, but I've got a rather large pain in my ass," she snapped.

He grinned. A moment later, her lips softened and began to curl into a soft smile. He sat and released a long breath. "We're in this together. Accept that because I'm not leaving you."

"Has anyone ever told you that you're stubborn?"

"Plenty. It's one of my finer qualities," he joked.

She didn't return the smile. "You deserve better than this."

"You assume we're going to die."

"She's powerful. I should've listened to you."

"But we have each other."

Melisse glanced at the sky. "Tell me more about what you felt. Tell me what made you defy Con to return."

"Power. Specifically, Druid magic. And malice. No matter where I went on Earth, I felt it." He propped one foot on the ground and rested an arm on his knee. "Each day it grew until I couldn't ignore it anymore. I'd hoped Esther would feel it, but she didn't."

"The doorway on Dreagan wasn't guarded?"

He twisted his lips. "Sebastian attempted to stop me."

"You were lucky to get past him. What if another King had been waiting for you on Zora?"

Henry thought about the fear, the certainty that she had been in trouble. "I would've found a way."

"All to find a Druid?"

The last time he had opened his heart to her, Melisse had made it clear how she felt about humans. He opened his mouth to tell her the whole truth, then thought better of it and simply nodded.

"What is so important about her?" Melisse asked.

"I think the thicket is her creation. This trap, as you call it, is all her. I wondered why a Druid wasn't aligning with dragons against those without magic. Her hatred of dragons answered that."

Melisse's expression hardened. "Then she has to be stopped. Someone with that kind of revulsion for dragons needs to be taken down."

"Nearly all humans on Zora either hate or fear the dragons. That can be laid at the feet of Villette, who has a vendetta against all of them."

"I've not had the pleasure of meeting her yet. Star Person or not, she has stirred up things here that are unforgiveable."

Henry agreed with her. It had come as a shock to everyone that the Star People had once enslaved dragons before one of them secretly created Earth to set them free. Villette had been after the dragons ever since. "We have two other Star People on our side."

"Lotti is still learning her abilities. She's gained a lot of ground, but will it be enough in time?"

"Don't forget Erith. Death has finally learned of her origins, and we know which side she'll choose."

Melisse lifted one shoulder in a shrug. "We don't know how many other Star People are out there. They could join Villette."

"They could join us. Or stay out of it. We can't make decisions based on what they *might* do. We need to fight the adversary before us. And right now, that is this Druid. If the other humans on Zora have been taught to hate dragons, then it seems logical that's why she has taken it upon herself to harm them."

"Do you have suggestions on how we can stop her?"

Henry shook his head. "Not a clue. You?"

"Besides hunting her down? No."

"If she's trapping dragons, then she must be doing something with them. Perhaps holding them somewhere."

Melisse bit her bottom lip. "That might be easy for the Pinks and the other small dragons, but not the bigger ones. You don't think she's killing them, do you?"

"Let's hope not."

"If she created the thicket, and she's holding dragons, then she likely lives here."

"It's a good possibility."

"Are you going to help me look?"

Henry took out some water from his pack and handed her a bottle. "It seems I am."

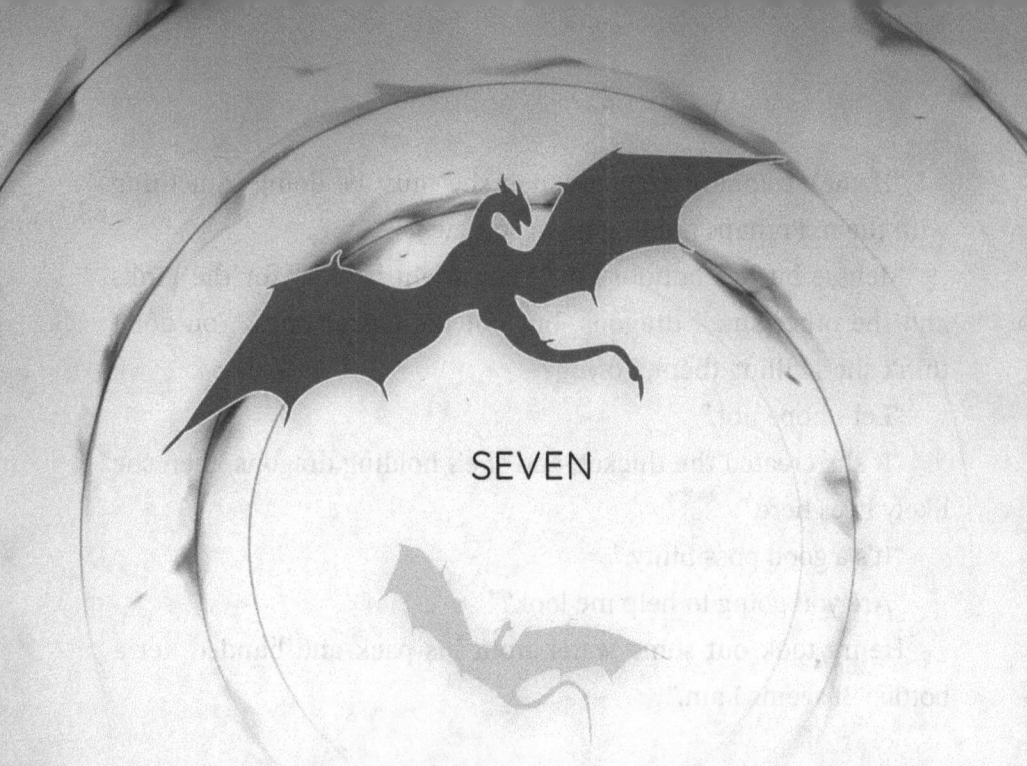

SEVEN

The agony made her want to scream. Somehow, she kept her bellow from escaping. She lifted her hand across her body toward her injured shoulder but stopped from touching it. She looked down at the blackened skin and charred remnants of her shirt. Even breathing was torture.

She forced her feet to move to the water jug. After pouring some into a bowl, she paused, leaning on her good arm. All she wanted to do was sit. But not until she had seen to the wound.

She used anything she could—the counter, a chair, the table, the wall—to get to her shelf of plants, hurriedly snapping off leaves and petals and dropping them into a stone mortar. It took more effort than expected, which caused her to pause and catch her breath. The longer she stood there, the harder it was to remain on her feet.

Sheer force of will had gotten her to this point. It would get her through the rest. Her hand shook as she found the dried herbs and added more to the bowl. As she put away the last bottle, it slipped from her fingers and fell to the floor, shattering and spilling. She ignored it and concentrated on using what little energy she had left to grind the contents with the pestle.

What should've taken a few moments took three times as long. Mostly because she had to stop and rest often. Any tiny movement that pulled her skin or the muscles around her neck and shoulder sent shooting pain through her.

Finally, she had everything ground and tucked the mortar into the crook of her uninjured arm, retracing her steps to the basin. Sweat trickled down her face by the time she reached it. Time wasn't dulling the ache. In fact, it seemed to be getting worse.

It took four tries to bring the mortar to the bowl and another two before she dumped the contents into the water. She held her palm over the bowl and pushed her magic into it. The water began to gradually swirl, growing faster as everything mixed together.

She rubbed her cheek against her uninjured shoulder and dropped strips of cloth into the water. When the water stopped churning, she took the strips out and laid them over her blackened skin. The contact made her clench her teeth, but she could no longer hold back her cry of pain.

Yet she kept at it until she'd used every strip. Then she leaned against the counter and turned toward her bed, shoving off and hoping it was enough to get her to it. Her legs gave out after the second step. She fell to the floor and lay on her back, blinking up at the rafters as the herbs began lessening the pain.

Who was the man who had deflected her magic? *How* had he hurt her?

He didn't have dragon blood. That had surprised her as much as his handsome face. It had been so long since she had seen another human. She'd thought the dragons had wiped them all out. Obviously, the outside world had changed if humans had dragon blood. She wasn't even sure how that was possible. But there was no denying the woman she had trapped.

She closed her eyes. Melisse. That was what the man had called the woman with dragon blood. Their relationship was more than just a casual acquaintance, and she needed to know more about Melisse. About *him*. That would be easy enough. Though she would need to be careful. She had made a mistake in disregarding him once. Look what that had gotten her. She wouldn't make that error next time.

His face filled her mind. How long had it been since she had spoken to another? Been seen?

Touched?

Her lids lifted as she thought about their encounter. He hadn't been surprised by her. It was almost as if he had known she was there. Could that be possible? Could he have actually sensed her?

She thought about how he had stepped between her and Melisse. What was it about the woman that held such sway over him? Did he have feelings for her? Did he love her?

Love. That was a word she hadn't thought about in so very long. She wouldn't now, either. Nothing good ever came of it.

She would talk to him soon. First, she had to heal.

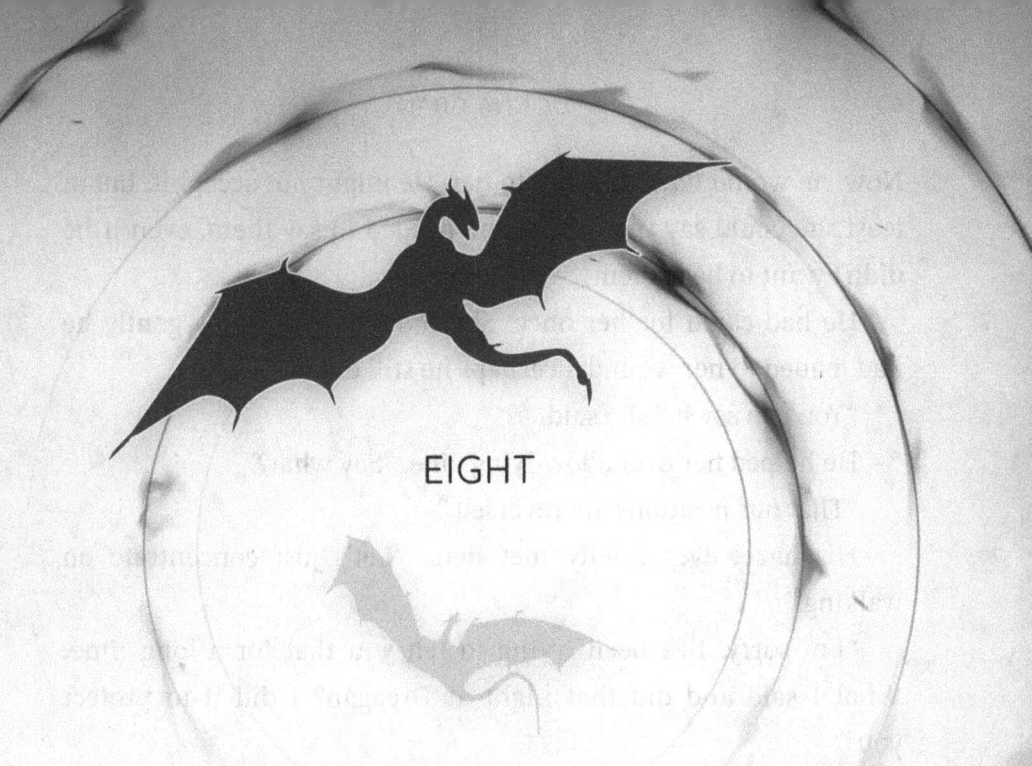

EIGHT

They were on the move again. Melisse still couldn't put much weight on her injured leg, but the fact that it had stopped bleeding helped. The way the fabric of her pants had stiffened where the blood had dried irritated her. If she still had magic, she would've changed them out with barely a thought. Instead, she had to walk around with the material scraping against her skin—at least the dry part. Some of the fabric was still wet and stuck to her skin. She wasn't sure which was worse.

She glanced at Henry. He had his arm around her for support once more, but she knew he wouldn't be touching her if he had any other option. She had meant it earlier. He deserved better than being stuck in the vine forest with her. But she relished every moment she had with him. He had to talk to her. Was she a horrible person for being glad he was there? She hoped not.

Neither had spoken about the past. Or her harsh words recently. She suspected that was just how he wanted it, but there were things she needed to say. She had tried to apologize before.

Now, he would *have* to listen to her. He might not accept it, but at least she could say the words. She needed to say them, even if he didn't want to hear them.

He had cared for her once. She thought about how gently he had tended to her wounds. Perhaps he still did.

"You can say it," she said.

He helped her over a low-lying vine. "Say what?"

"That our positions are reversed."

His hazel eyes briefly met hers. "Let's just concentrate on walking."

"I'm sorry. I've been trying to tell you that for a long time. What I said and did that night at Dreagan? I did it to protect you."

"You could've told me you were going after the Druid locked in the dungeon. I would've helped."

She had gone over that night in her head again and again. "It had nothing to do with whether I trusted you."

"Because you didn't."

"I had to do it alone."

He snorted. "You mean you didn't want a human without magic getting in your way."

"That's not what I meant." Why was it that every time she tried to explain, she only made things worse?

"You said what you needed to say. Let's drop it."

But she didn't want to let it go. He still resented her. "All I've heard from everyone at Dreagan is how great you are. You're intelligent, cunning, and trustworthy. You're a true friend. The Dragon Kings call few humans friends. You are part of their family, and it has nothing to do with your sister being mated to one of them and everything to do with you."

"Tell me," he said after a beat of silence, "how do you feel now that you can't shift or use your magic?"

She inwardly winced at his question. He knew exactly how she felt. "This isn't about me."

"But it is. You said that, without magic, you didn't have a reason to go on. It's easy for those who have magic to tell those of us who don't that it isn't everything and life has more meaning. But it's all a bloody lie. I've willingly remained friends with the Kings and became involved in a world of magic that includes Druids and Fae. I'm even supposedly important because of my bloodline. But that means fuck all when I don't have magic to go along with it."

"You have it now."

A muscle in his jaw jumped. He said nothing as he ducked beneath a vine and helped her under it. Only when they were walking again did he continue. "I don't know what I have."

"I know what I saw. That was magic. You stopped hers from reaching you." Melisse glanced his way again. His brow was puckered in thought. "Did you feel anything?"

He adjusted his grip on her. "How is your pain? Do you need more ibuprofen?"

"I'm fine." She was hurt that he didn't want to talk about it with her. She had thought they might get past things if she apologized and attempted to explain. But it wasn't enough. He was the one who didn't trust her now.

She couldn't say for certain why she hadn't told him the truth that night at Dreagan. Maybe she thought he might try to stop her. By alerting Con and the others, he had attempted to in the end. But she had gotten the evil Druid and stopped him from hurting anyone else.

Only a few had known of her existence at that time, and no one had been sure what she would do. The magic of Earth had told her she needed to take out the Druid to save those at Dreagan. And she'd be lying if she said she hadn't considered taking out her anger on the Kings. She still grappled with her bitterness and resentment most days. But on whose shoulders did the blame for that truly lay?

They walked in silence after that. Melisse wished she had the right words for Henry, but she could never find them. That seemed to be her misfortune from the beginning. Things always began well enough but ended badly. Would that be how it went with the Kings? Should she strike out on her own and save everyone a lot of heartache?

That might be for the best. It wasn't as if she had cemented herself as part of the Kings. She thought about the twins. Eurwen and Brandr were of two worlds, yet they chose to inhabit another realm. Perhaps that's what she should do, too—before everyone learned about her past, the events her parents had desperately tried to keep from everyone. Including her.

Melisse waited as Henry turned sideways and maneuvered past some tightly twisted vines. Once he was through, he reached out a hand to her and nodded. She linked her fingers with his and put a little weight on her injured leg. Pain shot through it. She overcompensated when she leaned onto her good leg, and it caused her to bump against a vine, one of the thorns snagging her shirt.

"I fucking hate these things," she said, wrapping a hand around it to try to yank it off.

Henry's hand covered hers, stilling her. "It might be best if we don't damage them."

"Why?"

"Gut instinct."

Melisse looked at the vines again and reluctantly released the thorn. She wasn't really angry at them. They hadn't taken her powers. Or had they? She stared at the barbs coming off the vines as they walked.

"What if it's the thorns?"

"Hmm?" he asked distractedly.

"The thorns. What if they're the reason I lost my magic?"

Henry's eyes met hers for a heartbeat. "Did you feel anything before you were cut?"

"Not that I remember. I had no reason to shift or use magic, so I can't be sure." She thought for a moment. "I do remember getting really tired once I was cut. I couldn't keep my eyes open."

"And now?"

She shrugged. "I'm still tired, but not like before. Though I can't say for certain if it's because of my injuries and the blood loss or something else."

"Could be either. Or both." He shrugged. "Just to be safe, stay away from the thorns."

Melisse barked out a laugh. "That might be a tad difficult."

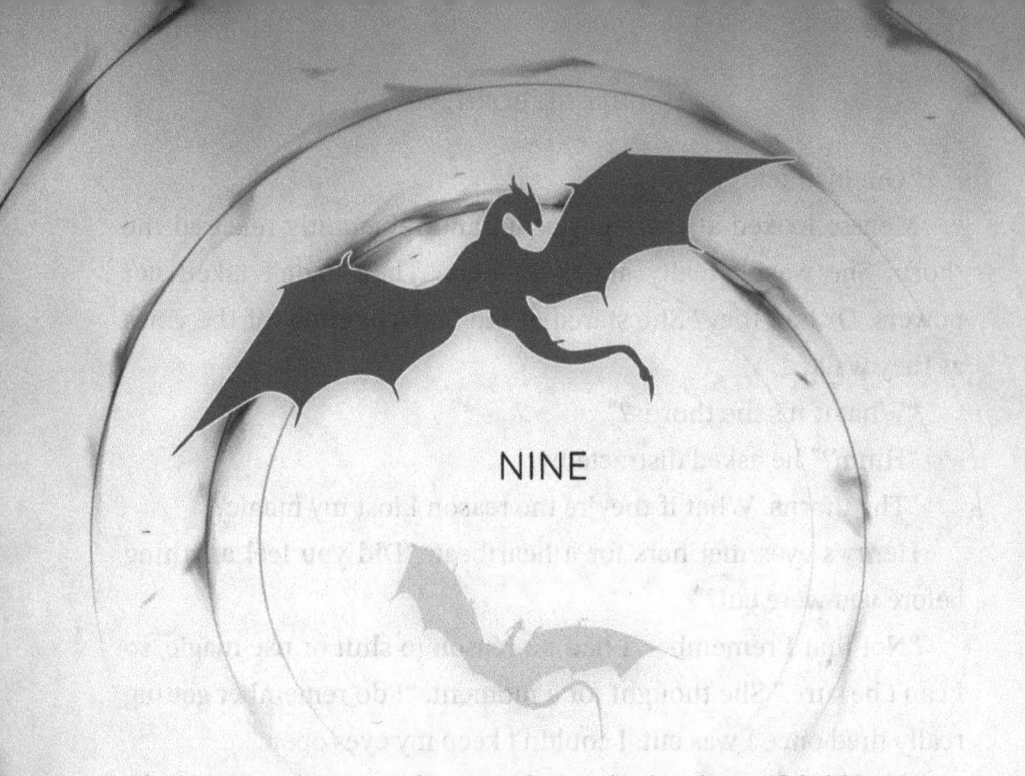

NINE

They were getting nowhere. At least, that's what it felt like. Henry debated his decision to remain in the thicket every step they took. Some color had returned to Melisse's face, and she seemed more aware than when he'd first found her. Though her wounds still weren't healing as they should with her magical blood.

He eyed one of the thorns as they passed. The only things around were the vines and spikes. It made sense that the barbs would emit a poison, but shouldn't it also affect him? Was it the poison that had taken Melisse's magic? Was that why he now had the ability? He wasn't comfortable even considering that. He had felt something, but for all he knew, it could've been the Druid's magic brushing over him and nothing more. If some kind of toxin in the thorns had affected Melisse's abilities, then every dragon needed to be made aware of that.

"I should rest," Melisse said.

He chastised himself for letting his mind wander instead of paying attention to her injuries. "Of course."

He shifted them to a low, curving vine she could sit on. Henry surreptitiously looked her over. Her breathing was elevated, and her brow was damp. The bleeding might have been dealt with, but she was far from okay. Henry knew dragons had to stay out of the valley, but what about Fae? It was difficult to tell if he could call for Rhi and have her not be affected. There was no way to know at the moment if only Melisse's dragon blood was being hampered or if the toxins might also be detrimental to the Fae.

Did he take that chance? Rhi was mated to Con and wouldn't die until he did, but that didn't mean she was immune to injury. And if she was harmed in some way, Con would retaliate swiftly. Any King would with their mate in jeopardy. There was also the moment Con had prevented Rhi from going into the valley with him.

Henry didn't know what that was about. There hadn't been time to ask, and he wasn't sure if either of them would've told him if there had been. Con's reaction might have been precautious, but Henry thought it was more than that. Though he didn't doubt for a moment that if he called to Rhi, she would come for them.

That time wasn't now. He would wait until he didn't have another choice. Until then, he would do whatever was necessary to keep Melisse alive.

Melisse blew out a long breath and closed her eyes. "If I never see another bramble again, it'll be too soon."

"I know what you mean." He scanned the area but didn't feel the Druid. He hadn't since their encounter. Was she the only one about? Since he couldn't tell one way or another, it would be wise to assume there were more so he wouldn't be surprised.

"Do you sense her?"

His head swung back to Melisse to find her whitish gaze on him. "No."

"You knew she was near last time. I should've listened to you. I'm sorry."

"We wouldn't have gotten far. It was better that we stood our ground."

Melisse grinned. "Is that what we did? I thought I got my arse handed to me."

She was so beautiful it hurt to look at her sometimes. And when she smiled, it felt like the sun was shining on him. "We did pretty well."

"You did," she corrected.

Henry slid his rucksack off and dug inside for a protein bar. He broke it in half and handed her a portion.

"Thanks." She took a bite. "How many of these do you have?"

"Four after this."

She nodded and lowered her gaze as she continued to nibble on the bar.

Henry barely tasted his. It was nourishment, which they both needed. He looked toward the sky. The sun hadn't peeked from behind the clouds since he arrived, but he wasn't sure if it was the northern climate or if the Druid had some part in it. Nothing about the vine forest felt natural. But he couldn't linger on that. He could do nothing about it, so he needed to turn his thoughts to something he *could* do. Like getting Melisse out while also searching for the Pink and any other dragons about.

Henry suspected the youngling was already dead. Melisse probably did, too, but she wouldn't admit it. At least not to him. He was out of his element here. Actually, he'd been out of his element since the first moment he realized that Banan wasn't a man at all, but a dragon who could change forms.

And Henry had believed his days as a spy were filled with unusual events. Nothing had even come close to what he had lived with the past few years at Dreagan. He would never be able to return to a normal life. His friends—his new family—had shown him how dull that existence had been.

Sure, enemies were always attacking the Kings, which usually meant some new evil to eliminate. And Henry went into each battle knowing it might be his last. But he was standing with those protecting Earth. He would gladly sacrifice everything for that.

His gaze returned to Melisse. He regretted his reaction to her apology earlier. It had been uncalled for. And it was time he told her that. It was time he told her *everything*.

"I had an ordinary life," he said into the quiet. "But a happy one. My parents were as average as you can imagine. As I grew older and then joined MI5, I felt the responsibility to protect my sister from every bad thing in the world fell to me."

Melisse frowned, and he shot her a crooked smile before continuing. "I know. It was an asinine thing to think, much less actually believe I could achieve. Add in the fact that I was away for days and weeks at a time, and that made it even more difficult to keep tabs on Esther. I wanted her to share all her secrets, but I kept every last one of mine. Then she found out that I was MI5. It seemed like a glorious vocation to her, and she showed interest. I was horrified because I knew the toll it took on agents. That wasn't the life I wanted for my sister."

He broke off a small piece of the protein bar and popped it into his mouth. Once he swallowed, he said, "What I should've done is give her the facts and let her make her own decision, but I was in protection mode and decided that wasn't the job for her. It left her no choice but to lie to me. I never knew that MI5 had contacted her to offer a job. She joined without my knowledge. I was so busy hiding the things in my life I didn't want her to know that I couldn't see her doing the same. Maybe if I had, she wouldn't have gotten dragged into the middle of a magical war against the Dragon Kings."

"She got out of it, though," Melisse said.

Henry didn't like to think about those dark days. "Barely. I was powerless. Literally. I could do nothing but rail against the unfairness of it all. But none of the Dragon Kings gave up on saving her. So many tried ways to bring her out of whatever magic had her in its grip. And they eventually succeeded. The relief I felt once Esther opened her eyes was immense. Things became very clear to me then. She was an adult, and I needed to treat her as one and trust her to make her own decisions. My vow to protect her had been made naïvely. And foolishly."

"You did it out of love."

He met Melisse's gaze. "I did. Just as I know you didn't want me with you that night at Dreagan. You were worried I might get injured. I know that now, just as I knew it then. The problem wasn't you or the way you worded things. It was me. Or my lack of magic. I felt inadequate and in the way. Unfortunately, I took that out on you. You never owed me an apology. I'm the one who should've begged for your forgiveness for overreacting and pushing you away. I'm sorry."

Her gaze briefly dropped to the ground. "Some of the blame needs to come my way. The way I framed those words that night caused you pain."

"It wouldn't have mattered how you said it."

She gave him a small smile. "Are we friends again?"

"We've never stopped being friends."

Her face lit up. "You have no idea how happy that makes me."

The need to lean over and seal their talk with a kiss was overwhelming, but Henry somehow managed to keep his lips to himself. Still, it was difficult holding her so tightly against him as they walked and not be reminded of the things she made him feel. But they weren't in a place where they could give in to those emotions. With Melisse's injuries and the Druid, they had to concentrate on staying alive and getting back to the others.

Henry looked at his hand. Did he have magic? He knew nothing about it. Oh, he had seen others use it, heard them talk about it, but he had no idea how to wield it. If he had somehow done something to the Druid, it had been luck. And he couldn't depend on that going forward. He needed to practice, but the Druid might be watching, and he didn't want to alert her or anyone else to how ill-prepared he was for battle. He would just have to trust that the magic would be there when he needed it.

Assuming he even had it.

It was enough to make his head ache.

Once they finished eating, Henry wrapped his arm around her again as they continued their journey. The air didn't stir with wind, rain, or snow. It was if they had entered a void. A part of Zora, yet not a part of the realm. It was magic he didn't know or understand. He had many questions for the Druid if they ever had a chance to talk.

Earth had powerful Druids, but none that came close to what he felt with this one. Given the strange happenings on the Isle of Skye, anything he learned here might help his friends there—if he and Melisse ever made it out of the valley.

"How long does it take a human's injuries to heal?" Melisse asked.

Henry shrugged. "Depends on the severity of the wound. I had a friend who cut off the tip of his finger while chopping veggies. It took months for that to heal enough that he didn't have to wear a bandage."

"Months," she murmured despondently. "It's very clear to me now how I've taken my magic and abilities for granted."

"Once you're out of the thicket, it'll return."

"You don't know that."

"And you don't know that it won't."

She shot him a side-eye and braced her free hand between two thorns as they skirted a grouping of vines. "Granted, I am thinking about the future and what might happen, but right now, I'm more concerned with our current predicament. The fact is, you have magic. It's going to come down to you."

"I don't know that I have any magic."

"You do. You were able to block the Druid's."

Henry swallowed. "I don't know what I did when we faced off."

"It doesn't matter. You did it. Which means you'll probably have to do it again. She'll be back."

"I know."

"She was interested in you."

It was Henry's turn to give the side-eye.

"Even you had to notice the appreciative look she gave you."

Henry shook his head. "She was sizing me up."

"She did a lot more than that," Melisse insisted. "Pay attention when she appears next time. You'll see."

"I bet she'll be after my head."

"Or maybe she won't. Maybe you killed her."

Henry frowned. "That's stretching things a bit. Maybe I blocked her magic. *Maybe.*"

"I think you did more than that."

"You were behind me. You couldn't see."

Melisse turned her head to him. "I saw you. You put yourself between us."

"I wasn't going to let her harm you. Not then and not in the future."

"Let's be pragmatic, shall we?"

"Yes, let's."

Melisse paused. "It was her magic that drew you to this place. My first instinct was to make sure she could never harm another dragon."

"As anyone in your shoes would."

"What if I was wrong? What if this situation calls for something with more finesse. Done by someone who has been in dangerous situations before."

He sighed, knowing exactly what she meant. "You saw her hatred clear as day. Same as me."

"Sure. That was impossible to miss since it was directed at me," Melisse stated sharply. Then she softened her tone and said, "Only you felt her. That tells me you're meant to be here. Do you deny that?"

"I do not."

"What else did you feel? What made you risk everything to find this Druid?"

Henry hesitated.

"Do you think you were meant to kill her?" Melisse pressed.

"I...I don't think so. I don't know."

"You do. If you don't want to tell me, that's fine. But at least admit it to yourself."

Henry maneuvered them around a tricky section of brambles. "Yes, I felt the Druid's magic. Yes, I knew I had to get here. And yes, I knew that if she wasn't stopped, the repercussions wouldn't just be here on Zora but also on Earth."

"Stopped. As in kill? You want to kill her? Mind you, I'm all for that after what she just did to me—and all the other dragons. If she's responsible."

"I don't know if stop means taking her life. She's powerful. Very powerful. The Kings need those kinds of allies when going up against Villette."

"Then convince her to join us."

Henry's head snapped to Melisse. "I might have brokered deals in the past, but this is way outside my expertise."

Melisse pulled away from him to lean against a vine. "You're a Druid, Henry. You know when she's near. Her magic brought you here, and you stood against her. That tells me all I need to know."

"It wasn't just her magic that brought me here."

Melisse waved away his words. "Dragons are being taken, harmed, or worse...killed. We know what's happening to me. It doesn't matter if it's from being cut by the dreadful thorns or something else. I can't shift to fly us out of here. I can't defeat her without magic. I'm not sure even Con could do that in my situation. It comes down to you. Whether by magic, conversation, or both."

"I'm not here to convert her. I'm here for you."

"I may not be savable."

"Don't," he warned.

Her lips curved into a small, sad smile. "Refusing to hear the truth doesn't make it less real."

"We *will* get out of here."

"I think she would let you go. I recognized the animosity in her gaze. I held the same kind of loathing for the Dragon Kings for a long, long time. If the dragons can't stop her, someone has to. *You* have to."

Henry shook his head. "We do this together."

"I knew there was nothing you could do to help me that night at Dreagan. I had to do that on my own. Soon, you'll realize there is nothing I can do to help you now. This falls to you. Even if I wish otherwise."

He closed the distance between them until they were nearly touching. "I felt Druid magic." His gaze lowered to her mouth for a heartbeat, and desire and longing surged through him. "I sensed the Druid's threat, her malice. But I would've run a gauntlet of dragons to get here. Because I knew you were in danger. I'm here for you."

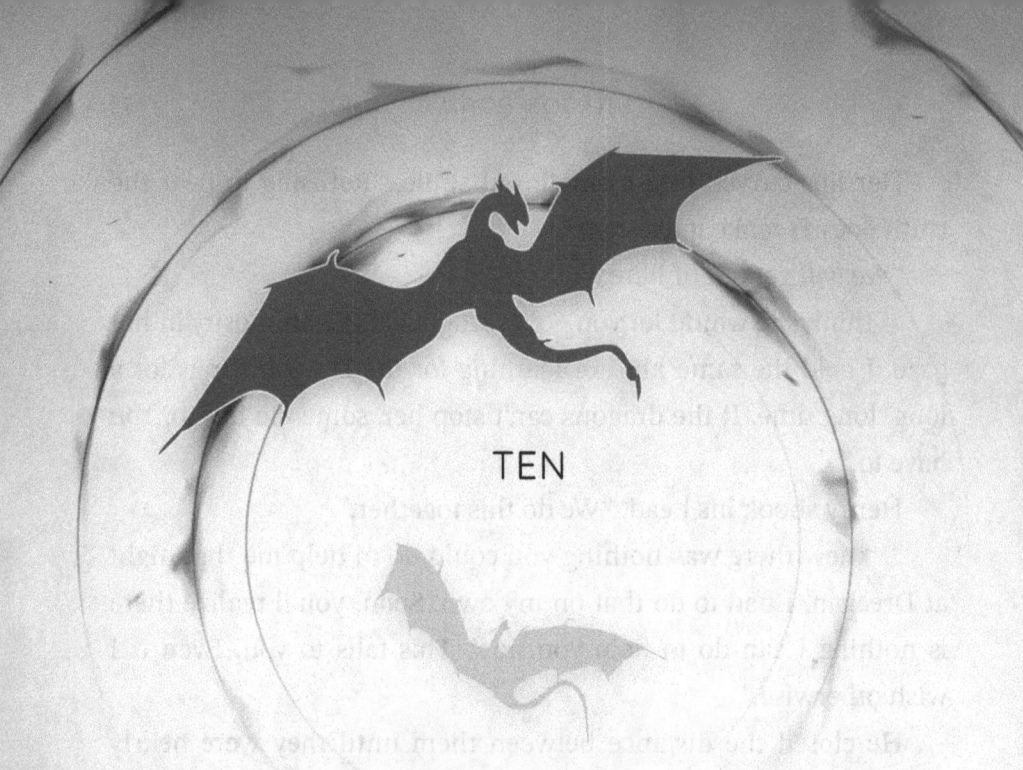

TEN

Henry's words rang in Melisse's head for hours. Even now, they stunned her. She hadn't been able to form a response. Not even when his eyes dropped to her mouth a second time. She thought he might kiss her, wished he would, but he had simply put his arm around her once more and started walking. She had no choice but to hobble along beside him.

I'm here for you.

Did he really mean it? Had he truly tricked Sebastian and ignored Con's order to return to face an unknown Druid...for *her*?

Melisse had been brokenhearted when she believed he had only ventured into the valley for the Druid. Now that she knew the truth, she was distraught that he had risked his life for her. She wanted him to live. Because while it might not be obvious to him, she had come to understand that she wouldn't be leaving the brambles.

Her leg ached incessantly. It was a pain unlike anything she thought possible. How did humans handle such things while their bodies took weeks or months to heal? It seemed improbable that mortals could function much less thrive as a culture. Yet they somehow did. She hadn't known how to treat the wounds, but Henry had been quick and methodical in his ministrations. Did mortals carry medical kids around in case they got injured? Now that she knew the difference between having an injury and being untreated, she was thankful that Henry had the kit.

The drop in temperature as the dim light started to fade warned that night was approaching. She saw no sun or moon through the thick blanket of clouds that never seemed to move. The only way to guess the time was by the fading light and the falling temps. She gritted her teeth as each step jarred her leg. The laceration on her arm throbbed from gripping Henry. She forgot about her palm for a bit until she set it down too hard on a vine, sending pain exploding through her arm.

Sweat ran down her face even as the coldness dried it. She thought about taking off her jacket but knew it would be foolish with night falling. Melisse found it better to prop the top of her boot on the ground and then limp forward without putting much weight on her injured leg. It was definitely better than holding it up and hopping.

Suddenly, Henry stopped and lowered her to the ground. She couldn't hold back her sigh of relief. His gaze raked over her as a frown marred his brow. He squatted down and rummaged through his rucksack as she looked around him to the tangle of vines. How far had they gone? They had traveled all day, so surely they had covered a fair bit of distance. Yet she couldn't tell. All the vines looked the same, which made it impossible to gauge any type of expanse. For all she knew, they had only gone a hundred feet or so.

"This is as good a spot as any to rest for the night," Henry said.

She accepted the water he handed her, and it took all her will not to drain the entire bottle. After taking a few drinks, she handed it back to him.

I'm here for you.

Her stomach fluttered as his words rolled through her mind. She would do the same for him. Without hesitation. She stared at him, her eyes lovingly running along the lines of his profile before dropping to his hands. They had touched more in the last few hours than they ever had. He was the one who held her up and got her over difficult sections.

"Let me check your wounds," he said as he opened the med kit.

She watched his large hands tenderly cup her hand in his as he gently peeled away the bandages. He brought her palm closer to his face and turned it this way and that to look at the scrapes. All the while, she felt the brush of his breath across her skin.

"The bleeding stopped."

"That's good." She lifted her eyes to his face, watching the lines of concentration there as he put on a new bandage.

His gaze met hers as he lowered her hand to her lap. He said nothing as he shifted to his haunches on her other side and waited for her to sit up and remove her right arm from her jacket, helping to cause minimal pain. Their eyes were still locked when his fingers gripped her elbow. She could feel his warmth of his touch through her shirt. His hand softly skimmed upward until he brushed against the bandage.

He dropped to his knees, bringing him closer. She wanted to reach up and brush her fingers over the dark stubble along his jaw, drawing his head down to press their lips together. She yearned for the feel of their bodies touching, the heat of desire swirling around them as their tongues tangled.

His other hand rose, and the pads of his fingers skimmed across her temple, brushing her hair from her face. Henry blinked and jerked his hand away. He focused his attention on her arm. She leaned her head back against the vine and closed her eyes, but she could still feel him. His fingers, his breath.

There was something between them. There had been from the moment they met, and no amount of time or distance had altered that.

"The bleeding has stopped on this one, as well," he said softly.

All too soon, he had her arm bandaged and moved away. She opened her eyes to find him watching her. If only she knew what was going through his mind. They had shared things that day, stuff both had needed to say.

At one time, she'd thought him forever lost to her. Now, she knew there was still a chance. He cared for her, had gotten past the Kings on Dreagan, and then convinced Con to let him come into the valley. For her.

His throat bobbed as he swallowed. "I need to take a look at your leg."

"All right."

"A proper look. While there is still some light."

She frowned and repeated, "All right."

"Can you lie on your stomach?"

"Oh. Of course." She felt foolish for not realizing what he needed. It made sense that he couldn't see the wound with her sitting as she was. She gingerly moved onto her stomach.

"I patched you in a hurry, and we've been walking all day. The clotting bandage should've worked, but in case it didn't, I have tools to stitch you."

She placed her arms, one over the other, then rested her cheek atop them. Henry gradually pulled the material hardened with her dried blood away from the wound.

"This can't be comfortable."

Melisse chuckled as her eyes fell closed. "It isn't. Though, sometimes, I focus on it instead of the pain."

"Try to keep your leg limp for me." He paused. "You should've told me you needed more for the pain."

"I don't think the pills work. At least I didn't feel the pain diminish."

He grunted. "They help keep the swelling down. I'm alternating two different kinds that should take the edge off some."

"Maybe it did. I've never had anything like this before, so I have nothing to compare it to."

He pressed on her leg near the wound, causing her to hiss. "Sorry," he said quickly.

She turned to put her forehead on her arms and did her best to keep her leg muscles loose. His fingers barely grazed her as he carefully removed the bandage. He drew out a small torch and turned it on to study her injury.

"What's the verdict?" she asked after a long stretch of silence.

"Well, the bleeding has stopped, and I don't see any signs of infection. I'm going to give you some antibiotics anyway."

She didn't have a clue what those were, but if he said she needed them, she would take them. Being off her leg did wonders for the pain. Henry spent extra time tending to the wound there. She was drifting off to sleep when he put on a new bandage and helped her sit back up.

"I cut off the part of your pants with the dried blood. Well, not all the material that had blood on it," he amended, "just the largest part. I'll put my shirt around the exposed area to keep you warm."

Her gaze immediately dropped to his chest as he shrugged out of his coat. "You're going to need your clothes."

"I'll be fine."

Melisse could only stare as he began unbuttoning his long-sleeve shirt to reveal the tee beneath it. Her mouth went dry when he quickly—and all too efficiently—removed the button-down and then the tee. She feasted her eyes on the wide expanse of his shoulders and the corded sinew of his arms and chest that tapered to a narrow waist. But that was all she got. He had his shirt buttoned and his coat back on in short order.

"You all right?"

She jerked at his voice and found him kneeling in front of her with his T-shirt in hand. "I'm fine," she managed.

He raised his brows and waited. She lifted her toes so her foot rocked back on her heel to give him room to wind the shirt around her leg and gently tie it off.

She smiled. "That feels so much better. Thank you."

He flashed her a crooked grin and then took a bottle from the kit, dumping two large pills onto his palm. He put that bottle away and took out another, adding two more tablets to his hand. "The big ones are the antibiotics. The others are for the pain."

She accepted them and the water he offered. Fastidiously, he put everything back into the kit and replaced it in the rucksack. Only after she'd gotten the pills down did he hand her half a protein bar. Then he chose a spot across from her, their legs brushing.

His head tilted back so he could look at the sky. "Perhaps we should be happy we don't have to worry about rain or snow."

"The monotony of this place is grating, though."

"That, it is."

They fell into silence. She was exhausted and longed for sleep, but it was difficult to give in to it when the Druid was still out there, waiting to make her next move. Besides, Henry needed as much rest as she did. He might not show it, but she was aware of it. Maybe she could get him to let her take the first watch.

Her parents came into her thoughts, and she wondered how they would have handled the situation. Her father had been the calm one and took time to consider and plan his moves. Her mother reacted first. They were opposites who had found the greatest gift of all: love.

"What is it?" Henry asked.

She looked at him, her brows raised. "Hmm?"

"You're smiling. What are you thinking about?"

"I'm thinking about my parents."

Surprise flashed over his face. "I didn't think you remembered them."

"I didn't. Not at first. The longer I've been free, the more has come back to me. Con was told much that wasn't true." She paused and drew in a long breath. She wanted to share what she knew with Henry. "My father's name was Lennox. He was a Silver and the King of Kings. Mum's name was Ailis. She was a Dark Fae and the first to ever build a doorway to reach across realms."

"Wow. That's incredible. What made her attempt such a thing?"

Melisse rotated the protein bar in her fingers. "Loneliness and the urge to explore. She didn't fit in with the Dark. She only became one because of her aunt, and once her aunt died, she had nothing. Mum used to tell me the story of how she found Earth. She said she had been drawn to the stars for as long as she could remember. She knew other worlds were out there waiting to be discovered, and she wanted to find one."

"How many did she visit?"

"I don't think I ever asked. I know she found Earth first and encountered my father almost immediately. She often said that if any other King had found her, she would likely be dead. But he was different."

Henry nodded for her to continue. "Do you know how they met?"

"He was swimming and surfaced to find a strange being." Melisse grinned, recalling how his eyes had always twinkled as he stared at her mum while telling the story. "He knew there was no other like her on Earth. So, he began climbing out of the water, and she formed orbs, ready to do battle. Before she could, he shifted into his human form."

Henry's mouth dropped open in shock. "Bloody hell. That's the first time a King shifted."

"It is. He was bombarded with all new sensations and experiences. He said it was overwhelming, but she helped him through it. Despite their differences, my parents realized they could learn things about each other. Mum showed him the Fae doorway and even teleported him a few places. He didn't like that," she added with a laugh. "Dad took her to his mountain to hide her from others as they shared the similarities and differences between their cultures and realms. And...they fell in love."

Henry shook his head, smiling. "You remember all of that?"

"It began as small snatches of memories. Over time, I've remembered more and more to fill in the blanks. I remember most things."

"Can you give me an example? What was it like on Earth during that time?"

She settled more comfortably. "There were certain places on the realm where dragons were scarce. When Mum and I would get stir-crazy in the mountain and need to see the sky, we would go there. There was one particular ice cave far to the north that we all loved. Mum created a Fae doorway so I had somewhere to go if I ever needed to escape quickly."

"Why would you need to escape?"

"No one knew about us. No one, save Osric."

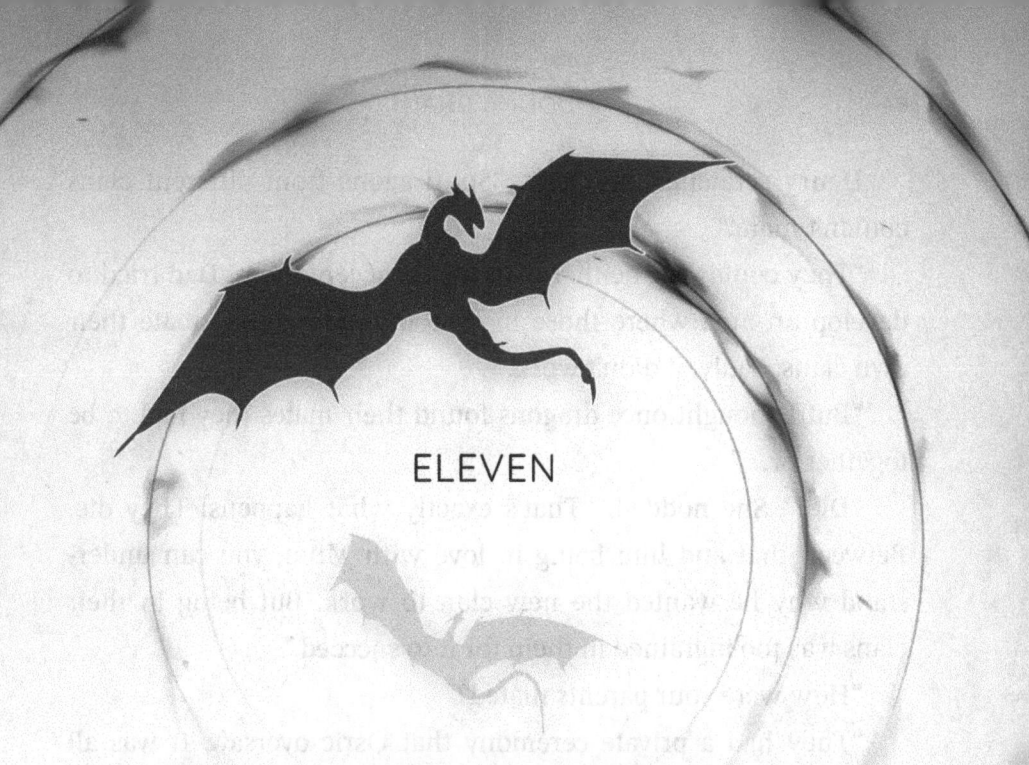

ELEVEN

Henry couldn't believe Melisse remembered her past. Or that she was sharing it with him. He stretched out his legs and reclined against the base of a vine while trying to rein in the dozens of questions he had. "Who was Osric?"

"My father's closest and dearest friend. They were more like brothers, actually." Melisse smiled as her gaze lowered to her lap. She sat there for a moment before looking at him again. "He was the King of Blacks. He, too, shifted in Mum's presence. He kept their secret and watched over Mum when Dad was away. I called him my uncle. My family might have been small, but it was amazing."

"Were your parents mated?"

"Not in the traditional dragon way. That would mean Dad had to alert the other Kings of Mum's presence, and that wouldn't have gone over well. Dad actually attempted to do away with the clans, or at least allow dragons who'd found their mates in other clans to be together. But it nearly resulted in a civil war."

Henry scratched his neck. "So, dragons from different clans couldn't mate?"

"They could, but neither clan would accept them. Dad tried to develop an area where those in that situation could create their own clans. Sadly, it didn't work."

"But I thought once dragons found their mates they had to be together or..."

"Die?" She nodded. "That's exactly what happens. They die. Between that and him being in love with Mum, you can understand why he wanted the new clan to work. But being in their clans was too ingrained in them for it to succeed."

"How were your parents mated?"

"They had a private ceremony that Osric oversaw. It was all they dared. Plus, it wasn't as if my parents had another place to go. Dad didn't feel right leaving the dragons, and Mum refused to return to the Fae Realm."

That got Henry's attention. "Why?"

"She stole a book from the Dark king's library. If she returned, she would be found and imprisoned."

"Or worse."

Melisse nodded. "Exactly."

"They could've found another realm."

"It was something they talked about often. Even with me. Osric told them to take me and find somewhere else. If Mum could build the doorway once, she could do it as needed until we found safety and freedom."

Henry felt sorry for Lennox. To find such a love and have a family, only to forever have to hide in fear of how the dragons would react. "So, you stayed."

"We stayed," Melisse replied with a nod. "No one dared to enter

Dad's mountain without an invitation. That meant we were safe from being discovered as long as we remained within."

"Except you didn't."

"I loved that mountain. It was our home. My home. I had my own space, as did my parents. Mum created a place that was cozy and comfortable. But, yes. There were times we chafed at being so confined. We left to one of the places that was ours. Sometimes, it was in the sand and the sea, playing in the water and climbing the cliffs. Other times, it was in the snow. One of my favorites was the desert, where we slid down the giant sand dunes to the bottom. Life was good."

Henry watched her face as she spoke. There was a spark of joy in her gaze that he hadn't seen before as she allowed her memories to surface. Then her smile slipped a little, and he knew what was coming.

"Life was so very good," she continued as her gaze slid to the side and a faraway look appeared. "I didn't realize it at the time, of course. I was too young. Now, looking back, I recognize it. Long for it. I believed the love I saw my parents share was what everyone found. The way they gazed at each other and shared secret smiles. How they always reached for each other, even in passing, just to let their fingers brush. There was always laughter. At least while I was awake."

Melisse paused and took a drink of water. She slowly screwed the lid on and shook her head absently. "I never went to sleep when they thought I did. Sometimes, I read. Other times, I played. And when I heard their voices, I snuck closer to make out their words. They were usually discussing me—or rather that they couldn't keep me in the mountain forever. It was the only time I'd heard them quarrel, and it was a recurring argument. What to do with me when I got old enough to want a family of my own. That generally led to the statement that it wouldn't happen on Earth, which led to the question of where we could go."

Henry wished he had sat closer. He wanted to reach across the space and take Melisse's hand in his.

"They could never decide on anything. I was appalled by the idea of leaving my home. I didn't understand their concern. Now, though, I know why it kept them up each night debating different options and possibilities. That went on for nearly a year." Melisse glanced at him, their gazes meeting briefly. "They never mentioned it to me, so I pretended I knew nothing. Life went on, and I believed everything would work out. How bloody naïve I was."

Dozens of questions filled Henry's mind, but he didn't allow any to pass his lips. He instinctively knew to remain quiet, that whatever Melisse was about to share was critical. The Kings believed they knew why Melisse had been imprisoned in Con's mountain, but he suspected that none of them knew what she had shared with him.

Melisse's chest lifted as she inhaled deeply. She swallowed as sadness snuffed out her happiness. "Dad explained his position to me. I knew the hierarchy of the dragons within the clans and among the Kings. I had seen him and Osric shift into their true forms. I even tried it, but I couldn't transform. Yet I had magic. I got some things from Mum's Fae side and others from Dad's dragon side. They both worked with me, and I was a willing—if not overzealous—student. As with most children, I didn't have any inkling of the goings-on for the dragons other than what my father shared. Though I did see them in the distance sometimes. We might share the same world, but they were separate from me.

I never thought of them as part of my life. It was a child's thinking.

"The three of us were supposed to go to the ice cave together, but Dad got called away at the last minute. There were more dragons headed north to the secluded location we always visited, so Dad asked Osric to accompany us. We used the doorway because Osric was fascinated by everything Fae and wanted to learn. I think he wanted us to travel to another realm just so he could follow and see what it was like." She grinned, but it was fleeting. "Osric kept watch over Mum and me. No dragons came near us, which meant we had the area to ourselves. We spent some time working on my magic before we took a break and had a snowball fight. Osric joined in the fun."

Henry realized his hands were balled into fists with tension. He spread his fingers and forced his body to relax, but it only lasted a breath before he tensed again.

"Osric threw a rather large snowball that flattened Mum. She came up laughing and sent one at him, but she added a bit of magic to make it go faster. He wasn't able to dodge it and ended up being clobbered with the snow. I was very keen to mimic my parents and become as proficient in magic as they were, so I immediately balled up some snow and used magic as I hefted it at Osric. He was laughing as he turned to the side, causing it to crash into his shoulder. He then fell into the snow. I thought he was being dramatic, so I bent to gather more snow, even as Mum rushed to him. Everything slowed after that. It was like the universe just...stopped. I'll never forget the look of panic and horror in her eyes when Mum looked at me. My perfect world came to an end that day. Because I'd killed a Dragon King."

Henry squeezed his eyes shut, his heart breaking for young

Melisse. As half-dragon and half-Fae, he could only imagine how powerful and uncontrollable her magic had been. All she'd done was attempt to copy her mother. He opened his eyes to find her quickly brushing away a tear.

"I rushed to Osric and shook him even as Mum gathered me in her arms. She tried to carry me back to the doorway, but I fought her to return to Osric. The next thing I knew, Dad was there. I expect him to fix Osric somehow, to make things right again. Instead, he dropped to his knees next to his friend and cried. Osric returned to his true form. The Blacks somehow knew their King was gone and called Dad to them. But I refused to leave Osric.

"In the end, I didn't have a choice. One minute, I was clinging to his scales, screaming for him to wake up, and then the world went dark. When I opened my eyes next, I was in my bed. I found Mum in the main tunnel of the mountain, standing with her arms around herself and tears coursing down her face. We felt the dragons' outrage. They wanted to know who had killed Osric. It wasn't one of the Blacks, so it had to be another King. They demanded an answer and looked to my father to supply it. But he couldn't give it to them without alerting them to my presence as well as Mum's."

Henry rose and moved to sit beside her. He took her hand in his, and she laid her head on his shoulder.

She sniffed and dashed away another tear. "I ran back to the doorway to return to Osric, but it was gone. Mum had destroyed it. I'd thought that if my magic had hurt him, maybe all I had to do was find a way to reverse it. The logic of a child of eleven. I begged Mum to show me how, but she kept saying there wasn't a way to bring someone back. I cried for the loss of Osric, never realizing what my actions had set into motion.

"The dragons expected Dad to investigate and uncover which of the Kings had killed Osric. The new King of Blacks was relentless in his search for answers. My father wouldn't give me up, which put him in a terrible position. It wasn't long before the Kings accused him of killing his best friend. There were those who saw my father elsewhere when Osric died, but it didn't matter. The Blacks wanted someone to blame, and Dad willingly stepped into that role to save me."

"Because he loved you," Henry said.

She sniffed again. "That doesn't make it any easier to bear. Mum offered to take his place, but he wouldn't let her. We spent our last three nights holding each other and crying until I fell asleep. Then they began making plans. The day the Kings came for Dad, my parents walked me to a place in the back of the cave. It wasn't easy to get to and hidden unless you knew where to look. It was where Mum and I were supposed to wait for Dad's return— still in the cave but hidden. Just in case.

"Neither of them mentioned what might happen if Dad didn't come back, and I couldn't get the words out. I figured it was better if I didn't know. Besides, Dad was the King of Kings. He would survive. He would talk reason into the other Kings." She licked her lips. "Dad hugged and kissed me and then turned to Mum. They clung to each other. That's the only way to describe it. He spoke to her, but it was a whisper, and I never made out the words. They shared a long, slow kiss. Then, he was gone. That's when Mum began crying. I felt so small, so insignificant. So useless. Everything that was happening was my fault."

Henry squeezed her hand. "It was an accident."

"Caused by me. Mum told me that the magic of the realm had chosen Dad as King of Kings and it would stand with him now, knowing Osric's death had been an accident. She assured me that he would win against any who came for him."

Henry's heart was pounding in his chest as he waited for her to continue. Her tears freely dripped from her face, soaking into the sleeve of his coat.

"The sound of that battle still plays in my head," Melisse said. "The roars, the shaking of the earth. It went on for what felt like days. Then, suddenly, there was silence. Mum's legs crumpled as she dropped to the floor and wailed. I'd never heard a sound so anguished before. And I knew Dad wouldn't be coming home. I wanted to ask her what would become of us, but I couldn't talk. Eventually, she got to her feet and grabbed my hand. She told me we were going away, that she planned to create another doorway somewhere. We were so intent on each other and our grief that we didn't realize we were no longer alone.

"I saw the Gold first. Mum teleported us around the cavern, but never outside of it. Then we were beside the hiding place. Mum told me that she couldn't get outside the mountain because something was blocking her. We both knew it was the Gold somehow. She shoved me into the hiding place. I thought she would join me like we had planned, but she encased me inside. The Gold came up behind her. She spun to attack, but dragon fire engulfed her before she could. The new King of Kings paid no attention to what was left of my mother. All he did was stare at me. He tried to get to me so he could kill me, but whatever magic had been used kept him out. At first, I was glad, because I was safe. But it soon became apparent that the hiding place was my prison. The mountain I loved became my jail. And the dragons I had revered were my jailers."

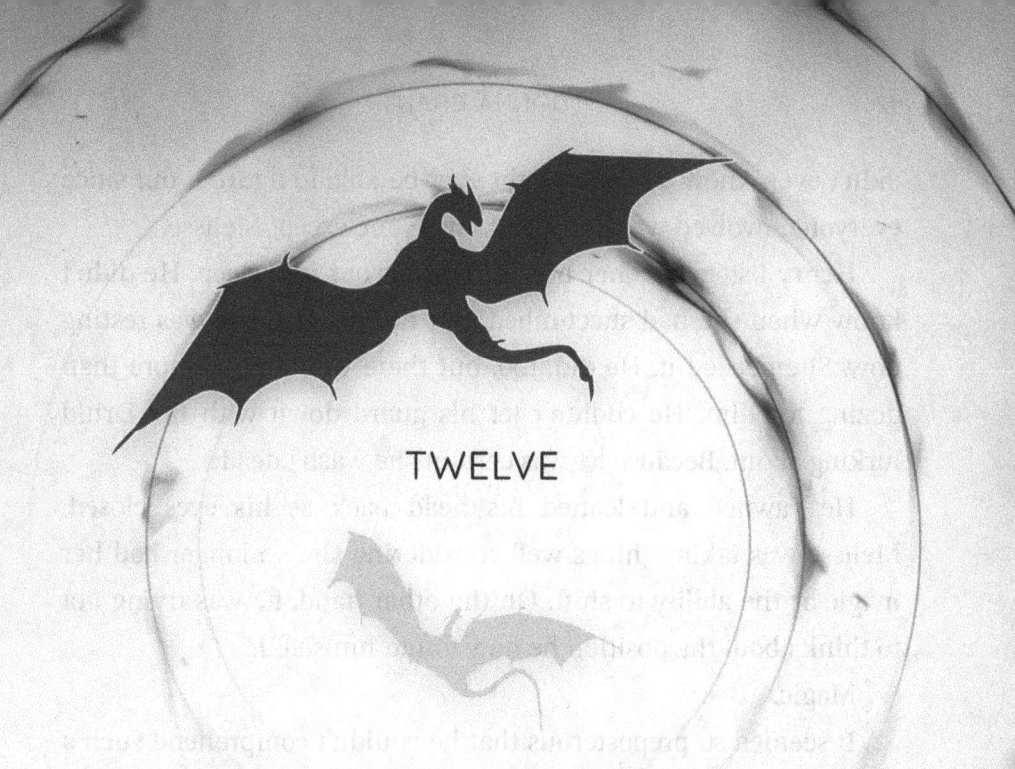

TWELVE

Melisse's silent tears cut through Henry, and her words hung in the air between them. She had been but a child when everything happened. When she accidentally took a life. It was easy for him to look back and criticize her parents for not getting her away from Earth as soon as Osric died, but they couldn't have known what would happen.

However, they could've planned for the worst. Just in case.

Con was immensely powerful, but Henry didn't think he could stand against the Kings if they all attacked him at once. Lennox should've realized that, too. Maybe he had. He hadn't been made the King of Kings without having the intelligence and strength to hold the position. He must have known he would die. Perhaps he and Ailis had even talked about it out of earshot of Melisse.

Ailis could've taken Melisse to one of their special places and waited for word from Lennox—if he survived. Why had they stayed in the mountain? That was where Henry kept getting hung up. He was missing something—something Melisse probably didn't even know. No one might ever be able to figure it out since everyone involved was long dead. Everyone except Melisse.

Henry listened to her breathing even out into sleep. He didn't know when she had succumbed, but he was glad she was resting now. She needed it. He did, too, but there wouldn't be more than dozing for him. He couldn't let his guard down with the Druid lurking about. Because he was certain she wasn't dead.

He yawned and leaned his head back as his eyes closed. Melisse was taking things well considering she no longer had her magic or the ability to shift. On the other hand, he was trying not to think about the position he now found himself in.

Magic.

It seemed so preposterous that he couldn't comprehend such a thing. It had happened so quickly, and then he'd had to see to Melisse and her injuries while putting distance between them and the Druid. Therefore, he hadn't taken much time to think about any of it. Now that he could, he wasn't sure he wanted to.

For so many years, he'd felt as if he was standing just outside the circle, always looking in but never truly a part of anything. He could admit that was his issue and not because of anything his friends had done or said. Ever. But now...if he *did* have magic? That changed *everything*.

At least for however long it lasted.

He might have only had magic while in the valley. Because he would stake his life on Melisse's abilities returning as soon as she was out of the brambles. And if that was the case, then there was no reason to think his magic would last.

Henry shoved that thought aside. None of it mattered. One way or another, they would leave the tangle of vines behind. That didn't give him much time to learn what magic he had or how to wield it, but he had no idea where to begin. Which was laughable. On Earth, he was surrounded by magical beings daily, from Dragon Kings to the Fae, Reapers to Star People, and then the Druids. He must have subconsciously picked up some things. He blew out a breath. He better have.

He searched through his memories for the times he had been around Druids and dissected each one, looking for something, anything that could help him. He tucked things away that appeared to be useful to take a deeper look later.

Melisse's head began to slide from his shoulder. He gently turned her so he cradled the top half of her body in his arms. She sighed and turned her head toward his chest. He stared down at her for a long moment, thinking over the traumatic events of her life before tearing his gaze away.

His feelings for Melisse were deep and strong. They had been from the start. He never should've pushed her away simply because she reminded him that he was mortal and without magic. She had endured more than anyone could imagine, and it hadn't turned her bitter. There was anger there—and likely would be for some time—but she had given the Kings a chance. Even Con, who had kept her a secret from all.

Could Henry have been so forgiving?

Could anyone?

He didn't think so. The ones who had taken her parents were long gone. She couldn't confront them, but other Dragon Kings were about. There was a comparison between her and the dragons on Zora.

Melisse's parents had been slain while she was imprisoned. The dragons had lost the Kings and their home to humans when they were sent away. How was it that Melisse could get past that while the dragons held on to generational resentment that only seemed to worsen? It was something to consider and look into deeper.

His eyes grew heavy. Henry leaned his head back and dozed. As soon as it grew light enough, he would have them up and moving. Sooner or later, they had to reach the edge of the valley. At least he hoped they were headed in the right direction.

Suddenly, something yanked him from sleep. His eyes snapped open as he stared around him. He could feel the Druid. She was close. He didn't like that she had snuck up on them. How long had she been there? No matter how he tried, he couldn't determine if she was alone. Maybe if he understood how he sensed her, he could expand it.

Something kept pulling his gaze straight across from him. One moment, the space was empty. The next, she was there. She now wore rust-colored clothing: a tight-fitting coat and a loose split skirt that hit at her ankles. The Druid met Henry's gaze before backing up.

Henry hesitated for only a moment before following. He gently laid Melisse on the ground and jumped to his feet. He walked to where he had seen the Druid, but he didn't go farther. He wasn't about to leave Melisse defenseless. She must want to talk, otherwise, the Druid could've attacked while he slept.

"This is as far as I'm going," Henry stated.

She emerged from the darkness. "Who are you?"

"You've never encountered another Druid?"

Her black brows snapped together. "Druid?" she said, testing the word. "I've never heard such a term."

"What do you and others call yourselves?"

"There are no others like me."

He was stunned that she would give up such information. *If* she could be believed. "You mean here?"

"I mean anywhere."

"That isn't true. I sense other Druids."

Her head tilted to the side. "How?"

Henry glanced over his shoulder to check on Melisse.

"She's safe from me. For now," the Druid promised.

"I don't know how I sense Druids. I just do. Where I come from, some Druids have special abilities like being able to see the future, talk to trees, or even heal."

"That isn't possible."

He turned to the side so he could see Melisse better. Only a fool would take the word of an enemy. "I assure you it is."

"Where do you come from where there are such things? Your accent is strange."

Henry licked his lips, unsure what to divulge. He decided on the truth. "I'm not from here. My home is far, far away."

"Then why are you in my valley?"

"I sensed you and your magic." He swung his head to Melisse. "I knew she was in danger."

The Druid snorted. "You're a fool to feel anything but contempt for her. Do you know what she is?"

"I do." He looked at the Druid. "Though I don't think you're aware of what she *really* is."

"She's a dragon." The Druid all but spat the words. The venom in them was palpable. "Her trying to appear human won't stop me from accomplishing my task."

Henry eyed her. "What task?"

"Ridding Zora of dragons."

"That's an impossible undertaking."

She smiled, the movement cold and malevolent. "It doesn't matter how long it takes. I will do it. I've already taken thousands."

Thousands? He kept his face neutral, but inside, he was stunned. When the Kings discovered this, they would raze the brambles to the ground, taking her with it. "Why would you do such a thing?"

"Retaliation."

"For what?"

She lovingly ran a hand along one of the vines. "How are the dragons able to look like us?"

"How do you know I'm not one of them?"

"You still have magic."

It was just as he and Melisse had suspected. "It's the thorns, isn't it?"

She shot him a devilish grin. "Maybe. Answer my question. How are the dragons able to change shape?"

"Not all can. Only a special few."

"Did you help them achieve this feat?"

Henry slowly shook his head. "I did not, but you should know they'll retaliate swiftly."

"They can try."

He had gotten some answers, but not nearly enough. The only way he could learn anything was by asking. "Who are you?"

"Apparently, a Druid."

"What is your name?"

"You didn't share yours," she replied.

He hesitated before he said, "Henry."

"Why are you helping a dragon, Henry?"

"She's my friend."

"You should be careful about who you choose as a friend."

"Melisse has done nothing to you."

The Druid shrugged one shoulder, her lips twisting. "She's a dragon. That's enough for me."

"She's half-dragon, half-Fae."

"I don't know or care what a Fae is. The fact that she has dragon blood is all I need to know."

Henry glanced at Melisse to find her still sleeping. "You should stop this assault on the dragons and return to your people."

"I don't have any people. I'm the last human on Zora." She pointed at Melisse, fury tightening her face. "They have no right to change shapes into my kind."

"You're wrong about the humans. There are hundreds of thousands on Zora."

"Stop lying!"

"I'm not. You can see for yourself."

She sneered at him. "You would say anything if you thought it would keep me from harming her."

"I'm trying to help you."

"Why?"

"So you don't die." As soon as the words were out, he knew they were true. He didn't want her to die. She was important, but he hadn't figured out how yet.

The Druid laughed. "I won't be the one to die."

"I wouldn't be so sure."

"I had a mind to let you go free."

He shrugged. "Do what you have to do. Just as I will."

"We could've been friends."

"Yes. We could have."

"What a pity," she said in a soft voice.

He saw her turning to leave and hurriedly said, "You never told me your name."

"I'll give you one chance. Walk away now. Leave the dragon, and I'll let you return to your friends."

"I'm not leaving Melisse."

The Druid held his gaze for a long moment. "So be it."

She was gone in an instant. Henry returned to Melisse and lowered himself beside her. A lot about his conversation with the Druid disturbed him, but the one thing he kept focusing on was that she thought she was the last human. How was that even possible?

He raised his hands and looked at his palms. From this moment until they were out of the valley, he would have to be ready for an attack. It could come from anywhere. He'd had a chance to connect with the Druid, and he had failed.

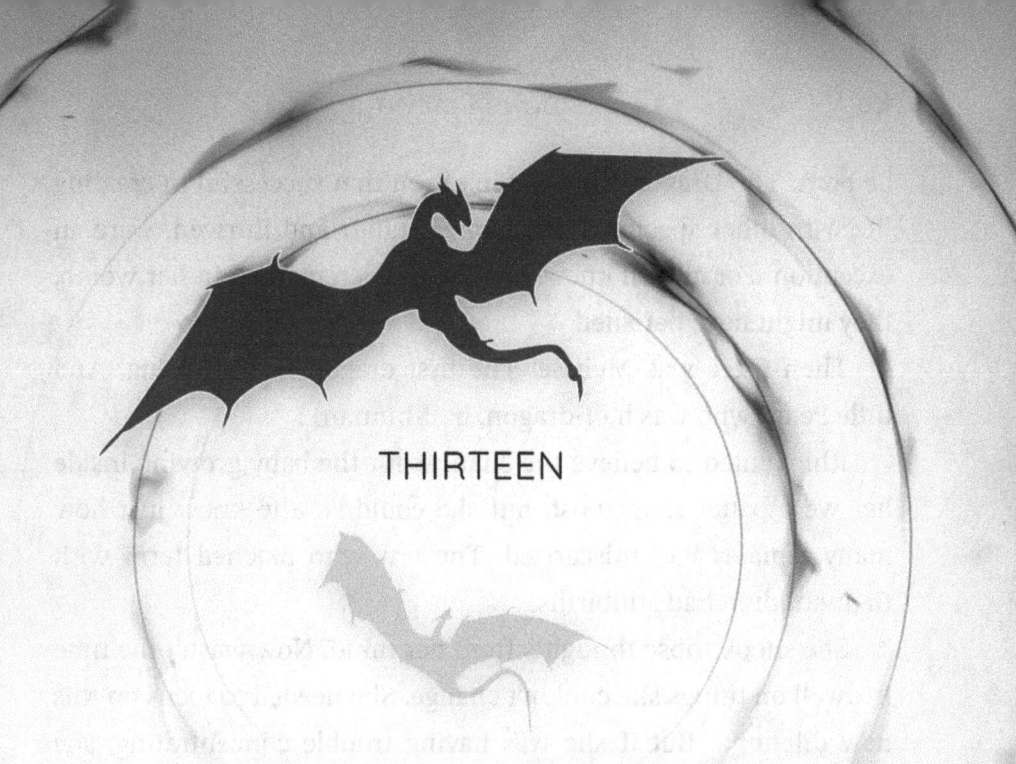

THIRTEEN

Just when they didn't think another shoe could drop, it did. Rhi thought she would get used to such a thing after so many decades of battling enemies. But she hadn't. She watched Con pace, her mate glancing every few seconds at the enormous brambles with their giant thorns.

She knew that look. He was about to go in after Henry and Melisse. Con felt responsible for Melisse. He had kept her a secret from everyone from the moment he became King of Kings, and nothing Rhi had said since Melisse regained her freedom had relieved him of the burden he continued to carry.

His shoulders were broad and strong, but everyone had a breaking point. He could only lug around so much before he stumbled. She clenched her hand into a fist so she didn't place it over her stomach. They hadn't told anyone that she was pregnant. And there were several reasons for that decision.

It wasn't the best time for a bairn, but it wasn't as if they had been trying. There was also a good chance the baby would never be born. The Dragon Kings hadn't been that successful in creating life with other species. Their twins, Brandr and Eurwen, were an exception. For all Rhi knew, had the twins remained in her womb, they might have perished.

Then there was Melisse. The first dragon/Fae offspring. And little Pearl, who was half-dragon, half-human.

Rhi wanted to believe the chances for the baby growing inside her were better than most, but she couldn't. She knew just how many females had miscarried. The few who reached term with their children had stillbirths.

She shook those thoughts from her mind. Now wasn't the time to dwell on things she couldn't change. She needed to focus on this new dilemma. But if she was having trouble concentrating, she suspected Con was, too.

He pivoted, his black gaze meeting hers. His lips were compressed, his face set in grim lines. "I doona like this," he said as he neared.

"You can't go after them."

"We doona know what's happening in there. What if they're in trouble?"

She took hold of his arm before he could turn to continue pacing. "You can't go in there. No other dragons can."

"I doona want you in there either."

"I'm not going, but there is someone who can."

The lines smoothed on his face. "Lotti."

"Aye."

Con ran a hand over his mouth and chin, allowing her to see his weariness. "Another enemy? This realm was for the dragons, yet it feels as if everything and everyone is pushing them out."

"Maybe that is exactly what's happening. We can't know that for sure. Not yet, anyway."

"We're stretched too thin." He shook his head. "I see the worry on everyone's faces."

Rhi cupped his face in her hands. "This is what Villette wants. She wants you to feel cornered, to believe you're defeated. We're not. You've never backed down from anyone, and we're certainly not going to start now."

"We?" he asked with a grin.

"We. Always and forever *we*."

He pulled her against him, his gaze fierce as he looked at her. "Always and forever."

"I'll return shortly with Lotti, and then we'll find Melisse and Henry."

He slid his hand to the back of her neck and held her head as their lips pressed together for a lingering kiss. She leaned back and winked before teleporting to Iron Hall. The underground city was gradually coming back to life as the Kings went through it, repairing the ruins.

Rhi appeared in the main section of the city, what most called the common room. Every stairway and hall led back to the center. Her gaze flitted upward to the mammoth tree above and its intertwining roots that held it steady, allowing sunlight to pour into the pool below. She heard voices to the left and followed them.

Tamlyn was in the middle of her lessons with the children. Rhi smiled at the Banshee and moved on before the kids noticed her. Each of the children seated there had been saved from execution at the nearby city of Stonemore, and all simply because they had magic. Iron Hall had been a refuge for Tamlyn and her friends, Sian and Jenefer. Now, it was home to anyone with magic.

A few doors down, Rhi entered Sian's retreat. The Alchemist had tables lining the walls, each with an assortment of glass bottles. Rhi had no idea what kind of experiments Sian conducted, but she was exceptional at her craft. If there was an ailment, Sian had concocted a remedy.

Rhi moved on. More voices led her farther down the corridor. That's where she found Lotti and Alasdair training. The King of Amethysts saw her first. Alasdair halted in their training and motioned Rhi forward.

"Sorry to interrupt," she told them as she approached. "We have an issue."

Alasdair's brow furrowed. "Is it Villette?"

"We're not sure what it is." Rhi paused. "Word hasn't gone out yet, but it will soon. Melisse joined Evander in the north. A clan of Pinks were nearby, and a youngling disappeared into a valley of brambles. Apparently, if any dragon goes in, they're never seen again. And Melisse went in after the Pink."

"I take it Con tried to contact her?" Alasdair said.

Rhi nodded. "So has Evander. She hasn't responded."

Lotti bobbed her head of blond hair, the ends just brushing her shoulders. "You think this is something the Star People created?"

"We're not sure," Rhi admitted. "Henry is on Zora. He said he felt Druid magic coming through the Fae doorway on Earth and had for some time. Told us it had only grown stronger. He went in after Melisse. Something's off about all of this. Something I can't quite put my finger on."

Alasdair crossed his arms over his chest. "Druids on Zora. Makes sense, I suppose."

Lotti glanced at Alasdair before turning to Rhi. "What do you need us to do?"

"Actually, I need you," Rhi told her. "We're not letting any more dragons enter the brambles. Only a small portion of it is on our side of the border. The rest extends north in a wide valley."

Lotti's turquoise gaze was steady. "You want me to find them."

"You may be the only one who can."

"What are we waiting for? Let's go," Lotti said.

Rhi didn't bother asking if Alasdair was coming. He would want to remain with his mate. Rhi laid her hands on each of them and jumped everyone. Teleporting was one of Lotti's many abilities, but it wasn't always easy for her to achieve, and there was no time to waste.

They arrived to find Con still pacing, his gaze locked on the vines.

"Bloody hell," Alasdair murmured when he caught sight of the enormous plants.

Lotti immediately made her way to the thicket, stopping just before she entered. She studied the vines for a moment. They waited for Lotti to continue on, but she didn't budge. Finally, after several minutes, she turned on her heel and made her way to the three of them.

"What's wrong?" Con asked.

Lotti's brow was puckered in a deep frown. "I can't enter."

"What?" Rhi and Con asked in unison.

Alasdair studied the thicket. "If this is a Druid, they shouldn't be able to keep a Star Person out."

"They are," Lotti stated. "There's a barrier there that refuses to let me through. I'm sorry. It looks like I won't be going in after Melisse and Henry."

Rhi faced Con. "That leaves me."

"Nay," he stated firmly.

She felt Alasdair's and Lotti's gazes on her, but she didn't look away from her mate. "We don't have a choice. One or both of them could be in trouble."

"What about Tamlyn? Or even Jeyra. Neither is a dragon," Lotti said.

"But they're both dragon mates," Alasdair pointed out. His gaze swung to Con. "Does that matter?"

Rhi shrugged. "We hadn't thought of that."

"Should that make a difference?" Lotti asked.

Con threw up his hands in frustration. "You know as much as we do. Dragons are the ones disappearing. The Pink I finally managed to get something out of told me that dragons are able to walk in easily, but they're never seen again. And all communication ceases. I watched Henry enter without an issue, so we know it isna just dragons who can get in."

"He's not mated to a dragon, though. That could make a difference," Alasdair pointed out.

Lotti shrugged. "Alasdair and I haven't done the ceremony yet either. I should've been able to enter."

"We're grasping at fucking straws," Con said as he glared at the vines.

Rhi slid her hand into his. "Then we continue looking for a way to get inside and find Henry and Melisse. We could ask Esha if she would be willing to go in after them."

"Nay," he said with a shake of his head. "No King will stand by while their mate enters such a perilous area where no one comes back out. Lotti was our best bet because she is a Star Person."

Alasdair offered, "I'll fly over it. Maybe I'll see something."

"We'll both go," Lotti said. "I'll make sure we're cloaked so no one can see us."

Reluctantly, Con nodded in agreement.

Once Alasdair had shifted and took flight with Lotti on his back, Rhi said, "We have to tell Eurwen and Brandr. Our son needs to return to Cairnkeep. We need every dragon we can get."

"He wouldn't be out there exploring if he didn't think there was something to find." Con sighed. "Were we wrong in no' ridding Earth of humans when we had the chance? The dragons could've stayed. They wouldn't hate us as they do now or be fighting for yet another home."

"Don't second-guess decisions. It never does any good."

He wrapped an arm around her and pulled her close. "We're doing everything we can no' to be drawn into war, but I'm beginning to think we willna have a choice."

"The dragons will join us if that happens."

Con's head turned to the side and the dragons in the distance. "I'm no' so sure."

"They will if they want to keep their home."

"Humans and dragons really can no' share a world, can they?"

Rhi watched Evander fly closer, his brass scales bright against the gray sky. "I think they could if a bitter, power-hungry bitch wasn't spewing her vitriol-filled propaganda."

Con chuckled, his lips softening. "Villette better watch out for you."

"She better," Rhi replied with a grin.

He kissed the side of her head and said, "I want your promise that you willna go into the brambles, lass."

"I can't give that. If Melisse and Henry are in trouble and I'm the only one who can get to them, then I most certainly will."

"What about the bairn?"

Rhi swallowed and leaned back to look at him. "I want our

child more than anything, but Henry and Melisse need us. You would do it if the situations were reversed. Don't ask me to sit on the sidelines when you never have before."

"I'm no' the one carrying our child," he argued.

"Con, sweetheart," she began.

He released a long sigh and looked over her head. "I know. You doona need to say it. That doesna mean I have to like it."

"I'll be careful. I promise."

"I know you will."

She tried to pull out of his arms.

"What are you doing?" he demanded.

Rhi shot him a flat look. "Going after our friends."

"No' until everything else has been attempted."

"Constantine."

"Rhiannon."

Their argument was interrupted by the arrival of Evander. No sooner had the King of Brass landed than the ground trembled with the arrival of Alasdair and Lotti.

"I couldna see anything," Alasdair stated angrily after he returned to human form.

Lotti shrugged helplessly. "Me, neither."

"I flew us as low as I could, and still nothing."

Evander nodded as he raked a hand through his short, dark hair. "I did the same earlier, but I didna cross the boundary. I was hoping you two would see more."

"The vines blanket everything," Alasdair said and jerked his chin to the bowl-shaped area they stood in. "Except here. I swept the entire area, but only one time up and back. I'm no' giving up, though. We'll head up again now."

Rhi stepped out of Con's arms. "That's my cue."

He didn't stop her this time. She gave him a smile before walking to the edge of the vines. The closer she got, the more apprehension filled her stomach until she thought she might be sick. This wasn't someplace she wanted to be, but she would go because that's what family did for each other. Her steps slowed as she reached the brambles. She didn't look back. If she did and saw Con's face, she might never go after their friends. Rhi took a breath and lifted her foot.

"Wait!" Con shouted.

Her boot was already lowering when he snatched her by the waist and drew her back. "Con," she admonished.

He was shaking as he held her back to his front, his arms locked tightly around her. "If this place traps dragons, you would be trapped in there, too, love. You're carrying my child."

"Half-dragon," she murmured as realization hit. She turned in his arms and held him close, her heart thudding against her ribs.

"We'll find another way to bring Henry and Melisse home," Con promised.

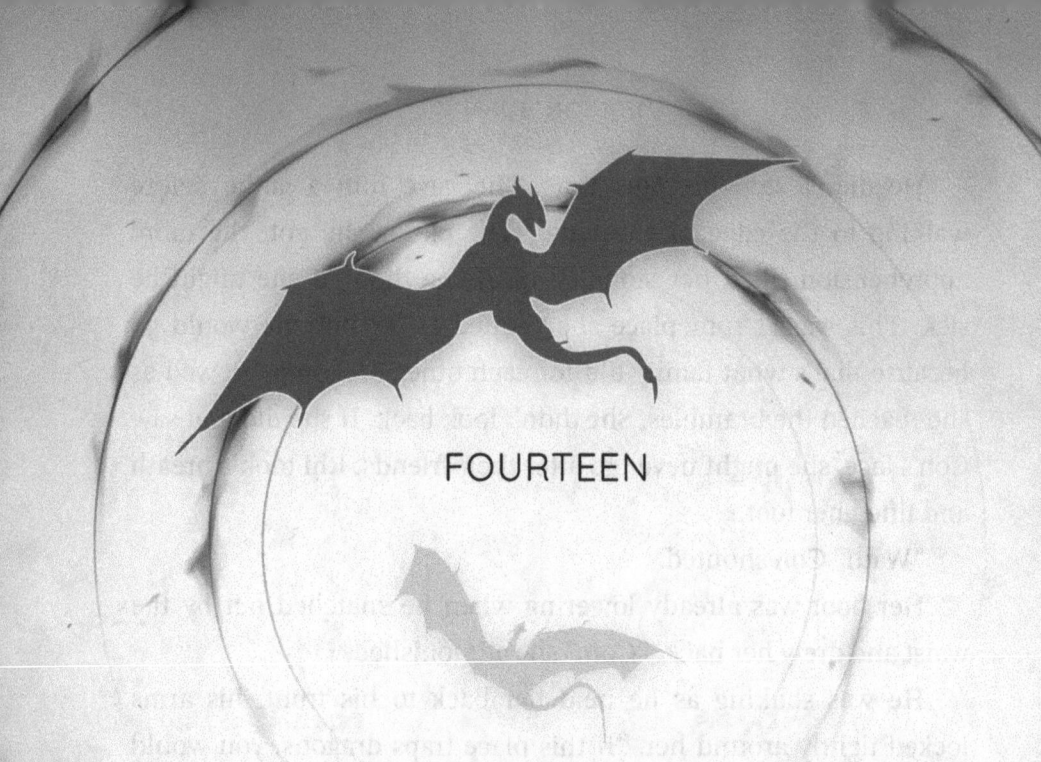

FOURTEEN

It felt as if a fog had descended over Melisse. She struggled to keep her eyes open. When Henry woke her, she had been sure she'd only slept for a few minutes, but a glance at the sky showed she had slumbered the entire night. She should've felt rested, restored.

She was anything but.

Neither said much as they split half a protein bar. She didn't ask how many were left. If they were each only getting a quarter now, that pretty much said everything. Melisse was mildly surprised that Henry didn't ask questions about her childhood or the time she was imprisoned, but she was thankful. It took too much effort to stay upright. She didn't have the wherewithal to talk and hobble at the same time.

Perhaps she should've been worried that he was lost in his thoughts. She told herself she would ask later. When she felt better. For the moment, she needed to concentrate. Her injuries burned as if they were on fire.

The food she had eaten tasted like cardboard, and it had taken everything she had to swallow it, along with another dose of pills. In fact, she had probably drunk too much water just to wash everything down. If Henry noticed, he didn't mention it.

He might be deep in his thoughts, but his hold was firm. He continued to take great care in helping her over and through difficult sections. Which seemed to be every foot or two. At times, he detoured just so they could weave through the vines instead of climbing or ducking. She tried not to lean too heavily on him but couldn't help it. She gave up after a short while and fisted her hand in his jacket for a tighter hold, which only aggravated her shoulder more.

The hours dragged endlessly. She went as far as she could before she begged to stop and rest. Henry leaned her against a vine as he had the day before, but it wasn't enough. Her legs trembled, warning that she was about to fall. She lowered herself to the ground, uncaring and unmindful of any thorns. Her need was too great. Thankfully, she didn't get another cut. The moment she was settled, her eyes slid shut on their own. It seemed only a heartbeat later that Henry woke her to get up and start walking again.

Each time she rested, it became harder and harder to stand, much less shake off the sleep. Worry settled in her stomach as heavy as a stone. Was this normal? Did humans react like so when injured? Shouldn't she feel better now that the bleeding had halted? She desperately wanted to ask but was afraid the answer wouldn't be what she wanted to hear.

What she *needed* to hear.

Lunch came and went. She declined the bit of bar Henry offered, but he forced it on her, along with more pills. She thought he said something about her needing the food in her stomach, but she wasn't sure if he had actually spoken. Somehow, Melisse got the food and pills down before sleep claimed her. Then Henry helped her stand once more. Her eyes were so heavy that she had to close them as she walked. It was only when her head fell forward, jerking her awake, that she realized she had fallen asleep. Henry studied her and tightened his arm around her.

They needed to continue. She wanted to go on, get out of the valley, and far from the Druid. But she couldn't. There was no use denying it any longer.

"I need to rest," Melisse said, hating herself for being so weak.

"We just stopped for lunch."

"That was hours ago."

His frown deepened. "That was five minutes ago."

Tears burned her eyes, but she refused to let them fall. She simply nodded and focused her gaze ahead, determined to stay awake and bear the pain. Henry would get them out. She knew he would.

If the morning had felt never-ending, the afternoon was a relentless torture that seemed determined to end her. Her body was broken, and her mind was following. She knew it yet could do nothing. She longed to take to the skies and fly far, far away, never to see this horrid place again.

Then she thought about the Pink youngling she had promised to locate. How many other dragons had been caught in this ghastly place, suffering as she was? How many more would follow if something wasn't done to stop the Druid? The dragons had borne more than enough. They weren't out there roaming the realm and feasting upon humans.

What if that was the problem? What if everything could be fixed by simply allowing the dragons to be who and what they were? Zora was meant to be theirs—the entire realm, not just a section of it. The border needed to be dropped so the dragons could spread across Zora. The mortals who were killing other humans with magic would be put in their place quickly. Melisse grinned as she imagined the terror they would experience.

Every mortal who had killed others because they were different, who hunted dragons and sought to harm them, should know fear. The kind that froze people in their tracks. It was what they deserved, after all.

As suddenly as the taste of vengeance had filled her, it vanished. Neither of her parents would've ever condoned such actions. Nor would any of the Dragon Kings—and they'd had the chance to wipe the humans from the world. She dashed away a tear.

The fingers gripping Henry's jacket slipped, causing Melisse to lose her balance. She tried to overcorrect even as Henry fought to right her. That's when her left leg buckled. She clamped her lips closed to halt the cry of pain when she landed on her injured leg.

"We're stopping for the day," Henry said.

That was a good thing because Melisse had no intention of getting back up. Shooting pains ran through her leg. Henry helped her find a spot against a vine that didn't have thorns. She closed her eyes, hoping to fall asleep and get away from the discomfort, but there was no release for her now.

The throbbing moved in time with her heartbeat. Her eyes burned from fatigue to the point where she couldn't keep them open, but she couldn't sleep either. Eventually, the aching began to subside. That's when she heard a sound she couldn't make out. Melisse cracked open an eye to find Henry kneeling while doing something on the ground. She forced open her lids and looked around to discover that he was drawing.

"What is that?" she asked.

"Something I've seen in my head all day. I had to get it out, so I drew it."

Melisse noticed the small knife in his hand and tried to make out what he was drawing. "Is it a pattern?"

"Aye."

She turned her head to see that it enclosed her in a large circle. "What is it?"

"A shield knot. Celtic origins," Henry answered as he hurried to complete the design.

Melisse shook her head in an effort to remove the fog currently making it impossible to think clearly. "A what?"

"It's for protection. One large shield that we will both be inside of, with seven smaller ones outside it. Don't ask me how I know. I've never studied this before. The knowledge is just there."

"Will it work?"

"Druids once used them. So, it should."

Melisse flattened her hand on the packed earth. Henry had dug his blade far into the ground. The pattern was embedded deep. It would take a lot to erase the design.

He stood and surveyed his work. "Done." Then his hazel eyes swung to her as he folded the knife and put it in his pocket. "It's time to change your bandages."

Her palm and arm were first. Then came her leg. She couldn't hold back the wince when she moved onto her stomach. It didn't matter how careful Henry was, anytime he got close to her leg wound, she couldn't hold back her moan of pain. Just the removal of the bandage was excruciating.

"Bloody hell," he murmured.

Melisse looked over her shoulder at him. "What is it?"

"All your wounds are infected. Your palm and arm were minimal, but this one is serious."

"The antibiotics aren't working?"

"Apparently not."

She dropped her forehead to the ground and fought to keep her cries of discomfort to a minimum as he spread something on her wound and then replaced the bandage.

"At least it isn't bleeding," Henry said.

Melisse might not know much about human physiology, but she knew infections weren't good. That explained why everything felt as if it were on fire, though. Henry helped her into a sitting position and put his hand on her forehead, then her cheek.

"You're warm."

"We've been moving all day."

His lips compressed into a tight line as he met her gaze. "We didn't get very far today."

Emotion choked Melisse. "I'll do better tomorrow."

"We're not going anywhere until the infection is dealt with. You never should've been moved."

"We can't stay in one place. The Druid will find us."

Henry turned his head from one side to the other, looking at their surroundings. Then he slowly swung around to her. "My guess is we'll be here for a few days."

"We should keep moving."

"You can't."

"Then leave me. I have this," she said and motioned to the shield knot. "You'll travel faster without me. Go get help."

Henry ignored her and pulled out more pills. He held them out to her, his brows rising when she didn't immediately accept them or the water. Only after she'd swallowed the pills did he speak. "We've already decided I'm not leaving you."

"You decided that before. We're having the conversation again."

"Fine. We had it," he stated. "I'm still not going. And what good would it do? It isn't as if I can bring any of the Kings. Dragons have to stay out."

Her eyelids were growing heavy again. "I was talking about you finding the Pink, not getting the Kings."

"Do you understand how dire the situation is?"

"Of course, I do," she replied angrily. "Trust me. I'm *very* aware."

Henry shook his head. "You're ill. Right now, I'm attempting to keep the fever at bay and rid your body of the infection."

"You may not be able to if it is magic induced."

"It is."

That jarred her awake. "What? How do you know that?"

"The Druid."

Melisse searched his face. "When?"

"Last night while you slept. She told me if I left you, she would spare me."

"I'm really coming to despise this woman."

"She believes she's the only human left."

Melisse shrugged. "She's obviously delusional. What else did she say?"

"She had no idea what a Druid was."

"You believe her?"

Henry sat and pulled his rucksack close. "She believes it. That's what matters."

"Does that mean we don't have to worry about other Druids?"

"I think so. There's more she didn't tell me, though her hatred of dragons runs very deep. She wants to know how you are able to shift forms."

A shiver ran down Melisse's spine. "Did you tell her?"

"I did not. She only knows you're half-dragon and half-Fae."

She released a breath. "Maybe you should've taken her offer and left."

"We've been over that."

"I'm serious. Look at me. Look at this place. I can't stand. I can barely stay awake. We may never get out if you remain with me."

He gazed at the half-empty water bottle in his hands before lifting his gaze to her. "Would some time alone with me be so bad?"

"Never," she answered softly. It was exactly what she wanted.

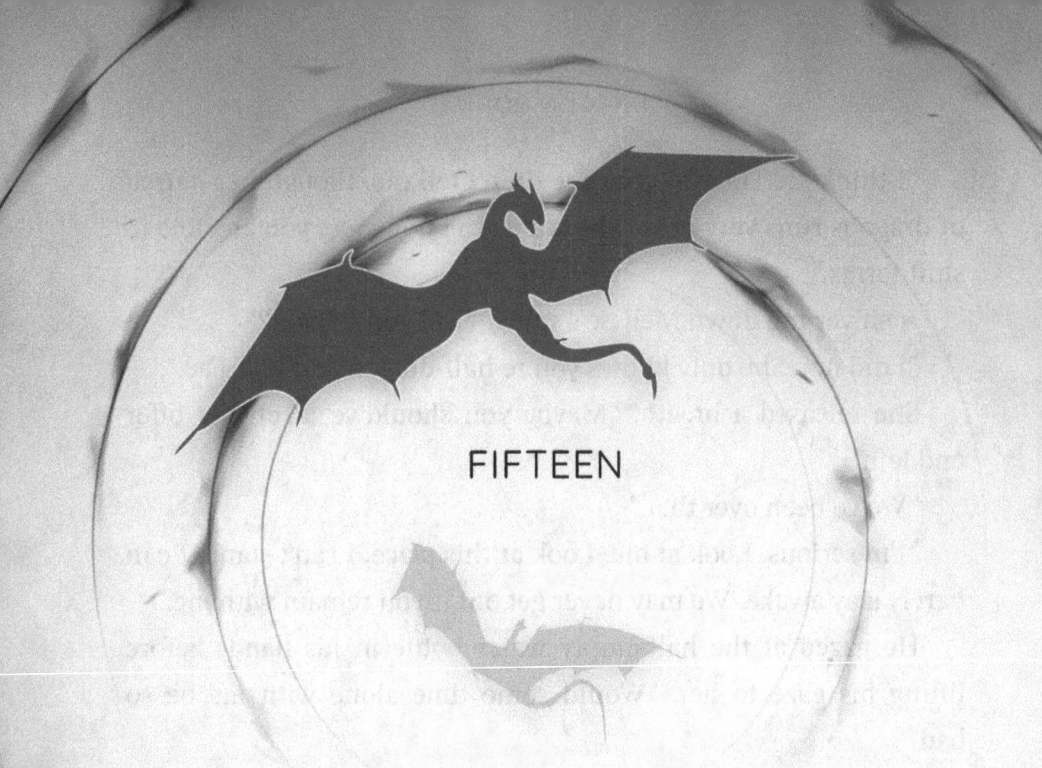

FIFTEEN

The instant Melisse fell asleep, Henry moved outside the protection shield. He circled the area, learning every dip and curve of the vines. He spent hours moving through each location in one direction, before switching and going in the other. He knew where to jump, where to duck, where to slide, and where to weave through the brambles. And all the while, he practiced reaching for his magic, feeling it rush through his body.

There was no denying he had it now.

He didn't use any magic because he worried it might attract the Druid. She had found them the previous night. Whether that was because she could locate anything in the valley or if she detected his magic specifically had yet to be determined. He wasn't going to take any chances. He wanted her to wonder how powerful he was.

Even as he pondered that question himself.

The more he identified his magic, the quicker and easier it answered him. For the smallest of moments, he allowed himself to wonder how he would live without it after he left the brambles.

Then, he hastily shut down those thoughts. He would deal with that when the time came. He had power now. That was where he needed to direct his attention.

Henry removed his coat to let the air cool his heated skin as he continued his run of the area. Every so often, he widened the perimeter to put more and more of the region to memory. He also found a route he could easily use with Melisse if the need arose.

He went as far as he dared before pausing and creating another shield knot. It wasn't as large as the one that encircled Melisse, but it would suffice. He drew smaller ones around the newest knot, large enough for him and Melisse to stand in comfortably, then depicted more that led back to Melisse. It would give them some protection. He couldn't be sure how much, but something was better than nothing. The Druid had made her intentions clear. She was formidable, but he wouldn't go down without a fight.

After a quick pause to check on Melisse, Henry walked the largest knot once more. He wished he knew how he had known about the shield knot, but he would probably never know the answer to that or how he now had magic. And pondering it wasn't doing anyone any good.

Henry ran once more around the perimeter as fast as he dared before he returned to Melisse. She hadn't moved that he could see. With the way she was sitting with her head bent to the side, she would eventually fall over. He carefully laid her on the ground and covered her with his coat since the temperature had dropped more. He was worried about her infections and the fact that she couldn't keep her eyes open. His real concern was what would happen when she didn't wake. He would carry her if he had to.

He lowered himself beside Melisse. It had grown dark quickly. His eyes were getting used to the dimness, but he wasn't confident that he could pick out everything in the shadows. He saved the batteries of his torch in case he needed them.

Henry debated whether to call for Rhi. She wasn't a dragon, but she was mated to one. That could have an effect, and he didn't want to trap her in the brambles with them. He broke off a bit of the bar and ate. There was a small portion left of one Melisse had barely eaten earlier. He saved it for her. She would need the nutrients, especially with her body fighting the infection. His stomach growled with hunger. The protein bars had to last for as long as he could make them while still giving each of them enough energy to keep going. Right now, the more pressing issue was the water.

"There's a way out," he said softly, as much for Melisse's benefit as his. "We'll find it."

Henry stretched out on his back with his body alongside Melisse. He searched the dark sky, but no matter how hard he looked in the moonless night, no stars or dragon shadows could be seen. How close were they to the edge of the thicket?

He'd pushed Melisse as hard as he dared but realized early on that she was giving all she had. The more he moved her, the longer it would take for her wounds to heal. If they healed at all. If only he knew what the toxins from the thorns did to dragons. He could only speculate, which wouldn't do Melisse any good.

The seeds of worry had fully sprouted. His apprehension that he wouldn't get Melisse out of the valley in time for her magic to return and heal her was through the roof. He didn't want to contemplate that she might die. But he couldn't stop the thoughts once they formed.

Henry blew out a breath. It puffed out around him in a little cloud before vanishing. He shivered now that his body had cooled from the exertion. Instead of putting his coat on, Henry slid his arm beneath Melisse and moved her head to his chest to share her body heat. She didn't so much as stir. He held her with one arm and put the other behind his head.

His thoughts drifted, trying to sort through their many problems. He settled on the Druid. If she called the valley home, there had to be a water source somewhere—for her and the vines. The area was still and silent, but it wasn't a desert. If he could locate water, then there would be sustenance. But did he look for that or continue searching for a way out? He couldn't do both, and once a decision was made, there would be no turning back.

All Melisse wanted to do was find the Pink. Henry wanted to do that, too, but he had to see to her first. Once she was safe, he intended to return to find all the dragons that had gone missing. If they were alive. Fuck. He hoped they were alive. But he had his doubts. He had seen the kind of animosity the Druid had. Nothing good ever came from that.

Ever.

He had believed he was drawn to the vine forest to find the Druid and Melisse, but he had also thought it would somehow help the Kings if he could do both. Maybe there had been a chance of that if he had gotten there before Melisse went into the brambles. Now? He sighed. Now, he wasn't sure of anything. Maybe he'd gotten it all wrong concerning the Druid.

Except that wasn't true either. He'd known she was powerful, just as he'd known Melisse was in danger. He squeezed his eyes shut as the tangle of questions and concerns knotted even more. He had to unravel them. Slowly, methodically. He took a deep breath and gradually released it, then thought of the dragons that had gone missing.

It would be easy to hide a Pink, they were small enough. But their size didn't mean they weren't dangerous. They were still powerful. Unless the thorns could cut through scales. As for hiding other dragons? Some of the vines would easily tower over many dragons, but not all of them. Even if the thorns couldn't cut through scales, the dragons would still be in the valley. He would be able to hear them if they were there. Wouldn't he?

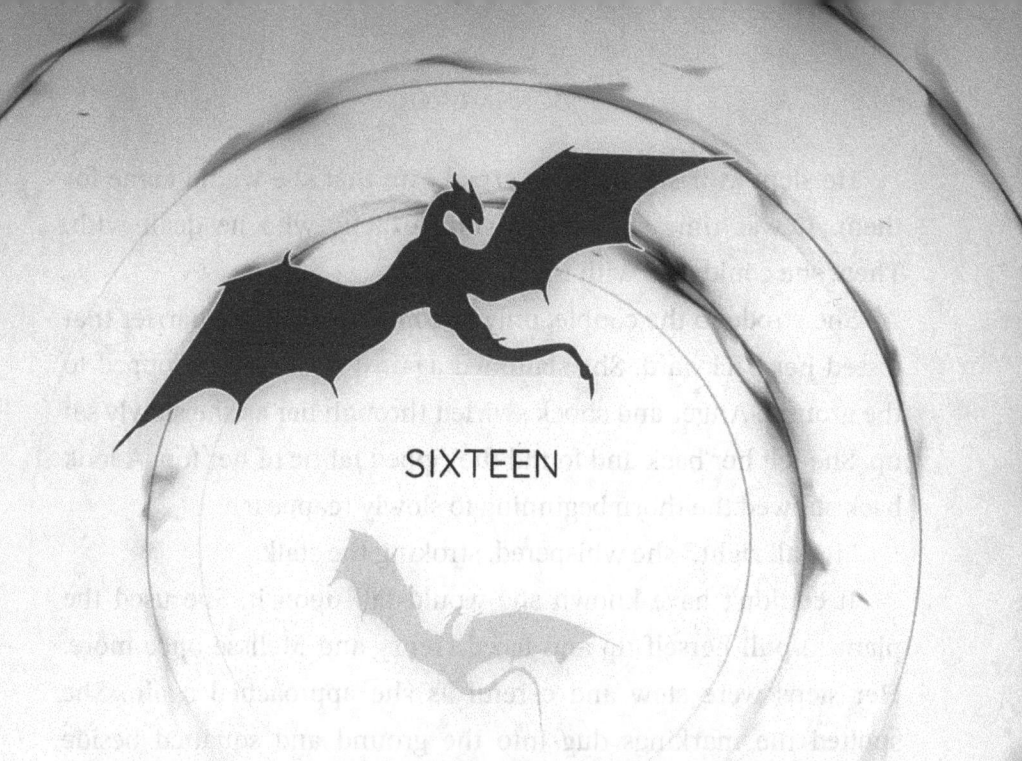

SIXTEEN

She stood silently watching Henry and Melisse. It boggled her mind that he could care so deeply for a being that had such wickedness within them. She wrinkled her nose in disgust when Henry gathered Melisse against his chest like a lover.

Her husband had once held her in such a manner. She jerked at the memory that came out of nowhere. It had been so long since she had thought about him. Henry's actions stirred the long-forgotten memories. Or maybe it was Henry himself that'd brought up the past. She couldn't remember her husband's name, but she could see his smile and hear his booming laugh. His face, however, was a blur. They had been happy once. Though she couldn't remember how long ago that had been.

She walked closer to the couple. Henry had ignored her warning and remained. She hadn't wanted to hurt him, but she would now. Did he believe himself stronger? Did he really think he could best her? He had gotten in a strike because she was unprepared. That wouldn't happen again.

He slept as if she hadn't warned him that she would come for them. It was time she showed him exactly who he dealt with. Then, she could deal with the dragon.

She strode to the couple, only to come up against a barrier that tossed her backward. She slammed against a vine and dropped to the ground. Anger and shock swirled through her as she slowly sat up. She felt her back and found the ripped fabric of her top. A look back showed the thorn beginning to slowly reappear.

"It's all right," she whispered, stroking the stalk.

It couldn't have known she would fall upon it. She used the plant to pull herself up and faced Henry and Melisse once more. Her steps were slow and careful as she approached again. She spotted the markings dug into the ground and squatted beside them. Tentatively, she put her hand out and felt resistance the closer she came to the pattern.

Straightening, she followed the design. That was when she came across some smaller ones, forcing her to move farther away. This was magic she had never seen before. Henry had called her a Druid and inferred he was one, too. Was this Druid magic?

It had to be. It certainly wasn't dragon magic. She took that from the beasts as soon as they entered her domain. They were rendered helpless, vulnerable. Fearful.

Just as she had once been.

Her rage simmered. Henry may have kept himself and the female safe for the time being, but it wouldn't always be so. And she intended to strike as soon as they ventured from the markings.

She couldn't take her eyes off the way the dragon lay against Henry, or his arm that held her close. He knew what Melisse was, and still he stood beside her. The dragon must have done something to convince him that he was safe with her. Because she couldn't fathom anyone willingly being near such a being, no matter if they looked harmless and beautiful as a human or not. A dragon was still a dragon.

She returned to her spot to watch and waited for the moment she could attack.

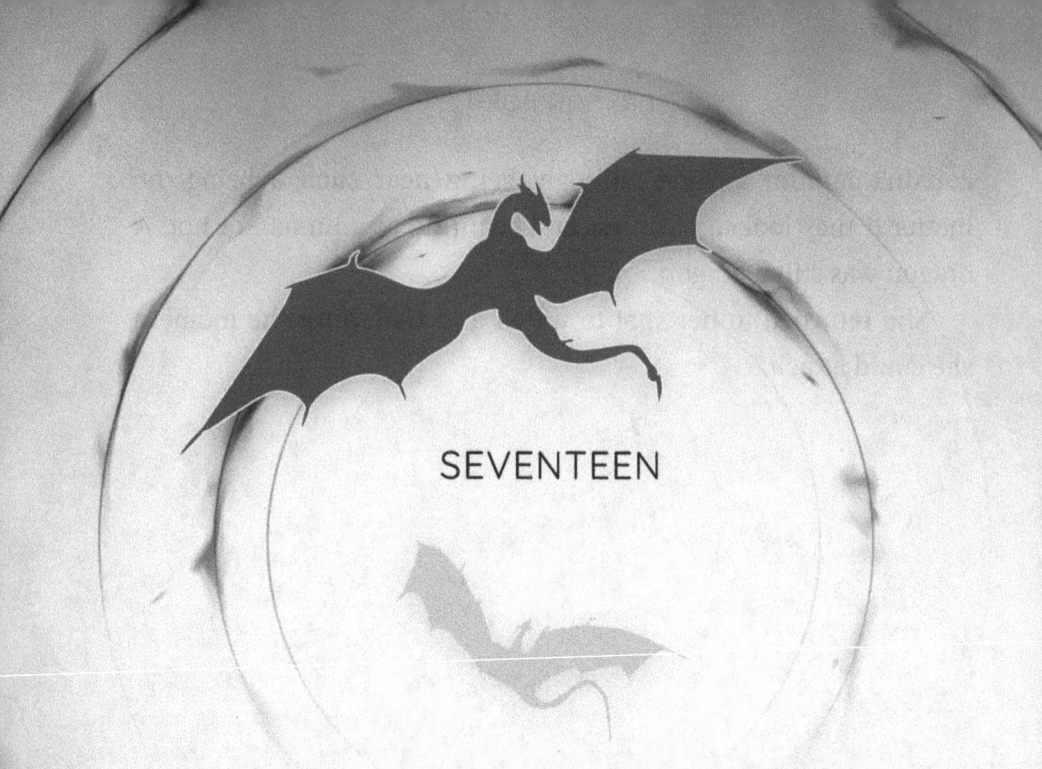

SEVENTEEN

Henry woke, but he didn't open his eyes. The Druid was near. Had she approached the shield knot? He thought about trying to talk to her again. If he could build a rapport, maybe he could discern what caused her to hate the dragons so. The chances of him altering her feelings in the short time he had were slim, though.

He also wanted to see if she could cross the barrier. The more time that passed without her getting closer, the more he believed the shield was working. It was one of the reasons he had lay down. He wanted the Druid to believe they were exposed and attempt an attack. Maybe she had. He wished he knew for sure.

So far, the Druid had only come to him at night. He wouldn't count on that in the future. Nor could he and Melisse remain where they were for too long. He could feel the heat radiating off her.

Henry gently rolled her to her back as he came up on his elbow over her. As soon as he felt her brow, he knew the fever had taken hold. He wasn't a healer. Hell, he wasn't even supposed to have magic. He ran a hand down his face and rose to his knees, as if that would supply answers.

"What do I do? *What do I do?*" he whispered as he looked around helplessly.

A memory flashed in his mind of the Skye Druids standing around one of their own who was injured. Henry remembered them chanting something. It was an ancient spell, one that had been forgotten by many and would likely never have never uttered again if the MacLeod Druids hadn't retained and shared it.

It usually took several Druids for such a spell to work, and he only had himself. Then again, he hadn't had magic before. What would it hurt to try?

Henry swallowed and rubbed his hands together as he fought to remember the words. He closed his eyes and concentrated on his memory. He recalled a few, but it wasn't enough. He had to get it just right. It was a long shot, even if he could remember the entire healing spell. But he was desperate.

He ran through the memory again and again. He slowed it, rewound it, as he picked up a word here and there. Each time he replayed that moment, he was able to string more words together until he had a sentence. But some words were too difficult to make out. He didn't stop, though. Didn't quit until he could say the spell in time with the memory. It was almost as if the Skye Druids were with him now, their magic and chanting joining his.

The mantra fell from his lips over and over, his words getting louder and stronger until he was nearly shouting. He knew the Druid was nearby, but he didn't care. Melisse was the only one who mattered.

His throat was raw, and his voice hoarse when he finally halted. He lowered his arms and slowly opened his eyes. There was no outward sign that Melisse was healed, so he felt her forehead. It was still warm, but the heat from before had lessened.

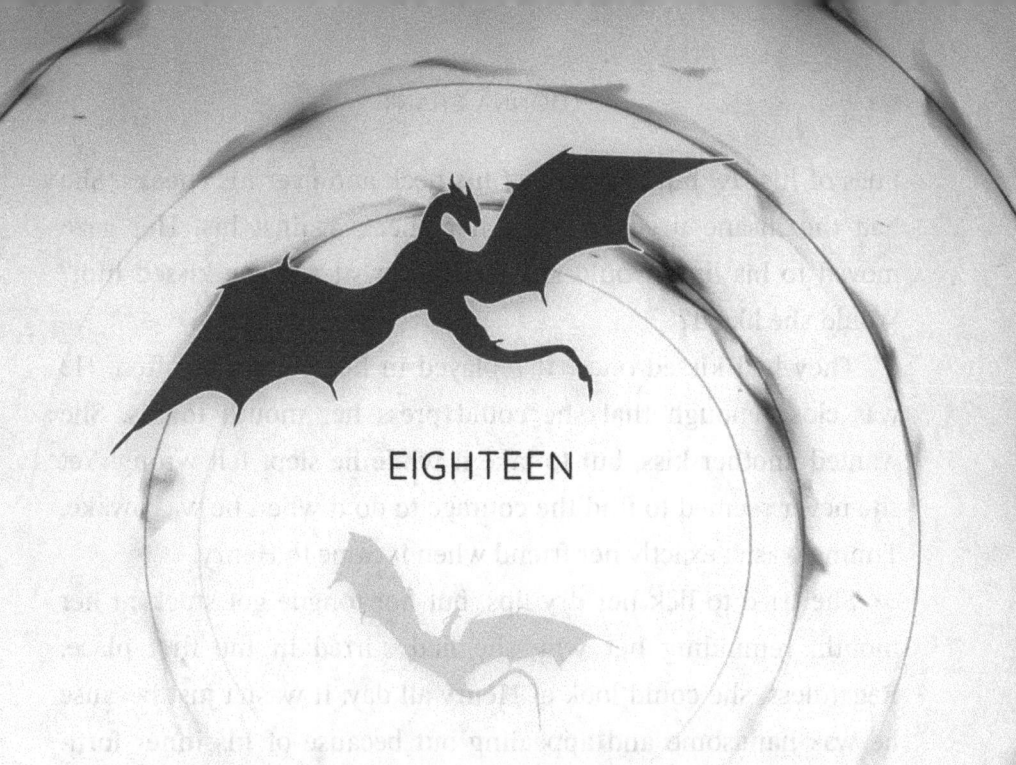

EIGHTEEN

A rhythmic beat pulled Melisse from the dark depths of sleep. She opened her eyes and found the world moving slightly up and down. She frowned. No. It wasn't the landscape moving. It was her head. And the beating was a heartbeat.

She lowered her gaze to jean-clad legs and boots. Henry. As soon as she realized his chest was her pillow, she felt the heaviness of his arm holding her. It was a most comfortable spot. And warm. It would be so easy to slip back into sleep. It beckoned her like a silent lover, urging her to return. Yet her mouth was so dry that it nearly became unbearable. Sleep would have to wait until she wet her mouth.

However, that meant moving out of Henry's embrace and possibly waking him. She didn't want to do either. So, she tried to forget about her parched throat and drift off to dreamland, but it was now out of reach.

Melisse slowly moved her head until she glimpsed Henry's face. His beard was thicker, the bristles covering not just the hard lines of his jaw but also part of his neck and over his cheeks. She had the insane urge to brush her cheek against his. Her gaze moved to his lips. Would she feel the bristles if she kissed him? Would she like it?

They had kissed once. It replayed in her memories often. He was close enough that she could press her mouth to his. She wanted another kiss, but to take it while he slept felt wrong. Yet she never seemed to find the courage to do it when he was awake. Timing wasn't exactly her friend when it came to Henry.

She tried to lick her dry lips, but her tongue got stuck in her mouth, reminding her why she had stirred in the first place. Regardless, she could look at Henry all day. It wasn't just because he was handsome and appealing but because of his inner fortitude, his love for those he cared about, and the innate search for justice that drove him in everything he did.

He might have believed himself lacking because he didn't have magic, but Henry was special. She had recognized that immediately. Her parents would've liked him. And she believed Henry would've gotten on well with them, too. Her thoughts of family had her attention drifting to the Dragon Kings. Con had said the Kings and their mates were Melisse's family now. She hadn't exactly acted as one of them, though she hadn't rejected them either. She missed the tight family bond. It was there, waiting for her if she reached out.

But a part of her, a small, tiny dot in the back of her mind, reared its ugly head on occasion, reminding her that she had the capacity to hurt—nay, kill—as she had done with Osric. Surely, the Kings would fear that. At least, they should. All the others before them had. She had expected for those at Dreagan to be cold toward her, shun her. Even after Con offered her a place with them, the worry persisted—along with a fear that they might change their minds about wanting her around.

If she made it out of the thicket, she was going to stop keeping to the outskirts of the Kings and truly be a part of them. First, she had to heal and actually make it out of the brambles alive.

Melisse slowly rose onto her elbow. Henry's arm slid from her back. He shifted in his sleep and turned his head away from her. As she sat up, something dropped to her lap. She realized it was his coat that had been draped over her. She softly covered him with it and quietly moved onto her knees. His rucksack was near enough that she could reach over and unzip it. There was a small bit of water left in one bottle. She downed that, eager for more.

She licked her lips as she screwed the cap back on and tucked the bottle into the bag. Her fingers brushed another container. She longed to pull it out and drink her fill. She'd never gone hungry or thirsty. It was a new sensation, and she didn't like the thoughts it produced. Or the lies she told in order to convince herself she could take the water.

Her eyes darted to Henry. He had come into this hellish place to find her and stop the Druid. He'd risked his life by remaining with her. He had doctored her injuries and practically carried her through the dense vines. And she wanted to ignore all of that and drink what could possibly be their last bit of hydration.

Melisse turned back to the rucksack and found the water bottle in her hand. She didn't remember latching onto it or drawing it out. She released it as if it had scalded her, then shoved the pack away.

Her attention moved past Henry and the rucksack to take in the area around her. She vaguely remembered being here, and as soon as she saw the formation drawn into the dirt, she recalled

Henry telling her that it was a shield knot. He must have been right about it protecting them because they were both still alive.

Melisse glanced upward. The clouds seemed darker, heavier. She wasn't sure if it was morning or noon. It was light enough that the night had fallen away. She stared at the clouds, willing them to part so she could see even a smidgen of the sky, perhaps feel a brief ray of sunlight.

Having been imprisoned deep within a mountain, she had gone eons without sunlight. Now, she craved it at all times. But the clouds wouldn't part for her. She jerked when she thought she saw a large shadow within the clouds. It had to be one of the Kings. Excitement coursed through her—a heady feeling. She searched the clouds for another glimpse but none came. It didn't take long for her to realize that it must be her imagination. She sat back on her haunches and was immediately assaulted by pain. Melisse carefully lowered herself to her bottom to relieve the throbbing.

She considered returning to Henry's side, but now that she was awake, sleep was the last thing she wanted. Nor did she wish to do anything to rouse Henry. He needed the rest while he could. She leaned back on her hand and came into contact with something soft. Melisse jerked away and twisted around to find a delicate green bud protruding from the ground.

Her eyes moved beyond it to see more, and then more. All within the shield knot. The majority of the greenery outlined Henry and where she had lain. Melisse lightly ran her palm over the sprouts. It was the first burst of color she had seen within the thicket.

Henry drew in a deep breath and yawned as he rubbed his eyes with his thumb and forefinger. He stilled when he realized she was no longer beside him. He jerked into a sitting position, his head swiveling until he found her.

"What's wrong?" he asked.

"I was hoping you would know."

"Know what?"

She motioned around her, indicating the buds.

Henry got to his feet and turned in a slow circle to take it all in. Then he squatted and lightly caressed one of the sprouts. "They're just within the shield knot," he murmured. His gaze lifted to meet hers as he lowered a knee to the ground. "How do you feel?"

Melisse took a moment to take stock of her body. "Apparently, sleep is what I needed. I feel rested. Awake. The drowsiness seems to have faded."

"Is your fever gone?"

"I don't know," she said with a shrug.

He scooted over and placed his hand on her forehead. "You're still a little warm, but I think the worst has passed. What about your wounds?"

She held out her hand in answer. Henry unwound the bandage. Cool air hit her palm, but it was the pink skin where the scrapes were healing that surprised her.

"Let me see your arm," Henry said, a note of urgency in his voice.

Melisse removed her jacket and turned so he could reach her right arm. She didn't have the same view as she had with her palm, so she watched his face instead. He gave nothing away as he softly pressed on her arm.

"Do you feel that?" he asked.

"It twinges a little. Is it healing?"

Henry didn't answer as he motioned for her to turn onto her

stomach. She complied and waited as he untied his tee shirt from around her leg to expose the area he had cut away from her pants. Next, she felt him removing the bandage. Then...silence.

"Tell me," she urged.

He plopped onto his bottom. "Shit."

Melisse rolled to her left side to find him staring at her leg with a glazed look. "What is it?"

He ran a hand down his face and looked at her. "Your fever was getting out of control last night. Between that and the infection, I knew I had to do something. I wished that I had healing magic. And that brought up a memory. I was on the Isle of Skye recently with my sister, helping the Druids with some issues. There was a battle, and many were injured. They didn't wait for the Healers to arrive. Instead, they used a chant the MacLeod Druids shared. It's ancient and died out as Druid magic faded."

"But the MacLeod Druids are from the past."

"Exactly," Henry said with a nod. "I was there to witness the Skye Druids gathering around and using the chant to begin healing those in need. I have a pretty good memory for things like that. It came in handy working for MI5, and I had nothing to lose in trying it. I wasn't even sure I had gotten all the words right. For all I knew, some of them were wrong or not in the correct order."

Melisse smiled. "I'd say you accomplished exactly what you wanted to do. Not only do I feel better, and my wounds are healing, but look at this," she said, spreading her hands to indicate the new sprouts.

"I would've done anything to make you feel better."

She reached over and covered his hand with hers. "Thank you."

"You're welcome." He squeezed her hand before releasing her.

"The leg injury was the worst. It looks much better, but it's far from being healed."

Melisse returned to her stomach so he could do whatever he did to her wound, before applying a new bandage and retying the shirt in place. Henry covered her arm and palm with new bandages, as well.

"Just being cautious," he told her.

"What now?"

Henry shrugged with a shake of his head as they sat facing each other. "I wish I knew. She was here last night. I felt her."

"She didn't try to speak to you?"

"I think she's done talking to me."

Melisse twisted her lips. "Maybe. I think the shield knot kept her out."

"I made us a path of little ones to another knot, but it's smaller than this one. We have more room here."

"We can't remain here forever."

"I know."

She blew out a breath. "Do you think we're close to getting out of the valley?"

"There's a way to find out," he said, looking over her head.

Melisse turned to see that he was staring at one of the vines towering far over them before arching. Her head snapped back around. "You can't be serious?"

"Do you have a better idea?"

Her lips parted, but her mind went blank.

"I'll be fine. Besides, we need to get an idea of where we are, and that vine will allow that."

"If you don't fall."

His lips split into a wide grin as he jumped to his feet. "Have some faith."

"Henry," she called and stood as he walked around her.

He turned to face her. "We're going to get out of here."

"I know."

Her stomach fluttered when his gaze lowered to her mouth. She leaned toward him, and just for a moment, he moved toward her. Then he suddenly turned and began the climb up the vine, using the thorns like ladder rungs.

"Don't fall," she whispered. "Don't you dare fall."

NINETEEN

Henry feared few things. And heights wasn't one of them. At least not until he began the climb up the vine, using only the thorns. He'd worried they wouldn't hold his weight. Or worse, refuse to allow him to scale them.

The brambles had done nothing to make him think they were anything but plants. For all he knew, the Druid's magic had crafted them, which got them to grow as large as they had. If they were a byproduct of her power, then they could turn against him.

Even if they were native to the land and had nothing to do with the Druid, they were still alive. Trees had voices and spoke to some Druids. That meant other plants could, as well. He had taken special care with the vines from the moment he entered the thicket. The last thing he wanted was for them to turn against him and Melisse.

He reached for a giant thorn and wrapped his fingers around it. Henry always tested his grip to make sure it would hold before pulling himself up. The higher he went, the sparser the spikes

became. He glanced down to find Melisse in the same spot he'd left
her with her head tilted back to watch him.

The urge to kiss her had been great. He almost had. Now, he
wished he had given in to the need. He found his footing and
reached for another barb. Some were in good locations, while
others required him to shimmy to the side in order to grab hold.

He studied the next section. The thorns were widely spaced. It
would be tricky. Doable, but tricky.

"Don't fall," he told himself.

Henry stretched out his right hand and got a grip. It wasn't the
best, but he had a hold of it. Then, he moved his foot to a spike,
nestling his arch at the vine's base to move up another rung. He
repeated the steps again and again, taking it section by section.

The next time he looked down, he could no longer make out
Melisse's face. He had known the vine was tall, but he hadn't been
able to gauge the exact height from the ground. He took in the area
around him and saw that he was even with most of the brambles.
But there was still more to climb.

He extended his hand for the next thorn and managed to brush
it with the pads of his fingers. He lunged upward in an effort to
grasp it, but he slid off. He had no choice but to jump from his
current perch on a thorn to reach the next one. He launched
himself upward with enough force to get a firm grip but flailed as
he sought a foothold.

Henry held on to the barb with one hand and wound his arm
around the vine so he didn't swing. His legs followed. He pulled
himself up with one arm and shimmied along the stalk. It was
agonizing and exhausting work before he could finally put his foot
on a thorn.

Only when he was stable did he press his forehead against the vine and draw in a steadying breath. His heart was still pounding when he lifted his gaze once more. He frowned as he stared at the thorns. He had been sure they were much farther apart than what he saw now. Henry wouldn't question it, however. Maybe it had been the angle of where he stood that had hidden them before.

He climbed carefully, meticulously. Left foot. Right hand. Right foot. Left hand. Over and over.

Sweat beaded his skin. He was glad he hadn't worn his coat. His palms grew slick, causing him to wipe them on his pant legs to maintain his firm hold. During one such break, he looked out.

He could see over the vines in the valley to the surrounding mountains now. A smile curved his lips. He had known he could get above the brambles. He looked in the direction they had been traveling and saw that the edge of the thicket was maybe a hard day's walk. That was if they weren't attacked. Quicker if they could run.

Henry looked to the north and saw the brambles fading into the horizon. A glance to the right proved they were too far away to attempt an exit in that direction. Shock went through him when he looked to the south and saw how deep they had traveled into the vines. They were far outside dragon land. Con would keep the Kings within the border until he had no other choice.

They had one chance to gain their freedom. The Druid had to know they'd attempt it. And she wouldn't allow them to leave easily. They would be ready for whatever came at them.

Henry took one last look around before beginning the long climb down. His hands were tired, and all the muscles in his body twinged at being used in such a fashion. He took his time, but his foot still slipped.

He slammed against the vine and lost his grip. Henry

attempted to reach for the thorn again but had lost his momentum. He grabbed the vine's thick base and searched for another foothold.

Movement near his face caught his attention. He could only watch as a thorn slowly extended outward. He didn't waste any time grabbing hold of it. As he kicked out with his foot, he connected with the side of another that hadn't been there before. He stepped on it.

"I knew it," he said with a grin. "Thank you."

There were no more incidents the rest of the way. When Henry jumped to the ground and turned to Melisse, she threw her arms around him.

"Don't do that again," she whispered.

Henry loosened his arms and leaned back so he could look at her. "The vine didn't let me fall. It grew thorns to make things easier."

"How? Why?" she asked in confusion.

Henry shrugged and put his hand on the stem. "I don't know, but I'm thankful."

"Please tell me you saw what you needed."

"I did." He bent and whispered, "We're about a day's journey to the edge. We'll need to move fast when we go."

"What are we waiting for?"

"We've already lost a lot of time today, and you're still injured."

Melisse put her full weight on her right leg. She only winced a little, but that was all he needed to see.

"We'll do better if you rest today and let your body heal some more. We'll set out first thing in the morning," he told her.

"I don't like slowing you down."

Henry shrugged off her words. "It happens to the best of us.

Now, get off that leg and let it heal. We don't want the fever returning."

"I don't think we need to worry about that after what you did last night."

"I'd rather not test it, if you please."

She pulled a face that turned into a grin. "You're very demanding. How did I not know that?"

"There's a lot you don't know about me. Just as there is much I don't know about you."

"I'm an open book. Ask. But know that for each question, I get one of my own."

"Deal."

She hobbled to the side and gingerly lowered herself to the ground with her injured leg outstretched. Henry noticed that she sat against the brambles without hesitation now. It could be because there was nowhere else to lean, or because she trusted that she wouldn't be skewered just for sitting there.

Henry decided to remain next to the vine he had climbed. His legs were outstretched to the point where his and Melisse's feet nearly touched. "What was your favorite thing about your mum?"

"Hmm," Melisse said as she contemplated his question. "I think her courage in going for her dreams, wherever they took her. Few would've opened that doorway without knowing where they would end up."

"Aye, but look what she got by being so adventurous. You and your father."

"She was killed in the end."

Henry pulled his rucksack close. "Everything has a beginning and an end. Even the Dragon Kings. That ending may be far in the future, but it will happen. What about your dad? What was your favorite thing about him?"

"That he loved wholly and completely. All he wanted was peace. He worked tirelessly for it while he was King."

Henry opened another protein bar and tore off half for her since she hadn't eaten the night before. She caught it when he tossed it to her. A bottle of water followed. "What was it like being imprisoned all those years? If it's too difficult to talk about, then forget I asked."

"No one has ever asked." She looked down at the bar and nibbled on a corner then lowered her hand to her lap. "I went in as a child, and the magic somehow aged me. I wasn't even aware of it. I couldn't move, but I could hear the world around me. King after King took that mountain, and they each came to stand and stare at me. None ever tried to free me after the first, though he had wanted to kill me. I don't know what my parents did to ensure that didn't happen. They only saw me as a weapon, a danger. No one spoke to me. Until Con."

Henry's brows raised. "Really?"

"It wasn't really to *me*, I don't think. At least, not at first. It was after the war with the humans when the dragons were sent away and most of the Kings took to their mountains for dragon sleep. Con remained awake. He was utterly alone during that time. It took a toll on him.

"Sometimes, he would shift into his human form and pace. Other times, he would bellow and curse the day the mortals arrived. Then there were the moments when depression took him. The only thing that kept him going was the Kings. They counted on him, and he latched onto that. I don't remember exactly when he spoke. I drifted in and out of sleep but became aware of his voice. He could've spoken for hours for all I knew. I thought someone was there with him, but it wasn't long until I understood he was alone."

Henry crossed one ankle over the other. "What did he say?"

"Everything and nothing. He was lonely, angry, and frustrated. He debated with himself whether to wipe out the humans. If he did it while the Kings slept, then he would be the only one the magic punished. He was willing to accept that penalty, knowing one of the Kings would wake to challenge him for King of Kings."

"He never did it."

Melisse took another small bite. "He found a reason each time to allow the mortals to live. I don't know how, but he did."

"And now we're right back to a similar situation on another realm."

"Maybe because there's supposed to be a different outcome."

Henry shook his head. "There's no stopping what's happening here, is there?"

"Villette has had centuries to cultivate the mortals' hatred for the dragons. They're beyond reason now."

"Con doesn't believe that. None of the Kings do."

Melisse propped her left foot on the ground and rested her elbow on her knee. "They will soon enough."

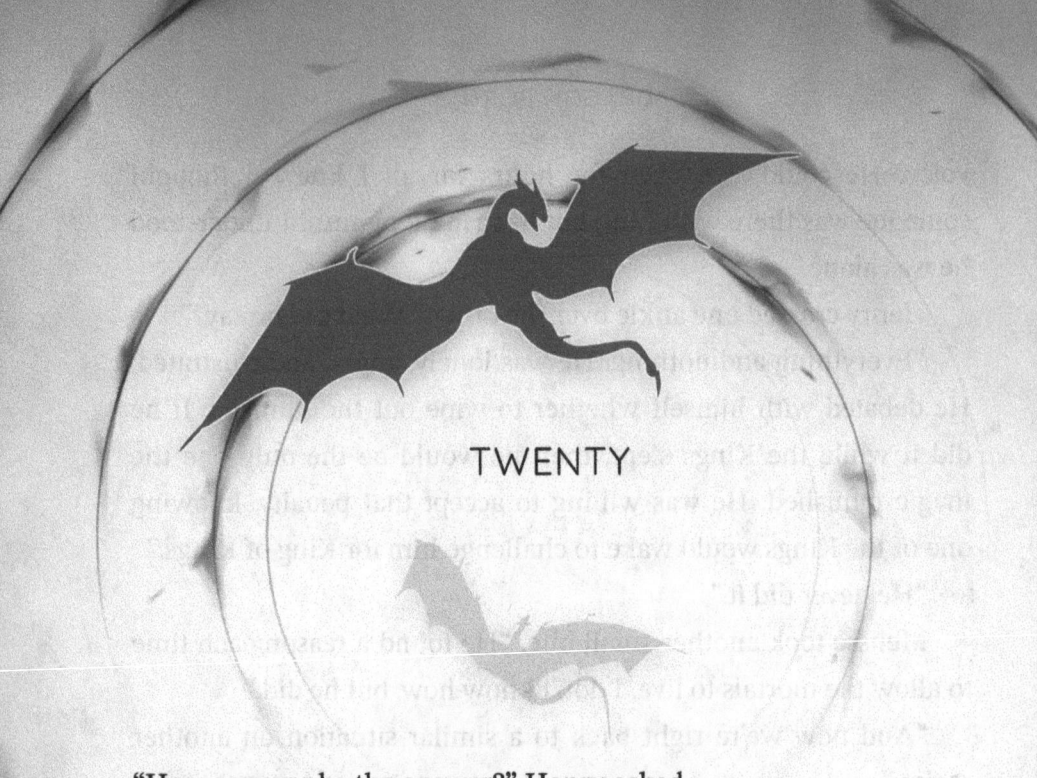

TWENTY

"How can war be the answer?" Henry asked.

Melisse swallowed the bite. "I never said it was."

"You implied it."

"I said there's no stopping Villette. She's made her intentions clear. The mortals' loathing of the dragons runs too deep for them to change suddenly. It's gone through generations, festered. Taken root deep inside them. It's part of them. Like magic is part of the dragons, the Fae, and the Druids."

Henry blew out a breath. "Like the dragons hate the Kings."

"Exactly. It can't—and won't—be altered easily. I'll give it to Villette, she was smart in planning and implementing her scheme. The humans will rise up against the dragons. Sooner or later, they'll cross the borders. If they do..." She didn't complete her thought. She couldn't say the words.

Henry was silent as he finished his bar. Finally, he asked, "What of the elves? As far as we know, Villette's reach doesn't extend to them."

"Someone abhors dragons enough to have tried to kill Kendrick while he was there."

"It could be argued that he broke the rule of no dragons crossing the border."

Melisse shifted positions. "Kendrick used that reasoning. He also gained permission from the elves to remain and help them hunt the invisible foe. That might have been fine, but then an elf fell in love with him. To make matters worse, Esha left Shecrish to live with Kendrick."

"And the elves gathered for an attack as retaliation. Had Esha's sister not warned her and Kendrick, and had they not summoned the Kings, it could have been disastrous." Henry shrugged. "Nikolai shares information with Esther, who then tells me."

"It's good that you know what's going on. It'll save time having to explain everything. The fact is, those with magic on the human side have been ostracized and shunned. They've been hunted and killed, simply for being different. They have something in common with the dragons. There's a good possibility they'll join us."

Henry's lips pinched. "You're still talking battle."

"If there was a way for Eurwen, Brandr, Con, and the others to stop what's happening, they would have done it. All they're doing now is mitigating things. It does nothing but prolong the inevitable. I don't make light of any of this. No one wants war except Villette. She has made the mortals believe they have a chance of taking down the dragons."

"She can. Even against a King."

Melisse leaned her head back against the vine. A thorn sticking out helped to prop her head up as she leaned to the side. "We don't know that for sure. She hasn't taken a King's life yet. The Star People are more powerful than the dragons. But you forget that we have two of them on our side now. Erith might have only just learned about her origins, but she won't be here alone. Cael will stand with her, and I suspect many of the Reapers will, too. Then there's Lotti. Without her, we wouldn't know what we do about the Star People."

"You're assuming none of the other Star People will join Villette."

"Eurielle aided Lotti. There's a lot of animosity between Eurielle and Villette."

"That doesn't mean she'll help us," Henry pointed out.

Melisse drank some water before tossing the bottle to him. "True. My bet is that Eurielle won't help Villette, though. We're not without friends. There's no way Villette could've anticipated any of this."

"She might be formidable, but she isn't all-knowing. Thankfully."

"Enough about the issues on Zora," she said with a grin. "It's time for my questions. You asked five."

He quirked a brow and shot her a questioning look. "I'm sure I didn't."

"Shall I repeat them back to you?"

"No, no," he said, waving his hand as he grinned. "We made a deal. Ask away."

She bit her lip as she stared at him. "It's odd. I feel as if I've known you for years, but we've not spent much time together, and I don't really know much about you. I want to know everything."

"That could take a while," he teased.

"How did you come to be friends with the Kings?"

Henry's brows rose, then he puffed out his cheeks and released a breath. "It feels like a lifetime ago." He snorted a laugh. "I was on a mission for MI5, surveilling a person of interest. He suspected he was being watched and was jittery and constantly looking around. I wasn't surprised when he went into his favorite pub. It was crowded that night because of the football match, so I followed him. Next thing I knew, someone shoved me from behind. A fight ensued, with men surrounding me. I held my own for a bit, but the odds were stacked against me, and it was only a matter of time before one of them got the advantage. I went down, and they pummeled me. Suddenly, they were gone. I saw a guy fighting against them and jumped up to join him." Henry shrugged. "Before long, it was over. Or we thought it was. A fifth man came at me with a knife, and Banan stopped him. I had lost the man I was tailing, but my partner was still on him. So, Banan and I left the pub just as the police arrived. He saved my life. I owed him, and I told him as much. A friendship developed from there."

"But you didn't know he was a King."

"Not until he called me to help him track down the men who kidnapped Jane. He had never asked for anything before that, and I wasn't about to fail in getting him what he needed. I'll never forget the first time I saw a dragon. I wasn't sure if we had stepped onto a movie set with some impressive animatronics or what. Soon, I learned the truth about who and what Banan and those at Dreagan were. All my life, I had felt a calling to do something good for the world. I had a chance to do that with them."

Melisse smiled as she listened to him. "I would've loved to see your face when you saw them shift the first time."

"I'm sure I looked like a right idiot," he said with a laugh.

She was sure he hadn't. If there was one thing she knew about Henry, it was that he was anything but an idiot. "You wanted to help them, even though you didn't have magic. That's impressive."

"Not really," he stated. "They were the big picture I had always suspected was out there. I had to be a part of it. I didn't give them a choice, really." He laughed. "It helped that they needed someone in the human world who could get information. That didn't last long, though. Corruption runs through everything, and MI5 was no exception. That was when I turned my attention to helping the Kings full time instead of between missions."

"Then your sister and Nikolai fell in love."

Henry's smile was crooked as he glanced at the sky. "I was shocked but thrilled. I knew that, no matter what happened to me, she would always have a family. But Esther discovered much more than love. She found our lineage."

His smile faded, and a small frown formed in the middle of his brow. Melisse wanted to smooth it away. "TruthSeeker and JusticeBringer. The duo meant to keep the Druids in line. It seems policing ran in your blood deeper than you knew."

"It felt good knowing we had a connection to the Druids, but we still didn't have magic. I think that mattered to me more than it did to Esther. I wish that was all we had to be concerned about, but there was so much more."

"Will you tell me?" she asked softly.

He bowed his head in a nod. "Of course. Esther found out that the people we thought were our parents actually adopted us. More than our names had been changed, however. Our birthdates had been switched and actually altered on our birth certificates. The more Esther and I dug into our pasts, the more we uncovered. We're descendants of the Clacher family, which was systematically wiped away by a *drough* named Deirdre."

Melisse nodded to let him know she knew about the evil Druid the Warriors and Druids of MacLeod Castle had fought against.

"Our parents were part of some others who were hiding who their children really were for decades. Even after Deirdre was defeated, it was so ingrained in them that they couldn't come out of hiding. The woman who took care of us before we were adopted believed someone was looking for us and wiped away all evidence of me and Esther. Supposedly, each time a TruthSeeker and JusticeBringer die, the next in line is activated, for lack of a better word. Except the ones before us were killed well before we were born."

"In other words, you were born into your roles. You wouldn't have known that as an infant."

Henry's lips twisted. "I suppose not. Esther went to visit the Isle of Eigg, where we were born."

"You didn't accompany her?"

"Not then. I went later after I scoured every document I could get my hands on about us, the woman who cared for us, and our birth parents. Names were always changed, which made it nearly impossible to find answers. Ryder worked his skills and magic with electronics, though."

Melisse softened her lips. "Your ties to the Dragon Kings have allowed you to gain knowledge you possibly never would've found."

"I know I wouldn't have."

"And now? Would you change anything in the past?"

His lips quirked in a grin. "Do you mean would I change things so I wasn't on Zora with you?"

"Aye."

"Never," he replied firmly.

Melisse watched him rise and walk to her. He motioned for her to scoot forward and then sat behind her, his legs on either side of hers. She sighed as he tugged her to lean back against him. She relaxed, her body sinking into his.

"Never," he repeated.

She smiled. She was so overcome with joy that her heart nearly burst from her chest. "I'm glad."

"I would do anything for you."

Melisse wished she was still looking into his eyes. "I feared I had done irreparable damage to our friendship."

"I was the ass."

"Justifiably. I was wrong to speak so to you."

He pressed the side of his face against hers. "It's in the past. Let it remain there."

"You're right. We've moved on." She loved the feel of his whiskers against her cheek. "I still have one more question."

"Haven't you used all five?"

She felt his smile, even as one pulled at her lips. "Probably."

"Ask away."

"What will you do once we make it out?"

There was a long stretch of silence before he said, "There are Druids here. I feel their magic in other places. I could be of help."

"But Esther isn't here, and you two are a team."

"Precisely. The dragons are stirred enough as it is. It wouldn't be wise for Esther to come or for me to remain."

The happiness from earlier shriveled as she became crestfallen. "That makes sense."

"Anything could happen. I'm only laying out the facts as I see them now. Tomorrow is a different day."

"Mm-hmm."

"There is another option."

She stared at their boots. "What's that?"

"If I have to return to Earth, you could come with me."

Her heart skipped a beat. The words made her deliriously happy, but would it be right for her to leave Zora while it was in such turmoil? Everyone with magic needed to be here for when the war ignited.

"I know," Henry said, his voice barely a whisper in her ear. "We're pulled in different directions. But we'll figure it out."

She nodded. If he thought that, then there was something between them, and that was enough to keep her feelings for him as strong as ever.

TWENTY-ONE

The vines hid her, keeping her from view. But she was close enough to see the expressions on the couple's faces and hear Henry's and Melisse's words. It was a game they played. It had to be. She had trapped them within her domain, yet they acted as if everything would work out.

As if they would get free.

Even more concerning was Melisse. She no longer looked as if she were about to succumb to the poison.

Her gaze caught the green that dotted the ground within the circle where the pair reclined like lovers. She bent, placed her hand on the cold, hard earth, and closed her eyes as she reached out with her magic. Her hand jerked away when she felt the sheer power of the new growth. It was unlike anything she had experienced before.

Slowly, she stood, her gaze sliding to Henry. The Druid. The word was foreign. Then again, so were Melisse and Henry. Their manner of dress, mannerisms, speech. She had wanted to like

Henry since he wasn't a dragon. It was difficult to admit, but for a moment, she'd thought she might have...what was the word again? Oh, yes. A friend. Not a true friend, but at least someone to hold conversations with. His arrival caused her to realize how lonely she had been.

It was an emotion she bore, maybe not easily but stoically, because she was the last human. There was no use bemoaning something that couldn't be altered.

Then Melisse arrived, looking human but affected like the dragons who had entered her domain.

Then there was Henry, claiming to be a Druid while telling her she was one, as well.

She had been ill-prepared for a confrontation with him. He was powerful. He had proven that time and again. Was he the reason Melisse looked almost healed? Her gaze dropped to the sprouts. Something had certainly happened within the confines of his drawing. And to think she had consented for him to leave the valley unharmed. He'd sealed his fate when he threw her offer away.

Yet she couldn't seem to turn away from the pair. She was mesmerized by the way they watched each other and shared smiles. Even now, as Henry cradled Melisse with his body, he seemingly couldn't stop touching her. Her hair, hands, and face. As if that simple contact was the difference between life and death.

And the dragon relished every second. The way Melisse's eyes closed in rapture when his cheek moved alongside hers.

Rage began to boil within her. Melisse was a dragon and, therefore, deserved nothing but death. Certainly not love or affection. Never that. As for Henry...she would force him to watch. He would attempt to stop her, of course, but she wasn't without surprises.

Her focus returned to the pair as the dragon held up her left palm. Their voices were low, but she could just make out the words.

"They're healing nicely," Henry said after removing the bandage. "The skin is pink and puckered. You'll likely have scars."

Melisse turned her head to glance at him, excitement brightening her face. "Do you really think so?"

"You want scars?" he asked with a chuckle.

Melisse rubbed the thumb of her right hand over her other palm. "I have plenty of them, but none that anyone can see. I want these to show."

"Why?" His brow furrowed as he leaned to the side to watch her.

"Scars prove that someone has survived. They'll be a reminder of what happened here." She looked at him. "About who came to my aid."

The two stared into each other's eyes for a long moment. Then Henry's head lowered. Melisse's lids closed, and her lips parted.

She couldn't bear to see any more. She stalked forward. The vines parted as she neared, opening to reveal her. The image of the two of them about to kiss replayed in her mind as the fires of her anger swelled.

"If you want scars, dragon, I'll give them to you."

The couple jerked apart. Anger and frustration filled Melisse's nearly white eyes. Henry rose, determination tightening his face. She didn't stop until she reached the perimeter of the etching.

"What do you want?" Melisse demanded as she climbed to her feet.

She noticed the dragon was careful not to put too much pressure on her injured leg. A weakness. Not something anyone should show an enemy. She grinned. "What I always get when a dragon enters my domain."

"That is about to stop."

"But it won't."

Henry moved to stand between them, forcing her gaze to him. She was really tired of him getting between her and her quarry. Whatever leniency she'd considered, whatever kinship there had once been, was gone.

"Help me understand why you have such hatred for dragons," he bade.

She raked her gaze over him. "You don't need to understand anything."

"Something happened to you," he went on as if she hadn't spoken. "A dragon must have hurt you."

A brief memory flared, one with fire.

"They hurt someone you loved," Henry said, his voice softer.

It was as if his mere words threw open a door. Long-buried memories spewed out, assaulting her. The screams, the heat. The stench of burning flesh. On the heels of that was the soul-ripping despair and agonizing anguish.

The gut-wrenching grief.

The past rose up and swallowed her, yanking her back to that harrowing day. She couldn't breathe, couldn't move.

"Share your story," Henry urged.

His voice pulled her to the present before she was sucked away. She fisted her hands when she felt them shaking. Sweat beaded her brow, but somehow, she forced a smile and laughed. Her enemies couldn't see weakness. She refused to allow that. "Like you two have shared yours to each other? Will we be friends after? Which of you will kiss me? Bed me?"

"Enough," Melisse bit out as she moved to the side. Fury brightened her whitish eyes. "I get it. You hate me. Fine. Hate me. I haven't done anything to you, but I'll take whatever you throw my way."

"If it wasn't for Henry, you would already be right where I want you."

Henry held up his hands, palms out in a calming gesture. "We can help you."

"You think I want your assistance?" As if she would take the help of a *dragon*! She began laughing softly, the sound growing louder and longer as she stared at the pair. "I need nothing from you."

"You didn't harm me," Henry stated as he lowered his hands to his sides.

She wound an arm around a vine and stroked her fingers along it in an effort to stop shaking. The memories were there, waiting to take her again. She pushed them back. "That was before you refused my offer to leave."

"You didn't harm me because I didn't have dragon blood. If you can differentiate between me and a dragon, then that tells me you aren't evil. Only someone who kills everyone they encounter has such a heart."

She snorted cynically. "A heart?"

"Morality. Compassion. Mercy. Call it whatever you want," he said. "I saw it when we first spoke. I wouldn't leave someone I cared about. I don't think you would either."

"You assume quite a lot for someone who knows nothing about me."

"Then tell me."

As furious as she was at him for not leaving, despite the hate she carried for the dragon, she couldn't deny that she enjoyed the banter. She didn't know how many years had passed since she had last spoken with another human instead of the one-sided conversations she had with the vines.

But to call forth those memories that had broken free? To willingly take herself back to that day? No. Never. She couldn't.

She *wouldn't*.

"We all have pasts," Melisse said, her voice softer—kind, even. "We've all been hurt."

Her gaze snapped to the dragon. "You wouldn't know the meaning of the word."

"Did you hear Melisse's story?" Henry demanded, his nostrils flaring. "She was imprisoned for thousands of years because others didn't understand who she was. A half-dragon, half-Fae."

She gave him a flat look. "Dragon blood is dragon blood. No matter what it's mixed with." Besides, she had no idea what a Fae was.

"You must have heard Henry's story," Melisse added. "His family was hunted to near extinction simply because they regulated the Druids."

Fae. Druids. They spoke as if she was supposed to know what those words meant. Henry had said she was Druid. But how could he know?

He caught her gaze. His voice was low and soft as he asked, "What did the dragons do to you?"

"Don't," she warned.

"I want to understand why you carry such animosity toward dragons, that's all."

She shook her head, but it was too late. The memories rushed her again. She gripped the vine tighter as she shied away, but there was no escaping them now. The screams boomed and rolled in her mind. They had once resonated through the air louder than a dragon's roar.

Momma!

She squeezed her eyes closed against the voice but it reverberated through her mind just like the screams. She drew in a deep breath, but the air was filled with thick smoke, choking her. She coughed and opened her eyes, ready to run. Only the air was clear. There was no fire, no smoke. No dragons.

Except Melisse.

"Who was taken from you?" Henry asked in that same gentle voice. He had moved a step closer, his gaze intent on her face.

"Everyone."

TWENTY-TWO

Henry moved forward another half an inch. He held the Druid's gray eyes. He was surprised he had gotten that much out of her, but he wasn't going to stop now. He had one hand behind him, his fingers splayed to keep Melisse from speaking.

"How?" he pressed.

The Druid's gaze went distant again. He didn't know what memories were rolling through her, but he could guess they were excruciating if the misery that creased her face was any indication.

Her lips parted as she gripped the vine tighter. A long stretch of silence passed before she said, "The sky was a brilliant blue. The first snowfall had dusted the valley the night before. It was a day like any other. Until we were attacked. Our village was small, not nearly enough of us to fend off such enemies."

Henry willed her to keep going. Her eyes were open and unblinking. The vines had retracted their thorns and wound together like a chair to cradle her. He glanced at Melisse, their gazes meeting briefly.

"They attempted to surround us, but some of us got away. There was only one direction to go. But there wasn't time to talk about what to do. We just...ran." She swallowed loudly. "I had my nieces by the hands, pulling them along with me. I thought the invaders would stop when we reached the dragon border."

Henry dropped his chin to his chest. He knew what was next.

"They kept coming. We crossed the border, intending to wait until they left so we could return. We never got the chance."

At her pause, Henry looked up to find the Druid's face contorted with rage and such anguish that he wanted to tell her to stop, to shove the memories back where they'd been. But it was too late for that. He should've known something like this must have happened, especially this close to the boundary line. Melisse took his hand. He looked over. She shook her head as if knowing he wanted the Druid to cease her tale. Henry remained silent and let the Druid continue her story.

"We watched the sky for dragons, but it was clear. None were close. Then, the attackers crossed the border and sent us farther onto dragon land. Everything happened so fast. A dragon swooped in out of nowhere, its roars deafening. It flew so close that the wind from one beat of its wings sent me flying to the side. I lost hold of my nieces. I called out to them, but everyone was screaming and running from the dragon, straight to the invaders— at least the ones who remained.

"I looked for my husband. He was fighting one of the attackers. I caught a glimpse of my daughter behind him. She was crying and screaming for me, her arm reaching out. I called her to me, and she ran my way just as the dragon flew at us again. There was no time to send her back, no time to warn her. The blaze cut a path between my family and me. The heat of it was so intense it blistered my skin. The flames were too high for me to get through, too thick to see through.

"I shielded my face with my hands and kept searching. I found one of my nieces with a spear through her back. Those who attacked us were either dead or running for their lives then. My family and those from the village were gone. The dragon came back around. I turned and raced across the border to safety."

Melisse squeezed Henry's hand. He returned the gesture, his heart as heavy as hers.

The Druid blinked and seemed to come back to herself, her grief palpable. She met Henry's gaze. "I swore payback that day. I've been hunting dragons ever since. Eventually, I'll snare the one responsible for taking my family."

Henry slowly released a breath. "I'm so very sorry for what happened. What color was the dragon?"

A brow rose on the Druid's forehead. "Do you intend to bring it to me?"

"I can help you get justice."

"How would you do that?"

Everything hinged on what he said next. He couldn't give her false hope, but he knew Con would uncover which dragon was responsible. "I can investigate and determine who it was."

"For what? Just to give me a name?"

"They would be punished."

The Druid snorted a laugh. "By whose standards? A dragon's? No, thank you. It's mine or not at all."

"Investigating crimes is what I do. Let me do this for you. For your family and your village."

"You say that as if you're getting out of here."

Henry shrugged. "What difference does it make if you tell me the color of the dragon if I'm not? You've already shared your story."

"Fine," she said after a pause. "It was peach with gold wings."

Henry's stomach dropped to his feet like a stone at the same moment he heard Melisse's quick inhale.

Because the Druid had just described Eurwen.

TWENTY-THREE

The first inclination Melisse had was to say that Eurwen could never harm a human. But she didn't know Con and Rhi's daughter. Melisse barely knew the Kings. Yet it didn't sound like something Eurwen would do.

"You know who it is," the Druid stated, her steely eyes locked on Henry.

He shook his head. "I didn't say that."

"I saw it on your face." The Druid slowly stood from the vine chair.

The fury and utter violence that radiated from her gave Melisse pause. She didn't have much experience with Druids, but she couldn't help but think that this one was different in more ways than just the magic she wielded.

Melisse wanted to back away, but there was nowhere to go. Henry's markings kept them protected—and imprisoned them. Not that they had somewhere to escape to. The Druid made sure they were trapped in the valley. Like a bug caught in a spider's web.

Something flashed in the Druid's hands. Melisse lowered her gaze and saw sparks firing from the Druid's fingertips. This would end badly. If Melisse still had her magic, she would shift and put an end to the woman as quickly and effectively as she could. Unfortunately, that wasn't an option.

Melisse tugged on Henry's hand. The Druid's fixation on him made her nervous. Their new enemy had so much loathing for dragons that she pretended Melisse wasn't there. That had been fine a few moments ago, but things had changed. And not for the better.

Henry swallowed, never taking his eyes off the Druid as the sparks ignited, coming quicker from her fingertips. Unease filled Melisse when the Druid's eyes seemed to take on an unholy light.

"I shut those memories away," the Druid stated in a hard voice. "Tucked them into a place I never had to go again. You have no idea how long it took me to get past them!" The Druid inhaled deeply as her rage built. "You pushed and pushed. I should've known better than to believe you would ever help me."

Henry quickly said, "I can help. I *will*."

"Right." The Druid's laugh was humorless. "Then tell me who the dragon is."

"It could be a couple of dragons," Melisse said, trying to take some of the burden off Henry. She knew it was a mistake the second the Druid turned those frightening eyes on her. If looks could kill, she would have been flayed alive.

Henry shot Melisse a quick look before telling the Druid, "She's right. There are a few with that coloring that I'm aware of. It's a rare color, to be sure. That's what you saw on my face."

The lies rolled off his tongue easily. But would they be enough to stop the building tension? Melisse sure hoped so.

When the Druid spoke, her voice was as frigid as the weather. "I hear their screams again. The stink of burning flesh fills my nose even now. My skin blisters from the heat of that fire. And for you to deceive me? My life was shattered. Obliterated. Everything I knew and loved was taken in an instant." She moved until her toes reached the outer edge of the knotwork. "The only thing that kept me going was vengeance. To pay back the dragons tenfold for what had been done to me."

"We know the color of the dragon that attacked now," Henry said in an even, calm voice.

Movement out of the corner of Melisse's eye caught her attention. She looked over to see the vines weaving quickly. Some rose skyward while others slithered like snakes over the ground. She tried to pull Henry so they could get away.

Henry turned his head, catching sight of the vines, but he wouldn't budge. "I can't begin to understand your pain, and I'm not pretending to. However, I am a man of my word. I will help find the dragon responsible."

"Oh, you're going to help, all right," the Druid said. "You're going to tell me everything I want to know about the dragons—including how they can change shapes."

Melisse might not have her dragon magic, but she was half-Fae. Besides, she wouldn't stand behind Henry and let him take the brunt of the Druid's anger. Not when Melisse was her intended target. She released Henry's hand and came to stand even with him, waiting until the Druid's gaze slid to her. "He can't tell you anything because he knows nothing. I, however, do. Not that you'll get anything from me."

"I beg to differ."

"Beg all you want," Melisse taunted, even adding a smile to punctuate her words.

"What the fuck are you doing?" Henry asked beneath his breath.

It was impossible to ignore the vines since they were all moving now, but somehow, Melisse kept her gaze locked on the Druid. "You've gotten away with your retribution for too long. It's all about to come to an end."

"By whom? You?" The Druid laughed and slowly shook her head. "As fun as this has been, I've grown bored with both of you." Her stormy eyes returned to Henry. "You should've run when you had the chance."

The minute she finished speaking, the Druid noticed the brambles moving. She didn't seem fazed by it, and that made Melisse even more nervous. The vines grew tighter together, blocking out light as Melisse moved closer to Henry and searched for a glimmer of Fae magic, even the smallest particle. All she needed was one iota of it.

"Don't," Henry said close to her ear.

She barely heard him over the creaking and groaning of the moving vines. Melisse met his gaze.

"*Trust me*," he mouthed.

Melisse nodded, but she continued searching for her magic. She had once used Fae and dragon magic separately. Or were her memories jumbled? She was half of each, which meant that only half her magic should be affected by whatever the forest did to dragons.

Unless there was no differentiating her magic. But she was

sure she had once separated the two. It was so long ago, though, and she couldn't be certain.

"Shit," Henry whispered. "Get ready."

The wrath that swarmed around the Druid now was unmistakable. The sparks at her fingertips grew bigger, thicker. Then they began moving around her sluggishly in an X pattern, growing faster as more joined. Until it looked like two long flames of fire crossing her front and back. Henry laced his fingers with Melisse's as the Druid leaned her head back and held her arms out at her sides.

Suddenly, she slammed her hand against the ground. Sparks arched from the Druid's fingers toward the shield knot. Then across it. Melisse and Henry took a half-step back when a crack exploded from the ground beneath the Druid's hand. The single fissure became two, then six, and continued on as it widened and shot straight for them. Melisse held her breath as it inched closer to the drawing in the ground. The Druid smiled and straightened, the flames still circling her as the knotwork line broke.

And with it went their safety.

Melisse had no time to react before being thrown backward and crashing into a vine. She hit the ground hard, but immediately jumped to her feet. She spotted Henry with his arms outstretched, palms facing the Druid as they battled, magic against magic. Melisse was in awe of Henry. He didn't give the Druid an inch, but he was struggling. The Druid's magic was formidable, and she was unleashing all of it on Henry.

Once more, Melisse searched for her Fae magic as she rushed to Henry's side. She dug deep. It had to be within her. Somewhere. If only it would answer. Henry needed her. She was a Fae and a dragon. She had the magic of two mighty beings flowing in her veins. She could do this. She *would* find it.

Melisse felt a tingle. She grasped onto it and coaxed it out. It was weak and barely what anyone would call power, but it was all she had. She lifted her hands and pushed the meager magic to join with Henry's.

The Druid's lips peeled back in a sneer as sparks came right at Melisse's face. She leaned to the side to avoid them, but a few managed to land in her hair. Melisse smelled burnt hair and chose to ignore it, focusing on her magic instead. It might be the only thing that gave them time to find a way out. And right now, that was all she could hope for.

Henry's teeth were clenched, his lips pulled back as he fought against the intensity of the Druid's clout. The vines continued moving. They hadn't come after her and Henry, but they did persist in weaving around them. Melisse noticed the vines weren't just tightening around them at the edge of the shield knot, but the brambles also created a dome over them. The only area still open was where their magic flowed and met. But even that was shrinking. The Druid must have noticed it, too, because she let out a bellow of rage.

Then, the vines sealed the hole. Henry and Melisse halted their magic and waited, just in case the Druid managed to break through. Seconds passed with nothing. Not even a sound from the other side. Henry lowered his arms, and they each took a moment to look around before their gazes turned upward to the open hole large enough to allow light to spill into the sphere.

"I'm not sure if they did this to help us or to trap us," Melisse whispered as she smothered her smoking hair to put out the sparks.

Henry walked to the side and trailed his hand along the vines. Not a single thorn showed anywhere within the perimeter. "They helped us. Didn't you hear her outraged scream?"

"I did, but these are the same plants whose thorns have poison designed to harm dragons."

Hazel eyes met hers. "The thorns are gone."

"Why?"

He shrugged. "I don't know. Does it matter?"

"They don't like me."

"The Druid doesn't like you."

"The vines are hers."

That made him pause. "If they were, they wouldn't have kept her away from us. At first, I thought she controlled them, but if that were the case, they wouldn't have helped me on the climb. I don't know if they're a byproduct of her magic or if they were plants already in the valley and her ability has turned them into what they are now." He looked from the brambles to her. "They haven't attacked either of us. Not once."

Melisse had to concede that.

"They're not going to harm us," Henry continued. "I believe they'll keep us from her. At least, for a little while."

Melisse looked up at the small bit of sky above her. "Which means we're trapped."

"Think of it as a safe room."

"You knew from the beginning that we shouldn't harm them. How?"

He shrugged and walked to her. "A feeling." He took her hands. "You used magic."

"Fae magic. And barely much of anything. It took a lot just to muster that."

"It helped. Thank you. I wondered if you'd be able to reach your Fae magic. It makes sense that you can."

"You didn't say anything before."

He gave her a flat look. "You were injured. You needed to concentrate on getting better."

"I am now, which means I can attempt to reach my Fae magic again."

"You think you could teleport us out of here?"

Melisse twisted her lips ruefully. "That was one aspect I didn't master before my parents died. And once I was released, I was too busy seeing the world."

"And shifting for the first time."

"Yes." How she wished her father could've seen that. He had always told her he thought she could change forms from Fae to dragon. He'd been right.

Henry ran the back of his fingers over her cheek. "You're one incredible woman."

"I've done nothing but fumble my way from one catastrophe to another."

"I wish you could see yourself through my eyes. You'd see the beautiful, resilient, formidable warrior I can't get enough of."

Her heart melted as she gazed up at him. "If you don't kiss me, I might go up in flames."

His lips curved into a quick smile before his mouth met hers.

TWENTY-FOUR

How many times had Henry dreamed of taking Melisse in his arms? How many times had he recounted their kiss?

And craved more.

Ached.

Yearned.

His fingers slid into the long, silver strands of her hair as their mouths brushed softly. He kissed her again, lingering before he slid his tongue past her lips. Need, fierce and demanding, pounded through him as their tongues tangled in an intimate dance. She sank against him, her breasts pressed to his chest. His hands slid down her back and held her close as he deepened the kiss.

She moaned, and it was his undoing. His blood thrummed fervently in his veins and rushed straight to his cock. Her hands gripped him tightly as if she feared he might let go. Didn't she realize that she had his heart? Surely, she had to know that he had been hers from their first kiss. He could think of no other, wanted no one but her.

Melisse.

Exquisite, exotic. Evocative.

The way she looked at him made Henry believe he could take on the world and win. Her whitish eyes held warmth and curiosity for all things. And when she turned them on him, the longing and passion reflected there made him forget everything but her.

The feelings she wrought. And what could develop between them.

If given the chance.

Against all odds, they were together in an unholy place with a vengeful Druid. And still alive.

His body burned for her. He yearned to strip off her clothes so he could touch and kiss every inch of her. He needed hours to worship her body and show her just how much he adored her. He wanted to shower her with orgasms until she was so sated she couldn't move.

But no matter how much he lusted to sink into her, their first time wouldn't be in a place that had sapped her magic and nearly succeeded in taking her life.

Henry gradually ended the kiss then lifted his head. His balls tightened when he saw her swollen lips. Her eyes were still closed, a dazed expression on her face.

Slowly, her lids lifted, and their gazes met. "Why did you stop?"

Her desire-roughened voice was enough to test a saint. And he was far from one. He'd hungered. "Is this really where you want our first time to be?"

She flattened her hands on his chest and smoothed them downward, pausing at the waist of his jeans. "If you really wish to know, I would've preferred for us to have already been together."

He grinned and ran the pads of his fingers along her jaw.

"But," she said, licking her lips and looking to the side, "you're right. This isn't the right place for us."

Inwardly, he groaned. If she had pushed to continue, he would've caved. A part of him really wished she had said that the place didn't matter.

She turned her face to him. "*When*—not if—we get out of here, we're going somewhere private where we won't be disturbed."

"I like the sound of that."

The pulse at her throat beat wildly. Her gaze lowered to his mouth, and her hands dropped to his hips. He grew harder for her, his arousal aching for her touch.

"If we're not...then you have to stop looking at me like that," he warned. "I only have so much control, and it's about to snap."

"I'm not sure I can release you." She inhaled, causing her breasts to rub against his chest.

Henry was losing a battle he didn't want to win. "Then don't."

"This place is filled with too much hate."

Her voice had dropped to a whisper. His hands moved to her shoulders and then down to her waist. "We can change that."

"Now, who is tempting whom?" she asked with a devilish grin.

"I need weeks—no, months—to do all the things I want to do to your body."

She sighed. "I have a few ideas of my own."

It was too much. If Henry didn't stop this now, they would be naked in seconds. He shook his head and stepped away from her. It was one of the hardest things he had ever done after finally holding her, kissing her again. But there would be more. He would make sure of it. "I've waited this long. What's a few more hours?"

"This is simply paused," Melisse said. "Until we get out."

"Until we get out," he repeated.

She put her hands on her hips and turned to look at the vines. "So. What now?"

It was a good question. One he didn't have an answer to. But it was either turn his attention to that or give in to the desire. He cleared his throat and turned to the problem. "I don't know how long the vines will be able to keep her out. We need a plan."

"What are our options?"

The longer Con stared at the brambles, the more uneasy he became. There was a malicious presence here. How was it that no one had noticed it? Why hadn't he detected it? Or had the dragons recognized it and just dealt with it?

Nay. That theory didn't work. They would've alerted Eurwen or Brandr. It had to be that the dragons hadn't known. He had to believe that. Otherwise, his daughter had agreed to send Evander and Melisse here, knowing what awaited them. There was much he was still learning about his daughter, but that didn't sound like her.

"Talk to me."

He turned his head as Rhi came up behind him, wrapping her arms around his waist and laying her cheek against his shoulder blade. "There isna much to say, my love."

"This is me you're talking to, sweetheart. You don't have to sugarcoat anything."

"I'm fucking scared. Is that what you want to hear?" The words came out harsh, his voice cracking from the pressure he felt pushing down on his shoulders, threatening to crush him.

Rhi walked around to stand in front of him. "That's exactly what I want to hear. We don't keep secrets anymore. Remember?"

"I have a bad feeling. And it's only growing the longer Henry and Melisse are in there." He jerked his chin to the giant vines.

She drew in a long breath and slowly released it. "We're all worried and terrified. But this isn't just your problem. This is on all of us. We're not on Earth anymore. It doesn't all fall to you."

"If it's the Kings, their mates, Henry, or Melisse—or you and our children—it always falls to me."

Rhi's silver eyes sparkled with annoyance.

"*Us*," he corrected, belatedly realizing why she was upset. "It falls to us."

"Better."

He looked past her to the valley. "I doona know what to do."

"It's a good thing you don't need to decide on your own. Eurwen is on her way. I also think we should have Brandr return."

Con shook his head. "I've no' changed my mind. We leave him to his business."

"He's needed. All he has to do is call my name, and I can jump to him. I'll teleport him here within moments—and back again if that's what he wants. It's that simple."

"It was his decision to go. We leave him."

"He would change his mind if he knew what was happening here."

Con took her hands. "Eurwen updates him on everything. As do I. He knows, love. I want him back, too."

"Is it that obvious that I miss him?" she asked in a soft voice.

He pulled her against him and held her tightly. "Only because I feel the same. He'll return when he wants to."

"I know. I'm glad you stopped me from entering the vines. I

should've thought about our unborn child having dragon blood. I could've put the baby at risk."

"But you didna go in. Everything is fine."

"We'll have to tell the others about the pregnancy eventually."

"I know."

She was silent for a long moment. "I want to fight alongside you and the others. It's where I belong."

"You're also growing a life." He gently took her face in his hands and tilted her head back so he could look into her eyes. "That trumps everything else."

Rhi sniffed and pulled away. "Eurwen is here."

Con turned and saw their daughter's peach scales. Her gold wings blinked in the sunlight before she floated to the ground. She didn't shift until after she'd landed. She took one step as a dragon, and with the next, she was in her human form, her golden hair tied back from her face in a loose ponytail. The flowy skirts she preferred were gone, replaced by denim and a thick, white sweater.

"You should've called me here when Henry arrived," she said as she joined them.

Con met her silver gaze, the same as Rhi's. "Time wasna on our side. I made a decision. If anything happens to him, I'll accept the blame."

"Not just you," Rhi said. "I sided with Henry going after Melisse and the Druid."

Eurwen crossed her arms over her chest and looked at the thick brambles. Con watched her. She didn't seem alarmed by them.

And he wasn't the only one to notice.

"You knew about this place?" Rhi asked.

Eurwen nodded once. "Brandr and I know every inch of the dragons' land."

"Are the dragons aware that they can no' come out once they enter?" Con pressed.

Eurwen wouldn't meet his gaze. "We alerted them to such."

"Yet the Pinks use this area because they have so few places elsewhere." The more Con thought about that, the more troubled he became. What was his daughter hiding?

"You blame me," Eurwen stated.

"I'm no' laying blame. I'm trying to sort this out."

"This is Zora. Brandr and I make the decisions here," Eurwen replied.

Rhi moved between them. "All right. Let's not go there. Eurwen," she said, looking at their daughter, "your father just said he isn't laying blame. He also isn't trying to undermine you." Then Rhi's gaze swung to him. "If the dragons knew this place was dangerous, then they came of their own free will. That's no one's fault but theirs."

"It is if the Pinks doona have safer areas to roam." He ran a hand down his face. "Regardless, that isna the issue. The problem is that Melisse went searching for a youngling who vanished in there," he said, pointing to the valley. "None of us can contact her."

Eurwen shook her head. "There's no use trying. No dragon can be reached once in there."

"We're not leaving Henry and Melisse—or the Pink—in there," Rhi asserted.

Eurwen dropped her arms. "That leaves few alternatives since dragons can't step inside."

"Nor can Lotti. She already tried," Con said. When Eurwen looked at Rhi, he added, "Nor can your mother."

Eurwen's brows rose. "We can ask other mates."

"We might not have another choice. Henry said there's a Druid in there," Rhi said.

Eurwen shrugged. "I know nothing of Druids on Zora."

"But you do know this place." Con didn't understand why Eurwen was so uncomfortable about the region. Was it because dragons had disappeared? Or was it something more?

"I've already said as much."

Rhi glanced at the vines. "Has there always been a portion of it across the border onto dragon land?"

"Nay."

One word. But it said much. Con almost pressed Eurwen for more, but he knew the stubborn look she wore. It was one Rhi often used. He would get nothing more about the past from Eurwen at the moment. He wouldn't give up, though. There was a story, and he would learn what it was.

"Have you tried removing it before it expands anymore?" Rhi queried.

Eurwen eyed Evander, who continued to fly over the brambles on their side of the border. "I didn't realize it had spread this far onto our side."

Rhi looked at him and said, "We should do something about that."

"Aye. But when? We've no idea where Melisse and Henry are or if they're even together. No' to mention the Pink and any other dragons who might be within that jungle," Con explained.

Eurwen faced the vines. "If there are dragons there, they're long dead."

TWENTY-FIVE

Melisse wasn't sure what woke her. She was still on her side, but instead of lying on Henry's chest as she had been, his coat pillowed her head. She sat, using her hand to prop herself up, then looked around the...whatever it was they were in. Globe? Sphere? She located the outline of a body squatting near where the ground had split from the Druid's magic.

"Henry?"

He turned to her, then got to his feet and walked over. "I'm here."

"What were you doing?"

"Just looking." He sat beside her, but his gaze lifted to the opening above them that showed the dark clouds of night.

She shifted onto her bottom and crossed her legs as they sat shoulder to shoulder. They had talked for hours, tossing around one idea after another until they fell asleep. "There's something on your mind."

"I'm going over everything she told us."

"And?" Melisse pressed when he didn't continue.

Henry bent his knees and wrapped his arms around them, one hand gripping the other wrist. "I'm not sure. Something isn't adding up."

"What's not to add up? Her village was attacked, they escaped the only way they could, and, unfortunately, they broke the one rule the dragons have: don't cross the border."

Henry's gaze swung to her. "And everyone died but her?"

Melisse hated not having her enhanced dragon vision. She could only make out his silhouette, but she knew by the uncertainty in his voice that his face was lined with concern. His lips were likely pinched, his brow deeply furrowed. "Some would call her lucky."

"Do you really think the dragon would take out everyone but the Druid?"

Melisse didn't miss the way Henry purposefully didn't say Eurwen's name. Just in case. "If we're going by what the Druid told us, it sounds like the flames might have hidden her."

"What dragon do you know would fail to spot all intruders? Because you know that's what the Druid and her people were labeled."

"None." Especially not a Queen like Eurwen. "If that's the case, then why was the Druid allowed to go free?"

"We may never know."

"Let's say, for argument's sake, that the Druid was allowed to live. What would the dragon's reasoning be?"

Henry shrugged, shaking his head slowly as he looked forward. "Regret for taking the others' lives, maybe?"

"Hmm. Doubtful.

"Yeah, I don't buy that either. The Druid and her villagers

crossed the border. The reason doesn't matter." Henry stretched out his legs and leaned back on his hands. "If it wasn't because the dragon was remorseful, what does that leave?"

Melisse used her fingers to comb through the ends of her tangled hair. "What if the dragon didn't see her?"

"We considered that."

"I mean, what if the dragon *really* didn't see the Druid? Not because of the flames or smoke, but because the Druid was hidden from E—the dragon." Melisse inwardly winced at almost having said Eurwen's name.

Henry's lips twisted. "The Druid's magic is powerful, but is it potent enough to take on a dragon?"

"Take a look around us."

"The vines with their poison are different. I suspect they came after that fateful day."

Melisse blew out a breath. "Maybe one of the villagers helped the Druid without her knowledge. She said that not everyone came with her group. Perhaps someone lagged behind and offered what they could as help before they were killed. It might have been just enough time for the Druid to get back over the border and to safety."

"It's plausible."

"But you don't think that's what happened."

Henry's head swung to her. "It's hard to know. We've only heard one side of the story."

"It isn't as if we can contact the dragon to get their side."

"Not now."

Melisse used her hands to turn herself to face him. "I thought Esther was the TruthSeeker."

"She is, but that doesn't mean I don't find myself needing to know in certain situations. Like now."

"What does it matter if the Druid had help or not? She made it out alive. She lost her baby and everyone else, and hatred, deep and unrelenting, consumed her. There is no coming back from that."

"You did."

She parted her lips to answer but realized she couldn't. "My situation was different."

"Was it?" Henry pressed. "You lost your family. You saw your mother taken right in front of you. By a dragon. You were imprisoned. You, better than most, have reason to despise them. And you could wipe them out."

Melisse looked away. "Do you want me to admit that there were times in those long, unending years that I imagined ways to kill the dragons, starting with whoever the King of Kings was at the time? Will it please you to know that planning their deaths and thinking of different ways to make each and every one of them suffer was the only way I got through some days?"

"I don't pass judgment. Anyone in your position—including me—would have done the very same, I can assure you." His hand reached over and covered hers that now lay in her lap. "My point is, you got past it."

"Have I?"

"Do you still wish them dead?"

Her eyes closed. "There are times I forget. Those brief moments allow me to bask in the present." She looked at Henry. "Then something happens that makes me think of the past and all I've missed and my anger swallows me. It happened often after I left Dreagan to see the world."

"How frequent are the times you forget?"

"They used to happen rarely, but I'd say a few times a week now. Why?"

His fingers squeezed hers. "You're healing. You're allowing yourself to heal."

"Me?" she asked with a loud snort. "I'm not doing anything."

"The only way a person can heal is if they want it. If they seek it. You're here, on Zora, to help the dragons. That tells me you've come a lot further than you realize."

Melisse turned her hand up and interlaced her fingers with his.

"And," he continued, "you're earning the Kings' trust, which speaks volumes. If Con, for any reason, didn't believe you were here to fight for the dragons, he wouldn't have allowed you to come or offered Dreagan as your home."

"Or maybe he knows he can't stop me. Maybe everything he's done is because he fears I'll kill them all."

There was a smile in Henry's voice as he said, "I've known Con for a few years now, and while I'm not his closest friend, there are few things he's afraid of. He would stand between you and the dragons if he thought you were a danger to them. Instead, he asked you to come to Zora."

It made sense. Or perhaps, Melisse wanted it to be true so badly that she believed it. "And my...healing...makes you think you can get the Druid to halt her vengeance?"

"That's a chance we need to take."

"I've seen her revulsion, felt her disgust. She won't listen to anything as long as a dragon is near, and I'm not leaving you alone with her."

"She's been willing to speak to me in the past."

"I think we can safely say that opportunity has gone. You saw how furious she was when the vines kept her from us. I think you're firmly in her hate column now."

Henry got to his feet and began walking in a wide circle. "How long do you think she's been trapping dragons? Twenty years? More?"

"Druids aren't immortal, so I'd say fifteen. Maybe twenty."

"That's twenty years of dragons that have gone missing." Henry threw up his hands in agitation before letting them fall to his thighs. "Even if that's only one dragon a year, that's still twenty too many. Right?"

Melisse winced at the rise in his voice. "Agreed."

"How can we let even one more go through what you endured here? I watched the poison work its way through your body. It was horrible, but I know it's nothing compared to what you experienced."

"But we've talked about how it's doubtful the thorns can get through a dragon's scales."

Henry halted before her. "The Druid was shocked and outraged to learn that dragons could shift. The vines have poison that specifically harms dragons. Trust me, the poison is getting through the scales somehow. We have a hard enough time walking through the brambles. A dragon would shove through."

Her stomach tightened in dread. "Thinking that their scales would be defense enough."

"And not having any idea of what was happening until it was too late."

"I think I might be sick."

He dropped to his knees and sat back on his heels. "The Druid has a right to her anger, but all of this needs to stop. She has to let go of the past and move forward. Find some form of healing—if she can."

"You're asking a lot of her. Besides, if she wanted to heal another way, she would have."

"Do we have any other choice?"

"We can get the hell out of here and burn it all to the ground, her included."

The softening light from the hole above signaled morning and brought some of Henry's face into focus. "It may come to that, but I think we owe her a chance at life."

"You think the youngling is dead, don't you?"

Henry glanced away. "I do. I'm afraid you would be, too, if I hadn't been able to heal you."

"I wanted to save the Pink. I wanted to prove I could be useful."

"How could you ever doubt that you are? You're a half-dragon, half-Fae. There are only three of you in the entire universe."

Melisse realized that no one had feared that Eurwen and Brandr would destroy the Kings. Only her. Because she had killed a King. "I don't fit anywhere."

"You fit with me."

She grinned at him. "We do make a good team."

"You fit anywhere you want to be. The Kings welcomed you. All you have to do is allow yourself to become a part of the family."

He was right, of course. "Well, we did a lot of talking last night and this morning, and we haven't come up with a plan to get out yet."

"We have. We're going to talk to the Druid."

"Because that worked so well last time," Melisse said, motioning to the vine dome.

Henry shrugged. "Details."

"Important details. We need to know what to do when she attacks again."

He pulled her up with him and took her to the vines. "We can leave whenever we want."

"You sure?"

"Positive. I made a path through the brambles to the next shield knot."

Melisse glanced back where the ground had cracked. "I don't know that it will do us much good."

"It gives us a little time."

"You saw the path to the edge of the forest. You know how close it is. I say we make a run for it. If she comes at us during that, we'll fight her." When Henry frowned, Melisse sighed. "Fine, we'll try to talk to her. But you need to understand that you might not be able to save her."

Henry nodded toward the vines. "I'm trying to save everyone." Then he jerked his chin to the ground.

For the first time, Melisse looked at the greenery that had sprouted the day before. It now carpeted the entire circle in thick grass.

"Every living thing matters," Henry said.

Melisse looked into his eyes and smiled. "You're right. They do. We'll give your plan a go, but if anything goes wrong—"

"I know," he said over her.

They faced the vines together. Henry put his hand on them, and layer by layer, they began moving and shifting until there was an opening big enough for them to exit through.

"Ready?" Henry asked.

Melisse laid her hand on the smooth vines and silently sent a wave of gratitude through her palm. "Let's do this."

TWENTY-SIX

They were taking a huge chance leaving the safety of the vine cage, but Henry knew it was the right thing to do. The *only* thing to do.

He and Melisse couldn't remain in there forever. Besides, they needed to find Eurwen and hear her side of the story. As for the Druid, Henry knew his strategy hinged on her willingness to listen. And they were probably past that point.

But he had to try.

For her, for the vines, for the dragons.

For Zora.

Whatever happened, however it had happened, it would only get worse. The dragons had been kept away, fearing the vine forest, but also because they wouldn't cross the border. How much longer that last part held true was anyone's guess. And once the dragons decided it would be better to take out their anger on the Druid and the vines, it would be like a spark to dried wood. In an instant, Zora would be embroiled in war—the very thing Villette wanted.

Henry led Melisse through the vines as they hurriedly wove their way along. They kept their eyes peeled for the Druid because she was near. He had kept that part from Melisse. He probably shouldn't have, but the truth of the matter was that the Druid would remain until they attempted to leave. Be it this morning, the next, or ten days from now. She wanted retribution, and she intended to have it.

None of the smaller shield knots he had made had been disrupted. Yet. He paused on one to look behind them. The dome remained intact. Were the vines staying to distract the Druid? Henry hoped he wasn't wrong about them assisting them.

"Nothing," Melisse whispered when she reached him.

He nodded and went to the next part of the path that led to the large shield knot. One section required them to jump over a vine. He had looked for an easier route, but that one was it. Melisse didn't need to be carried anymore. Actually, her limp was barely noticeable now.

Yet when he reached the area where they needed to get over the four-foot-high section of vine, it wasn't there. Henry didn't stop to think about it. The path was correct. He was sure of it. Then he spotted the large shield knot. He sprinted the last bit of distance.

Once inside the knot, he tossed the last bottle of water to Melisse and let her drink before taking his share. She acted as a lookout for the Druid while he surveyed the vines in the direction they needed to go. It was tempting to remain where they were, but if they had even a slight advantage over the Druid, it was better to take it.

"Ready?" he called softly.

Melisse gave him a nod and came up next to him. She stayed a step or two behind as he took off. The terrain was uneven, but the brambles weren't clustered as tightly together as in other areas. At least that's what he thought until he saw them moving to open a path for them. He grinned and ran faster.

Because Melisse was still healing, he alternated his speed and made sure there were times they kept to a fast walk. They were making good time—better than he had hoped, actually. They rarely spoke. There was no need. As quiet as the forest was, sound carried, including their feet slapping the ground as they ran. But there was nothing to be done about that.

They paused for a break. Henry bent over, his hands on his knees, gulping in air. He couldn't imagine how he would feel if he hadn't kept up his five-mile runs each morning. Melisse tapped his shoulder. He looked up to find her gaze on something through the vines. Henry straightened and looked in that direction.

"*It's her,*" Melisse mouthed when she looked at him.

Henry motioned for them to get moving again. They walked quickly, keeping their footsteps as light as possible. The vines closed the path behind them as soon as they were out of the way, and the route ahead looked to be as straight as it could be.

When he thought they had put enough distance between them and the Druid, he started running again. Unfortunately, they didn't get far before Melisse gasped behind him. He turned to find her limping and immediately went to her.

"I'm fine," she whispered.

He ignored her and took out their last protein bar and the water. He shoved the remaining water at her as he broke the bar in half. They would need all the energy they could get to escape the forest and the Druid. They both sipped the water and devoured their portion of the bar, then got moving again.

Melisse was limping, but at least she could somewhat manage a run. The path wasn't wide enough to stand side by side, which kept them moving in single file, but it made traveling much easier. Also noticeably missing were any thorns they could run into.

Henry glanced back to find Melisse's limp more noticeable, but she motioned for him to keep going. He peered ahead of them. They had to be getting close to the edge of the valley. He leaned to the side to try to get a better view when something red-orange zipped past him. Melisse shouted his name just as another round of sparks came his way. He spun to find the Druid stalking toward them, fury in her gaze.

"Going somewhere?" she taunted.

Melisse lifted her hands as if to send a blast of magic, but nothing happened. Henry's stomach dropped like a stone when he saw the fiendish grin curving the Druid's lips. Her next bout of sparks was aimed at Melisse.

Henry didn't think twice as he shoved her behind him, his mind filled with ways to block the Druid's assault. To his shock, the sparks bounced off and fell harmlessly to the ground. The vines didn't interfere this time. They hurried out of the Druid's way, making her path to them easy.

"Henry," Melisse said.

He pushed her around and said, "Run."

She ran all out, her arms pumping hard as her feet slapped the ground. Henry was right on her heels. He saw sparks to his right and ducked as they struck a vine instead of him. He could've sworn he heard a high-pitched bellow.

More magic came their way. Some were way off the mark, but many were entirely too close for comfort. If they slowed even a little, it would be over. Henry felt a burn on his legs and looked down to find that sparks had landed on his jeans and caught fire. He swatted them out, never breaking stride.

Sparks landed to the left and the right of his feet. A few even hit his boots, but his rapid movements quickly extinguished them. He saw some arching over him and coming within breaths of landing on Melisse. It gave him time to dodge sideways and avoid most of them. A sting lit his face, neck, and scalp. He patted and swiped at the sparks, hoping he got them all.

His side ached. Melisse was having trouble keeping up the pace, but she pushed onward. He drew in a deep breath to fill his body with oxygen and keep going, but he felt his energy fading, along with his speed. He dug deep and pushed harder, even as he came up behind Melisse and urged her to go faster.

He caught a glimpse of the mountainside ahead of them. They had reached the end of the vine forest. It was only a hundred yards away.

"There it is," he said.

Melisse somehow ran faster. He was doing well keeping his legs pumping. The distance between him and Melisse grew as she surged toward the edge of the valley. He didn't look behind him. The Druid was still there.

"Don't stop," Henry told Melisse. "Keep going."

Sparks rained over him. There was no way to escape them. They were big—larger than he had seen since she had been standing right in front of him. Did that mean she was close? He took a chance and looked back. The Druid was right behind him, her intentions clear.

"Run, Melisse!" he bellowed.

He saw the sparks shoot from the Druid's hands and arch over him like a rocket. He followed the projection and shouted Melisse's name in warning. But it was too late. The sparks fell in a flurry of beautiful flickers and glimmers, pelting Melisse right as she reached the edge of the vine forest. She fell forward with a shout of pain, her back on fire.

Henry knew he was the next target. He should face the Druid, but he couldn't leave Melisse hurting. He ran faster while Melisse rolled on the ground to put out the flames. He was almost to her. He could see the smoke wafting from her burnt coat and hair.

Then something slammed into his shoulder, twisting him around. His feet tangled as his gaze met the Druid's. Agony spread through his chest as he was flung backward.

Shock allowed Melisse to forget her burns and get to Henry to grab his hands and drag him out of the vines so she could put out the flames. And all the while, the Druid stood and watched as she approached.

Melisse shook him, but he didn't stir. Tears burned her eyes. She put her hand beneath his nose but couldn't feel his breath. She couldn't lose him now. She wrapped her arms around him and let out a mournful cry.

The creaking of the vines pulled Melisse's attention back to the Druid. She got to her feet. If the Druid wanted a fight, Melisse would give it to her. But before she could return to the bramble, the vines sealed the area, preventing Melisse from getting in—and the Druid from getting out.

Melisse dropped to her knees beside Henry and sobbed. They had made it. He had gotten them out at the cost of his life. It was wrong. All of it. She should've been able to use her Fae magic. Why hadn't she learned how to teleport?

The one thing Melisse knew was that she needed help. It was time she turned to the family that had been waiting for her all along. She opened the mental link and shouted to all dragons in hopes someone might hear. She was out of the vines, but that didn't mean her magic had returned.

Still, she had another advantage she hadn't used. "Rhi! Help, please!"

"Melisse."

She looked up to find Rhi standing before her. Fresh tears came. The Light Fae said nothing as she touched both her and Henry. In the next moment, they were at Cairnkeep in Brandr's cottage that Con and Rhi were using.

The pain began to make itself known each time Melisse moved. She clutched Henry's hand. Then Con was there. And Eurwen. There were others. Melisse could hear their voices, but it was getting difficult to focus on anything as pain consumed her. Someone tried to pull her hand from Henry, but she latched on tighter.

Melisse let out a shout of agony when someone touched her shoulder. Almost instantly, it was gone. She shifted her shoulders, expecting pain, but it had vanished. Con. He had the ability to heal anything.

The King of Kings knelt beside Henry then, his black eyes meeting hers.

"He can't be gone," Melisse whispered.

Con drew in a breath and rested his hand on Henry. It felt like an eternity before Melisse saw Henry's chest rise. She crumpled over him for a heartbeat then threw herself at Con and embraced him.

"Thank you. Thank you so much," she said between wracking sobs.

"It's what family does," he told her.

TWENTY-SEVEN

Henry looked at his bare chest in the mirror. He rubbed his fingers over where he had felt the Druid's magic enter him. He was healed, his skin showing no indication that there was ever a wound. But he would never forget the searing pain that had pierced him like hundreds of daggers.

Voices reached him from outside the cottage. He didn't know how long he had been unconscious. He didn't even know how he had gotten to Cairnkeep or who had brought him. But he could guess. He listened, hoping to hear Melisse's voice with the others.

"It's driving me mad," Rhi stated.

"He'll come out when he's ready," Con replied.

He heard a long sigh before Rhi said, "You didn't see them."

As he suspected, Rhi had found them. Henry tuned out the rest of the conversation and ran a hand through his damp hair. The shower had felt amazing. He'd stayed beneath the spray for far too long, enjoying the heated water as it ran over his skin. But now it was time to face what had happened and get answers. He would uncover them.

No matter how deep he had to dig.

Or who he pissed off.

Henry slipped on the new olive sweater and jeans someone had laid over the chair. Even his boots were new. Again, most likely Rhi. She was always thinking of others like that. He needed to thank her. And Con, since the King of Kings had healed him. Henry tugged on the boots and stood as his gaze caught on his reflection in the mirror once more.

He ran a palm over his freshly shaven jaw. Flashes of the past few days ran through his mind. He lowered his eyes to stare at his palms. Then he fisted his hands, dropped them to his sides, and turned around. Now wasn't the time to wonder about whether he still had magic. He walked to the door and rested his hand on the knob. Then, with a deep breath, he opened it.

Rhi paused mid-stride, her gaze locked on his face. She gave him a tentative smile, one filled with concern and joy. Con was to Henry's right, leaning against the side of the cottage. Eurwen stood a few feet away, her arms crossed over her chest. Henry turned his head to the other side, but there was no sign of Melisse among the group of Kings.

Henry swung his gaze back to Con. "Where is she?"

"At the cliff. We'd like to know what happened. Melisse hasn't said much."

Henry shifted his attention to Eurwen, but she wouldn't look his way. "Soon," he promised and walked away to find Melisse.

No one stopped him. It wasn't as if he'd get far if they tried, but they knew he wouldn't leave without sharing what he had discovered. First, he had to see Melisse. He needed to know that she was all right. Con would've healed her, but his ability couldn't take away mental or emotional trauma.

As Henry walked down the slope, he finally saw Melisse standing alone on the cliff. She, too, had on new clothes, and her black-tipped silver hair no longer bore scorch marks. His steps quickened, even as he told himself not to rush to her. Much had occurred in the brambles for them, both as individuals and as a pair. Would she look at things—at *him*—differently now in the light of day?

His gaze never left her. He didn't care about the Kings flying overhead or the dragons in the distance. There was only Melisse.

There would only ever be her for him.

Suddenly, she turned. Their gazes clashed, and her mouth curved into a smile. The grip on his chest loosened, and he was finally able to breathe again. She started toward him. He couldn't slow his steps anymore. Then, she was in his arms. They clung to each other, their emotions too great and thick to speak.

They stood like that for a long time. She buried her face in his neck as he closed his eyes and savored the feel of her against him. They had made it out of the valley but not without help. Henry looked to the north. There was unfinished business there. But that was for later. Now was the time to rejoice in their survival.

He leaned away to cup her face and gazed into whitish eyes with silver threads. Then he pressed his mouth to hers for a lingering kiss. He had only meant it to be a small touch, but the moment her tongue slid against his lips, he couldn't resist deepening the kiss. Somehow, he got control of his desire and lowered his forehead to hers with a sigh. He could feel the others staring, impatiently waiting for details.

"I've never been so scared in my life," Melisse said.

Henry lifted his head to look at her. "You never have to see the vines again."

"That's not what I'm talking about. I thought you had died. Don't do that to me again."

He gave her a soft smile. "I can't promise that. Everything dies. Just as I will someday."

"No." She fisted her hands in his jumper and stared at his chest.

Henry covered her hands with his. He understood the riot of feelings within her because he'd dealt with them himself when he found her unconscious.

"Are you fully healed?" she asked softly.

"Not even a scar."

She pulled her left hand away and looked at it. "Con healed us, as I'm sure you guessed. I asked him to leave my scars." Her gaze lifted to his. "I called for Rhi once we were out of the valley. She brought us to Cairnkeep."

"Have you spoken to them?"

"You mean, have I asked Eurwen anything?" Melisse shook her head. "I was waiting for you."

He tucked a flyaway strand of hair behind her ear. "Have you shifted?"

"I'm scared to try. What about you? Have you tried magic?"

"I haven't worked up the courage yet."

She snorted a laugh. "What a pair we are."

"I'd like to say let's wait, but the question will be posed to us. And I'd like to have an answer." When she didn't reply, he asked, "Wouldn't you?"

"What if I can't?"

He tipped her chin up with his finger. "You will. Go on," he urged, "I'll be right here."

Her gaze shifted over his shoulder to where the others were likely watching.

"No one knows what we're doing," he said as he took a step back. "If you can't, we'll be the only ones to know."

Henry understood her fear and panic. He felt some of it himself, but if he lost the magic he had just found, it wouldn't be that big of a deal. Melisse not being able to shift was something much, much bigger.

Melisse's eyes met his. Maybe he shouldn't have pushed this now. It would probably be better to wait until they were alone or even when Melisse was by herself. Henry was about to tell her to forget it when a second later, a regal dragon with violet scales stood before him.

He had only ever seen her from afar. Now, he got to see her up close and personal. His lips parted in awe as he looked into her blue dragon eyes, the exact color of an afternoon sky. A mane of bony spikes grew like a crown at the back of her head. Her scales narrowed on her underside, and she had slightly different-shaped wings from the others and a long tail that lay half curled behind her.

She was exquisite and fearsome. There was no other way to describe her.

Then, Melisse was back in her Fae form, clothes and all. Henry could only blink at the quick shift. He had been studying her but forgot all that at her bright smile. She threw her arms around him, her delight infectious.

"I did it," she whispered.

"I knew you could."

Melisse leaned back and nodded as she became solemn. "Your turn."

Henry almost refused, but if she could do it, so could he. He called for his magic, tried to feel it as he had in the valley, but there was nothing. Not a whisper. "It's gone."

"I'm sorry."

"We're back to how things are supposed to be. I'm fine with that."

Melisse arched a brow. "Are you really?"

"I am," he assured. "Ready to face the others now?"

"Aye."

They walked to the cottage, where a small group waited for them. Eurwen finally met Henry's gaze but didn't hold it for long. He then looked at Con. The King of Kings gave him a nod and said something to the group of Kings nearby. Everyone but Eurwen's mate, Vaughn, walked away.

"Let's go inside," Rhi said when they reached the cottage. "There is food as well as tea."

"And whisky," Con added.

Henry's stomach growled, reminding him how little he had eaten over the past few days. As soon as he entered the cottage, the smell of the food was too much. He helped himself to a few items, so famished he nearly swallowed them whole.

"Perhaps we should wait so Henry can eat," Vaughn offered.

Henry shook his head and looked at the King of Teals. After he swallowed, he said, "It's better to get this lengthy story underway."

The only door inside the cottage was to the bathroom. It wasn't meant to hold more than two people, so six around the rectangular table made it crowded. Henry was next to Melisse on the bench while Con sat to Henry's right. Rhi took the chair across from

Henry with Vaughn next to her, and Eurwen on the other end of the table beside Melisse.

Rhi made a show of getting everyone drinks to allow him more time to eat. Henry cast a furtive look at the two Dragon Kings and one Queen, then the royal Light Fae, and a half-dragon, half-Fae. Each could've conjured whatever drink they wanted within seconds.

He was more than aware of how powerful the beings were, yet whatever he had always felt he lacked before was gone. The magic he had—or didn't have—wasn't what defined him. Esther had been trying to tell him that for so long, but he hadn't listened to her or anyone else. Now, he understood.

Magic had the ability to make things fun and interesting. Those who had it didn't know what it was like *not* to have it, and vice versa. He had experienced things on both sides, and while he'd only had the magic for a short time, it had opened his eyes in ways hearing it described never could.

He had *felt* it.

Used it.

And it had changed him.

Maybe being in the vines had healed the emptiness he'd carried since discovering his ancestors and his past. With or without magic, he would face the future differently.

Once everyone had their drink of choice, and Rhi had resumed her seat, Con looked at Melisse.

"I'm not sure where I should start," she said. "I saw nothing but the vines when I rushed in after the youngling. I heard nothing, saw nothing. I had no way of knowing the thorns were poisonous until much later."

Vaughn's brow furrowed as his Persian-blue eyes trained on Melisse. "Poison? Were you no' able to heal?"

"I could not. The poison only harms those with dragon blood, however."

Henry met her gaze and rested his hand on her thigh beneath the table. "Melisse was unconscious when I found her. She had a laceration on her upper right arm and several smaller ones on her left palm. From what I could tell, the poison caused lethargy."

"And considerable pain," Melisse added. "But it was the area itself that took my magic and prevented me from shifting."

Con crossed his arms over his chest. A muscle jumped in his jaw—the only thing showing his anger.

"That's why no dragon can contact others who venture into the brambles," Rhi said.

Henry nodded. "I thought it was the vines themselves, but it isn't. The Druid I felt lives in the valley among the brambles."

"It doesna matter what is affecting the dragons," Vaughn replied. "The vines are keeping the Druid safe. They must be removed."

Henry jerked his gaze to Vaughn. "No one is touching the vines."

Rhi nudged a glass of whisky to Henry and changed the subject. "You saw the Druid?"

"Saw and spoke to her." He downed Dreagan's finest and let it heat a trail to his stomach. He couldn't let the matter of the vines drop. They would discuss it again. "She had quite a story."

Melisse shrugged one shoulder. "It wasn't easy to get it out of her. She had a thing for Henry, though."

"She didn't," he interjected.

Melisse ignored him and continued. "She told him he could leave the valley unharmed so long as he left me."

"She didna care that you were only half-dragon?" Con asked.

Henry rested both arms on the table. "She was surprised and angered to learn that dragons could shift. She asked me how it was possible, but I never told her. Even when I explained that Melisse was half-Fae, the only thing that mattered to the Druid was the dragon blood Melisse carried."

"What's her name?" Rhi asked.

Melisse twisted her lips. "She refused to tell us."

"I've come across a few Druids on Earth with exceptional power," Henry said. "Eilish, Rhona, the MacLeod Druids. But they don't come close to this one."

Vaughn whistled softly. "We need to be careful, then. How do you know she's alone?"

"She had no idea what a Druid was," Henry explained. "She was baffled by my description, but also a little curious. There was a time I think I could've befriended her."

Rhi shifted in her chair. "Before you refused to leave Melisse."

He nodded. "Everything changed after that. One thing surprised me the most. She believes there are no more humans here."

Vaughn glanced around the table. "What would make her think that?"

"I think it's time we hear the story she shared with you two," Con said to Henry and Melisse.

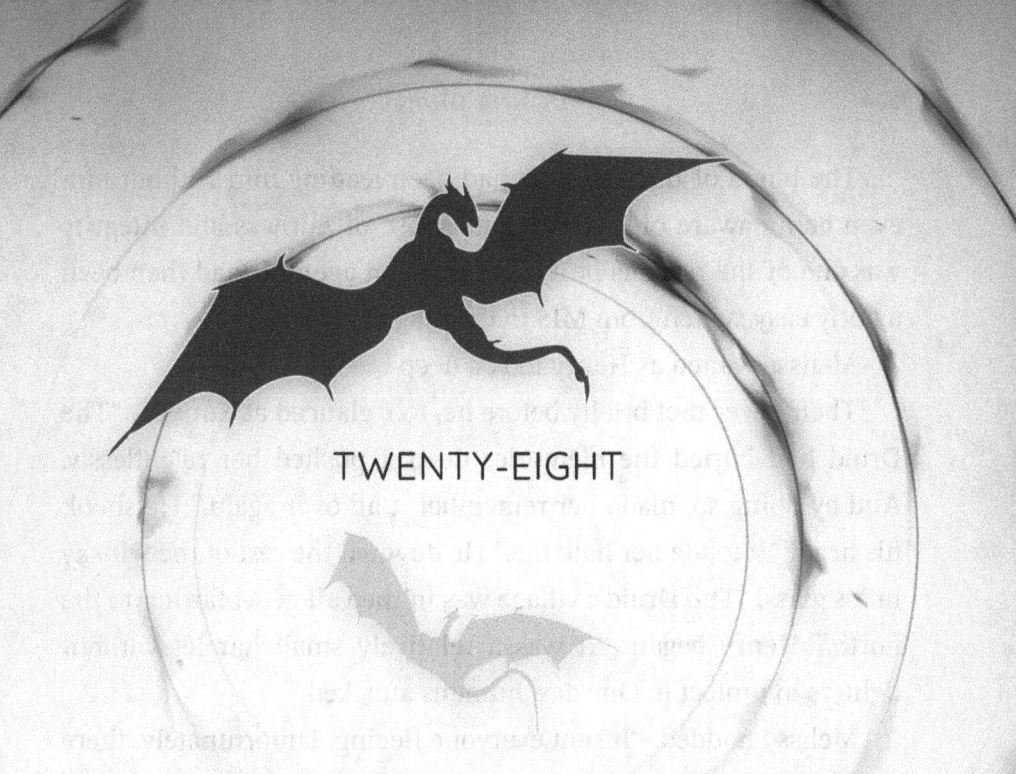

TWENTY-EIGHT

The tension around the table was impossible to ignore. It was palpable and growing more intense and tangible with each minute that passed.

And it would only get worse.

Melisse cut her eyes to Eurwen. The Dragon Queen sat stony like her father, with her hands clasped on the table. She hadn't uttered a single syllable yet. Melisse saw Eurwen's white knuckles as she gripped her fingers. Vaughn must have noticed, as well, because he covered Eurwen's hands with his and shot her a questioning look.

Everyone else's attention was on Henry. Melisse had done some digging on Henry and MI5. He'd had a great career with the agency, rising in the ranks rapidly. He was a man who rarely missed much. He had a knack for reading people and ensuring those who did wrong were swiftly brought to justice.

JusticeBringer.

The blood of his ancestors had been leading him without him even being aware of it. His innate sense of fairness and integrity was one of the reasons he'd excelled as an agent. It had then been a fairly easy switch from MI5 to the magical world.

Melisse waited as Henry took a deep breath.

Their gazes met briefly before he, too, glanced at Eurwen. "The Druid had buried the memories deep. I pushed her relentlessly. And by doing so, made her remember it all over again." He shook his head. "It made her hate me." He downed the rest of the whisky in his glass. "The Druid's village was in the valley, set farther to the north," Henry began. "It was a relatively small hamlet without fighters to protect it. One day, humans attacked."

Melisse nodded. "It sent everyone fleeing. Unfortunately, there weren't many places to go. The Druid, her family, and another small group fled toward the border. She hoped that by heading in that direction, the assailants wouldn't give chase."

"She was wrong," Henry said, picking up the story. "They were swarmed, and, doing what anyone would, they sought to live. So, they crossed the border. She had her nieces while her husband carried their daughter. She said they halted almost immediately across the border, but the invaders continued their assault, driving the villagers farther away from the boundary. Then, a dragon appeared."

Con closed his eyes and dipped his chin. Rhi swallowed loudly. Even Vaughn looked pained. Only Eurwen sat unfazed. Melisse remained quiet as Henry continued.

"It went after them. With the attackers coming at them on one front and the dragon on the other, there was no escape. Both of her nieces were killed by the humans. As the Druid told it, the dragon burned everyone, including her husband and daughter, along with the attackers that remained. Somehow, the Druid found herself the only one left alive."

Melisse linked her hand with Henry's on the table and said, "When she crossed over the border again, she discovered that her village had been decimated. No one was left. No one but her. That was the final straw for her, I think. She turned all that sadness and grief into rage. Toward dragons."

"She had to know what would happen if they crossed the boundary line," Vaughn said into the silence that followed. "All of them did. No human was supposed to cross. It's the law here."

Rhi shook her head. "They didn't have a choice. They were trying to save themselves. It was a no-win situation. The dragons can't be blamed for protecting their territory, and the humans can't be blamed for seeking safety."

"Dragon," Henry corrected as he glanced at Eurwen. "There was only one."

Con sat forward and rested his forearms on the table. "She told you what color dragon attacked."

It wasn't a question. Henry and Eurwen were staring at each other now. Melisse looked between them before answering. "She did. Peach with gold wings."

Con looked at his daughter. Gradually, Rhi and Vaughn did the same. Melisse was the last to turn her attention to the Dragon Queen.

"It isn't what you think," Eurwen said. She blew out a breath and looked between Henry and Melisse. "Neither of you have any right to judge me."

Melisse shrugged one shoulder. "We're not judging you. The

Druid is, and because of what happened, she's been trapping dragons since you took her family."

"We want to hear your side," Henry added.

Eurwen looked at each person at the table. "After what the humans did on Earth, do you really think I wouldn't defend the territory we had carved out for the dragons? Do you think Brandr and I wouldn't retaliate each time a mortal crossed the border, no matter the reason? Because if we allowed one, then others would follow. It's a slippery slope, and I refused to find myself on it."

"You and Brandr promised the dragons you would keep the humans away. You did what you had to do," Vaughn told her, shooting her a quick smile to let her know he supported her.

Melisse studied the wood grain on the table as she thought about the Druid and the animosity that consumed her. "Rhi's right. It was a no-win situation. The villagers took a chance, and it didn't go their way." Melisse met Eurwen's silver eyes. "It would've been kinder to take the Druid's life along with the others. To be left alone, to have watched her family be killed, to find her village destroyed along with everyone…it was too much for her. Dragons have suffered because you left her alive."

Eurwen rolled her eyes and slammed her hands on the table as she jerked to her feet. "Do you really think I could kill so easily?"

"No one is judging you," her mate stated.

Eurwen's laugh was hollow as she motioned to the table. "Every one of you is doing just that. You say you understand, but there is also condemnation in every gaze here. Especially yours," she said, nodding at Con.

"That's no' what you see," Con said. "It's regret and sadness that, even on a new realm with a border that is supposed to keep mortals out, you, Brandr, and the dragons have to deal with situations like these."

Something in Eurwen's voice caught Melisse's attention. She waited until Eurwen looked at her to ask, "Did you kill them?"

"No," Eurwen said with a shake of her head. "I used the fire to separate the villagers from the attackers. I saw all of it happening before they even reached the border. I had hoped the humans wouldn't cross it, but they did. Fortunately, I was the only one around to witness it." She slowly sank into her chair. "Once the invaders were dead, I took the mortals left alive and carried them to safety. They were screaming and terrified, and many were wounded, but I didn't hurt any of them."

Henry sat up straighter, impatience vibrating off him. "Took them where?"

"To the other side of the mountain. Close enough that they could get back to their village if they wanted, but far enough away that they wouldn't encounter the assailants again."

Melisse covered her mouth and nose with her hand as she gaped at Eurwen. She lowered her arm. "They're alive? If the Druid knows that, she'll stop attacking the dragons."

Confusion marred Eurwen's face. "I doubt they're still alive."

"The Druid's daughter might be," Henry said.

Con sat back again. "It would go a long way in mending the hurt the Druid has carried if we can return her daughter."

"That's impossible," Eurwen stated and shook her head. "This happened fifteen hundred years ago."

It was like a rug being yanked out from under Melisse. She could only stare in bewilderment.

"Druids, despite their magic, are mortal," Vaughn said. "How is this one still alive?"

Rhi nodded. "That's my question."

"Why did you leave the Druid?" Con asked his daughter.

Eurwen shrugged. "I never saw her."

Henry frowned. "Are you sure?"

"I searched for any mortal still alive. I wouldn't have left her."

Vaughn lifted his hands to stop any more questions. "Whoa. Hold up. Let's go back to how this Druid still lives."

"The MacLeod Druids have lived for hundreds of years," Rhi pointed out.

Vaughn's lips thinned. "Because of the magical barrier around the castle, and now because of the rings Con gave them, which allow them to leave the grounds and remain immortal."

"Could someone have given something like that to this Druid?" Rhi asked.

Con said, "Anything is possible. There are many with magic on Zora."

"There's also the Star People," Vaughn added.

Eurwen's lips twisted into an angry sneer. "Villette, you mean."

"The Star People have shown they like to interfere in the lives of others," Con said with a half-shrug. "It wouldna surprise me to know that one of them aided the Druid to become immortal. And to trap dragons."

Melisse shook her head. "We're forgetting the point. All this time, I was thinking the Druid had been luring and trapping dragons for twenty years max. But it's been much, much longer. How many dragons has she taken?"

"Are you sure she is only trapping them?" Rhi asked.

Henry briefly looked at Melisse. "I think it might be more than that. The poison was killing Melisse. If I hadn't attempted to heal her th—"

"You what?" the other four said in unison.

Melisse hadn't brought up Henry's magic because she wasn't sure he wanted the others to know. Based on the expressions on their faces that ranged from astonishment to disbelief to amazement to alarm, she was glad that she hadn't. The alarm came from Eurwen.

"You don't have magic," she stated.

Melisse took offense to her tone and raised a brow as she said, "Henry didn't. Not until he was inside the vine forest."

"Are you sure it isna the vines giving the Druid her power?" Con asked Henry. "Giving *you* power?"

Henry twisted his lips and shrugged. "The vines aided us, and then they shielded us from the Druid. But granted me magic? I don't think so."

"Shielded how?" Vaughn asked.

Melisse said, "They built a dome over us, locking together so tightly and deeply the Druid couldn't reach us."

"Nor could you get out," Rhi said.

"That's what I thought at first, but when we wanted to leave, they opened a doorway so we could escape."

Con held up his hand. "Wait. Let's go back to Henry having magic."

"My thoughts exactly," Eurwen muttered.

Con glanced at her but returned his attention to Henry. "Are you sure it was magic?"

"I saw it," Melisse said. "Mine was gone, but his wasn't."

Henry ran a hand over his jaw. "I found out by accident. The Druid attacked shortly after I found Melisse. I stepped between them and raised my hands on instinct."

Melisse grinned as she recalled that first encounter. "He not only blocked it, but whatever he did also sent her away for a time."

"I'd have liked to see that," Vaughn replied with a grin.

Henry pinched the bridge of his nose with his thumb and forefinger and squeezed his eyes closed for a heartbeat. "After the battle with the Druid, Melisse's leg was impaled on a thorn, and her wounds became infected. All of them. Nothing in the med kit worked. I was practically carrying her as we made our way through the vines. I couldn't keep Melisse awake, and getting around the brambles was difficult. An image kept popping into my head, and I had this insane urge to draw it. It was a compulsion, really. So, I did. I used my knife to cut into the dry ground, and halfway through, I knew what it was. A shield knot."

"Celtic protection," Con murmured.

"My hope was that it would keep the Druid out. I needed to rest, and so did Melisse. But Melisse was getting worse. While I was on Skye, I heard the Druids chanting a healing spell they'd learned from the MacLeod Druids." He paused. "The same impulse that made me draw the shield knot told me I had to remember the chant and do it right then."

Melisse threaded her fingers with his once more. Their gazes met, hers blurry from unshed tears. She owed him her life.

"I ran through that chant over and over in my head, mouthing the words and then saying them aloud. Some I knew were right, but others I knew weren't. Still, I kept going through that memory until each and every word was correct," Henry said.

Melisse swallowed past the huge knot of emotion in her throat. "He healed me."

"Not completely," he interjected as they stared at each other. "I must have gotten something wrong since the wounds were still there. The infection was gone, though."

Rhi reached across the table and touched Henry's arm. "The chant you're referring to is one done by several Druids. I've seen it. No single Druid who isn't a healer has ever had enough power to use it and have results."

"No' until Henry," Vaughn said, a grin on his face as he stared at Henry.

TWENTY-NINE

Hours later, after much talking and discussion, Con called it a day. Vaughn saw the relief on Henry's and Melisse's faces, and the two quickly attempted to get away. They didn't quite make it, though. Rhi trapped them at the door.

Con caught Vaughn's gaze as they stood. Vaughn nodded at Con, letting him know that he would keep an eye on Eurwen. She got quiet like her father when she listened and considered, but when she became withdrawn and closed, Vaughn knew something was troubling her.

Eurwen slid behind Melisse and Henry to exit the cottage. Vaughn followed but paused when someone touched his arm. He looked back to see Rhi staring after Eurwen, concern in her eyes.

"I know," he said and continued after his mate.

He wasn't surprised when Eurwen went to their cottage. They were the only two at Cairnkeep. The dragons accepted it because they were Brandr's and Eurwen's, but the idea of any other Kings, Queens, half-dragons, or humans living there had halted plans for any others. For now, those not patrolling stayed at Iron Hall, which was where Henry and Melisse would head when they got free of Rhi.

Eurwen left the door open. He entered their home and softly shut the door behind him, then leaned against it to wait. His mate stood in the middle of the cottage, letting her emotions show. The guilt and remorse clouding Eurwen's face gutted him.

"You couldna have known, love," he told her.

Her silver eyes speared him. "I should've looked harder. I could've made another pass. I could have returned."

"The Druid was back over the border by then. And we both know you wouldna have crossed it."

She shook her head and looked out the window.

Vaughn pushed away from the door and walked to her. He took her gently by the shoulders and waited for her to look at him. "What are you holding back?"

"I saw it all. I saw the invaders attack and slaughter the villagers. And I saw the group running to the border."

"Dragons stay on their land. Humans stay on theirs. No one judges you for not interfering."

"If I had stepped in earlier, I might have saved more."

Vaughn pulled her to his chest and wrapped his arms around her. "It never does any good to look at the past and question our decisions. It's too easy to condemn ourselves for making the wrong ones once we see the outcome of those choices. We doona have that option when we're confronted in the moment. We make the best decision we can and live with it."

"A Druid's life was destroyed. Her anguish twisted her heart into one of misery and retribution."

"That's on her. She's no' the only one who's lost everything.

Plenty of others have experienced that and doona allow it to turn them into something vengeful and evil."

Eurwen leaned her head back to look at him. "And how many dragons have succumbed because of my actions?"

"Did you send the invaders?"

Eurwen rolled her eyes. "Of course, not."

"Then that isna on you. The villagers scattered. Some toward the border. That was their decision. You helped them. The Druid saw none of that. She saw fire and heard screams."

"Making her believe I had killed her husband, daughter, and nieces."

Vaughn smoothed her golden blond hair from her face. "There's no saving this Druid. Her hate and resentment have warped her beyond redemption. Henry tried, and by pushing her to recall those memories, turned her against him."

"She relived it all again. Bloody hell. I can't imagine how I would react if I had to relive something so traumatic."

"What do you want to do? Talk to her? I doona think she will do much conversing."

Eurwen pulled out of his arms and sank onto the corner of their bed. "Brandr should be here."

"Call him back."

"I can't."

"You can," Vaughn insisted. "Do it, or I will."

Brandr looked at the setting sun as he stood atop a desert sand dune. He had traveled over a large portion of Zora, but there was still so much more to see. And he had a feeling he should return to

Cairnkeep soon. Eurwen kept him updated on what was going on there, and it seemed things got progressively worse every week. Yet things were different out here, far from dragon land and Stonehaven, where Villette lived. Quieter.

Calmer.

He had come across decent-sized villages, some doing better than others. There were larger towns where the villagers came to trade and barter. Then there were the cities. He wouldn't exactly call them metropolises, but there had been a couple of impressive ones, not just in their size but also in their architecture.

Brandr didn't spend time in every location he came across. He studied each one before deciding whether to venture inside or skirt around them. He always altered his clothing so he wouldn't stand out. Sometimes, he stayed in the market, milling about with the locals to listen to gossip.

Much could be discovered that way. But the best location to learn about a place was at an alehouse. It didn't matter if he sat with others or alone, it never took long for him to learn the history of a location.

Originally, he had set out to uncover who their nemesis was, never imagining that the Divine—as everyone called the leader— was more than he could've ever imagined. The Divine, who killed anyone with magic in Stonemore—including children—was actually named Villette.

Though none of them would have that information if it weren't for Lotti and Alasdair. But there was more. The Kings had discovered that Lotti and Villette were Star People. Learning who those powerful beings were and what they had done to dragons had sickened Brandr. He should've returned home then, but he kept traveling.

As he did, he had seen and learned many things. Some of it was expected, others not. He had hoped to locate Highvale. The city was supposed to be a mecca for those with magic since they were persecuted nearly everywhere else. Brandr had yet to find it, though.

It would be easier if he could fly. He could cover much more ground. Instead, he walked and teleported, thanks to his Fae blood. He wasn't able to jump across vast distances as other Fae did. He could only go as far as he could see, but that still allowed him to cover much territory.

The sky was absolutely stunning. He couldn't take his eyes off the spectacular display of colors. The clouds were a deep purple, the lavender sky fading to an inky blue between them. The bottom of the puffy clouds burned an arresting red the farthest from the setting sun while those closest were brilliant shades of orange. But the gorgeous yellow stretching across the horizon took his breath away.

Brandr remained rooted to that spot until the giant yellow ball sank below the horizon and took the last of the dramatic colors with it. He heard his sister's voice in his head and opened the mental link.

"Aye. I'm here," he said.

There was a pause. *"I think you need to come back."*

"What happened?" He knew she wouldn't ask that of him unless it was important.

"Do you remember when I saved those humans after they crossed the northern border ages ago?"

"The ones chased by invaders? Aye."

"I didn't get to all of them."

It was his turn to pause. *"How could you possibly know that? It's been, what? A millennium?"*

"Longer," she replied.

"Eurwen. Tell me. What is it?"

"It wasn't long after that incident that the giant brambles started appearing in the valley. We thought we'd warned the dragons away from that area after several went missing."

His brow furrowed as he searched his memories. *"Aye. We did warn them. Have others gone missing?"*

"The Pinks prefer that valley now since others don't venture to it, but the vines have grown over the border. They cover nearly the entire valley now."

Brandr fisted his hands in regret. *"The Pinks knew. All dragons did. We warned them about the dangers in that area."*

"A youngling disappeared into the vines while Melisse and Evander were patrolling the northern border. Melisse went in after the Pink to bring it home. Then Melisse went missing."

"What?!" Brandr bellowed.

Eurwen sighed, the sound filled with guilt and shame. *"It's a long story, brother."*

"Tell me every detail." He sat as she began the tale.

Brandr had no words by the time his sister finished. Henry, the vines, and a Druid. No. That wasn't right. Henry had said there were others on Zora. Brandr scrubbed a hand down his face.

"This Druid is killing dragons. How is that even possible?" he asked.

"Henry said she's the most powerful Druid he's ever come across."

"And he now has magic?"

"He did in the valley."

Brandr blew out a breath. *"This Druid needs to be dealt with once and for all."*

"It isn't as if we can go to her. Anyone with dragon blood who steps into those vines loses their magic."

"It returns, though. Right? Melisse has her magic again?"

Eurwen made an indistinct sound. *"She was able to shift, aye."*

"Fuck me. As if we didna have enough going on."

"I know. It keeps piling on, but we keep going."

Until something stopped them. Brandr knew it was inevitable, but he didn't give voice to those fears. He would stand firm with his sister and the other Kings to give the dragons hope. But that didn't mean he wasn't thinking and planning. *"I'm coming home. I shouldna have stayed gone for as long as I have."*

"You weren't out there on holiday. You were gathering information."

"I have quite a bit, too."

"I can't wait to hear it."

"See you soon."

The link severed. Brandr sat for a moment, taking the story in. He looked out over the rolling sand dunes—nothing but dark shapes against a darker sky. If there was a way for him to turn back time and change things, he would. There was no getting past his and Eurwen's arrogance in believing that things which happened outside their borders didn't concern them.

Maybe if they had taken an interest, they would've learned of Villette and the Star People before things turned so ugly. It was even possible that they could've stopped some of the hatred for dragons and anyone with magic. But that revulsion was so deeply rooted across Zora that he had begun to suspect there was no way to end it.

Did that mean dragons would go up against the humans? Just as his father and the other Kings had done on Earth? He and Eurwen had ripped the Dragon Kings to shreds countless times for sending the dragons away and handing the realm over to the mortals.

The irony now was that they might be faced with the same dilemma: fight and wipe out a race or give in and find the dragons a new home.

The difference this time was that they knew why things were happening on Zora. Villette was furious that her brother had freed the dragons from their enslavement and incited the humans on Earth as well as those on Zora. It didn't matter where the dragons went, Villette would be there stirring up hatred and bias.

It had to stop.

She needed to be stopped.

There was no more running for the dragons. This was their home, and they would fight for it.

Even if they lost.

THIRTY

Henry couldn't remember the last time he had been so damn tired. Until he arrived at Iron Hall with Melisse. He had expected Rhi to jump them to the underground city, but it had been Lotti since she was still learning her teleporting ability. She took Melisse first and then returned for Henry.

By the time he and Lotti arrived, it was already dusk. It prevented him from seeing the splendor of Raynia Canyon and appreciating all its glory, but he could see enough of the verdant walls to recognize its splendor.

"This way," Lotti called as she started toward the end of the narrowing canyon.

He wanted to stay and look around, but that would have to wait for the light of day. Henry hurried to catch up.

"I think the canyon is quite impressive. I prefer to arrive here and make my way inside." She paused and grinned at him. "Besides, I like seeing people's reaction the first time they enter Iron Hall."

Henry couldn't wait. They walked toward an ancient tree with exposed roots that protruded from a crack running down the canyon wall. Just behind the roots were the arched double doors to Iron Hall.

"Cullen told us the roots once knocked the door off its hinges and crumbled them to ruins," Lotti said as she opened a door and stepped through.

Since it was already darkening outside and there were lamps scattered around, it didn't take his eyes long to adjust. He halted at the entrance and took in the grandeur around him. The area was huge, but what first grabbed Henry's attention was the smooth and perfectly cut rectangular stones that glowed from within.

Steps carved from the mountain led him toward an enormous room, light filtering in from several hundred feet above. Henry had heard about the tree hanging by its roots on the cliff above. The complex root system reminded him of the vine forest. Water dripped from the roots into a large pool at the center of the chamber.

Henry turned in a circle to take in the entire room. There were numerous stairways and doors, reminding him that Iron Hall was a massive city with more sections being uncovered every day. Henry caught sight of one of the four giant heads carved out of the rock. The faces were neither male nor female. The artwork was phenomenal and incredibly intricate.

Lotti came up beside him. "This is north. It and its south counterpart have their eyes open. East and west have smiles, but their eyes are shut."

"There is something similar in a city on Earth called Cambodia."

"Alasdair said the same. You've been to Cambodia?"

Henry shook his head. "I've only seen pictures."

"If you like this, then you'll have fun exploring here," Lotti said.

"I'm not sure I'll be here that long."

"Oh, I think that has changed."

His head turned to her. "What do you mean?"

"You sensed the Druid when none of us could. You were the only one able to go in after Melisse. You spoke to the Druid and got information. You still have a part to play here, and you know it."

"The dragons aren't happy, though."

Her lips twisted. "There's no denying that. And I don't see that changing anytime soon. We're trying to help, and they're ignoring the Kings' overtures of reaching out. They hurt Alasdair particularly."

"Have Eurwen and Brandr not spoken to them?"

"I think it's better if I stay out of that discussion. Come," she said and headed for a set of stairs. "Melisse has already been shown her room. I'll take you to yours."

Separate rooms. What else did he expect? It wasn't as if they were lovers. Though he hoped that changed.

Lotti shot him a grin. "Don't worry. You two have been put near each other."

"Do you read minds?"

"Maybe," she teased, laughing.

He smiled, liking her immensely. They turned down a corridor. "You've experienced a lot of changes yourself recently. How are you handling all of it—if you don't mind me asking?"

"Not at all. I think I'd still be in the dark about my origins if not for Alasdair." She shrugged, her blond waves brushing her shoulders. "I take things day by day."

"That's really all anyone can do."

"I'll be ready when the time comes," she stated, meeting his gaze.

Henry bowed his head. "I have no doubt."

"What of you? I'd say you've had your life shaken more than once these last few years."

"You could say that. I don't think I've handled some things all that well."

She leaned closer and whispered, "Don't tell anyone, but neither have I."

Henry made an X over his heart with a finger. "Your secret is safe with me."

"And your magic? Do you still have it?"

"I don't think so."

"No matter. Remember who you are. Because it isn't the magic that makes the man. It's the man who makes the magic." Lotti halted next to a door. "You have many skills that go beyond any type of magical abilities."

He glanced at the floor. "Thank you. The same could be said for you."

"I'm a Star Person. Everything will come down to my power."

"Not just your magic. Your friends. We stand united."

Her lips split into a grin. "Alasdair speaks very highly of you. I see why. The Kings consider you a true friend. That isn't an easy feat."

"They're as much my family as my sister is. I would do anything for them."

"You've proven that already." Lotti motioned to the door. "This is your chamber." She then pointed back down the hallway the way they had come. "Melisse's is the third from here. No one will disturb either of you. If you need anything, follow this corridor back to the stairs and you'll run into one of us. Have a good night," she replied with a wink and turned on her heel.

Henry put his hand on the door handle to his room but paused, his gaze moving to Melisse's. He strode over and knocked, but no one answered. He tried again, rapping harder in case she didn't hear. Yet the door remained closed.

He had to consider that she might not be in her room yet. Or maybe she didn't want to see him. She had endured a lot and hadn't had much time alone since they'd arrived in Cairnkeep. He pivoted and made his way back to his room. When he opened the door, his gaze landed on Melisse sitting in one of the chairs.

She closed the book in her hand and set it aside as she sat forward with a smile. "Have fun exploring?"

"I barely got an eyeful," he said, closing the door. His blood heated at the sight of her, rushing through his veins like fire.

She rose in a fluid motion. "If you'd rather be alone, I can leave."

"Don't you dare."

Her lips softened. "I suppose that means you want me to stay."

"Want," he said as he walked to her. "Crave. Ache. Hunger. Take your pick."

"Hmm. Mine would be yearning."

He ran a finger from her arm down to her wrist. "I've been waiting for this moment for a long time."

"Too long," she whispered, her eyes darkening with desire.

His cock thickened. The need to crush his lips to hers was overwhelming. But he hesitated. "It's been a while for me, and I'm not entirely sure I can control myself. I need you too much. I'll be careful though."

She grinned and rose onto her tiptoes, her mouth near his as she whispered, "Don't you dare."

He set his hands on her waist and dragged her the last few inches to him until their bodies were pressed together. "I've dreamed of this moment for so long."

Her answer was to pull his head down to hers. Their lips met, and the walls of his control snapped. He lifted her and spun her to the wall as they shared a passionate, intense kiss. His hand reached for the wall, softening the impact of his pushing her back against it.

The flames of desire licked over them. His hands gripped her bottom, and her legs wrapped around his waist. It brought his arousal into contact with the junction of her thighs. Henry rocked against her, the urgency to sink into her wet heat almost too much to bear. She moaned at the movement and kissed him harder.

"I need you," she said between kisses. "Now."

He didn't have to be told twice. He turned to carry her to the bed when she tore her lips from his.

"Now. I need you inside me right this instant," she stated.

He released her so she could yank her pants off one leg as he unfastened his jeans and pushed them down so his aching rod sprang free. Then he had her legs around him once more. Their eyes were locked together as he guided his cock to her entrance.

A moan fell from her lips when he brushed against her sex. She was so wet it made his balls tighten. He pushed inside and withdrew before thrusting deep. She cried out, her nails digging into his back through his jumper.

He pumped his hips, sliding in and out of her wetness until

they were both panting. He felt his orgasm building rapidly. Each time he thrust into her tight, wet heat, he fought not to give in. Until the hitch in her breathing alerted him that she was close.

"Henry," she whispered, right before her body clamped around his cock.

He was lost then to the sheer power of the orgasm. Time was forgotten. It was only the two of them and the passion between them.

Henry had no idea how much time passed until he came back to himself. Her fingers were moving through his hair, and his face rested in the crook of her neck. He lifted his head and pulled out of her to see her face flushed and eyes closed.

"That was...I don't have words for how special it was," she murmured.

He had the words, but he wasn't sure now was the right time to say them. So, he kept his feelings to himself. "Maybe we should get some food to restore you. Because the night is just getting started."

Her lids lifted as she looked at him with a smile. "My thoughts exactly."

Henry turned to take them to the bed, but he couldn't walk normally with his pants pulled low. He ended up tripping, and they fell to the rug in a tangle of limbs and laughter. He rolled her onto her back and gave her a slow, deep kiss that had her arching against him. His cock was already hardening for her again, but he would take his time for their second go-round.

He moved away and yanked off his jumper, then removed his boots and pants until he stood naked before her. The need he saw in her eyes made his breath catch. She rose to her knees, set her hands on his legs, and slowly caressed upward toward his straining cock.

THIRTY-ONE

He was beautiful. Magnificent. Utterly flawless. Melisse had often fantasized about what Henry would look like nude, how he would feel as she ran her hands over him.

And now, here they were.

Finally.

She had been waiting and hoping for so long it almost didn't seem real. He had been inside her, his thick, hard length filling her, stretching her. But it wasn't enough. She would never get enough of him.

Her palms met a dusting of hair that shadowed his firm calves. She glided her hands higher to his corded thighs. Unable to help herself, she slid her palms around to the backs of his legs and found his tight bum.

She removed her pants and underwear and rose onto her knees, her face close to his arousal. It jumped, straining at her nearness. Her sex clenched in response. Her palms lightly stroked his hips and moved closer to his rod. She wound her fingers around him and heard his quick intake of breath. Her gaze lifted to his face.

His jaw was clenched, his eyes shut as his chest rose and fell rapidly. This man...this gorgeous, strong, loyal man, meant everything to her. She didn't think she could hide how she felt anymore. Was tonight the right time to tell him? Did she wait to say she loved him?

He cared about her. That much was obvious, but it might be too soon for him to have love in his heart. And she didn't want to do anything to drive him away. She had already done that and would rather not make that mistake again.

She caressed up the length of his shaft and circled the head of his cock with her finger. He moaned and tangled his hand in her hair. Her body shivered at his response. To know that she could wring such pleasure from him left her breathless and eager to give him more. So very much more.

Her hand moved slowly up and down his arousal. She marveled at the soft skin that encased steel. She could spend hours just on this one part of him, and she would. Later. For now, she needed to know how the rest of his gorgeous body felt.

She smoothed her palms down him one last time before flattening her hands near his hip bones. Her fingers dipped into the indents of sinew accentuated there. Henry's body was honed to perfection, each muscle expertly sharpened and refined.

Her exploration continued up his trim waist to the ridges and valleys of his chiseled abdomen. Then higher to his thick chest as she climbed to her feet. Slowly, she caressed his chest and the dusting of hair there. Her gaze followed her hands to his wide shoulders, thick with sinew, and then down his muscular arms.

Melisse looked into his face to find his hazel eyes locked on her. Her stomach quivered with excitement when she saw the desire reflected there. "I've hungered to see you just like this, to touch you."

"All you had to do was say as much."

His voice came out as a hoarse whisper that made her breath catch. She licked her lips, drawing his gaze to her mouth.

"I've dreamed of you," he continued. "So many nights I dreamed of this moment, but nothing could've prepared me for you."

His hand moved to the back of her neck as he splayed the other at the base of her spine. He removed her shirt and bra with nimble fingers. His lips touched hers softly, before he took her mouth in a deep, toe-curling kiss. Then, he trailed kisses down her neck and along her collarbone.

Henry was so overcome with emotion he shook. Melisse stood before him in all her stunning glory, open and willing, with need in her touch, and longing in her silvery white eyes. He didn't have to worry about waking to find his arms empty because this wasn't a dream.

He breathed in her scent of rain, oak moss, and wind. Her skin was soft, her sexy curves enough to make his knees weak. There was no evil after them, no impending war hovering. Time halted and cocooned them in their own bubble, tucked away from everyone and everything. Just the two of them—and their desire that wouldn't be denied.

He skimmed his palm down to cup her arse and pulled her against him, pressing his cock into her soft belly. Her moan shot straight to his groin. He rocked against her, and she whispered his name. Did she have any idea how she drove him mad with longing?

Gradually, he walked her back to the bed. The moment they reached it, he carefully laid her atop the mattress. Their eyes met as he put a knee on the covers. She held out her hands to him, and he was powerless to resist her. She called to his soul, to his very psyche.

Henry lay beside her, braced on his forearm, letting his gaze roam down her exquisite body. The quick taste he'd had of her had only whetted his appetite. And he knew that he would never get enough. Every kiss, every lick, every touch only made him crave her more. Eternity wouldn't be enough for him.

The sight of the red and black ink on her left leg drew his gaze. He traced a finger along the dragon tattoo that wound up her leg from the edge of its tail at her ankle to its head resting on her hip. Its wings were tucked against its body, and its gaze seemed to be looking directly at Melisse. His hand stilled when he thought the tattoo moved. His gaze jerked to Melisse's face to find her watching him.

Henry continued to trace the tattoo up the swell of her hip, to the indent of her waist, and then upward along her arm. He moved over her shoulder and neck. Then down the middle of her chest. Her lips parted when he circled a breast again and again, growing closer and closer to her straining nipple. Her breathing quickened. Then he flicked his finger over the taut tip. She sucked in a breath, which quickly turned into a groan when he cupped her breast and began thumbing the peak.

Her back arched, and her fingers dug into the covers. He bent, took the nipple into his mouth, and suckled.

Melisse was on fire. She clutched his head, unsure if she wanted to keep him there for more of the delicious torture or push him away because it was too much. In the end, it wasn't up to her. He released one nipple and moved to the other, repeating the tantalizing torment.

Her hips sought contact to help curb the need thundering through her. She turned toward him, but he grasped her hip and returned her to her back. A cry of pleasure fell from her lips as he suckled her nipple before circling the nub with his tongue.

Her sex clenched greedily. And there was only one man who could give her what she craved.

It was all Henry could do not to thrust into her. The desire seared him, the ache to join their bodies once more relentless and incessant. Her moans were driving him wild. And every time her hips sought contact, it tested his control.

He didn't know how long he could last. How could he have already had her, yet still feel like he would die without being inside her once more?

His hand caressed down her side into the indent of her waist and then moved over the curve of her hip. He trailed his lips down the center of her chest to her stomach. Her fingers were in his hair, half-pulling him back to her and half-shoving him lower. He knew what she sought. And he intended to give it to her.

Her nipples strained for his mouth, the air chilling the damp peaks, sending a shiver through her. His mouth and tongue left a hot trail as he slowly worked his way to her aching sex. Everywhere his hands touched, she burned for more.

She rocked her hips and moaned as she made contact with his chest. The pleasure that rolled through her was only a tease of what she knew was coming, what he had already wrung from her.

When his warm breath fanned over the junction of her thighs, she stilled, eagerly waiting for him. Would it be his mouth or his fingers that found her?

"Please," she begged when the moment stretched endlessly.

Henry fought against his need when he saw Melisse's wet, swollen folds. His cock demanded to be encased in her tight body again. She was ready for him. She was as fervent as he.

Before he gave in, he lowered his head and softly ran his tongue along her vulva. She moaned his name in response. Then he settled between her legs and found her swollen clit with his tongue.

Desire pooled low in her belly and tightened. Each flick of his tongue brought her closer to release. He expertly drew her to the edge and held her there. It was too much. Yet she never wanted it to stop.

She no longer had control of her body. Henry worked it now, taking her where he wanted her to go. And she willingly followed.

The pressure in her body built to a new level. She sought the orgasm that was just out of reach, aching to fall into that place where she drifted upon waves of pleasure. Before she could, she was taken to another new high.

Suddenly, he lifted his head. She whimpered, not ready for the bliss to end just yet. That sound quickly turned into a moan as he slid a finger inside her. A second soon joined the first. Then, he found that special place and began rubbing against it.

She gasped as the pleasure surged, hot and thick, through her body. It swelled, and the desire tightened in her belly. Then his tongue swirled around her clit again. That was all it took to send her careening into the climax.

Her breath caught in her lungs, a cry in her throat. Ripples of ecstasy rolled over her, each one sweeping her higher, farther. Deeper.

The feeling of Melisse's body clenching around his finger broke through his control. He rose over her and saw the look of pleasure on her face, the flush of rapture that would forever be ingrained in his mind.

Henry was inside her in one hard thrust. She gasped and blindly reached for him. Her body was still contracting from her orgasm as he began pumping into her. He grabbed her hips and shifted her so he could sink deeper.

Her eyes opened, and their gazes met. He pumped his hips faster until their bodies slapped together. She wound her legs around his waist and held on as he drove into her harder and deeper.

The way he slid inside her was amazing. He filled her completely. Each thrust was exactly what she needed. Hard or soft, fast or slow. She needed all of it.

She needed all of *him*.

Shock ran through her as another climax quickly built on the heels of the first. Henry quickened his tempo. She cried out as she flew back into the abyss of pleasure. She could feel him moving within her, drawing out the ecstasy until she was mindless with it. Until he buried himself deep with a shout.

She came back to herself with him slumped atop her as small aftershocks continued to run through her, causing her to tighten around his cock. Eventually, he lifted his head and grinned at her. She smiled back, feeling more content than she thought possible. Henry pulled out of her and rolled to his side. She shifted to face him and took his hand because she had to touch him.

"Woman, you may be the death of me, but it's going to be such a sweet death."

Melisse smoothed a lock of his hair away from his brow. "I have no words for what I experienced."

"I do," he said in a soft voice. "Perfectly wonderful."

She couldn't stop smiling. "It was incredible."

"Will you stay with me tonight?"

"Yes."

"And the night after? And the one after that?"

They shared a laugh. Her heart was full to bursting. Was this what her parents experienced? How she wished she could ask them. "I'll stay for however long you want me."

"Forever, then. Are you tired?" he asked, brushing the pad of his thumb over her lips.

She shook her head. "I'm relaxed and satisfied, but I don't think I can sleep now."

"What shall we do?" he asked, his eyes twinkling.

"How about a soak in the tub?"

His brows snapped together in surprise. "There's a tub?"

"Did you not look around?"

"I saw you. That's all I cared about."

And if it were possible, she fell even more in love with him.

THIRTY-TWO

Brandr hadn't realized how much he'd missed Cairnkeep until he stood on the mountain as dusk neared and looked around at his home. He had called to his mum, and Rhi had teleported to him instantly. It was hard to miss how excited she was that he'd turned to her. He hadn't wanted to take days to return to Eurwen when Rhi could get him there in seconds.

His mum had hugged him. It was still a bit awkward between them, but she was trying, and so would he. Con didn't embrace him, though Brandr could tell he wanted to. The King of Kings simply nodded, a smile on his lips.

"It's good that you're back," Con said.

Brandr looked around his cottage, expecting to see his twin. "Where's Eurwen?"

"With Vaughn, I believe," Rhi answered.

Brandr walked from the structure in search of his sister. Con and Rhi didn't follow, which he was thankful for. They must have realized that he and Eurwen needed some time to talk privately. Brandr went to her cottage as his first stop, but no one was there.

He then walked to the edge of the cliff and jumped, shifting as he did. He spread his wings and soared higher. It felt good to be in dragon form again. Brandr flew to Eurwen's favorite areas, but there was no sign of her.

He was about to call to her when he realized exactly where she would be. He turned north and flew quickly, covering miles in a heartbeat. He searched for her in the skies, even looked for Vaughn, but Brandr saw only Evander's brass scales. Brandr lowered his gaze to scan the mountains. There had been a time when he and Eurwen hadn't bothered to patrol the borders. The magic they used alerted them to anyone crossing, as well as their location. Usually, it was nothing more than animals. They'd had to tweak the magic to allow animals to pass through without notifying them. It hadn't been an easy fix, and in truth, they had never gotten it quite right.

But they hadn't needed to worry about plants or trees. Perhaps they should have. They should've been concerned about everything. If they had, they could have halted the vines from crossing. Even thinking that seemed preposterous.

Brandr caught sight of the valley from a distance. The last time he had laid eyes on the brambles, they'd looked harmless enough.

If only he had known...

As he flew closer, it became increasingly clear that they were more than just a little past the border. But how did they force a plant—or vine, in this instance—to keep to one side of a boundary line? That would be like telling the wind it could only blow in one direction. It was impossible.

Brandr spotted Eurwen standing before the vines, wearing a

long, dark gray skirt that tangled around her legs. He dove and sailed over her before soaring over the brambles. As he reached the border, he turned onto his side so his belly scraped against the invisible shield. He made a few passes over the brambles at different heights to get a better picture of the valley, then returned to his twin.

He landed and shifted, clothing himself at the same instant. Eurwen didn't even look his way. The air was frigid, and the clouds above them promised snow. The mountains were already dusted with it. Brandr closed the distance between them as he studied his sister.

"Don't look at me like that," she said when he reached her.

"Like what?"

"Worried."

He gently turned her to face him. "I am worried. I've felt your unease for some time now. I never wanted you to hold anything back."

"I didn't. I was always honest," she stated, her chin rising in defiance.

"I didna say you lied, but you repeatedly told me I didna need to return."

She shrugged and moved some hair out of her face. "You didn't. You had a good plan, and things were as good as they could be here."

"I should've come back. I knew it, and I didna follow my gut. I should've been here to help."

"To do what?"

He dragged her to him when she tried to pull away. After a moment, she sagged against him and wound her arms around him. "Nothing that happened that day was your fault. Doona carry that."

"It's too late for that," she murmured.

"Why are you here?" he demanded, for the first time wondering why she was alone. "You're no' thinking of going in there, are you?"

Eurwen stepped away and wiped at her eyes. "I need to talk to the Druid. She blames me. I want to explain."

"You're the last one who should face her. We've no idea what she could do to you. You would be defenseless."

"Just like she was that day. It seems only fair. Besides, she has a right to know what happened to her family."

Brandr shook her head. "No' from you. Where is Vaughn? Why is he no' here?"

"We had a fight."

"About?"

She motioned to the vines.

Brandr used the mental link to quickly alert Vaughn to Eurwen's intentions. Then Brandr's focus returned to his sister. "Let's return to Cairnkeep. There's nothing more to do here."

"I can't stop thinking about the Druid. She lost everyone."

"It happens every day."

Eurwen's head snapped to him, her silver eyes blazing with anger. "One day, you're going to find your mate. The person the world stands still for. The one you will do *anything* for. Even die. Try to imagine that."

"I have." It wasn't a lie. He'd been attempting to do that since Eurwen and Vaughn fell in love. He watched the couples both on Zora and Earth. And while he believed in love, he couldn't fathom its reach. He had a bond with Eurwen. Twins felt what the other did. Knew what they knew.

And yet, he hadn't been aware of her and Vaughn.

It had gutted him as few things had. He didn't know if Eurwen had intentionally kept it from him, or if their bond wasn't as strong as it'd once been.

Brandr glanced at the hulking vines. "I know our bond. I can imagine it."

"It is similar, but when you find your mate, you find...everything. Serenity, happiness, pleasure, and a million other emotions. Vaughn and I are two pieces of a puzzle that fit. Some people equate it to feeling whole. I never thought I was missing a part of myself, and I still don't. He just makes everything better. Brighter." She put her hand to her heart. "He is my everything." She then looked at the brambles. "Even if the Druid felt a tenth of the love I have for Vaughn for her husband, her world was obliterated. Add in her daughter and nieces, and...she was shattered."

"You can no' turn back time and return her family to her."

Eurwen faced the vine forest. "I owe her an apology."

"She's taken hundreds if no' thousands of dragons. She's the one who needs to apologize."

There was a beat of silence before his twin turned silver eyes on him. "I remember a time when you advised peace and forgiveness. When you urged me to forgive and show mercy."

He swallowed and looked away. "Those days are long gone."

"I caused you to harden your heart against others. I was your opposite in every way. You wanted leniency. I was ruthless and unforgiving. And angry. So very angry at what had happened to the dragons on Earth that I took it out on everyone and everything." She sighed. "I railed at Con and the Kings for countless years for not doing the right thing. I loathed the mere thought of them. And Rhi. It didn't matter that Erith explained a million times that our parents didn't know about us, I still hated them. But not you. You, my sweet brother, only had love in your heart."

Brandr forced his hands to unclench. He wasn't that person anymore, and he didn't like to talk about it. "I didna come to speak about the past."

"But that's exactly what we're facing now. The past," she insisted. "I remember how sure we were that we would be better than the Kings. That we wouldn't make the same mistakes. And we didn't. We made new ones."

"We did the best we could."

"And so did they. Don't," she barked when he opened his mouth to argue. "We know now that they did nothing to bring the mortals to Earth. Or Zora. That was all the Star People, specifically Villette."

Brandr looked into his sister's eyes. "That's right. We know the truth now."

"Forgive the Kings. Forgive our parents."

"I have."

She gave him a quelling look. "You know better than to try to lie to me."

"What do you want from me?"

"I want the kind, compassionate brother you once were before I changed you."

He scratched his forehead. "You sure think highly of yourself. You no more changed me than I changed you."

"On the contrary. Do you remember that huge fight we had? The one where you told me I needed to learn to forgive those who were innocent in hurting the dragons?"

She stared until he grudgingly nodded. How could he forget that quarrel? It had been one of the worst they'd ever had. "Aye. I remember."

"It was after that I came here." She pointed to a nearby peak. "Right there, actually. That's why I was here when the village was attacked. I heard your voice in my head, pleading for me to be understanding and offer clemency. I knew you thought I could never be redeemed, and I was beginning to think I wouldn't be either. So, that day, I did what you had been imploring for years. It felt good to save those people."

"No' everyone deserves mercy."

"You once believed differently."

He raised his brows and glared at her. "You think Villette deserves forgiveness? What about how she trapped Merrill? I doona think he could leave Stonemore if he tried. What about her bringing Alasdair's brother back to life and using him against Alasdair? How about Villette's vitriol against anyone with magic? Let's discuss her priests at Stonemore who have executed *children* simply because they were born different. Her list of crimes is endless."

"Agreed. It is. And she will be brought to justice."

"Justice," Brandr said in a low, dangerous voice. "No' leniency."

Eurwen's lips tightened in anger. "Forget Villette. I want to talk about the Druid."

"That place is a trap for dragons. It's a fucking miracle Melisse got out, and only because Henry managed to talk Con into letting him remain on Zora. That Druid is so full of hate and vengeance that it has kept her going for a millennium and a half!"

Brandr was yelling by the time he finished, but he didn't care.

To him, there was no way the Druid deserved anything less than death for what she had done. Plenty of others had their families ripped from them and didn't kill in retaliation.

"What happened to make you so...cold?" Eurwen asked softly.

Brandr blew out a breath. "Life."

"That's an excuse, not a reason. We've led the same life."

"You had it right all along." He shrugged. "Is that what you want me to admit? Fine, I admit it. You were right from the beginning. You made me see that. We never should've shown even an ounce of mercy. Look what it has gotten us. We're on the brink of war."

Eurwen took his hand. "I know you have a good heart. In truth, you're the better of us. You always have been."

He shook his head, but she continued talking.

"I was the one who was wrong. I should've admitted it after saving those here." She looked at the vines and sniffed as tears rolled down her face. "But I didn't. I kept it to myself. I didn't want to give you a reason to say '*I told you so.*' Maybe if I'd spoken about what I had done and how good it felt, things would be different."

"Or maybe we're two sides of the same coin. Black and white. Yin and Yang. Merciful and merciless. Forgiving and heartless."

She faced him as more tears rolled down her cheeks. "I know you. We shared a womb, remember? We may differ on some things, but I know your heart. You're a good person."

Brandr pulled her to him for another hug. He turned his head to the side and looked at the brambles. His gaze met those of another just inside the forest. At least, he thought so.

But when he blinked, no one was there.

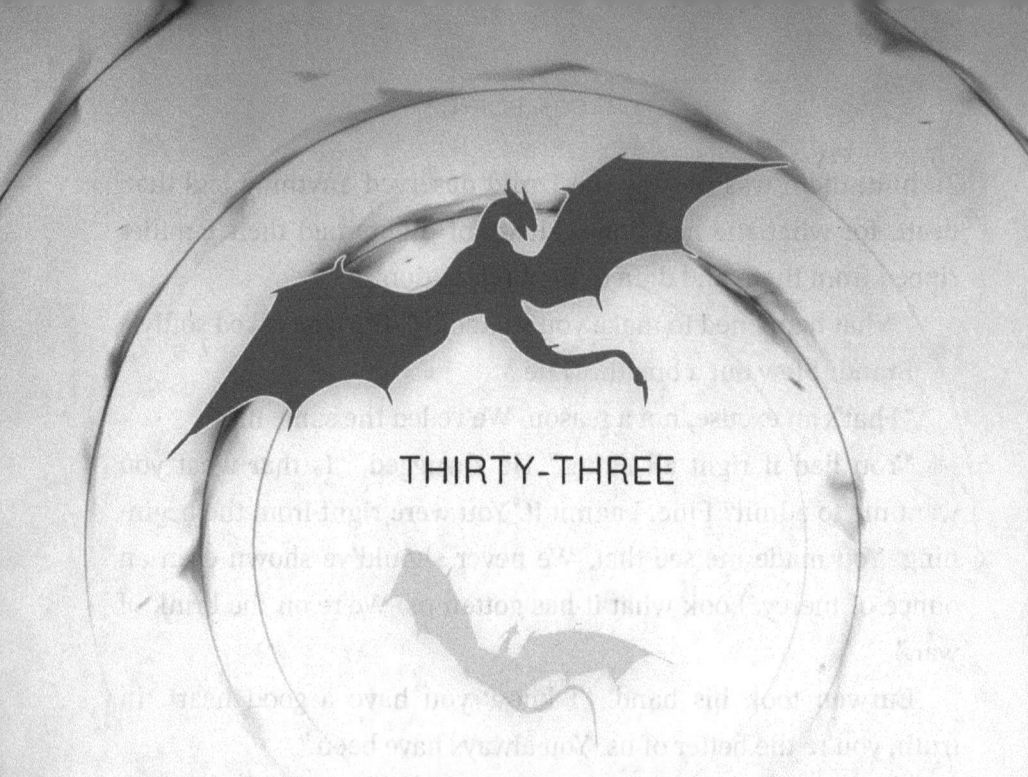

THIRTY-THREE

Henry reclined in the tub with Melisse resting against his chest. He was unsure what kind of metal it was crafted from, but it was an incredible heat conductor, much like copper, yet it was a stunning teal color. Heat spiraled from the water while he spread his arms along the rim. He and Melisse had spent a very soapy and seductive time washing each other thoroughly, before refilling the tub to relax as they were now.

For the first time, he took a good look around his room. It was huge. Bigger than many of his flats in London. The walls and floor were the same stone as could be found throughout the city, but someone had added a rug with a distinct antique-inspired motif that made him think of the ocean with its symphony of navy, teal, gray, and shots of copper.

There was a lot of empty space in the chamber that could be used for anything. He thought the area across from the bed in the corner would be great as a reading nook. It already held two chairs, but he would've put wider, comfier ones to sink into. The wall near the door would be a good place for a desk. Not that he would ever know. His time on Zora was limited. He knew that.

Accepted it.

His gaze briefly landed on the large bed with its deep blue comforter and pale gray sheets. He wondered how many of the rooms in Iron Hall had a touch of color added to them. He imagined quite a few. No one knew the exact size of Iron Hall yet since it was still being explored and the ruins repaired. He had a feeling there was much, much more to the underground city than any of them could conceive. Henry wouldn't mind exploring a bit himself if given the chance.

Melisse's head rolled to the side as she moved her feet, causing water to slosh softly. He watched her unusual, black-tipped-silver hair floating atop the water. He lifted a long strand.

"I don't know," she said.

He grinned. "Don't know what?"

"You're going to ask why my hair is silver and black. I don't know." She craned her head back to give him a quick smile, then looked forward once again.

Henry chuckled. "I *was* going to ask that. I'm guessing you got it from your mother?"

"She was a Dark Fae. As you know, all Fae are born with black hair and silver eyes, but once they turn Dark, their eyes become red—which hers were—and there is silver in their hair."

"I'm gathering she had that."

"She did."

"What coloring did your father have?"

She hesitated. "I can't remember."

"I shouldn't have asked." He inwardly kicked himself as he released her hair. "It was thoughtless of me."

"It's just that I used to remember every detail about them. There are still things I know with certainty. Like Mum's coloring or Dad's dragon color. But there are other memories that have faded. Like their faces." She paused. "Their voices."

He wrapped his arms around her. "I don't know the faces of my biological parents. I wish I did. I have lots of pictures of my adoptive parents, though."

"I wish I could have that."

"Have you spoken to any of the Kings? I know Tristan can get into someone's mind. That's how he helped Esther break free of the magic used on her. Perhaps he can find those memories for you."

Melisse languidly ran her fingers up and down his arm. "What would I do then? I can't paint or draw."

"But Nikolai can. Once he sees something, he can draw it."

"Nikolai won't be able to see into my memories, though."

Henry rested his cheek against her head. "Dreagan is the source of the magic on Earth. We're all surrounded by it on both realms. We can find someone to get it from your memories for Nikolai."

"That's asking a lot just to have pictures of my parents."

"I've learned that, in our family, someone is always willing to help."

She swallowed. "What if it doesn't work?"

"We won't know until we try."

"I don't know."

But he did. And Henry would make it happen. Melisse deserved to remember her parents. Besides, he knew everyone else was curious about them, as well. "Think on it," he told her.

"Blond," she suddenly said. "I think my father's hair was

blond. And his eyes were green. Yes! They were green. Not a deep green, but pale, like the first spring bulbs." She sighed softly. "He had the best laugh."

Henry smiled at her words. He was glad that she was recalling details of the past. Some would cause her pain, but others would make her happy. Those were the ones she would be able to cling to and recall when she needed them.

"I wonder what life would've been like had I not killed Osric."

"That was an accident," he reminded her.

Melisse lifted her hand to wipe her face, droplets of water sluicing back into the tub. "It doesn't change what happened."

"If he loved you as you said he did, he would hold no ill will toward you."

"You can't know that."

He kissed her temple. "I do. As for what life might have been like, I think it was only an eventuality for when the dragons learned about you and your mother. I suspect your parents knew that. Osric, too."

"What do you mean?"

"Even if you could've shifted back then, you weren't part of a clan. Your father couldn't take you to the Silvers, and Osric couldn't bring you to the Blacks."

She was quiet for a long moment. "I hadn't thought of that. Now that you bring it up, I recall there being discussions about how rigid the clans were in not allowing anyone not their color to join them."

Henry couldn't imagine what her parents had gone through, worrying and fretting while trying to plan her future. "It wouldn't have been fair to keep you in the mountain forever. Besides, that couldn't happen. Your father's reign would've eventually ended. I can guarantee your parents wanted you to have a future and a family of your own. They wanted you to be happy and free."

"That would've been impossible on Earth as well as on the Fae Realm. My birth made life much harder for them."

"Life is hard no matter who or where you are."

"Do you...do you think they regretted having me?"

"Never," he stated firmly. "You were a product of their love. They proved that in what you've told me about them. Osric, too."

She sat up and turned to face him. "What if I don't remember any of the bad times? What if my life wasn't as wonderful as I think it was?"

"It's what you recall now that matters." He took her hands in his and brought them to his lips to kiss. "You were loved and wanted, Melisse. Don't ever think differently."

It took a moment for her to nod. Henry got to his feet and pulled her with him. He stepped out and then lifted her to stand beside him. After they'd dried off, he tugged her to the bed. It didn't take long for her to drift off to sleep. Henry waited another hour to make sure she remained that way. Then he rose and quickly dressed before quietly slipping out the door.

He was halfway down the corridor when a shape moved from the shadows into the light of a wall torch. Henry recognized Lotti's blond waves. She slowly walked to the middle of the hall and waited. "Something wrong?" he asked when he reached her.

"Just waiting on you."

"I beg your pardon?" he asked, confused.

She crossed her arms over her chest and stared at him with her turquoise eyes. "You're going to need help getting to the Druid."

How the fuck did she know what he was about?

Lotti chuckled. "I don't read minds. It's just what I would do if

I could. Now, would you like for me to teleport you to the valley, or would you rather spend days trekking there, giving Melisse time to catch up?" Lotti looked behind him. "Especially since you've been so quiet about your departure."

He stared at her for a moment. "I'd love a ride. But what about Alasdair and the other Kings?"

"Don't worry. Alasdair knows what I'm doing. He's not happy. As a matter of fact, I've spent the last few hours going over why you need to do this."

"I have to admit, this is a surprise."

"I tried to go in after you and Melisse. Everyone, including me, believed I'd be fine in that place."

He widened his stance as shock went through him. "You tried to enter the vines?"

"And couldn't. It was like a wall there, preventing me."

"You couldn't break through?"

She shrugged. "I didn't try, truth be told. But I've been thinking about it ever since. The power of the Star People is pretty potent."

"Damned formidable, from what I've heard," he interjected.

"A Druid's magic shouldn't have stopped me."

"I agree. As powerful as that Druid is, I don't think she could stand in a fair fight with any of the dragons, much less a King. If that's the case, then a Star Person should easily be able to handle her."

"Which means this Druid isn't acting on her own."

The pit that had been in Henry's stomach since he and Melisse escaped tightened painfully. "The Druid believes she's the last human."

"That isn't to say she's in the valley alone, though. I know I'm still learning the extent of my abilities, but I keep coming back to one thing. That the only thing that could prevent me from entering that place is another Star Person."

"Bloody hell," Henry murmured.

Lotti nodded, her lips twisting ruefully. "I can't be sure. Yet. Which is why I want to return. Perhaps I can call them out."

"Fuck. You think it's Villette."

"Who else has a hatred for the dragons that runs as deep as the Druid's?"

Henry ran a hand down his face as he walked a few paces away, then paused and looked back at Lotti. "I was able to hold my own with the Druid, but I can't guarantee that will happen again. I don't feel any magic anymore."

"It might return when you enter the vines."

"Maybe. But even if that happens, I'm certain I won't stand a chance against Villette."

"Leave her to me," Lotti told him. "What do you intend to do with the Druid?"

"Talk to her. Try to convince her that the world isn't as she thinks it is. She needs to see it for herself. If I can get her to look."

"Then let's get you there and get moving with our theories." They turned and started walking before Lotti said, "I'm guessing Melisse has no idea what you're doing?"

Henry grimaced. "If she knew, she would insist on coming, and I don't want her to go through that again."

"It's her decision."

"I know. There will be hell to pay after this."

Lotti snorted as she glanced his way. "You can count on it."

"*If* it even works."

"It'll work."

They didn't speak again until they reached the main hall.

Henry spotted Alasdair talking to a dark-haired man seated on the stones framing the pool. As he and Lotti drew closer, the man faced them and turned black eyes—Con's eyes—to him. This was Brandr.

"Just who I was looking for," Brandr said when they reached him.

Alasdair motioned to Lotti. "Let's leave them to it."

"I'll wait for you outside," Lotti told Henry as she followed her mate.

Henry swung his gaze to Brandr as he pushed to his feet. Henry really hoped Con and Rhi's son didn't intend to keep him at Iron Hall.

"I hear you went to great lengths to get to my realm," Brandr said.

Henry nodded. "I did."

"You've done a lot for the Kings on Earth and continue to do much here. Thank you. I'm Brandr." He held out his hand.

Henry grasped it, and they shook. "Henry."

"It's good to finally meet you."

"Likewise. What can I do for you?"

Brandr drew in a deep breath and then slowly released it. "Can you stop the Druid?"

That took Henry aback. "I aim to try. I'd like to give her a chance to set aside her revenge and have a life."

"Do you think that's possible?"

"I won't know until I try."

Brandr considered that for a heartbeat. "What do you need from me?"

Henry had expected Brandr to try to talk him out of his plan. His relief was immense. "Don't let anyone harm the vines, and don't let anyone else enter once I'm in the forest. I can't do what I need to do if I'm worrying about others. Especially Melisse."

"I can no' promise the last part, but I'll do what I can. I also understand you want to protect the vines, but if you don't come out or something happens to you, there will be consequences."

"Understood." Henry looked back to the hallway that led to his room where Melisse slept, then left Iron Hall.

THIRTY-FOUR

"Are you sure about this?"

Henry glanced at Lotti, but her eyes were locked on an enormous thorn pointed at her face. "As sure as I can be."

"I know that feeling." She slid her gaze to him. "If you get into trouble, you know what to do."

It had been discussed before they left Iron Hall. The instant he felt he was in danger, he would call for Rhi. Henry didn't know if she would be able to hear him or get into the vines, though. And there wasn't a fallback if Rhi couldn't reach him.

He nodded once. "I do. What about you?"

"It won't be the first time I've faced Villette. I can only hope it will be the last."

"Do you really think that's the case?"

Lotti wrinkled her nose. "I don't. Villette has planned this for a very long time. Alasdair believes she has contingencies in place if certain things happen."

"I assume the same. No one who goes to such lengths isn't prepared for other eventualities."

"True. But she didn't expect me."

Henry grinned as he looked at the brambles. "There is that."

"I'd go with you if I could."

He met her gaze. "I know. We each have a part to play."

"That we do. Don't worry about us out here. We'll keep things under control. You focus on your strategy."

Henry swung his new rucksack onto his shoulder. It was packed with several water bottles and food. Just in case. He hoped he wouldn't need any of it, but he also recognized that it would take more than a few hours to find the Druid, much less talk to her.

So much rode on him accomplishing this task. He didn't know if everyone would agree with it, and it didn't matter. It was also why only a handful knew what was going on. He was the one putting himself at risk. He would be the one to pay the price if anything went wrong. His thoughts briefly slipped to Melisse. He had walked into deadly situations before. MI5 had trained him for just such instances.

He squared his shoulders. He would make it back to Melisse.

"Good luck," Lotti said.

He gave her a smile. "You, too."

Then he walked into the vines. The thorns started to retract as he approached, proving that the plant was sentient. To hurt one of them was to hurt them all. They probably originated from a single plant, which could be anywhere.

Henry walked among the towering brambles that made another path for him. The trail snaked northward. Was he being led to the Druid? Or someone else? He kept his guard up. No doubt the Druid still fumed about Melisse getting free. She would be looking to take out her anger on him. Hopefully, Henry would see her first, but considering that the Druid had lived in the valley for over a thousand years, he doubted that would be possible.

He walked for hours. There was no sign of the Druid—of anything other than the vines. He kept a steady pace, not too fast and not too slow. Every so often, he looked behind him. The path remained open. Would it still be there if he needed to leave in a hurry?

"At least you remember me," he said softly to the brambles.

Henry assumed the Druid remained in the valley. He had gotten the impression that she hadn't left because there was nothing out there. He couldn't help but wonder if she might have taken his suggestion and gone to explore. Though she had discarded his words promptly when he mentioned it. Most likely, she had forgotten all about it. Which meant she was still in the valley.

He looked up often, even knowing he wouldn't see anything but gray clouds. The stillness unsettled him now as much as it had the first time. *Silent as the grave* took on an entirely new meaning in the brambles.

The meager light soon began to fade. He had gone almost an entire day without sight of the Druid. He looked down at one point and came to a halt when he found small green shoots like those within the shield knot at his feet. Henry lowered onto one knee and gently ran his fingers over the greenery. He looked to the left and saw there was a trail of sprouts leading in that direction. Had they come from the shield knot? Had they somehow extended outward? He marveled at it for a moment longer before standing and continuing on the path the vines had made.

Henry walked until it became too dark to see. He had a torch in his rucksack, but he didn't want to use it. He found a good place to camp for the night and sank down to the ground, leaning against the base of a vine and pulling food from his pack.

Alasdair had handed him the rucksack, and Henry hadn't bothered to look inside once the King of Teals told him the contents. Now, he would discover everything Alasdair had packed. Besides four bottles of water, there were various protein bars, apples, and four carefully packaged bundles.

Henry opened the first to find a ham and cheese sandwich. He devoured it and finished off his second bottle of water. Then, before his eyes, water began to fill the bottle he had just finished. He chuckled and reached for an apple.

"Would've been nice if you'd told me, Alasdair," he mused.

Henry wadded up the wrapping for his sandwich and tucked it into his rucksack with everything but the apple. Only then did he bite into the fruit and stretch out his legs. He tried not to think about what Melisse was doing—and thinking—but his thoughts led him back to it again and again.

"I'm not going to tell you again to get out of my way," Melisse threatened.

Brandr stood before her with his arms crossed. "I'm trying to explain."

"You've wasted hours saying nothing." She was fast losing the last frayed thread of her patience. "I need to get to Henry."

"He didna wake you for a reason."

"And I don't care!" She shoved her hands into her hair and

turned around, looking for anyone who might side with her. Cullen and Tamlyn had made sure the kids were far away, and everyone else had soon followed.

Everyone except Brandr and Alasdair.

She dropped her hands and looked at the King of Teals. "How are you okay with letting Lotti go alone?"

"Because that is what she felt she must do," Alasdair answered.

Why wasn't he getting it? Melisse wanted to scream in frustration. "Don't you want to be with her?"

Alasdair gave her a dark look. "Of course."

"And yet, you're here," she snapped.

Brandr dropped his arms to his sides and took a step toward her. "Henry is trying to protect you."

"I don't need it!" Melisse looked between the two men, so angry it felt as if fire were coming out of the sides of her face. "One way or another, I'm going to get to him."

"Do you know why I'm no' with Lotti?" Alasdair asked. "Because I've been with her, I've fought alongside her. I know the power she wields. I've felt it." He held out his hands, palms up. "I know what she's capable of. And as hard as it is to accept, I know she's the only one who can stand against Villette. Would I change places with her in a heartbeat? You fucking bet I would."

Brandr caught her attention. "You know what happens to dragons within the vines. You're vulnerable and unable to defend yourself against magic. Henry isna. Nor is he worrying about protecting you or one of us, which would only hinder his plan. He's doing what we can no'. And nay, before you ask, I'm no' happy about it. But I'm damned glad he's here and willing to venture into that place."

Melisse squeezed her eyes closed and clenched her hands, wishing she could touch Henry. "I can't lose him."

"He was drawn here because of you. Trust in that," Alasdair said.

Brandr asked, "What is the one thing Henry has demanded of everyone?"

Melisse looked into his black eyes. "That the vines aren't hurt. He wants to help the Druid, but he won't allow the vines to be harmed."

"Which we will do if he doesna come out of that place," Alasdair stated.

Melisse hated the situation, but she grudgingly admitted they were right. Going into the vines again would cause more harm than good. There was nothing she could do. Not now, at least. But she would be prepared when that changed. She tried to walk around Brandr.

"Whoa. Where are you going?" he demanded.

She looked into his black eyes. "We need to get ready in case Villette is a part of this."

Brandr blew out a relieved breath. "Do you have an idea?"

"I think I do," she said with a smile.

Henry was dozing when magic brushed against him. His eyes snapped open. He swung his head to the right, surveyed the area, then looked left. When he slid his gaze back to the center, the Druid stood there.

She said nothing. Simply stared at him. Henry couldn't gauge her emotions. Sparks weren't flying from her fingers, which meant her anger was at least contained. For the moment. That could change in a second, though.

Her long, black strands were gathered at her neck in a queue, and her arms hung at her sides as she studied him. He debated whether to rise and decided to remain just as he was. He also opted to let her speak first.

The silence drew out for a considerable time before she said, "You should be dead."

"I nearly was."

There was another long pause. "Why have you returned?"

"For you."

"To kill me?" she asked, brows raised and her voice holding a hint of irritation.

Henry shook his head. "To talk."

"I think we've done enough of that."

"Have we?" He tried another tactic. "When was the last time you left the valley?"

"Why does that matter?"

"Humor me."

She glared at him. "I don't know."

"I know how long it's been since that fateful day you were attacked. Do you?"

"Time doesn't matter."

"It's been fifteen hundred years."

A frown marred her face before she quickly smoothed it away. "You're lying."

"Why would I lie?"

"I'm trying to figure that out."

Henry spread his arms. "I had no reason to return. But here I am. I spoke the truth before, and I will do so again."

"You expect me to trust you?"

"I ask that you listen to what I have to say."

She slowly shook her head. "Only a fool would return. You must have a death wish."

"On the contrary, I very much want to live."

The Druid's lips peeled back. "You think I'll let you return to your dragon? That won't happen."

"Then you'll die."

"You can try."

"I didn't say I'd be the one to take your life."

Her gaze narrowed. "Then you'll die with me."

"Maybe."

"What kind of man are you to care for dragons?"

He climbed to his feet then. "The same man who is here to help you."

THIRTY-FIVE

"Help me?" She couldn't believe his audacity.

Henry's hazel eyes swept about before coming to land on her. "Have you been surrounded by desolation so long that you've forgotten the feel of rain on your face? Catching snowflakes on your tongue or having the wind blow through your hair? Can you recall the smell of flowers? Basking in sunlight? Have you forgotten the myriad of colors a sunset and sunrise bring? The music of birdsong?"

"Why does any of that matter? How can it after I lost my family?"

"I am sorry for what you've suffered, but you aren't alone in such grief or loss."

Her stomach churned with righteous anger, her chest constricting with fury. How dare he? How. Dare. He? The urge to end his life was so great she shook with it. Magic rushed through her body and gathered in her palms, readying to do just that.

Then, a tiny voice in her mind made her hesitate. *He isn't a dragon.*

She took a step back, alarmed and deeply troubled at how swiftly—and willingly—she had been about to kill Henry. A human. Ice ran through her veins at the realization. That wasn't who she was.

"I don't have children, so I can't imagine how it feels to have them taken away," Henry continued. "But I know death. Sometimes, I think it shadows my every move, waiting to strike those nearest me and devour me in pain. There have been times it has."

She swallowed and flexed her fingers. The rage that'd had her in its grip just a few moments earlier dissipated like smoke. Her stomach churned with trepidation, making her queasy. "It isn't the same."

"You're right. It isn't. My family wasn't attacked."

"There is but one truth in my life. That is the destruction of dragons."

Henry sighed. "That will never happen."

"Maybe not, but I can take out many of them before my life comes to a close. And I'm all right with that."

"Why?" he asked, a deep frown furrowing his brow. "Why do you put all your anger on the dragons?"

A flare of irritation blossomed again, but she kept it under control. "Do I need to repeat my story?"

"I heard it fine the first time. I have just one question."

When he didn't immediately ask it, she motioned for him to continue. "Go on. Ask."

"Why isn't your wrath split between the dragons and the invaders?"

Her mind went blank for a moment as she tried to sort through Henry's words. They made sense. She heard them, but her mind couldn't grasp what he asked. Then it hit her. The army that had initially attacked and sent them fleeing. She hadn't forgotten about them. She'd told Henry that part of the story, but he was right. Why wasn't she furious with them?

Henry was far from finished. "If the dragon hadn't been there, the invaders would've been the ones to end your family's lives. As well as yours."

"You would say anything for the dragons," she bit out. Though she wasn't sure if she was mad at him for pointing out such facts or at herself for not having a better reply.

"It's true. The dragons are my friends. And I am theirs."

"How?" she asked in bewilderment. "They're killers."

He twisted his lips ruefully. "Everything has the potential to be evil or good. Sometimes, we're both at the same time." He motioned to the vines. "Their thorns can take a life. Some berries are poisonous. Humans kill. So do animals. Yet I walk among these vines, I eat fruit, I have animals as pets, and I have both human and dragon friends."

She looked away. For most of the day, she had stayed away from him because she hadn't decided what she would do with him. And this conversation forced her to look at things differently, which didn't sit well. She liked the world as it was. She knew where she belonged, and she had a purpose.

He wanted to take that from her.

But she wouldn't let him.

"And Druid friends," he added.

There was that word again. She was curious about it. Henry had called her a Druid. Yet she was wary. His objective was to get her to end her vengeance. She had been at it too long to halt it now.

Henry held her gaze. "I'd like to be your friend."

"Don't lie. You're only here to save the dragons."

"That's not entirely true. Yes, I want the dragons to be safe, but I also want to give you closure."

She snorted. His impudence knew no bounds. "Closure? And how would you do that?"

"By giving you the truth."

She searched for a hint of deceit, some doubt in his visage and tone. And found nothing. "It wouldn't be the truth I know."

"You only know a portion of that day. I discovered the rest. Just as I promised I would. I investigate, remember?"

"Then you know which dragon it is."

Henry hesitated. "I do."

After all this time, she was so close to...to what? He wouldn't send the dragon to her. She had always known which one it was. She had just waited for the time it ventured into her domain. It hadn't. Maybe it never would.

"I will tell you their side of that day," he offered.

She shook her head. She didn't want to hear denials or excuses, and that was all it would be. Her people had crossed the border. That was the only reason dragons needed to kill. It didn't matter that they were peaceful people who only had a few weapons for hunting.

There was no need for more. Not that night. Maybe not ever. She was done talking. Though she still wasn't sure what to do with Henry. She turned to walk away.

"Wait," he called. "I'm sorry. I didn't mean to push."

She didn't know why she paused at his words. It was nice to

actually speak with someone, but the heartache afterward was too much to endure. As were the questions bombarding her.

"You can ask me anything you want," Henry hurried to say. "Anything."

Her head swung to him. His features were hidden in shadow, but she didn't need to see him to hear his desperation. "Why should I?"

"Because you're curious. I'm the first human you've seen in over fifteen hundred years."

The fact that he was right meant she should leave. She would be a fool to believe anything he said. And yet, she did.

"Please," Henry added.

It wouldn't hurt to listen to whatever he had to say. Besides, she had questions. She faced him. He bent and took something out of his peculiar bag that made a noise she had never heard before. There was a click, and then light shone from a small device in his hand. She had seen him carry it the last time.

"It's a torch," he said, holding it out to her. "Take it. I have another."

"I don't need a light in the dark."

He shrugged. "I do, and I'd like to see you."

Her chin lifted. "There's no need for you to see me. I know where your affections lay. With a dragon."

Henry said nothing as he tossed the torch at her. She caught it on reflex, noting the cool metal that met her palm. She tentatively touched the light, expecting to be burned, but it did nothing. Was it some kind of magic? He sat and drew out the second torch, which he turned on and pointed at her.

"I'm not trying to seduce you." His gaze lowered. "My heart belongs to Melisse. It always has."

"How can you be in love with a dragon?" she asked without thinking.

"The same way I can be friends with them."

She sat, crossed her legs, and placed the torch in her lap with the beam pointed his way. She didn't need light to make it back to her cottage. The vines always opened the way for her, and there were no predators in her forest. But she couldn't see in the dark, and the light gave her the opportunity to see Henry's face.

He raised his arm to shield his eyes and winced. She realized the light was pointed directly at him and shifted it.

"Thank you." He lowered his arm. "Go on. Ask me something else. I know you have questions."

She swallowed, suddenly uncertain about remaining. There was much she wanted to know, but she was locked on the dragons and couldn't get away from them. "How are you friends with dragons?"

"I just told that story to Melisse," Henry said with a wry grin. "I was at a pub—er, a tavern. I'm not sure what you would've called it."

"I know what a tavern is."

He nodded once. "Good. I was tracking an individual there and didn't realize I had walked into a sort of trap. I was attacked. I was about to have a knife plunged into me when someone stepped in to help. It was Banan. I had no idea that he was anything more than human. Before I met him, I knew nothing of magic."

"How can that be? You have magic," she pointed out.

"That's a recent occurrence. In my world, there are a few places where magic thrives and people know of it. Most, however, believe it is nothing more than superstition and fantasy."

She found it curious that he said *in my world*. Was it a slip of the tongue, or another meaning about the dragons?

"Banan and I became fast friends. He discovered that I worked for a government organization, but he never said anything to me. Nor did he disclose who he really was. Not until the day someone kidnapped the woman he fell in love with. That's when he called me. I, of course, wanted to return the favor of him saving me and immediately found what he needed. I also joined him. That's when I first saw him shift."

She didn't have a clue what type of government organization he was talking about or the *calling* he kept mentioning. But she didn't need to in order to keep up with the story. "And it terrified you."

"It did," he acknowledged with a nod. "But Banan was my friend. He never threatened me or made me feel that I was in danger. Not even after he shifted. Once I saw the world of dragons and magic, I never wanted to leave."

"You expect me to believe that story when I know humans are gone?"

"If they're gone, how am I here?"

She couldn't answer that. Nor did she know how the dragons could shift.

"There is an entire realm for you to see and hundreds of thousands of people. There are also more humans with magic. I feel other Druids. Aren't you curious to see if I'm right? Don't you want to venture out and look at what's changed?" When she didn't answer, he said, "That's what I thought."

"Where do you live that dragons and humans interact in such a way? No one crosses their border, and they aren't supposed to cross into ours. That's the law."

Henry bent his knees and braced his feet on the ground. "I live in a place far, far from here."

"Dragons have their own land," she argued as her anger spiked. "They killed my family for daring to seek shelter with them. Nothing you say can be true, because if dragons leave their land, they can be hunted and killed. Just as humans are for venturing over the border. It is our way."

"There is much you don't know. Everything I've told you is the truth."

She jumped to her feet. The torch dropped to the ground and rolled, coming to a stop with its beam on Henry. "Where do you live?" She needed to know about this place. If there were dragons out in the world, then she could entice them to her.

"I'm from another realm."

She studied his face. Either he was a very good liar, or...he spoke the truth.

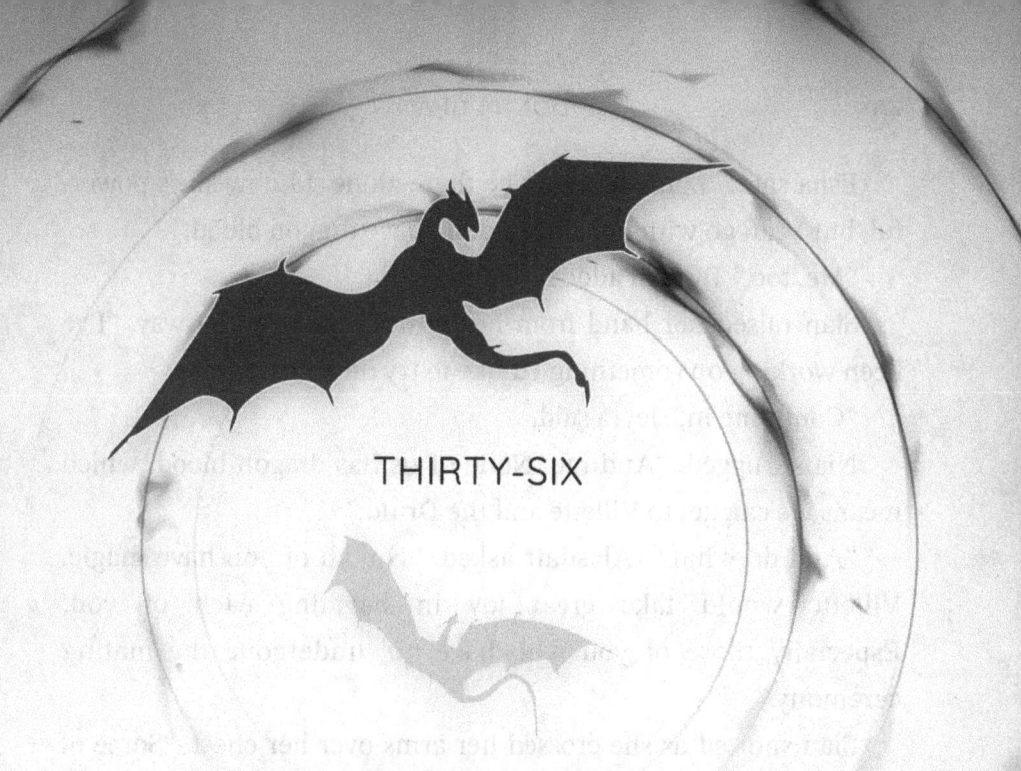

THIRTY-SIX

Melisse tried to imagine what her parents would do in her situation. She only had snatches of memories of them, but she was sure they would have chosen the same stance she now took, which found her in the common room at Iron Hall surrounded by Dragon Kings.

But she wasn't alone. Brandr and Alasdair stood with her. Lotti and Henry were there in spirit. She was furious that Henry had left without telling her, but she also understood why he did it. She would've fought and argued to go, even though it would've put them at a severe disadvantage once again. Here, at the hidden city, was where she was supposed to be right now.

Until I can get to him again.

"Fuck me," Cullen said.

"Villette?" Rhi asked with a frown.

Shaw shrugged, his face tight with irritation. "It makes sense."

"Aye, but we can no' fight her even if it is," Hector pointed out. "No' outside our borders."

Esha said, "Lotti shouldn't be there alone. I know she's power-ful, but I can go with her since I don't have dragon blood."

"Me, too," Tamlyn added.

Sian raised her hand from her position near a doorway. "I've been working on something I'd like to try on Villette."

"Count me in," Jeyra said.

Nia shrugged. "And me. None of us has dragon blood, which means we can get to Villette and the Druid."

"And do what?" Alasdair asked. "No' all of you have magic. Villette would take great joy in harming each of you. Especially those of you who have no' undergone the mating ceremony."

Sian snorted as she crossed her arms over her chest. "Some of us have skills other than magic."

"Your alchemy aside, Sian, we don't want to just anger Villette," Melisse said. She looked at the mates who had volun-teered. "We want to hurt her."

Varek crossed his arms over his head. "Look, we all know we're coming to a battle with her sooner or later. A few of us have already had run-ins with her. I want her dealt with as much as anyone, but Hector's right. The moment we cross the border, the war will be set in motion."

"Which is exactly what she wants," Evander stated.

Melisse noticed that neither Con nor Eurwen had spoken yet. She didn't know what to make of that. Then again, Brandr had remained silent, as well.

"Could we tempt her across the border?" Alasdair asked.

Vaughn blew out a breath. "This all hinges on Henry convincing the Druid to drop her revenge. This is a woman who has dedicated her life to trapping dragons and doing who knows what with them. I doona think Henry could do it even if he had ten thousand years."

"How much time are we giving him?" Eurwen asked.

Since Melisse hadn't been there, she glanced from Alasdair to Brandr. That was when she saw Brandr and Con staring at each other. She suspected the two were having a private conversation.

"It wasna discussed," Alasdair answered.

Melisse tried not to think about the chance that Henry would never return to her. If she lingered on that, she might lose what little courage she had left. Henry knew what he was doing. She had faith that he could get through to the Druid. But if he didn't...

"Henry made his decision," Con said in a clear voice. "We must trust that he knows what he's doing, even if we doona like it or agree. And we need to be ready for any outcome."

Brandr looked past his father to the other faces in the group. "We should be ready to back up Lotti and Henry because they'll likely need it. A few of us can cross the border, and no one is under any obligation to do more than they feel comfortable doing."

And just like that, it was decided. Melisse listened to the buzz around the room as mates talked among themselves while others came up with ideas of where they could be stationed to lend support. Eurwen pointed out that the borders still needed to be watched, which meant not every King would head north.

Melisse felt like the eye of a storm, the solitary figure who stood restlessly as chaos swirled around her. She should join the conversations to lend her opinions, but then the only thing that mattered was that she was headed north. She might not be able to go into the valley to aid Henry, but she would be there waiting.

Someone touched her arm. She turned her head to find Alasdair. The top part of his auburn hair was tied away from his face. He had stood calmly and spoken evenly to everyone, but he was far from either. His mate was also alone, and he wanted to be with her as much as Melisse wished to be with Henry.

"Are you good?" Alasdair asked.

She shook her head. "You?"

"Far from it." He blew out a long breath. "I should be. Lotti can handle herself, but it feels wrong no' being with her. It always feels wrong."

"Yet you didn't stop her. You got to say goodbye."

Alasdair's gaze intensified. "Henry should've told you, but we both know we would've had to restrain you to keep you from going with him."

"What if he dies? I'll never have gotten to say..." She trailed off, afraid to say the words aloud.

"Say what?" Alasdair pushed. "That you care about him?"

"Aye."

"That you love him?"

She looked away, only to find her gaze landing on couple after couple. Love. She knew what it looked like. She had seen it between her parents and so many of the Kings and their mates. The truth was that she'd never thought herself worthy of it. Not after accidentally taking Osric's life, which ended up costing her parents' theirs. How could anyone who had done something so horrible be loved?

But she loved Henry. She loved him so much it hurt.

Alasdair wrapped an arm around her shoulders and leaned down to whisper, "Tell him. Never, ever pass up an opportunity to tell those you care about how much you love them."

Because you never know when you might not get another chance was left unsaid. But she knew that all too well. She hadn't gotten to tell her mother goodbye, hadn't gotten to tell them how sorry she was or how much she loved them. Same with Osric. And now, Henry.

"He has to live," she said, her eyes swimming with tears.

Alasdair squeezed her shoulder. "He will. As will Lotti. We're going to make sure of it."

It was a reminder that she wasn't alone. Hadn't Henry said that to her? She wouldn't forget again. She looked up into Alasdair's face and forced her lips into what she hoped was a smile. "We will."

Henry watched the Druid's face carefully. She thought he lied. He couldn't blame her. If he hadn't known realms could be crossed, he'd likely laugh in someone's face if they said it could happen.

"I know it's difficult to believe," he said. "I thought it might be easier if you assumed I was from Zora."

She did nothing but stare at him with her intense gray gaze as if frozen.

He licked his lips and kept going in hopes she would continue listening. This could be his only shot, and he needed to get it right. He chose his words carefully. "Our worlds aren't much different. There are those with magic on mine. Druids, Fae—"

Her brows shot together in confusion.

"Melisse is half-Fae. They're a race of beings who look human but are born with magic. They can teleport, er, jump long distances. Sometimes, halfway around the world. They also build doorways to move from one realm to another. It's how we arrived here."

The Druid's frown was still in place, but there was curiosity in the tilt of her head.

He barreled on. "The Fae are more powerful than Druids, but the dragons are the most dominant of all magical beings on my world. Long, long ago, my realm—Earth—was the home of the dragons. Then, humans arrived. No one realized it until eons later, but they were taken from a planet of Druids and brought to Earth for the sole purpose of disrupting the dragons. Each clan of dragons was ruled by a King, and as those Kings approached the newcomers, they were able to shift from dragon to human form in order to communicate. The dragons opened their home to the mortals, and for a time, there was peace. It didn't last, however. A war began when humans tried to trick—and kill—one of the Kings."

The Druid grinned at that. So much for turning her hatred from the dragons.

"The Kings had the opportunity to rid their realm of all humans, but they didn't. Instead, they sent their family, friends, and clans away. To here. A realm created in Earth's image for them. They once more had a realm all to themselves. Then mortals began arriving inexplicably, causing the dragons to set up borders to keep them out. On my world, the Kings hid away for thousands of years until their existence was forgotten and they became myth and legend. It was only then that they ventured out to walk and live among us."

"Am I supposed to care that the dragons lost their homes and families?"

Henry fought a wave of frustration. He drew in a breath and shrugged. "You should. You lost yours. The entire reason the dragons have the border is so what happened on Earth doesn't happen here. And it is."

She frowned. "Explain."

"Go see for yourself. All you have to do is walk through any city, but don't let any of them know you have magic. They'll kill you for it."

She scoffed at his words.

"I'm not joking. There is a city to the west, built into a mountain. It's called Stonemore, and the Kings and others have rescued children being sacrificed for no other reason than because they were born with magic." If Henry thought that would elicit a reaction, he was wrong. He kept talking. "The dragons remain on their land, yet someone is stirring hatred for dragons and anyone with magic. We're on the brink of war—a war the dragons are desperate to stamp out."

"If they're so powerful, then they can wipe everyone out like you said."

"That isn't who they are," he argued. "They didn't do it on Earth. Why would they do it here?"

She leaned a shoulder against one of the stalks. "That's exactly who they are. If there really are other humans on Zora, then I applaud whoever is telling them the truth about the dragons. Everyone needs to be after them."

Henry slowly ran a hand down his face. If that story didn't make her see the plight of the dragons, then he needed to change tack. Her hatred ran too deep. He had to get her out so she could see the realm for herself. That was the only way she would believe anything he said.

"Tell me about your ancestors," he urged.

She blinked, obviously taken aback by his request. "My ancestors?"

"You had to get your magic from one of them. Did it come from your mum or your dad? Or was your entire village Druids?"

"I told you before. I don't know that word."

He motioned between them. "It's what we are. I can sense Druids. I sensed you all the way on my world. As soon as I arrived, I felt the other Druids—humans with magic. There are others. Perhaps you called yourselves something else."

"Nobody in my village had abilities like ours," she said.

He watched her glance at her hands and wondered why she didn't say *magic*. "When did you first notice your magic?"

"After."

He didn't need to ask what she meant. He knew it was after the loss of her family. He studied her tense form. "It just came about suddenly? Or did someone help you?"

"Why does that matter?"

She kept her voice smooth, but the slight stiffening of her body told him the question wasn't one she wanted to answer. Which meant she hadn't been alone. Lotti was right. Villette very well could be involved. But how much did the Druid know about Villette, her motives, or the Star People?

More importantly, how much could he get out of her?

"The truth is, I think I know who helped you," he said, watching the Druid carefully. "She's the one stirring hatred among the humans."

"I don't care. I want to know more about the Kings and their changing...no, shifting forms. How many of them are there? Are they stronger than the other dragons? Is Melisse one of them?"

THIRTY-SEVEN

The light of the double moons teased them through the thick, fast-moving clouds. Wind gusts swayed Melisse from her perch atop the mountain as she stared at the dark valley below, her hair blowing around her. The vines prevented her from seeing through them to the man she loved.

One who had willingly walked into danger for a second time.

A man she knew she might never see again.

She clung to the fact that Henry had found her in the jungle of brambles. He had run into the valley without hesitation because he was called to it. She no longer cared if he had come for her or the Druid. He was on Zora, and they had settled their differences. They had shared their thoughts and bodies.

If only she had told him her feelings. She'd thought they had time, but she—better than most—knew that time was an illusion fate teased. When someone was lonely or grieving, it stretched interminably.

And when they were blissfully, amazingly happy, fate sometimes only gave them a snippet.

"Come back to me, Henry," she whispered on the wind.

"He will."

Melisse spun around at the Irish voice to find Rhi. The Fae's face was pinched, her inky hair hastily pulled back in a low ponytail. "Why do you think that?"

"Because Henry is resourceful and shrewd. He relies on his wits and ability to read people. I don't think he's ever understood just how formidable he is. He never needed magic because his talents extend far and wide. Besides," Rhi said and stepped closer, "he has a reason to return. You."

Melisse glanced toward the valley, wondering where he was and if he was safe.

"I know Henry," Rhi said with a small smile. "There has been something between the two of you for some time."

"I almost ruined it."

Rhi gave a quick shake of her head. "You worked through it. He went back into that place for you, for the dragons. For everyone. Even the Druid. Justice has ruled Henry his entire life. He will always set wrongs to right and bring down those who must pay for their crimes. When he loves, he does it with his whole heart. He will move realms to return to you."

Melisse's heart skipped a beat at the idea that he could love her. "You can't know how he feels."

"You didn't see his face as he stood up to Con to get to you. He was prepared to fight to get into the vines. For you."

And because of the Druid. But Melisse knew what Rhi meant. All she had to do was look back at everything Henry had done since arriving on Zora. He had searched for her, stood between her and an attack, healed her, and gotten her out of the valley alive.

"Now," Rhi said as she swung her gaze to the valley, "has all your magic returned?"

"I believe so."

Rhi pressed her lips together. "Good. That's good."

"What do you think our chances are to finish Villette?"

"Slim." Rhi shrugged and pulled a strand of hair from her cheek to shove behind her ear. "Villette wants a showdown, and she'll make sure she gets it."

"You don't think the war can be avoided?"

Rhi shook her head. "I wish with all my heart it could. The Kings have fought enough battles, but Villette's need to put the dragons back in their place won't be denied."

Unless she could be stopped. If Melisse had the power, she would face Villette herself. Much as Henry had gone back into the vines. "We need more Star People to join us."

"We have Lotti and Erith."

And with her, at least some of the Reapers. Dragon Kings, Star People, Reapers, and whoever else they could get to join them. An impressive bunch, but would it be enough?

Rhi blew out a breath and faced her. "I didn't come just to talk about Henry."

"All right," Melisse said and looked at her.

"Brandr told me if Henry gets into trouble, they decided the best thing for him to do was call to me."

"That's what Brandr and Alasdair told me. You should be able to locate him."

"I'm sure I can, but I'm unable to go into the vines."

For a beat, Melisse simply stared at her in confusion. "Only those with dragon blood…oh!" Her mouth dropped open as it dawned on her. "You're pregnant."

"I am," Rhi confirmed with a brilliant smile. But it swiftly vanished. "We've not told anyone else. I thought you needed to know the reason if I didn't go after Henry."

Melisse shook her head. "You're right. You can't go. If the Druid learns of the bairn, there's no telling what she would do to you."

"Nor can I leave Henry."

"It might not come to that," she said to soothe Rhi. All the while, Melisse's mind raced to come up with another alternative. "Will you let me know if he does call to you?"

Rhi studied her for a long moment. "Not if it means you'll go in after him."

"I will if I have to, but the point is to ease the situation, not make it worse."

"Do you have a plan?"

"Not yet. I'm working on it."

Rhi reached out and squeezed her hand. "Then I'll tell you."

At the Druid's demands for information, Henry squeezed the bridge of his nose with this thumb and forefinger. "The Dragon Kings can only be killed by another King. Melisse, as I've told you, is half-Fae and half-dragon. It allows her to shift from her Fae form to dragon and back again."

"Then I'll turn the Kings against each other."

Henry sighed. Maybe he couldn't change the Druid's mind. Was it time to cut his losses and leave? No. He wouldn't give up yet. If she wanted knowledge, then he would give it to her. "Many others much more powerful than you have tried. Not a single one has succeeded."

"They weren't me."

"You'll have to leave the vines," he stated. "The Kings know what this place is now. They won't enter, and you can be damned sure that no other dragon will ever be caught again."

Her nostrils flared in response. "There are always those who believe they can escape. They will come."

"They won't."

"We'll see." She leaned a hip on a curving vine.

Henry cast a quick look around into the darkness but didn't see anyone else. "Have you been alone this entire time?"

"You know the answer to that."

"Most would've gone mad by now."

She shrugged, her face turned to the side. "I had something to focus on."

That she did. And she always brought their conversation back to the dragons, but if she could do that, so could he. "You never answered me earlier. Why not go after the invaders?" Silence met his query, but he continued. "Do you want to know what I think?"

"Nay, but you're going to tell me regardless."

"I think it was easier for you to latch onto the dragons and make them the villains. After all, you went to them for help, despite the law of the land—knowing that you might be killed on sight. You took that chance."

She slowly turned her head toward him. "We were being chased."

"Not by dragons. By *humans*."

"If they had caught us, it was death or enslavement. We had to run."

Henry folded his arms across his chest. "You broke the one law of Zora. No humans were ever to cross onto dragon land. The consequences were swift and deadly. The dragons did exactly what they were supposed to."

"Dragon. One," she stated angrily.

"The dragon did as it was supposed to," he amended. "I understand your anger at it for taking your family, but we both know it was only a matter of time before the invaders caught you. You said yourself, they were right behind you. They would've done what the dragon did. Is it fair to put all your rage onto one species?"

She flicked something off her sleeve before folding her hands in her lap. "You speak eloquently. You even pose a decent argument, but it doesn't change the facts."

"We both know if the dragon hadn't been there, the raiders would've caught you. All of you. Some would've died. Others would've been taken."

"That isn't what happened."

"It's what could've happened. It's what nearly happened. You won't admit it because you have told yourself you must hold on to your hate for the dragons. But I don't think your ire was directed solely at the dragon in the beginning, was it?"

She lifted her chin. "What if it wasn't?"

"Something or someone shifted your anger."

"The loss of my family and the fact that I'm the last of my kind was pretty much all I needed."

Henry drew in a long breath and slowly released it. "You aren't, and you never have been, the last human. Let me show you or go on your own. But *go*. *See*. Zora has many settlements."

"You think I'll leave my sanctuary so you can burn down the vines?"

"I would never harm them, and I'm not going to let anyone else hurt them either."

She snorted. "As if you could stop the dragons."

"If it wasn't for me, the valley would already be burning. They wanted to do it the moment Melisse and I got free."

"You barely got free. I struck both of you. I know what I delivered to you should've taken your life. Is it your magic that saved you?"

He lifted one shoulder. "I was healed by a dragon. Con is one of my friends. The very one who is holding off scorching the ground. For me."

The Druid blinked and looked away again. "The world you describe is nothing like the one I remember. It is a pleasant fabrication. But a misrepresentation."

"I give my word. The vines will be protected. Go see things for yourself. You'll discover that I'm not deceiving you." An idea came to him. "Unless you can't." As soon as the words were out, he realized the truth in them. "Bloody hell. You can't leave."

She cut her eyes to him. "This is my home. Why would I wish to leave?"

"What were you given to remain and trap the dragons? Magic? Immortality?"

The Druid snorted a laugh. "I only have your word on the passage of time. I would know if it had been that long."

"How?" he demanded as he climbed to his feet. "You can't see the sun, the moon, nor the stars. There are only those fucking clouds that never move. No wind, no rain, no snow. No sounds of animals or insects. Just silence. This place is a goddamn tomb, and you don't even realize it."

She slowly straightened, her chest rising and falling quickly. "Enough."

"Tell me I'm wrong," he goaded. "Tell me you're not forced to remain here."

There was no reply.

"Why would you give up your freedom?" he asked in astonishment.

The Druid seethed, her rage tangible. "For revenge!"

Henry held her gaze, waiting for her to continue, but she clamped her mouth shut. "You locked yourself in a prison, twisted your heart with hate and vengeance when you could've been with your family."

"I will see them when I die."

"That's the thing. They weren't killed. The dragon you assumed burned them actually took them to the other side of the mountain to freedom."

Sparks shot from the Druid's fingertips. "How dare you?" she bit out.

"I promised you the truth, and that's what I'm giving you."

"They died. I saw it."

"You saw flames," he argued. "You saw some bodies, but it was the attackers. Not your family."

She took a step back, visibly shaken. "You're lying."

"You were lied to," Henry continued, praying he was getting through to her. "Lied to and trapped even more thoroughly than any dragon. Let me help you break free from all of it."

The Druid pivoted and walked away. Henry watched her,

seeing the vines open a path for her. He hesitated before grabbing his bag and following. What did he have to lose?

THIRTY-EIGHT

Truth. Wasn't that what she'd always wanted? Wasn't that what kept her going?

But now...she wasn't sure of anything. Her head swam with the things Henry had told her. Could she believe him? That he came from another realm? What about the Fae? The Druids? The passage of time?

If she had been able to argue against any of it, she would have done so in a second. She wanted to, even tried to, but words failed to come. Did she dare believe any of it? That was the question that swam in frantic circles in her mind as she walked home. She made her way along the same path she had run that fateful day when her world fell apart. How many times had she walked it as the memories assaulted her, yanking her back to relive it time and again?

Too damn many to count.

She had finally shoved them away in the last vestiges of her heart where they'd be kept safe. And she hadn't risked revisiting them. Not until Henry dredged up the past—and the memories along with it.

Henry. She didn't know what to make of him. She had been sure she'd killed him. It didn't surprise her that the dragons could heal. They were made of magic, after all. But if she had almost killed him, why risk returning? He wasn't dimwitted, which meant he must have some purpose.

As he'd said, the dragons could've burned the entire valley. They hadn't. Yet. That hung over her like a death knell. Perhaps that was exactly what all of them wanted. Why, then, did Henry keep saying that he spoke only the truth? Why did it matter if she believed him? He'd been safe and free. Any sane person would've remained that way. Instead, he'd returned. Alone, at that.

She didn't stop until she reached her cottage. She left the door open for Henry. If he followed. Though she suspected he would. She stood in the middle of her home. As her gaze moved around the small space, vague, poignant images of her daughter filled the home. She heard her giggle in the distance. And with it, her husband's boisterous laugh.

A tear dropped onto her cheek, which she quickly swiped away. It would be so easy to get lost in the past and remain there with those she loved. She reached out to steady herself. Her fingers closed on the back of a chair. She gripped it tightly, refusing to be bowed.

She moved past those recollections to her encounter with the dragon. The memories were unclear and difficult to reach. She closed her eyes and heaved them up, one by one. She needed details, specifics that she hadn't dared think about in a very long time.

The screams and the fear were always there, hovering around

her. They came first and enveloped her like a net. She saw her husband. He was ahead, clutching their toddler daughter against his chest as he ran. He looked back often, their gazes meeting as she moved as fast as she could while urging her nieces' short legs to keep up. Others overtook her with wide, panicked eyes. She was too slow. She had to go faster.

She shuddered, recalling the urgency and the terror. She forced her memories to jump to when the dragon arrived. That's where she needed details. The roar filled her mind as if she were standing there once more. Then she was. When the dragon came around the mountain, she hadn't been able to look away from the enormous beast. It dove straight for them, its huge mouth open and showing its teeth. The wind from its wings blasted her, putting her off balance. She suddenly realized her hands were empty. Her gaze darted around, searching for her nieces. The screams of others drowned out her shouts. She stared in shock as her people rushed straight to the invaders to get away from the dragon.

Her frantic gaze landed on her husband who was valiantly fighting one of the attackers. Then she spotted their daughter. Her heart tore in two at the sight of her darling girl crying, her arms out toward her. Her only thought was to get to her daughter. She motioned the child to her. No sooner did her daughter start toward her than the dragon flew at them. Her husband turned to shield their daughter right as fire shot from the dragon's mouth. The flames carved the ground, cutting her off from them.

The air was filled with smoke and the screams of those burning alive. She jumped back as the blaze reached out to her, singeing her hair and clothes. She frantically scanned the writhing bodies as well as the charred ones for her husband or their daughter. There were no clothes left to tell who was who. No one could survive such a fire.

She had always assumed.

And why would she think any differently? No humans were supposed to cross the border for *any* reason. It was the law. If any did, the act was punishable by death. Which is exactly what'd happened to her family.

Hadn't it?

She hadn't seen the bodies, hadn't had time to search for her daughter or husband. She had run for her life. What if...?

The sound of a door clicking closed jerked her to the present. She knew the hope Henry's words gave would lead her down a trail of heartache, but she couldn't stop it. Didn't want to. What if her family had been saved? What if they'd lived? What if they had tried to find her?

Emotion choked her as she imagined all the firsts she'd missed with her daughter. She wanted to cry out, fall to her knees and pound the ground. What if? Two simple words, but they had her spiraling as nothing had before.

She realized her cheeks were wet. Her tears had dried up long ago, but they were back with a vengeance now.

What if...?

She drew in a shaky breath. If she trusted Henry, it could be her downfall. But what if she did, in fact, believe what he said. It wasn't as if she had much of a life now. He'd called the valley a tomb. He wasn't wrong. She was the walking dead, existing merely to take out her wrath on others.

"You were right," she said, her voice cracking. "My anger should've been divided to include the raiders. I never forgot them or the part they played. It doesn't make sense that they would escape my fury."

"It was out of your control."

She listened to his perfectly formed words. From the first moment she had heard his accent, she had known he was different. She just hadn't expected him to be from another realm. Not that it mattered now. She'd made her decision.

She turned to face him. He stood just inside the door, his hazel eyes locked on her. Truth or lie, he had come to her as no one else had. It was preposterous that a dragon would save her family. Just as it was preposterous that dragons could change forms.

If dragons could shift, then perhaps Henry *was* from another world. Maybe fifteen hundred years *had* passed since she'd lost it all. But if she dared to believe any of that, then she must also consider the possibility that the dragon hadn't burned her family alive.

One teeny thread of chance, hope, and she cleaved to it with all she was.

She glanced at the door and thought of Villette. "There isn't much time. You need to prepare."

Henry's brow furrowed as he searched her gaze. "For what?"

"You suspected I had help. You were right."

He took a tentative step forward. "Why are you telling me this?"

"You got what you wanted. You compelled me to look at things differently. There are aspects that have made me question and reconsider certain…things." She didn't want him to know that she was leaning toward believing all of it. She swallowed, suddenly so weary she could barely stand. "I am confined to the valley. Or, more precisely, to wherever the vines grow. I urged them over the border, and no one stopped me."

Henry slowly set down his bag. "I'll help you leave."

"I can't. That much was made clear. As long as I stay and trap dragons, I won't be disturbed or harmed."

"Who told you that?" he asked. "Was it a woman? One with burns on the right side of her face and neck?"

She wiped the remnants of her tears away. The only way he could describe Villette was if he'd had dealings with her. "Aye. She is as you describe."

"Fuck," Henry murmured, running a hand down his face and briefly turning away. "Villette is extremely dangerous."

She nearly laughed. "I know."

"I don't think you do. Her kind, the Star People I mentioned before, once enslaved the dragons. Her brother freed them and created my world, Earth, for them. Villette is responsible for bringing humans to Earth and Zora."

She nodded, recalling that he had spoken about that earlier.

"Villette is cultivating hate among the humans for the dragons. She has one of the Dragon Kings with her at Stonemore. She somehow even resurrected a long-dead dragon to fight for her—the brother of another King." Henry shook his head. "Bloody hell. She has her hands in everything."

"Then you should know that I don't kill the dragons that enter the valley. I alert her when I capture one, and she comes to take it away."

Shock ran through Henry, draining the color from his face. "Do you know what she does with them?"

"I assumed she killed them. She made it seem like that was what she did."

"Do you know where she takes them?"

She shrugged. "I never asked. I didn't care."

Henry put his hands on his hips and slowly shook his head from side to side as he stared at the floor. His gaze snapped back to her. "What happens if you leave the valley?"

"I never asked. Leaving wasn't an option I ever considered."

"And your magic? Was that from Villette, too?"

She shrugged. "I never had anything like it before. No one I knew could do such things. I'm not a..." She frowned, trying to recall the word. "A d...dr..."

"Druid," he supplied. "That is the magic you carry. All the humans on my world are descended from Druids."

"Then I will face Villette."

Henry's eyes widened as he gave a firm shake of his head. "No. You can't. She'll kill you with a thought. Star People don't have equals. Not even the Dragon Kings. They're incredibly powerful."

"Then the dragons are doomed."

He grinned. "I didn't say we were without friends and allies."

"I hope they get here soon because Villette is on her way."

His smile vanished. "What?"

"I summoned her."

"How?"

"As I always have."

"Which is?" he asked sharply.

"I concentrate on her. It isn't long after that she appears."

"But why would you call her?"

She halfway pulled out the chair her husband had made and sat. "To confront her."

"That's not a good idea. She has a terrible temper."

"I want answers. I need to know if she lied to me."

Henry blew out a breath. "Face her another day. Leave with me. I'll take you somewhere safe."

"So I can be hunted by the dragons or one of your friends for all I've done these past years?" She shook her head. "I'll remain here and face whatever comes."

In two strides, he stood before the table. "Don't do this. Please. You can still have a life."

"We both know that's not true. If you're correct, then the dragons have reason to want justice against me."

"And if I've lied?" he asked.

She rested one arm on the table. "Then you'll die with me. Be it by Villette's hand or the dragons when they realize you won't be returning and they set fire to the valley."

"There's a third option. I could take you to my world."

Her palm flattened and skimmed over the worn grains of wood. "Leave or hide. She'll be here any moment."

A muscle worked in Henry's jaw before he looked around the cottage and took the ladder to the loft above. He wasn't even settled yet when the knock sounded.

Her gaze jerked to the door. Maybe she had been premature in summoning Villette, but it was time for the truth. No matter how, she had to find it. She lifted her chin as magic rolled through her body. "Come in."

The door swung open. Villette stood in the doorway with her long, blond hair hanging to cover the right side of her face, hiding most of the burns. "Two dragons in one week. Impressive, Katla."

She let Villette think what she would. After all, the only reason she summoned Villette was when she had a dragon. "Especially when they can change appearance to look human." She watched Villette carefully, so she saw the quick flare of surprise.

"You have a Dragon King? Where? Which one is it?" she asked excitedly.

The first confirmation. Katla softly drummed her fingers on the table to hide the fact that her hand shook. Was it fear? Anger? Excitement? Maybe all of it. Now, it was time for the rest.

THIRTY-NINE

Henry's heart thudded against his ribs as his gaze locked on Villette through the slats in the loft floor. She sat so her left side was visible to Katla. Villette's blond hair was down and draped across most of the right side of her face, but he could still make out the burns. It made him wonder what type of fire could disfigure a being as powerful as Villette.

If she could be hurt and not heal herself, then they needed to figure out what was used so *they* could use it against her.

Henry fought the urge to adjust his left hip, which had begun to hurt. He ignored the irritation and the gnawing pain and remained perfectly still. He even kept his breathing soft and shallow despite his heart thudding loudly against his ribs.

His gaze slid to the Druid. Katla. At least he had a name now. She appeared unruffled by Villette's presence, but he saw the slight tremble in her hand. He had no idea what Katla intended. Perhaps that was exactly how she wanted things. She could turn him over to Villette, but he didn't think she would. Something in her gaze had told him she was starting to believe him. Had he done enough, though? Only time would tell.

"Which King?" Villette demanded, her voice rising.

Katla stared at her for a long stretch of time. "Why didn't you tell me about them?"

"I would've shared the knowledge if I thought you needed to know. I didn't expect them to fall prey to your domain."

"Don't you think I should've been prepared for one of them should they enter the valley?" Katla pressed.

Villette shrugged her shoulders indifferently. "No being with dragon blood can enter the vines without being...castrated, as it were."

"And the females?"

Villette's eyes fairly glittered with glee. "You got your hands on Eurwen, didn't you? Oh, this is better than I could've hoped."

Henry watched Villette trail her fingers along the tabletop as she stood and walked around it. He had a good angle. If he was confident in his magic, he could take a shot at her. But how much damage could he do to a Star Person? Would it be enough to buy him time to get himself and Katla out? He could make an accurate decision if he had more time to know his strengths and limits. But without that experience, he might do more harm than good. So, he remained hidden, waiting.

"I want more," Katla said.

Villette's head swung to her. "More?"

"As you said, I've caught two dragons in one week. I want to capture more. One every so often isn't enough anymore."

A smile broke over Villette's face. "Your need to wipe out the dragons is ravenous, isn't it? I like that."

"I want those responsible for my family's death to be brought down."

Henry noted how Katla hadn't called out the dragons.

Villette drew in a breath and faced Katla as she rested her hands on the back of a chair. "The valley is yours to do with as you please."

"I'll extend deeper into their territory," the Druid said.

"Don't be overeager," Villette warned. "Take it from me and go slow enough that you don't raise suspicions. By the time they notice anything, it'll be too late."

Henry fisted his hands, his anger churning in his gut like a black cloud. What else was Villette involved in that the dragons hadn't noticed? It could be anything. Bloody hell. He needed to get back to Melisse so he could tell her everything. The Kings needed to prepare.

Katla rose to her feet. "That's good advice, but it doesn't help me lure more than one in at a time."

"I'm sure you'll come up with something. Take me to your latest captive."

"One more thing," Katla said.

Villette's face hardened. "I don't like to be kept waiting."

"Take me with you this time. I want to see what you do with the dragons."

Blue eyes studied the Druid for a silent minute. "Why?"

"As you pointed out, I'm bloodthirsty. I want to end my enemies once and for all. This...dragon...spoke. I want to see it hurt. I *need* to see its life drained."

She was so convincing that Henry began to doubt which side Katla was on. Maybe he was the one getting played.

Villette considered her request. "Eurwen will attempt to say anything to get free. You can't believe anything that comes out of her mouth."

"I'm more concerned with the fact that dragons can now change shape and look like us."

"Not all of them." Villette paused, considering. "All right. I'll bring you just this once. Now, let's get our prisoner."

Villette was the first out of the cottage. Katla paused at the door and looked up, meeting Henry's gaze. Then she was gone, and the door closed behind her.

Henry released a breath but didn't move. Not yet. Not until he was sure they were gone. He counted out three minutes before pushing up on his hands and swinging his legs to the ladder. The soft creak of wood was the only sound as he climbed down with his bag over one shoulder. Once his feet were on the floor, he hurried to the window.

The few candles that burned cast large swaths of light but also left some of the interior in shadow. He kept to them as he tried to look out the open shutters to the outside. Henry caught the sound of the women walking away.

"Rhi," he said as loudly as he dared.

His patience was threadbare. He had to get to the Kings and Lotti and fill everyone in quickly before Villette realized there wasn't another dragon. Henry looked around, but there was no sign of Rhi. He called her name again, louder than before. It should reach her.

When another minute passed without the Fae's appearance, Henry slipped out of the hut. The vines shifted, opening a path for him that led away from Katla and Villette. He hoped it took him out of the valley. He broke into a run, pushing himself as hard as

he could, all the while trusting the vines that had saved him
before.

Something was wrong. No matter how many times she tried,
Melisse couldn't shake the feeling. Her gaze swept the valley in
hopes of seeing something, anything. There was nothing, just as
before. Why, then, did she know that something had gone awry?

She chanced a look at the ground where Rhi stood with Con
and a handful of other Kings. Eurwen and Vaughn were on the
mountain across from her. Melisse had no idea where Brandr was,
but she knew he was close. She shifted positions, her unease
growing by the second. Suddenly, Rhi was beside her.

"Henry called to me. He's inside the vines."

Melisse's stomach clenched painfully. Was he being attacked?
Was he hurt? Dying? She leaned forward, intent on jumping and
shifting to go to him, but Rhi grabbed her arm before she could.

"He didn't sound injured," Rhi quickly said. "He sounded
aggravated. Edgy. But not hurt."

That was a small comfort. "He still called for you. That means
something happened."

"It means he wants out."

"As I said, something happened." Melisse pulled from Rhi's
grasp and looked at the valley that seemed to stretch endlessly north.

Rhi stated, "You know you can't go in there."

"I can't stay here and do nothing." She looked at the Light Fae.
"You wouldn't if it was Con."

"No, I wouldn't. I would move mountains for Con."

Melisse nodded. "Then you understand."

"I do. What do you plan?"

"I don't know yet."

Rhi shot her a soft smile. "Good luck. We'll do all we can."

"I know."

Melisse hesitated for a heartbeat before shifting. There was still a small kernel of doubt in her mind that she couldn't, but it was quickly extinguished with her transformation. She then dove from the mountain and spread her wings to soar over the others before maneuvering to the vines. She flew alongside the border, her eyes searching beyond for any signs of Henry. If she spotted him, she would fly to him, regardless of where he was, no matter if she had to cross the border. She knew what that would risk, but she didn't care. War was coming anyway.

She didn't want to be the one to set off that chain of events, but she couldn't—wouldn't—leave Henry to such despicable people.

Back and forth, she flew. Waiting for what, she wasn't sure. But something was coming.

Lotti stood at the northernmost point of the valley with the mountains two steps at her back. The vines were a single step ahead. They felt different than before. She put out a hand and was able to touch one of the brambles. The last time, she hadn't been able to do even that much.

If she could touch them, then that meant she could enter the vine forest. And if she could enter, then Villette was there.

She didn't waste a second jumping to Jeyra's and then Esha's locations. If they were surprised to see her, they said nothing. It never even dawned on her to worry about teleporting the three of them together. She just did it, situating them in the middle of the valley. Two pairs of eyes were on her, waiting.

Lotti motioned for them to follow her, and they did without question. Jeyra wore the dragon eye mark on her shoulder that pronounced she had undergone the mating ceremony to her King and was bound to him, living for as long as he did. Lotti and Esha had not had their ceremonies yet. It would be up to Lotti to get Esha away if Villette turned her attention on the elf. Kendrick would never forgive her if something happened to his mate.

There was another question, though. One that no one dared to ask—not even her. Could a Star Person kill a mate with a mark? If a mated King died, then his wife would also die. That bond was supposed to keep the wives alive and, for all intents and purposes, immortal. The link hadn't been tested against a Star Person, however.

That niggled in Lotti's mind as she found an easy path through the vines. It was night, and while night, the low-hanging clouds kept the darkness from penetrating completely. She spotted the tangled brambles Melisse and Henry had talked about on either side of them. Yet their path was clear. As unobstructed as the one Henry had mentioned that'd led him and Melisse out of the valley.

Henry had suggested that the vines were sentient. Lotti had been inclined to believe before, but she was positive of it now. Even the huge thorns weren't visible near them. She noted their sharp points and could only imagine how having one prick her skin would feel. Hopefully, she wouldn't find out.

She picked up her pace to a jog, a sudden urgency filling the air and propelling her forward. The three of them moved as silently as ghosts through the valley, each ready and prepared for battle.

Jeyra's exceptional skills as a warrior made her a deadly enemy, as did the sword in her hand, while Esha's Sun Elf magic was spectacular to watch.

Lotti knew they wouldn't be enough to bring down Villette, but that wasn't the plan for tonight. That would come later. This was more of a test. They needed to know how far they could go against Villette because none of Lotti's friends were willing to test their magic on her.

Then there was the Druid. Lotti wasn't sure she could be saved. She would give Henry time to change the Druid's mind, but that would come down to the Druid. Lotti wouldn't hesitate to leave her behind to save Henry and the others. And after what all the Druid had done, maybe that was for the best.

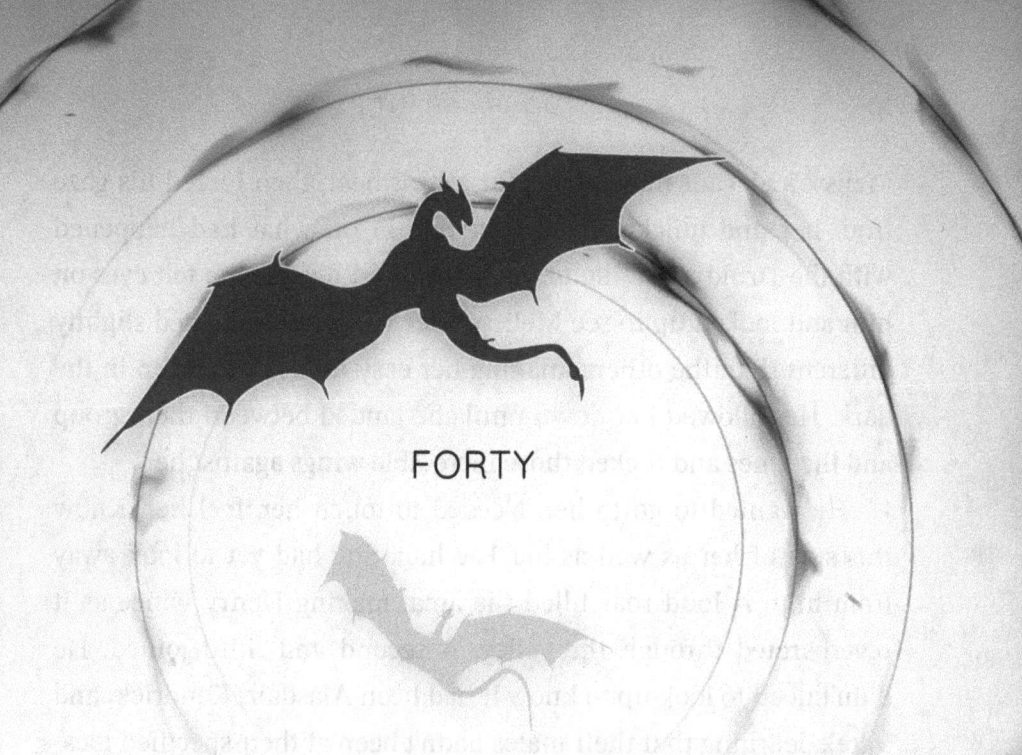

FORTY

Henry burst from the vines and came to a halt as he stared at the side of a mountain curving sharply upward. He was breathing heavily as he looked one way and then the other. Lotti was to the north, and everyone else to the south. He wasn't sure which was closer.

"Rhi," he called as loudly as he dared.

In a blink, the Fae stood before him. "Thank the stars," she said and reached for him.

Henry stepped back. "Take me to Lotti. Villette is here."

Rhi hesitated only a moment and then jumped them to the north. Except Lotti wasn't there. Jeyra and Esha weren't in their positions either. Rhi said nothing as she teleported him to the rest of the group across the border.

"Henry," Con said and turned to him.

But Henry's gaze was locked on the dragons overhead. The light of the two moons glistened on violet scales. He watched

Melisse's elegant movements for a heartbeat, then forced his gaze from her and quickly filled everyone in on what had happened with the Druid and Villette. As he finished his tale, he felt eyes on him and looked up to see Melisse. Her wings were shaped slightly different than the others, making her easy to pick out, even in the dark. He followed her down until she landed between their group and the vines and tucked those incredible wings against her.

He wanted to go to her. Needed to touch her, feel her. Know this side of her as well as her Fae half. She had yet to look away from him. A loud roar filled the area, making Henry wince as it reverberated through the valley. A second and third joined. He didn't need to look up to know it had been Alasdair, Kendrick, and Varek, learning that their mates hadn't been at their specified locations. There were two reasons they wouldn't be there.

They had either left on their own.

Or Villette had taken them.

"Is the Druid on our side?"

It took a second for Henry to realize that Con spoke to him. He met the King of King's gaze. "My gut says she is."

"She lied about having another dragon captured. That confirmed it for me," Rhi said.

Con looked at the brambles. "Then the Druid will face the wrath of Villette on her own."

"There's nothing we can do about that." Rhi shrugged. "She made her choice."

Henry took a step toward Melisse, the urge to speak with her nearly overriding everything else. "You're forgetting about Lotti and the others."

"Hardly," Con said, standing shoulder to shoulder with him to face the vine forest. "If Villette had seen Lotti, we would've heard or seen a skirmish. The fact that Lotti isna here tells me she ventured into the vines. Which makes sense if Villette is there."

Rhi moved up beside Con. "Then all we can do is wait."

"The Druid has a plan," Henry said. "We need to be ready for whatever that is."

He didn't wait for a reply as he walked to Melisse. Her head turned back to him, and she observed his approach. When he had nearly reached her, she shifted, returning to her Fae form, and waited for him to reach her. The black-tipped ends of her silver hair lifted in the cold breeze, and her eyes blazed with anger and disappointment. He had known she would be incensed by his actions, but he would do it all over again if it kept her safe.

When he stood in front of her, he had to force his arms to remain at his sides instead of reaching for her. He didn't know how much time they had before Villette realized what was going on, but he needed to know where they stood. "I know you're furious," he began.

"You don't know what I am since you didn't bother to ask. You left. While I slept."

"I won't apologize for doing what I thought I needed to do to protect you. I will always do that. But," he added when her mouth opened to speak, "you're right. I should've talked to you about it."

"Aye. You should have," she stated angrily. Then she blew out a breath. "I feared you..."

She didn't finish. She didn't need to. He understood exactly what she meant. He pulled her against him and closed his eyes at the feeling of her arms around him.

"I know. I'm sorry," he whispered. They stood in silence for a moment. Then he said, "I think my gamble paid off."

Melisse leaned back to look at his face. "Con relayed everything, though he condensed it to save time."

"I'll go into all the details later. Suffice it to say, the Druid is taking a chance with her life."

"I'm not sure I can feel any sympathy after what I endured."

He slid his hands down her arm and entwined his fingers with hers. "She let her hatred fester. She wasn't the first, and she won't be the last, but her eyes are open now."

"I saw something when I was in the air. The dome we were under. It's still standing."

"Katla is leading Villette to where a supposed dragon is being held."

"Who?" Melisse asked.

Henry glanced at the vines. "Katla. The Druid. That's her name. I think she's taking Villette to the dome. It makes sense. Villette wouldn't be able to see through it to know it was empty."

"I need to get up there to keep an eye on it and notify the others of your theory."

He pressed his lips to hers for a lingering kiss before reluctantly letting her go. "Be safe."

"You, too."

She moved back. He blinked, and then she was in the sky, her wings churning the air so forcibly that it caused him to take a step back just to remain on his feet. He watched her rise swiftly. She had a great vantage point, but he could see nothing over the towering vines. Nothing while he stood on the ground, anyway.

He turned to the side to look up at the mountain on his left and then the one on his right. Each of them would be a good lookout, but that was all he could do there. And even then, he would have to wait until the sun rose to truly see anything since he didn't have a dragon's eyesight.

Another whoosh of air hit him from behind. He stumbled forward and turned in time to see golden scales. Con soared upward, Rhi on his back. Soon, the King of Kings wove among the other dragons in the sky, circling the brambles. Henry looked to the vines once more. Everything that would happen would occur in the valley.

Even Lotti, Jeyra, and Esha were there. He might be a novice with magic, but he could do some good.

"You made it out twice. You want to test it a third time?" asked a deep voice from behind him.

Henry looked over his shoulder to find Brandr striding up. "I might be able to help."

"You have. More than any of us."

"Like you said, I've gotten out twice. I should be in there helping Lotti and the others."

Brandr shoved a hand through his longish black hair to get the strands out of his face. "With every second that passes, tension ratchets. Things are about to come to a head."

"All the more reason to go in."

"I'm no' going to stop you, but did you ever think that perhaps this is exactly where you were meant to be?"

Henry opened his mouth to reply, but Brandr lifted a hand to quiet him. His face went stony as his gaze locked on the vines. Henry followed Brandr's gaze, but he saw nothing.

"Listen," Brandr said softly.

Henry shook his head. He was about to say he couldn't hear anything when a soft creak and then a groan reached him. He knew that sound. The vines were moving.

Melisse kept her gaze on the dome. That was why it took her time to realize that the vines closest to Henry and Brandr were beginning to move away. They slithered like snakes but with such rapid movement it was difficult to keep up with them.

"Down the middle!" Evander's voice shouted in her head.

She, like every other dragon, looked toward the middle of the valley. She caught sight of the trail that hadn't been there before. Melisse looked down the path but didn't see any movement. She had to circle around for another look. Her gaze darted to the dome again. For just a moment, she thought she saw sparks.

Lotti held up her hand to let the others know something was ahead, but they'd already slowed. Whether they sensed or heard it, she didn't know. Her steps halted. Suddenly, two more paths opened, veering from hers. She looked back at Jeyra and Esha. Jeyra motioned that she would take the path to the left. Esha pointed to the right.

They soon disappeared into the vines. Lotti continued onward. She could make out voices now. She knew one immediately. Villette. This wasn't their first encounter, and as much as she wished it would be their last, she didn't think it would be. But they had an advantage today. That was enough to make Lotti smile.

The vines moved stealthily, but Katla still heard them. Then again, she knew the vines like no one else did. She wanted to glance over her shoulder at Villette. Somehow, she kept her gaze forward until they reached the dome. If Villette heard the plants moving, she didn't say anything.

"What did Eurwen say to you exactly?" Villette asked.

It was by sheer will alone that Katla kept her fingers from curling into fists. She halted at the dome and turned to Villette. "A number of things."

"Such as?"

"That there were human settlements all over Zora."

Villette's hair kept her face hidden as she investigated the dome. "Hmm."

Katla's fury mounted, roiling through her. "Are there?"

"A few."

Tears of outrage and resentment burned her eyes, but she held the emotions in check. Barely. It wouldn't last much longer. Then again, she didn't need it to. "I thought I was the last."

Villette laughed and cast a quick glance at her. "I did tell you that, didn't I? I'd forgotten. Oh, well. It doesn't matter. Your kind breed quickly and indiscriminately. The population swells no matter how many times I trim it back."

Trim it back. The words reverberated in Katla's head like a bell. She stared at Villette, the person she had once thought of as a savior, a friend. The one who had helped her put her life back together again.

But it had all been a sham. And she had fallen into it so easily. It hadn't taken more than a few words.

The moment Villette disappeared around the side of the dome,

Katla lifted her hand and shot sparks into the air. She hoped it was a good enough sign for Henry and whoever else might be looking.

"This is magnificent," Villette said as she reemerged from around the other side of the dome. "The vines created the perfect confinement. Not that Eurwen would get far with the poison in her system and no magic." She nodded to the dome. "Open it. I want my prize."

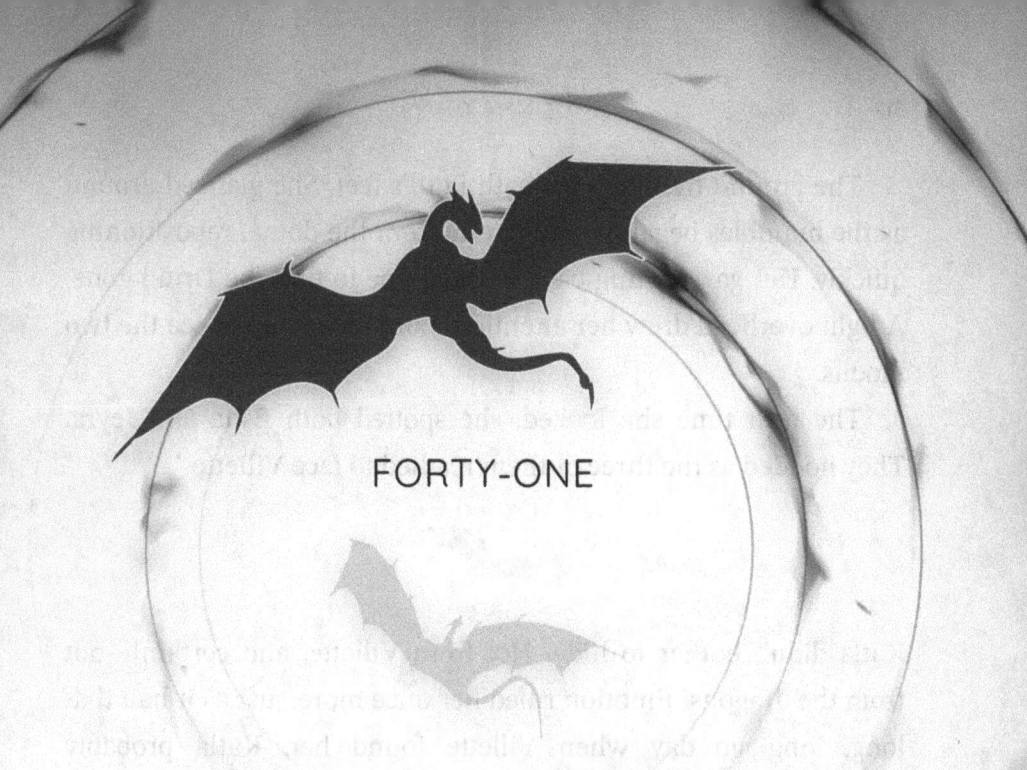

FORTY-ONE

When she spotted two women, Lotti realized why the vines hadn't opened a path for her. She recognized Villette easily. The other must be the Druid. Lotti silently moved behind Villette. The only thing separating them was the brambles. Villette was oblivious to the hostility the Druid directed at her.

The Druid clenched her hands into fists, but not before Lotti saw sparks shoot from her fingertips. Villette's gaze was on the dome, confident that everything was in hand as it had always been. That overconfidence, the hubris, would be Villette's downfall. Lotti intended to use it against her nemesis now, but she wasn't sure if it would be enough to bring down Villette once and for all.

Lotti barely had time to wonder if the vines had brought Esha and Jeyra near when the brambles making up the dome shifted to open and create an entrance. Villette smiled expectantly and ducked inside. Almost immediately, the vines locked her in. It wouldn't hold her. Not nearly long enough.

The ground trembled beneath Lotti's feet. She glanced around as the brambles began moving away from the dome, repositioning quickly. Her gaze swung back to the dome to find the Druid gone. A light overhead drew her attention. Lotti looked up to see the two moons.

The next time she looked, she spotted both Esha and Jeyra. They nodded as the three of them readied to face Villette.

Katla didn't bother to hide. Not from Villette, and certainly not from the dragons. Emotion ruled her once more, just as it had that long, long-ago day when Villette found her. Katla probably should've learned her lesson. Then again, maybe this was just who she was.

She wanted to right the wrongs done to so many. And not just by Villette. By herself, as well.

The vines had pulled back from the border to behind the dome. Katla spotted sprouts of green stretching outward in all directions from the etching in the ground. Henry had brought life to the valley, where she had only brought death and destruction. That wasn't the person she'd been, the mother she had been.

She saw herself through Villette's eyes and was disgusted. Appalled.

Horrified.

Katla looked across the bare expanse of ground toward the border. Dragons flew in a mesmerizing pattern, barely missing each other as they watched the scene unfold. Her gaze lowered, and she discerned two male figures standing together. She recognized Henry. The other was one she had spied on earlier.

A rageful scream suddenly permeated from the dome behind her. Katla turned her back to the dragons and prepared for Villette's wrath. A heartbeat later, the dome exploded violently. Katla ducked on instinct and called to her magic to protect her, just as bits of vine and thorns hurtled toward her. The remnants of the dome smacked the ground as Katla straightened. Her gaze connected with Villette's.

Katla lifted her chin defiantly and welcomed the magic that flowed into her hands.

"Hold."

Con's voice was firm and unyielding in Melisse's head. They had a chance at Villette, and she wanted to take it. Melisse dipped her wing and swung around sharply. It would be so easy to slip over the border and take her shot at Villette. They could end this clash today.

"Hold," Con repeated.

Melisse growled her frustration. The others obeyed without question. Even Eurwen held her position in the air. Melisse was older than all of them, but she was the greenest in battle. And for just a moment, she contemplated disregarding Con. He wasn't her King. Then she thought about her father. He had once held Con's position, and her father had demanded the same obedience. So, she begrudgingly stayed where she was.

The howl of rage from Villette reverberated around the valley. They waited on tenterhooks to see her reaction. Melisse had to give the Druid credit. She hadn't run. In fact, she stood her ground.

Villette lifted her gaze and looked at each of the dragons. Melisse knew the instant Villette's gaze moved to her. It lingered for a moment as if putting her to memory before sliding away. That look made Melisse's scales crawl with unease.

Brandr kept his gaze on Villette. She seethed with blatant indignation. The tension heightened. The air crackled with outrage. Sparks shot from the Druid's fingers as she raised her hands. But Villette was faster. A blast of magic slammed into the Druid and tossed her far and high. She smashed into the ground behind Brandr, bounced once, and rolled a few times before coming to a stop, unmoving.

Then all hell broke loose as Villette strode toward the border, hurling magic at the dragons.

They did their best to evade Villette's magic. Melisse opened her mouth, but instead of fire, a cone of burning venom shot from her. Villette dodged it. Kendrick was grazed, and Villette zeroed in on him. He had no choice but to camouflage himself to avoid most of the strikes.

Brandr started toward Villette when Eurwen was suddenly tossed back against the mountain, her roar of pain deafening. She managed to get back into the air and use her ability to shield herself.

He shifted and jumped into the air, then dove between Villette and Con. Brandr called to his power and sent her blast harmlessly to the side before it could reach his father.

Henry wanted to do something instead of standing around. Katla was unmoving and likely dead. He couldn't help her now. No one could. Brandr was doing a good job of deflecting Villette's magic, but she was quick and powerful, and he couldn't be everywhere at once.

A roar stopped abruptly. Henry looked up to see Varek plummeting from above. Shaw caught him and held on until Varek shook off the magic and could fly on his own again. Just as relief went through Henry, he winced as Kendrick got hit. Then Cullen. Then Eurwen, a second time.

Rhi hurled orbs of Fae magic from Con's back, a few hitting their mark. Until Villette's aim locked on her. Henry watched in horror as the blast knocked Rhi off, and she tumbled toward the ground. Con dove after her, but Brandr reached her first.

They outnumbered Villette, but she was dealing blow after blow. Henry stepped forward but paused to glance at his hands. He didn't have magic now that he was out of the vines. The only thing he could do was pull her attention to him. It might give everyone enough time to focus all they had on Villette.

Henry's head jerked up when a roar of pain filled the air. Dread filled him as he helplessly watched Villette strike Alasdair over and over, sending him crashing backward into the mountainside. The impact sent rock raining down. Henry dodged one, only to trip over another and fall. He rolled onto his back to see a huge boulder headed straight for him—and an unconscious Alasdair right behind it.

There was no time to get away. This was it. This was how he would die. Henry thought about Melisse and the short time they'd had together. He raised his hands to reach out toward Melisse. Except magic pooled in his palms. Somehow, he managed to halt the boulder, but there was nothing he could do about Alasdair. Henry tossed the rock aside and braced for impact.

He felt a whoosh of air and looked up to find Alasdair flying to meet the others. Relief surged through Henry. His heart raced uncontrollably as he sat up and spotted Lotti, Esha, and Jeyra emerging from the vines behind Villette. He jerked his gaze to her, but she had no idea the trio was there. It gave them an advantage. Too bad they didn't have more.

Henry looked at the boulder he had stopped and tossed to the side. Jumping to his feet, he urged his magic to him. But nothing happened. He tried again, focusing everything on his magic.

Still nothing.

Something flew above him. He felt the tremor and looked up to see Melisse hit the mountain. His heart felt as if someone had reached into his chest and squeezed it when her wing crumpled and she dropped. Henry jerked out his arms, intent on stopping her as he had the boulder, but the magic failed him again. He had no choice but to get out of the way as she continued to bounce against the mountain, battering her body on the way down.

She landed with a thud, unmoving. He stared in shock at her broken wings. Then rocks she had dislodged pelted her. A boulder headed straight toward her head. Magic rushed through his arms. He caught it, just before it slammed into her.

This time, he knew exactly where to throw it.

His magic felt strong and clear as he faced Villette, who had a smile on her face as she delivered blow after blow to the dragons.

Henry used everything he had to heave the boulder. It struck Villette, knocking her sideways.

Lotti kept her attention on Villette. The glee on her nemesis's face as she hurt the others was like a knife twisting in Lotti's heart. She wanted to make herself known immediately, but Jeyra had held her hand up for them to wait.

Lotti wasn't waiting anymore.

She stepped from the vines. Villette shoved the boulder off her and unsteadily got to her feet. Villette's gaze locked on Henry, but before she could retaliate, Jeyra moved from the brambles and sent her sword flying through the air. It impaled Villette through the side.

Villette released a bellow of fury and swung toward Jeyra, right as Esha unleashed her elven magic. The golden glow of it arched slightly and then enveloped Villette from behind, bringing her to one knee.

Lotti had kept tight control of her anger while she watched her mate and friends get struck again and again. Villette had been toying with them. But Lotti had no intention of playing with her enemy. Villette shrieked in outrage as she yanked the sword out, her chest heaving.

"My turn," Lotti said.

Villette's head snapped to the side. She attempted to get to her feet as Lotti released a barrage of magic. Lotti didn't relent, even when Villette's magic clashed with hers.

Then the others joined in. Varek sent energy-draining shadows to swarm Villette, while Shaw used illusions to confuse her. Con doused her with fire.

They were weakening her, Lotti could feel it.

Henry could see the tide turning in their favor. They were going to defeat Villette. No one had believed it possible, but it was happening right before his eyes. He silently urged the others on as he added his magic to theirs.

Then Lotti suddenly went flying back into the vines. A roar of agony came from a dragon. Henry saw Shaw struggling to stay in the air. One by one, the dragons were struck. Henry lowered his arms. Villette stood, her arms raised above her head, her fingers spread as magic shot from each of them.

Everyone attempted to regroup, but Henry knew they wouldn't do it in time. This was his chance to pull Villette's attention to him. He started forward when movement caught his attention out of the corner of his eye. Katla strode to Villette. The moment she reached her, the Druid put her hands on Villette's head and sparks erupted.

Villette grabbed Katla and pummeled her with magic, but the Druid wouldn't release her. The sparks became bigger and more intense as they swarmed Villette and then Katla until neither could be seen. The light became brighter and brighter until it exploded.

Henry raised his arm to shield his face until the light faded. When he chanced a look, both were gone. He immediately rushed to Melisse. She hadn't moved since her fall. He put a hand on her scales, unsure what to do. Could she heal herself? He looked for Con and saw everyone tending to themselves and their mates.

"Melisse," Henry said. "I need you to come back to me. It's over." For now, at least. "Return to your Fae form if you can."

Her breathing quickened, and her eyelids lifted. He stared into bright blue dragon eyes and smiled. "There you are. You had me worried. Can you shift back?"

A moment later, she lay naked beside him.

Henry yanked off his coat and laid it over her. "Do you hurt?"

"Yes," she croaked.

"It'll be all right. Give yourself time to heal."

She reached for him. He threaded their fingers and brought her hand against his chest. After another minute, she rolled partway onto her back and looked up at him with her whitish eyes.

He leaned over her. "I love you."

Her eyes flared in surprise before she smiled. "I love you, too."

"I know."

"You do?"

"I've been paying attention," he whispered, then placed his lips on hers.

FORTY-TWO

The morning sun was bright, the sky clear. Evidence of the battle lay all around them, but they were all alive. Melisse still hurt, but her body had healed. Con offered to hurry it along, but she needed to make sure she was the same as she had been before she went into the vines.

The Kings looked for Katla, while Henry, Lotti, and a few other mates searched the valley and the Druid's home. So far, she was nowhere to be found. Neither was Villette. No one yet dared to declare Villette dead, but everyone suspected the Druid likely was.

Melisse had to admit that Katla's death went a long way in making up for the pain she'd caused the dragons over the centuries. Henry had done what he'd set out to do. He had put enough doubt in the Druid's mind to cause her to question things, which had, thankfully, ended with Katla fighting on their side.

Her gaze searched for Henry as she flew near the border. The clouds over the valley had receded. Melisse didn't know the reason, and she really didn't care. She caught sight of Henry making his way back to the border with the others. Her heart missed a beat as she remembered his declaration of love.

She glided to the ground and shifted once she landed to wait for Henry. She spied Brandr standing alone and walked to him. He looked pensive as he stared at the brambles in the distance. His head swung to her as she neared.

"Would you rather be alone?" she asked.

"Just thinking about what happened here. I wish we had proof about Villette one way or the other."

"I'm sure we will get some soon. She'll want us to know if she's alive."

He grunted. "How are you feeling?"

"Like I took a fall."

"I bet," he said with a quick grin as he faced her. "You're healing?"

She nodded. "Oddly, shifting helped."

"Interesting. I'll try and remember that if I'm ever in a similar situation." He scratched his cheek. "We've no' really had a chance to talk, but I'd like to change that. Eurwen and I would like to sit down with you and compare our...abilities, if you will. See what we have that's alike and what's different. There might be things we can do that you can no' that we could teach you, and vice versa."

"I'd like that. I've felt rather disconnected from everyone. That is partly my fault." She shrugged and glanced away. "I wasn't sure I belonged anywhere, so I kept myself separate. Con and the Kings did everything they could to make me feel welcome. I don't blame them. How I've been is my fault."

Brandr's shoulders rose as he drew in a breath. "I understand. It's one of the reasons Eurwen and I came here. It was easier. Cowardly, too, if I'm being honest. It wasna fair to our parents, or us, to keep our existence from them. That's finished, though. We've moved on. Or at least Eurwen has. I'm trying."

"I think you're doing a good job. From the few hours I've seen," she said with a teasing grin.

He chuckled. "Oh, you're going to fit in well."

Their conversation ended as the Kings descended and landed around them. Everyone stood waiting for the others to return. It took longer than Melisse liked, but finally, Henry emerged from the vines. His face split into a wide grin when he saw her. She made her way to him, meeting him at the border. He crossed and pulled her into his arms for a long, heated kiss.

"I'm ready for a few weeks of just us," he said as he pulled back to look into her eyes. "No interruptions. No demands. Just you laid out naked on the bed so I can have my way with you. But first, we need to talk."

"Yes, we do."

"I should've talked to you about my plans to go to Katla instead of slipping away. I knew you would want to come."

"I would have, but I might have understood your reasoning for going alone. We'll never know, though, because you didn't give me a chance."

"I know. I thought it was the right thing to do at the time. It won't happen again."

She sighed. "It'd better not. From either of us."

"You have my word."

"And mine." She gave him a quick kiss. "Now that that's out of the way. I take it you didn't locate the Druid?"

Henry shook his head, his grin fading. "There's no trace of Katla or Villette, at least that we can find. I take it you didn't fare any better?"

"Nothing."

Henry glanced up and froze. Then he turned her around. Melisse looked up to see about forty dragons atop the mountains, watching them.

She cleared her throat and said loud enough for the others, "Um...we have company."

Brandr was the first to follow her gaze. He said nothing as he shifted and took to the skies. Eurwen followed a moment later. As soon as the two were in the air, the dragons jumped from their perches and joined them.

"Are they talking?" Henry asked.

Melisse shook her head. "Not that I can hear."

"I wonder how much they saw," Esha stated.

Con twisted his lips. "I'd be happy if they realized what we did today."

"Let's hope they have." Vaughn watched Eurwen.

Alasdair said, "I think we can call this a win. We're all still here, and whether Villette is alive or no', we hurt her. To that, I suggest we join the others at Iron Hall where I hear a feast awaits."

Lotti and Rhi jumped many to the hidden city, but Melisse lingered. Once she and Henry were alone, she turned to him. "I thought I'd fly us."

"You want me to ride?" Henry asked.

She nodded, wondering if she should've asked first. "If you don't want to I ca—"

He yanked her to him and kissed her, then smiled down at her. "Oh, I want to."

"All right. I promise not to make any sudden movements that might knock you off."

"I trust you. Shift. I want an unfettered view of you."

Exhilaration shot through her. Had her mother been as excited to see her father? Had her dad been as thrilled as she was at that very moment? She suspected he had been. A piece of her heart would always ache at how her parents had died—Osric, too—but she could turn to her memories with fondness now. And perhaps, one day, she might no longer feel responsible. But that would take time and a lot of inner-healing work. She was ready for that now. Just as she was ready to see what was in store for her and Henry.

She released her dragon form. It happened as quickly and seamlessly as one breath following another. She towered over Henry as she looked down to see his lips softening into a smile, wonder in his gaze. She remained still as he slowly walked around her, caressing her leg, her wing, her tail, and then around to the other side before he stood in front of her.

"Wow," he murmured.

She lowered so he could climb her arm and onto her back. After he was settled, she stood. She liked how his hands felt on her scales. She even enjoyed the weight of him. For so long, she had felt as if the world were crowded around her, confining her. She had broken through the pain and misery to find hope and love.

And so many possibilities just waiting to be experienced.

Melisse jumped into the air and unfurled her wings, rapidly flapping them to take them higher. She glanced back at the vines. Alasdair had called the battle a win, but it wasn't. A youngling was still missing. Melisse hadn't found the Pink, but she wouldn't stop looking. She had made a promise, after all.

The flight to Iron Hall was as exhilarating for her as it was for Henry. She felt it in his touch and heard his shouts of delight when she took them high and then soared low over the land. She wasn't ready for it to end when they reached the eastern border at

Raynia Canyon. She descended gradually. When she landed, Henry slid from her back. She'd shifted into her Fae form before he even landed.

Then she was in his arms, his kiss hungry and urgent as his hands smoothed down her back and over her arse to yank her against him. Desire burned through her veins. She clung to him as he rocked his erection against her stomach.

They were breathing heavily when the kiss ended, her fingers still twisted in his coat. She swallowed, her body aching to finish what they'd started.

"Fuck," he growled hoarsely. "I should've waited until we were in our room to do that."

She became ridiculously happy that he had said *our* room. "No one is around."

"Don't tempt me."

Melisse looked into his heavy-lidded eyes. "I don't think anyone will mind if we're a little late to the festivities." She smoothed her hand down his front to his thick arousal.

"Now. Let's go inside now."

"Or...we can stay right here," she said and stepped out of his arms, shimmying out of her coat.

Melisse saw something big and black move out of the corner of her eye. She turned her head and locked gazes with the huge beast, its green eyes watching them as it sat, the end of its long tail lazily moving back and forth.

"Please tell me that's Cullen's pet wildcat," Henry said in a soft voice.

She shrugged and looked at the black-on-black-spotted fur. "That might be Nari."

"It's a big as a fucking lion."

"Maybe we should go inside," Melisse said.

Henry took her hand. "I think I'd feel better without a wildcat watching me so…"

"Ravenously?"

"Yes. That."

She laughed as they walked across the border to the canyon. As they climbed down, she told Henry about her conversation with Brandr.

"That's brilliant," Henry said while walking to the hidden doors. "I'm happy for you."

Melisse pulled him to a stop before they entered the city. "What about you? What will you do?"

"I don't know."

That's what she'd feared he might say. "You proved how valuable you are here. That should allow you to remain."

"Maybe, but I also have duties on Earth."

"Then I'll go with you."

Henry cupped her face, his thumb brushing over her lower lip. "You're needed here."

"I don't want us to be apart."

He stepped closer so their bodies were together. "We'll figure it out. If Balladyn can be with Rhona on Skye and return to the Reapers when he's needed, there's no reason the two of us can't figure something out."

"We do have the Fae doorway."

"That does make things easy." He grinned. "The dragons need to be on your side. Having humans—or anyone in human form—coming onto their land, no matter the reason, isn't helping. I'll stay for as long as I'm able and return as often as I can."

"Nay."

His brows drew together. "Do you want a set time? What if I remain on Earth for a week? We can try that."

"That isn't what I mean. We stay together. If you're needed on Earth, then I'll go with you. If I have to return here, then you come with me. I think we've both earned that, don't you?"

"Definitely." He rested his forehead on hers. "I love you."

She wound her arms around his neck and kissed him. "I love you."

"There you two are," Tamlyn said as she poked her head out the doors. "We're all waiting for you. Con was about to send out a search party."

Henry linked their fingers together as they made their way to her.

"I heard there's also some announcement coming from Rhi," Tamlyn added after she closed the doors behind them.

Melisse ducked her head and tried to hide her smile.

"What do you know?" Henry whispered.

She met his gaze. "It's good news. Trust me."

"Always," Henry replied with a squeeze of his hand.

"I found them!" Tamlyn shouted as she hurried around Melisse.

There was a loud cheer from the common room as she and Henry descended the steps. She looked over the smiling faces and knew that she had not only found her place, but also her family.

And her mate.

Somewhere out in the universe, her parents were smiling. Their love had spanned realms. She looked at Henry. As had hers.

He gave her a slow, sexy smile and wrapped an arm around her as everyone surrounded them.

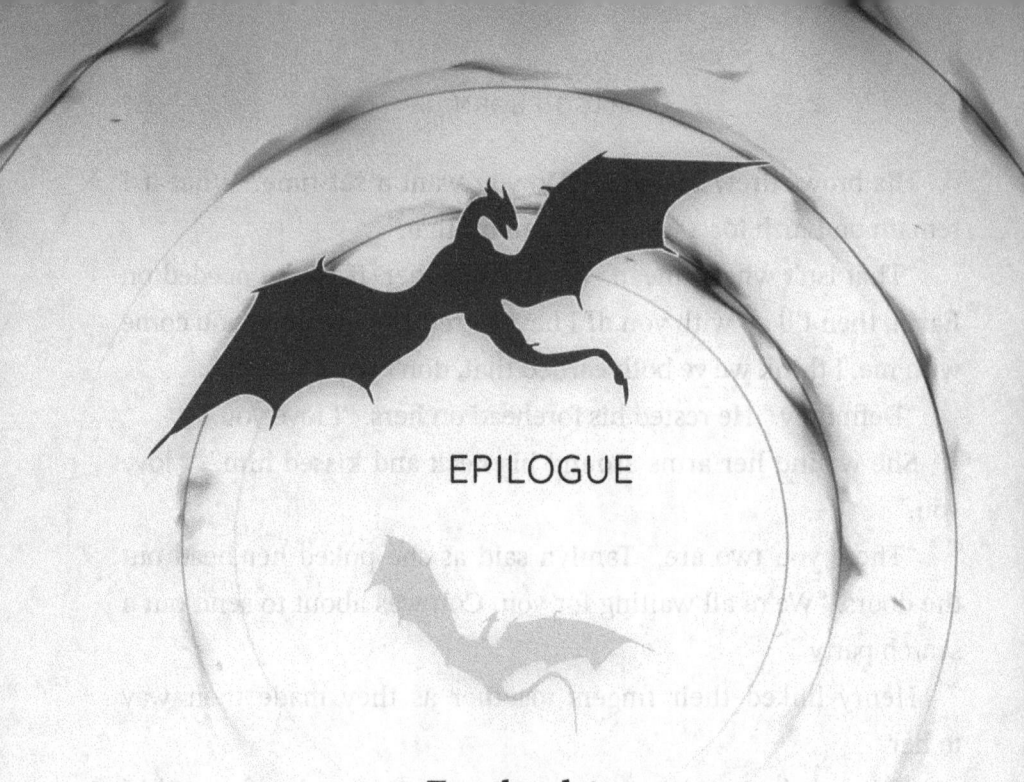

EPILOGUE

Two days later…

Henry sat on the edge of the canyon, watching Melisse, Brandr, and Eurwen test their magic as half-Fae and half-dragon. They had many similarities, but there were also differences. Things on Zora had been quiet, allowing him and Melisse to spend a lot of time together. Everyone knew it was just a lull.

"Do you mind if I join you?"

He looked up at the deep brogue and saw Con. "Not at all."

The King of Kings sat beside him and watched the trio below for a long moment. "I wondered if I'd ever see Melisse so at ease. She's happy."

"We both are."

"That much is obvious to everyone." Con glanced his way, a grin in place. "I'm pleased for you both. We all are."

Henry leaned back on his hands and studied Con's profile. "But?"

"No buts," Con replied. Then he looked at Henry. "I give you my word."

"Maybe not a but. Still, you're concerned about something."

Con's black gaze held his. "I'm always worried and considering the possibilities with our adversaries. Comes with the job title."

"You want to know how long I intend to remain on Zora."

"Nay. Melisse informed me what the two of you decided. I think it's the best answer as long as it works."

Now Henry was confused. "Then what?"

"Your magic."

"Ah." He hadn't thought much about it since leaving the valley behind. Odd since he'd spent the past years agonizing over the fact that he didn't have any.

Con turned his head to watch the twins and Melisse again. "You may no' have it once you leave Zora. You should be prepared for that." He paused. "You're important to us regardless of whether your sister is mated to a King or you have magic or no'." Con's gaze slid back to him. "Whether you are Melisse's mate or no'. You understand that, right?"

Henry sat up and nodded. "It took coming here to learn that, but yes, I do."

"You're family, Henry. You were from the moment you accepted us for who we were. You will *always* be family."

"Thank you."

Con climbed to his feet. "There's been a message from Earth. It seems you and Melisse will need to return."

"Skye Druids?" Henry asked as he stood.

Con nodded. "Sounds as if things are getting worse. Let me know if you need anything." He held out his hand.

Henry shook it. Once Con walked away Henry looked down

into the canyon to find Melisse staring up at him. He didn't think it was possible to love someone more every day, but that's exactly what happened. The more he learned about her, the more he loved her.

He'd never expected that defying an order from the King of Kings would give him not only the love of his life, but also the peace that had always eluded him. Peace that had been within his grasp all along. He'd just been too caught up in other things to realize it.

Henry made his way down the canyon wall. When he reached the bottom, Melisse was at his side. He gave her a lingering kiss in greeting.

"What is it?" she asked.

"Time for us to return to Earth."

She gave him a bright smile. "I'm ready when you are."

Stonemore

Merrill reclined on the bed, one foot on the floor as he flipped through a book. He couldn't concentrate on the words. Or maybe he just didn't care. That was increasingly becoming an issue. He didn't seem to care about much of anything anymore.

He thought about Dreagan and the life he'd had on Earth. He recalled fond memories with the Kings, especially Varek, who he was closest with, but it didn't stir anything else in him. He had searched Stonemore, or at least the parts he could get access to, though he didn't know what he was looking for. Maybe nothing.

Should he have left with Alasdair?

Merrill second-guessed his every decision of late. The rage that had remained buried for eons had been let loose when he arrived on Zora, and there was no securing it away again. It always simmered just beneath the surface, looking for a reason—*any* reason—to be unleashed.

He should be worried about that, but he wasn't. Just as he should be concerned with the fact that Villette hid things from him. He despised her. But she was useful.

For now.

Alasdair's warning about her intentions was never far, though. Maybe Merrill could take her, or perhaps he couldn't. Again, he didn't care.

Whatever happened, happened.

The door to his chamber burst open. Villette staggered inside with her clothes torn and charred. Most of her hair was singed nearly to her scalp, and the burn scars on her face were inflamed and blistered.

He sat up as she reached for him. He didn't go to her as she dropped to one knee and then turned to fall onto her back on the rug. She let out a yelp of pain and writhed in agony. He pushed to his feet and stood to peer down at her. If there was one smell he knew, it was dragon fire.

"You tangled with the Kings," he said.

She said nothing as she continued to thrash about. He spotted blood on her dress, along with a slice in the material wide enough to be from a sword.

He squatted beside her and waited until her blue eyes focused on him. "Bad idea."

Katla was jarred awake by something splashing onto her cheek. There was another on her forehead, and then another on her lips. She turned her head to the side and reached up to find liquid running down her cheek. She opened her eyes and blinked, startled to see a blue sky through clouds as more raindrops fell. She slowly sat up and took stock of her body.

Everything appeared to be in order, and nothing hurt. But how was that possible? She had felt Villette's power. And she had welcomed the expected death from attacking the Star Person. Maybe she was dead. She watched the drops of rain soak into her clothes. Would that happen if her life had ended?

She got up and looked around. Tall grass was beneath her feet. She bent and ran her hands over the blades, taking in the color and following it until she spotted the trees. They were a bounty of vibrant orange, red, and yellow foliage. Autumn. The season was autumn.

It had been so long since she had seen such colors that she hurriedly walked to the trees and plucked leaves from the ground to hold like a bouquet. She ambled through the forest. The sounds suddenly descended upon her all at once. She was mesmerized by the rustle of a brisk wind ruffling the branches, gently tugging the leaves free to dance upon the air before lazily gliding to the ground. There were various birds and even chirping that she recognized, though she couldn't think of the animal.

She didn't even care about the rain. The shower was soft, as if welcoming her back into the world. If that's what was happening. Katla didn't much care. She was surrounded by everything alive and vibrant. She didn't deserve to be here, but she couldn't turn away either. She scraped her palm against the bark of a tree. She bent to smell a flower clinging to the last remnants of summer. She watched birds flutter from one tree to another.

Every step was something new—well, not *new*. A reminder of her long-ago life.

Katla didn't know how long she meandered through the forest before she spotted a tall wall and an imposing gate. Beyond it was a city built into the side of a mountain. She heard voices over the other side of the gate. Could it be possible that she had found humans? She had to know.

"Hold," commanded a male voice above as she walked from the tree line.

She paused and lifted her face to see a helmeted head peering down at her. "What city is this?"

"Stonemore. What business do you have here?"

She'd heard that name before. This was where Villette lived. Henry had warned her about the city. She smiled up at the soldier, a plan forming. "I'm surprising someone."

THE END

Thank you for reading **DRAGON BORN**. I hope you enjoyed Melisse and Henry's book as much as I loved writing it. Their story was a long time coming.

If you want more Dragon King stories, then I have a treat for you. A special duology adjacent to the series that will take place

between Dragon Born and the next Dragon King book. Keep
reading for a peek at THE BASTARD KING.

BUY THE BASTARD KING NOW
at www.DonnaGrant.com

* * *

If you love the Dragon King series, you'll love the next Dark
Universe book set in the Skye Druids series, STILL OF THE
NIGHT...

BUY STILL OF THE NIGHT NOW
at www.DonnaGrant.com

* * *

To find out when new books release
SIGN UP FOR MY NEWSLETTER today at
https://www.tinyurl.com/DonnaGrantNews

* * *

Join my Facebook group, Donna Grant Groupies, for exclusive
giveaways and sneak peeks of future books.
https://bit.ly/DGGroupies

* * *

Keep reading for a peek of THE BASTARD KING and a glimpse at
STILL OF THE NIGHT...

SNEAK PEEK AT THE BASTARD KING

THE BASTARD DUOLOGY, BOOK 1

With just one fiery embrace I could destroy her...or love her until the end of time.

I am fire and death. My very presence brings terror and panic. For most, I am the last thing they will ever see. For there is only one thing I live for — freeing my kin.

Every action, every battle brings me a step closer. Nothing distracts me from my purpose.

Until she crosses my path.

Brave and fearless, she holds me utterly enthralled. I have to know her. Her past and her future. But especially the secrets she keeps closely guarded.

One taste of her lips, and I'm caught. Trapped. Seized. The

more I'm with her, the harder it is to leave. But I have sworn allegiance to another who promises to free the dragons.

Her or my kin. It was once an easy choice.

Before my heart got involved.

A dragon without a family. An outcast running from her past. They might be able to stop the impending doom—if they learn to trust each other. A Dragon King duology from *New York Times* and *USA Today* bestselling author Donna Grant.

Keep reading for a sneak peek at THE BASTARD KING...

THE BASTARD KING EXCERPT

The berries in his hand were forgotten as Derek watched the woman run away hunched over. She jumped onto a boulder and straightened as if to declare her presence. The jingle of armor announced the soldiers before he saw them racing after her.

He couldn't remember the last time a human had been friendly. Men avoided him. Women only wanted in his bed. But not a single one had ever put themselves into harm's way for him?

Until her.

Derek rose to his feet. He looked from the soldiers to the woman. The path she took only led one place. And he knew what the soldiers were about. None of this involved him. He had no reason to meddle. But she intrigued him. He couldn't remember the last time he had been fascinated by anyone. Especially a human.

He started running, slowly at first but increased his speed. Derek kept her in his sights, and just as he expected, she ran toward the blocked valley near the wetland. Was she leading them there on purpose? She was fast. Not as fast as him, but faster than the soldiers. She could have outdistanced them quickly, but she hadn't. Instead, she had slowed so they could keep up. How...odd.

She wanted them in that part of the valley for a purpose. Five against one wasn't good odds. Maybe there were others waiting to help her. His curiosity was raised now. Nothing was going to stop him from seeing the outcome.

Derek diverted and took another route that cut through the marshland. His feet slapped through the water, spraying it as he ran. He arrived, waiting within the thick mist when the woman rushed into the valley. She slid to a halt and spun to face her pursuers. Long, dark hair had come loose from its binding and hung to her waist. She stood with her feet apart, her hands at her sides. Her chest heaved from the exertion while her gaze was locked on the approaching soldiers.

"Seems you have nowhere to go," a female soldier stated.

The woman smiled softly. "I'm the one who stopped."

"Because no one goes in there." The soldier jerked her chin toward the swamp.

Derek was well hidden. But everyone knew the swamp was a dangerous place.

Because of *him*.

The silence was broken by a crossbow being fired. The woman leaned to the side just before the bolt struck her. Derek marveled at her ability to dodge it. In seconds, the soldiers surrounded her. He took a step forward, only to stop. He was curious about the human, but it didn't go farther than that.

She ducked and dodged, spun and sidestepped. She even managed to block a few blows, but she was up against weapons with only her wits. A part of him wanted to help. As he was considering it, she suddenly jerked at the impact of a quarrel into her chest. There was a slight tightening of her face before she ducked a sword going for her head. Another blade cut along her thigh when she lunged. One of the soldiers stabbed her in the back.

It was a blood bath. And he had seen enough. Derek shifted into his true form. He stalked forward, knocking over trees as he did. The mist swirled around him as if trying to keep him hidden. It parted when he pushed onward, revealing his face first.

Four of the soldiers caught sight of him and froze. The female leader was too intent on the woman to take notice. She swung her sword down and around, embedding it deep in the woman's side. Derek growled. She lifted her eyes to meet his. Her face drained of color as she tugged her blade free.

The woman dropped to her knees before listing to the side and rolling onto her back. The scent of blood filled the air. Derek stood over her. He didn't know why. There was no saving the human. Not that he would if he could. He looked down. Her eyes were open, but she didn't show any surprise or fear to see him. She must already be dead.

And that infuriated him.

"We're leaving," the female soldier announced. "We're sorry to intrude in your territory. We had to take care of business."

Derek looked at her and let smoke roll from his nostrils. His fury grew. With the woman for not getting away when she had the chance. With the soldiers for ganging up on her and killing her. And for himself for not intervening before it was too late. He drew in a deep breath, feeling the fire within his chest flare and expand. They tried to run, but it was pointless. One breath of fire took them instantly.

He could have made them suffer. Maybe he should have. Derek looked down at the female again. Her eyes were closed now. Her injuries were fatal. He hadn't even gotten a chance to thank her. It wasn't something he did. There had been no need for her to warn him, but she hadn't known that. She deserved better than this.

Derek returned to human form and squatted naked beside her. Why had she brought the soldiers here? There hadn't been anyone to help her. She should've escaped when she had the chance. Why hadn't she?

Her blood spilled into the packed earth as mist curled out from the swamp to lick at her boots. Derek tugged a lock of hair free that had fallen across her face. He dropped one knee to the ground. Her hair was like aged mahogany, rich and deep. The strands were cool against his fingers

Her oval face was beguiling. Her full lips could have lured him into temptation with the barest of smiles. Dark brows arched pleasingly over large eyes. He had looked briefly into the clear brown eyes, but he could describe every detail. They had been bright like a sunrising shining through them. Swirling in the dark rays was bronze and amber all trapped by a ring of thick black.

He skimmed the back of his knuckles along her cheekbone. Who was she? He would never know. And that was a pity.

She was attractive, but more than that, she had been brave and kind. Not something he described about anyone, much less humans.

Derek straightened, but he didn't walk away. He stared at her a long moment before he bent and gathered her in his arms. He walked past what was left of the soldiers to the path used by animals to ascend the mountain. She deserved a warrior's death, and while he couldn't give her that, he could give her the next best thing. Derek carried her up to the top and gently laid her on the slab of rock.

He stared at her face to commit it to memory. Then he looked down at her body. She was dressed in all black. Her shirt was threadbare at the wrists and holes stitched. Her pants were in little better condition. It seemed she spent most of her coin on her boots. They were of solid craftsmanship that would've lasted her years.

The wind picked up the ends of her hair and danced it around. Derek took a step back. He let his gaze take in the view. He stood on the northern most point of the Tunris range. Ahead of him stretched rolling valleys of grass that went on for miles. Beyond that was a lake and land as wild as his heart.

He would give her the burial she deserved so that her ashes could be scattered into the beauty of the realm. Perhaps that would allow her to one day return as fierce as she had been that day.

Derek's eyes lowered to her face again. He couldn't fathom why she hadn't let her speed take her far from the area. She shouldn't have stayed. He had decimated humans time and again, and he would continue to do so in order to free the dragons. And yet, he was greatly saddened to see this one dead.

"Dederick."

He fisted his hands at the command that filled his mind. He didn't dare ignore it. His life was pledged to that of Stonemore, and if Villette summoned him, then he must go to her. Derek debated on whether to incinerate the human now or wait. He had seen other mortals gather round their dead. She deserved at least that. If he didn't have time to watch her body burn, then he would do it when he returned.

Derek held out his hand and created an area around the slab with magic so no one could get near her. He looked at the silver cuff at his wrist. No matter how many times he traveled by Villette's magic, it felt wrong.

He caught sight of his nudity and reluctantly used his magic to clothe himself. He spent most of his time doing what he wanted. But there were other times, like now, where he bent to another's rules. His gaze lingered on the dead human a moment more.

Derek touched the cuff. One moment he was outside, and the next, he was stood in the center of a chamber deep within a mountain. Flames danced in the enormous hearth, the red-orange glow reaching out toward him along the floor with flickering fingers.

He knew this chamber well since it was where he met Villette. There were no windows. A single door marred the simple walls. Despite its size, the room only had one chair. There was no need to use his enhanced abilities. He turned his head to the left and found his mistress sprawled on a chair covered in fur pelts.

"Took you too long."

Derek frowned at the pain in her voice. He caught a glimpse of new burns that covered her face, arms, and torso. "What happened?"

"Nothing for you to worry about."

He drew in a breath and smelled a familiar scent of dragon fire. "You fought dragons?"

"I said not to worry about it."

He curled his hands into fists when she didn't elaborate. Villette wasn't just his leader. She had saved him. He owed her his allegiance *and* his life. Both, he gave freely.

She sighed loudly. "I've already given you my word that you will be by my side when we free your kin."

"Tell me who did this to you. I will hunt them down."

"I want that pleasure," she stated icily. She cut her eyes to him. "Has there been anything out of the ordinary that has happened?"

Derek observed her for a silent moment. He could tell her about the female, but then he would have to explain why he cared. Villette would become worried, and there was no need for that. "Nay."

"You need to be extra vigilant. Don't get far from the marsh."

"You expect someone to come?"

"I'm being cautions. It's how we've gotten this far."

Someone had spooked her, and she wasn't giving him any information. Villette was one of the most powerful beings alive. She was a Star Person, moving among realms by mere thought alone. She ruled Stonemore as the Divine. Few knew her as anything other than the Divine's right hand. Villette had gained influence and dominion by weaving a complex web of deception and trickery to gain the upper hand in the battle for Zora.

And she was winning.

There had been setbacks before, but they were getting closer to freeing the dragons. He could feel it.

"I'll see it done," he declared.

She swallowed, a grimace of pain creasing her face. "Dederick," she called.

He hated that name, but he bit back his response. "Aye?"

"The next time I call, come immediately." She slowly sat up, but it cost her much as she began shaking. "I may need you soon. Don't let me down."

"I would never," he vowed.

"Check the swamp. I want you to be sure no one has found it."

He took a step to her. "No one has."

"Check the entire area. Go. Now," she bit out.

Derek bowed his head and touched the cuff. Seeing Villette injured worried him. Something had spooked her, and he wished she would tell him who or what that was. In the meantime, he would do as she asked.

He reappeared atop the mountain only to stare in disbelief at the empty stone slab.

BUY THE BASTARD KING NOW
at www.DonnaGrant.com

GLIMPSE AT THE NEXT DARK UNIVERSE BOOK

STILL OF THE NIGHT, SKYE DRUIDS SERIES, BOOK 5

SKYE DRUIDS

COMING SOON

NEW YORK TIMES BESTSELLING AUTHOR
DONNA GRANT

Forest child they call me. It is within the woods that I find solace and feel the magic of my ancestors. For I am a Druid. One who can trace her roots from the very first to call the Isle of Skye home.

The isle draws many to its magical shores. It drew him. Imposing, bold, and handsome. We fell hard and fast that summer. Then he left with the tide to the city.

I learned to live with the cracks and fissures on my pieced-together heart, the scars only I can feel.

Until the day he walks back into my life asking for a second chance. I yearn to give it to him. How can I not? He's the only one I've ever loved.

The only one I will ever love.

But there is a darkness growing on the isle—a treacherous evil that has targeted him. I've lost him once.

I won't lose him again.

A Druid with a secret past. A man looking for a second chance. Return to Scotland and *New York Times* and *USA Today* bestselling author Donna Grant's Skye Druids, where magic and danger intertwine and a tale of love, sacrifice, and second chances unfolds.

BUY STILL OF THE NIGHT NOW
at www.DonnaGrant.com

ABOUT THE AUTHOR

New York Times and *USA Today* bestselling author Donna Grant® has been praised for her "totally addictive" and "unique and sensual" stories.

She's written more than one hundred novels spanning multiple genres of romance including the bestselling Dragon Kings® series that features a thrilling combination of Druids, Fae, and immortal Highlanders who are dark, dangerous, and irresistible. She lives in Texas with her dog and a cat.

www.DonnaGrant.com
www.MotherofDragonsBooks.com

facebook.com/AuthorDonnaGrant
instagram.com/dgauthor
bookbub.com/authors/donna-grant
goodreads.com/donna_grant
pinterest.com/donnagrant1